STEPHEN:
UNLIKELY MARTYR

KATHERYN MADDOX HADDAD

A COMMENTARY IN NARRATIVE FORM

DEDICATION

Dedicated to all Muslims, Hindus, Buddhists and
all others
in our modern world
who have become Christians
at risk of their lives.

YOU ARE OUR HEROES!

OTHER BOOKS BY THIS AUTHOR

HISTORICAL NOVELS & STORYBOOKS
Series of 8: They Met Jesus
Ongoing Series of 8: Intrepid Men of God
Mysteries of the Empire with Klaudius & Hektor
Christmas: They Rocked the Cradle that Rocked the World
Series of 8: A Child's Life of Christ
Series of 10: A Child's Bible Heroes
Series of 8: A Child's Bible Kids
Series of 10: A Child's Bible Ladies

HISTORICAL RESEARCH BIBLE
for Novel, Screenwriter, Documentary & Thesis Writers

TOPICAL
Applied Christianity: Handbook 500 Good Works
Christianity or Islam? The Contrast
The Holy Spirit: 592 Verses Examined
The Road to Heaven
Inside the Hearts of Bible Women-Reader+Audio+Leader
Revelation: A Love Letter From God
Worship Changes Since 1st Century + Worship 1sr Century Way
Was Jesus God? (Why Evil)
365 Life-Changing Scriptures Day by Date
The Road to Heaven
The Lord's Supper: 52 Readings with Prayers

FUN BOOKS
Bible Puzzles, Bible Song Book, Bible Numbers

TOUCHING GOD SERIES
365 Golden Bible Thoughts: God's Heart to Yours
365 Pearls of Wisdom: God's Soul to Yours
365 Silver-Winged Prayers: Your Spirit to God's

-SURVEY SERIES: EASY BIBLE WORKBOOKS
→Old Testament & New Testament Surveys
→Questions You Have Asked-Part I & II

Genealogy: How to Climb Your Family Tree Without Falling Out
Volume I & 2: Beginner-Intermediate & Colonial-Medieval

NORTHERN LIGHTS PUBLISHING HOUSE

Cover design by Sharon A. Lavy. Images from DepositPhotos.
ISBN- 978-1-948462-61-7
Printed in the United States

TABLE OF CONTENTS

MAP 1 OF MEDITERRANEAN
PLACES MENTIONED IN THIS NOVEL

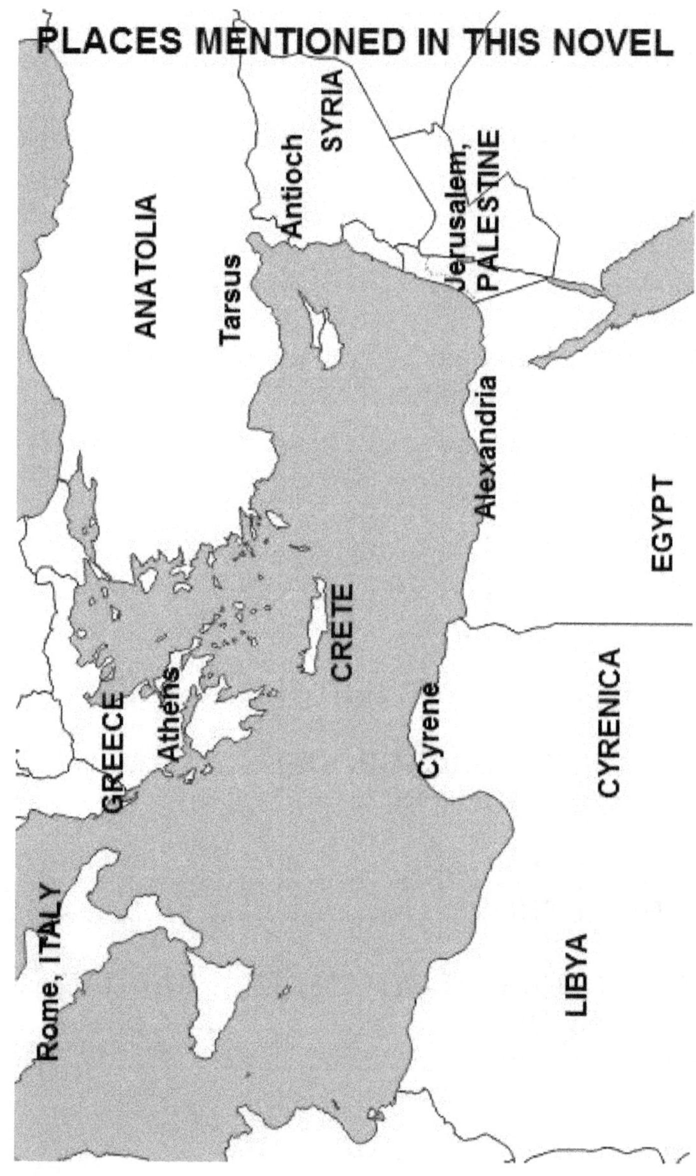

1 ~ ABRAHAM'S CRUCIFIXION

"**H**urry, Stephen! They're crucifying Abraham."

Seventeen-year-old Stephen looks up from his anvil, his eyes wide. "What?"

He throws the small iron bar back into the hot forge, drops his sledgehammer and tongs to the dirt floor, and runs out onto the street.

"Along the road to Seleucia," Ahab shouts, leading the way.

They run through the market and along the River Orontes toward the road leading out of Antioch and to the seaport twelve *milles* west.

Stephen's chest heaves, and his breath comes fast and hard. His face turns dark red as his strong muscles strain to go where he does not want to go. Beads of perspiration form on his head and down into his sparse young man's black beard.

They race out the western gate of Antioch and down to the bottom of the hill on which the great showplace city—third in magnificence and size only to Alexandria and Rome—is built.

They see the gathering mob ahead of them shouting, and shaking their fists, or laughing in scorn.

Stephen's eyes mist, and he stumbles, though there is nothing to trip over except the awful thing that should not be happening to his very best friend.

He and Ahab slow and stand at the outer edge of the mob.

Abraham's hands and legs are bound by chains.

"No! No!" he calls out.

Abraham falls to his knees, clasps his hands together, and holds them up to the centurion in charge.

"Please. Not this. I do not deserve it. You cannot do this to me. Please. Please. I have a mother to support and two little brothers. Please, I beg you. Oh, I beg you."

Abraham, the same age as Stephen, drops his head to the cobblestone street, his skinny body trembling. His pleas have the hoarseness of a youth whose voice has recently changed to that of a man.

A legionnaire grabs the condemned and jerks him up.

"Get going there."

Abraham stumbles on blubbering and begging as he goes.

"All right. This is far enough," the centurion barks.

The procession stops. Abraham looks toward the upright beam already in the ground.

"No! Please! No!"

A legionnaire pushes young Abraham onto the ground. His head hits the crossbeam there waiting for the condemned criminal.

His screams become shrill. A legionnaire unlocks the chains around his wrists. Another joins him, and they stretch Abraham's hands to opposite ends of the cross beam.

"Hand me a spike, someone," the second legionnaire calls out, easily holding down Abraham's struggling arm with one hand and reaching up for a spike with the other.

"No!" Abraham shrieks. "No. Please. No. Ahhhhh!"

The first spike is driven into his wrist.

Abraham reaches with his free hand to rescue his wounded one.

The first legionnaire grabs it and holds it in place on the other side of the crossbeam.

"Ahhhhh! Ahhhhh!"

The mallet finds its mark over and over until the criminal is secured to his cross.

Abraham kicks until the legionnaires force him to stand, one at each end of the beam. They push him backward toward the upright beam, and every time he takes a step, the spikes stretch the wounds so that his young blood flows more freely.

"Nooooo!" Abraham screeches. "Nooooo!" His eyes are wide, the veins in his neck swell.

Once at the upright beam, the legionnaires, both much taller than Abraham, lift him up far enough that the crossbeam fits neatly into the notch, thus connecting the two pieces.

A third legionnaire grabs Abraham's feet, so they do not dangle and pull his entire weight down until the rips in his wrists grow so large his hands are freed.

The third legionnaire places Abraham's feet over the bottom

upright beam, but he kicks the legionnaire in the face.

Two of his colleagues come to the rescue and hold Abraham's feet down so the job can be completed.

Now, with the large spike securely through Abraham's feet and into the upright beam, they back away and wait for someone to nail his crime over his head.

BLASPHEMY

"Nooooo," Abraham screeches in an unsteady voice that tapers off into the horrifying abyss he has been condemned to.

During the entire process, Stephen has had his head turned. Indeed, his entire body faces away from his friend. When Abraham screams in pain, Stephen puts his hands over his ears.

"Okay, men," he hears the centurion say. "Settle in. Only two shifts for this—one for day, one for night. It's going to take him two or three days to die."

Stephen waits until he thinks the legionnaires are at rest, then gradually turns around to see what he does not want to see.

"No, no, no," Stephen mumbles in his adolescent voice forcing its way into manhood.

He puts his big hands on top of his head. He squints, presses his lips hard together, and mumbles still, "No, no, no."

The tears. The unwanted tears that betray his cowardice and shame. He squints his eyes closed, hoping the whole thing will go away.

"No, No." This time it is not him.

Stephen opens his eyes, and they meet the eyes of his friend.

"Please, Stephen. Get me down," young Abraham cries. "I hurt. Please. Oh, please. I cannot breathe. I hurt so bad."

"Shut up," one of the legionnaires calls up.

"Crying for your mother?" a bystander taunts

"Not so arrogant now, are you?" another tells the condemned.

"I did not mean to. It wasn't me. I was home when it happened. I do not even own a hammer that big."

"How do you know it required a big hammer? Or any kind of hammer, you fool?" the high priest of Tyche, guardian goddess of Antioch, bellows. "Your own words condemn you."

"Abraham," Stephen cries, walking closer to his friend. "Why did you do it? There are other things we were ...."

"So, you know about it too?" the centurion calls over to

Stephen. "I suppose all you Jews knew. You're nothing but trouble."

One of the city magistrates walks toward the two friends of the condemned.

"You know you're not allowed down in Daphne where the sacred cleansing baths and groves are. How did you sneak into the temple of Tyche and deface her riverfront image?"

The centurion turns and looks toward Stephen and Ahab. "Arrest them too."

Stephen pivots and sprints back toward the city gate. He charges through the market, dodging in and out of side alleys. He does not know where Ahab is. All he knows is that his life on earth—like Abraham's—is about to end.

He does not head toward his locksmith shop. Instead, he runs up one of the foothills of Mount Silipius toward Ezekiel's scribe school.

He scarcely feels his feet touch the ground.

"Father!" he shouts as he draws closer. He rushes inside the mud-brick building, past the students sitting on the floor with their tablets and styluses and to a back room.

"What is it, Son?" Ezekiel asks, rushing after him.

Stephen leans his hands on his knees and looks up, panting. "They're crucifying Abraham. And they think Ahab and I were in on it."

"In on what?"

"Defacing the statue of Tyche."

"Well, were you?"

"Of course, not. But they're looking for us now to crucify us too. What are we going to do?"

Ezekiel turns in a circle, his head on his thick graying hair.

"Sir, what is it?" Achaius, the oldest of Ezekiel's hired staff, asks, following them into the back room.

"They're after us."

"Us, who?" Achaius says, pulling at his long, leathery nose.

"Us Jews," Ezekiel interjects.

"No, Father. Just Ahab and me."

"I have seen it happen before," Ezekiel replies, trying to keep his voice calm. "They will blame all the Jews."

"What are you going to do?" Achaius asks his employer.

"Leave. We've got to leave Antioch. It is mid-morning. We cannot go until dark."

"We won't be able to get past the city gate," Stephen objects.

"The guards will be watching for me."

"We will walk east across the hills outside of the city and down on the other side of the hills."

"Do you want Secundus, Justice, and Trophimus to help me alert the other Jews?" Achaius asks.

"They will have to decide for themselves whether or not to leave and where they could go."

"Well, we're leaving with you," Achaius declares.

"Dismiss the school and tell the other teachers what is happening. You can go along with us if you like."

"What about Mother? Will she want to leave?" Stephen asks. "She's only Jew by conversion; she wasn't born one of us."

"She will want to help protect you. Now, let us get out of here."

Ezekiel glances at Achaius. "Just leave the writing supplies behind. They will be easy enough to replace."

He ducks out a back door of his scribe school, Stephen following close. Both look around to see if they have been spotted. They work their way along the same ridge of the foothill where Ezekiel's school is.

Ezekiel strains and breathes hard, his bulky weight trying to hold him back.

"What about my smithing tools, Father?"

"If you think you can go back there without being spotted, you can grab a few of your smaller tools. But I would rather you not even try."

Shortly, they come to the gate leading into their home compound. Stephen, the locksmith of the family, pulls out a key he keeps around his neck. They hear the rattle of a handle on the other side.

Before he can unlock it, the gate is opened by a slender, petite woman with dark hair, square face and sparkling eyes.

Her smile disappears.

"What's wrong?" she asks, looking first at her husband of twenty-nine years, then their late-born son.

"Tullia, Stephen's in danger."

"They caught Abraham, Mother. They're, they're…"

"They're crucifying the young man," Ezekiel says, finishing for their son.

"Oh, no," Tullia says. She looks at Stephen and reaches up to hold his reddened face in her hands.

Mother and son stare at each other a moment. Stephen breaks away and walks over to the reflecting pool in the middle of their courtyard. He sits on the raised rim.

"Well, we have a lot to do," Tullia says, looking back at Ezekiel. "Of course, we will return to Tarsus. It is the only reasonable thing to do."

"I believe you are right," he replies. "Well, we need to decide what we can take with us. Hopefully, the ship will allow us to take a pack animal with us."

"I thought we could take our horses and carriage up to Tarsus, dear," Tullia replies.

"Too easy for the soldiers to follow us. It's a one-week trip up to Tarsus. Too much risk walking. We shall go by ship."

"Well, I will run to the market and get cheese and bread for the trip, and a few fresh grapes, apricots, and apples."

"Mother, do not do it."

"I will be fine, Stephen. Remember, I am part Hittite, and my father was the famous Athenodorus. No one dares bother me." She forces a smile and a wink.

"Well, then, maybe we could go together," Stephen says, standing.

"To the market? That would be fine. You can carry my basket."

"Well, there. But also to my shop."

"You'll be recognized, Son," Ezekiel interjects.

"I am taller than Mother, but not that much taller. I can wear one of her robes with a hood."

"And that bushy black beard of yours?" Tullia says with a grin.

"I will put a veil over my head."

"The shop owners will wonder who you are," Tullia objects.

"Just do not answer them when they ask. Just wink at them and walk away."

Tullia looks over at Ezekiel and shrugs her shoulders.

"Might work," he responds. "He will need his tools, especially the ones he uses for the intricate locks he makes."

Shortly, Tullia and Stephen leave the compound. "I will have our pack mule ready when you get back. And enough food to keep him happy for the two days aboard the ship."

They walk across the foothill, then down a familiar path closer to the city. They walk toward the market.

"Where is everyone?" Stephen asks.

Tullia does not answer.

Stephen looks up at the sky. She can hear sniffs from

behind the veil.

"They're all down watching Abraham die," he whispers. "Why did he have to do it, Mother?"

"He thought he was pleasing Jehovah," she replies. "Now, let us stop talking."

With most of the produce stands left unattended while the merchants run go to the excitement at the city gate, Tullia selects what she wants for the trip and puts them in the basket Stephen is carrying for her. Each time, she places a few copper coins on the stool where the merchant normally sits.

"Okay, while everyone is gone, let us slip over to your shop."

As they walk, they hear shouting down at the riverfront.

Stephen, half boy and half man, sobs and is glad for his mother's veil that hides the part of him he cannot control.

"Okay, start at the beginning of the alphabet with me," she whispers.

As they follow the example of his mother's famous philosophy father, Stephen manages to maintain control of his emotions.

When they arrive at the shop, Tullia stands outside to watch for anyone looking their way. It does not take Stephen long.

They head back toward home when they hear shouting behind them.

"Hey, you!"

They stop. Stephen freezes in place.

"Run, Mother. Run!"

2 ~ THE ESCAPE

*T*ullia looks over toward the sprawling city to her left, then toward the mountains on her right.

"What? I did not hear anything."

She takes hold of both his wrists and looks up into his frightened eyes that she cannot see.

"As long as we are careful, no one will suspect who you are."

"Hey, you," they both hear this time.

Tullia looks behind her and sees two men approaching.

"Oh, Lucius, it's you. And Nicholas."

"Yes, we heard what is happening," Nicholas says, now only one man-length from them. "I suppose you are leaving like so many of the other Jews. Where are you going? To the safety of Jerusalem?"

"It is better that you not know," Tullia says.

"You might try Cyrene," Lucius says. "That is where I was born and raised. Well, may your Jehovah go with you," he says, turning away.

"Yes, be at peace," Nicholas says.

"May he be your God too someday," Tullia says, calling after both men.

They hurry on the rest of the way home. The remainder of the afternoon is spent sorting and deciding what to take with them, creating individual bundles for each of them to carry, and one large bundle to be carried by the pack mule.

Periodically one of them climbs to the roof to see if anyone in authority is headed in their direction.

Stephen paces. He fights back unmanly tears. "Why, Abraham?" he mumbles now and then. "You had so much to live for. You were the smartest of all of us. We needed you to lead us. Why, Abraham? Why?"

"Son, we live in a dangerous world," Ezekiel says, taking a break from the sorting and packing.

"Abraham was just trying to save their soul by destroying Tyche's statue. She's not a goddess. How can people believe that?"

"People do not like to admit they're wrong, and their ego gets in the way. Plus, she is the guardian goddess of Antioch, and no one wants to defy her and her priests and be crucified for treason."

"Like Abraham," Stephen whispers.

He sits back on the ledge of the reflecting pool, slumps, puts his elbows on his knees, and drops his head into his hands. And sobs.

Ezekiel sits next to him and puts his arm over his shoulders. His son lets him and puts his head on his father's shoulder.

"Do you think he is dead yet, Father?" he whispers.

"No. It takes a long time to die by crucifixion. They die a little bit from losing their blood, but mostly they suffocate slowly because their lungs cannot work right in that position. It's a slow death. That is why they crucify the most dangerous criminals."

Stephen lifts his head, his eyes now puffed and red. "But Abraham wasn't dangerous." He draws his sleeve across his nose. "He is just a kid like me."

He stands once again. He stares at the sky above the open courtyard of what will soon no longer be their home.

"Why, God?" he shouts, his arms outstretched toward heaven. "Why? He had all those plans to defeat the pagan Gentiles and make everyone worship only you. Why did you let it happen, God? Now his work will go undone. Why, God? Why?"

Ezekiel resumes his work.

Just before dark, Trophimus, Secundus, and Justus join Ezekiel and his family. They pray to Jehovah for protection on their journey, and that there will be a ship ready to leave for Tarsus when they arrive at the port of Seleucia.

When the shadows are long and only a faint glow of red shows from below the horizon, they prepare to leave.

Being just inside the city wall at the foot of Mount Silipius, Ezekiel puts up a ladder on their rooftop that extends to the top of the higher wall.

He checks and sees Achaius has taken a wagon out the east gate and around along the outside of the city wall to where

Tullia had hung a rope as a signal. It is in place for the escapees.

Ezekiel lowers their belongings to Achaius, who packs them on the mule.

The six on Ezekiel's roof now climb up the ladder to the top of the wall, then down another longer ladder to the wagon below because the second ladder is not long enough to reach the ground. Then they drop to the ground.

Achaius unhitches the mule. Leaving the wagon behind, they work their way across the foot of the mountain behind the city of Antioch, then along the outside of the north wall.

They reach the Orontes and stay in the shadows away from the distant torchlight. Stephen thinks he hears groaning. *Oh, Abraham....*

They wade across the river at a place known to be shallow and continue west.

I am deserting you, Abraham. I am such a coward. I am so ashamed.

They walk all night. Without speaking, they walk. In silence, they walk. The silence of confusion and wondering why.

At early dawn, while the sky is still gray, they smell the salt of the Great Sea. They hear the squawking of seagulls and the clanging of bells signaling crews to do whatever they are supposed to do. Different bells signal other ships that they are on their way in or out of the port.

"Wait here," Achaius tells the others. "Sit over here and rest. I will find a ship to Tarsus for us."

Ezekiel pulls out his money pouch. "Here is enough for the seven of us."

"I will go with him," Justus says. "I am twenty years younger than him and have good eyes. I will keep watch for any legionnaires that may be looking for us."

They do not know how long they wait. They close their eyes, and moments later, the two teachers on Ezekiel's staff reappear. The sky is red now.

"We're in luck," Achaius says. "I talked one of them headed for Ephesus into dropping us off at Tarsus on their way. It's going to be his last trip of the season before he docks his ship for the winter. So, God must be with us."

"Will they take our pack mule?" Ezekiel asks.

"Yes, they said they would, but do not expect them to feed it."

As they follow Achaius to the ship, Secundus steps over to

his employer. "Why are we going to Tarsus, if I may ask?"

"That is where my father was taken as a slave when Pompey conquered Jerusalem. I was born and raised in Tarsus. I married Tullia there. Stephen was born there. It's our home. We are going back home."

Ezekiel leads their pack mule to the wide gangplank and hesitates. A sailor walks down and takes the reins.

"I am good with animals," he says.

Once onboard, they watch their mule being led to a stall along the guard rail, and a bar placed across the front of the stall.

The sailor returns.

"Welcome board the *Marmore Viridi*. We take Syria's green marble to Rome and bring back lumber from the mountains to their north." The sailor grins as though his status among the passengers will grow just in the saying.

Stephen's family looks around, steadying their legs as they do.

"Someone has to stay with the mule at all times," the sailor continues. "The rest of you can go below deck."

"I will watch him," Stephen says.

He works his way over to the stall, testing his legs as the ship sways back and forth on harbor waves. He takes the tackle off the mule, pats it on the nose, then sits in front of it on the deck.

He watches sailors give instructions to passengers as they board. He watches his family and associates disappear below deck into the darkness. As dark as his heart and Abraham's future. Through misty eyes, he watches as his world and the world of Abraham shifts and groans before it gives in and dies.

He watches as the sailors go about their business of preparing to set sail.

"Weigh anchor!"

Stephen hears the metallic scraping of chains on the cleat.

"Cast off down-hauls!"

Crewmen rush to their posts to begin unfurling the sails.

"Haul away on the halyard!"

A sailor scales the mizzen mast and soon is in the bird's nest high above.

Stephen stands and looks toward Antioch, his home for the past five years. His home since he had been a mere boy of twelve. The city that now looks smaller than it had a few moments earlier.

Bells ring. The other ships know to stay put until the *Marmore Viridi* is out in the open sea.

If Abraham had just stayed put. If Abraham had just not thought he could make a difference by himself. God, help Abraham die fast. Do not let him suffer, God. Can you at least do that much for him? He did it for you, you know, God. He did it for you.

They hear another bell, and the crew members leave the sail rigging for other duties. He sees the sailing master deftly handle the helm wheel, flanked by who Stephen assumes to be the captain on one side of him and the quartermaster on the other.

So self-important they look up there. Like they can command the world. Well, they cannot. They cannot. Just like Abraham, he thought he could command Tyche's high priests, but he was wrong. Oh, Abraham, my friend....

Stephen lays his head back onto his raised knees.

"Son."

Stephen opens his eyes. Had he been asleep? The sun is much higher now.

"Your mother wanted me to give you these fresh grapes. They need to be eaten before they spoil. Come on, Son. Let us walk over to the rail and allow the morning breeze to cleanse our minds."

Stephen obeys.

"You know, Abraham kind of reminded me of my father," Ezekiel begins.

"I was named after him. But I do not think I am like he was, am I, Father? Tell me again how he came to be a slave."

"Well, Son, we Jews are a stubborn people. I guess we always had to be in order to survive. But sometimes it hurt instead of helped our survival."

"Like when Pompey tried to put us under the control of Rome."

"Yes, like that. Of course, we weren't about to give up control of our own country. But he was stronger than we realized. His soldiers killed tens of thousands of our people right there in Jerusalem."

"How did Grandfather Stephen survive?"

"Your grandfather was a talker, not a fighter. As a young lawyer of twenty-one, he thought he could convince the soldiers to turn around and leave."

"Father, that is crazy."

"Your grandfather was an arrogant young man, just like a lot of other young men are."

"Like Abraham..." Stephen's eyes begin to water, but he

gets control of them.

"Luckily, the soldier he wanted to argue with was a centurion with some authority and an odd sense of humor in the middle of battle. He told his men to hang back, and stood and laughed at your grandfather as he declared Jewish supremacy."

" 'He will be good entertainment in someone's household. Bind him. He's going to Rome.' "

"Those were his exact words?"

"Indeed, they were. Your grandfather never forgot them. In the blink of an eye, he went from promising lawyer to hopeless slave for the rest of his life."

"Then what?"

"In Rome, he was bought by a teacher of philosophy and taken to Tarsus to tutor his son in Hebrew and oratory. But, once again, your grandfather couldn't control his tongue. It took the father a couple of years to realize Stephen was trying to convert his son to Judaism by teaching him the speeches of Moses."

"My grandfather was a stubborn man," Stephen says, smiling for the first time in a day.

"Well, he sold your grandfather to a tribune heading for Britannia. He was with the tribune seven years, serving as his scribe. He kept trying to convince the Celts to change their religion, just making them mad."

Ezekiel watches the waves a while.

"Next, the legion was out posted in Germanica," he continues. "Your grandfather did the same thing there, and only stirred up more trouble. Eventually, the tribune who owned him retired and did not want to take your grandfather with him. No one else at the outpost wanted him."

"'Cause he had a reputation as a troublemaker. Right, Father?" Stephen finishes for his father, unexpected laughter in his voice.

"So, he was sold to a lumber dealer in the Taurus Mountains."

"Hey, what are you two men up to?" Tullia strides over and stands between the two most important men in her life.

She looks over the waves. "Ah, it will be nice being home again. Do not you think so, Sweetheart?"

Both men reply that it will be.

While his parents talk about possible plans, Stephen turns and watches the four scribes who had helped build his father's school. They are lined up, seated along the animal stalls. He decides to walk around alone.

"Stephen, if you are still hungry, here is some cheese. And I know you are hungry," Tullia says as he passes near her, "so I needn't ask. Here, take it."

Stephen obeys and stuffs half of what she hands him into his mouth.

"Your grandfather should have stuffed his mouth more often, and he wouldn't have ended up in the Taurus Mountains," Ezekiel says, watching his son devour his food.

"So, how did you come about?" Stephen spits.

"Me? During my father's six years in the forest, he learned the blacksmith trade to keep the woodcutters supplied with axes and saws. He met my mother—a slave cook—and they were allowed to marry. She was one of the slave cooks. I was born the next year. He named me Ezekiel after the prophet who predicted the Jews' release from slavery in Babylon and return to Jerusalem."

"Father," Stephen says with a grin. "Tell me about Cleopatra again. Isn't that when...."

"Indeed, it was, Son, but that was five years after I was born. When the magistrates of Taurus learned Queen Cleopatra was coming in her famous luxury barge, they ordered trees cut and brought down out of the mountains to lay across the dock and up the road into the city. Her barge was pulled by thousands of slaves along those rolling logs."

"And Grandfather Stephen actually caught the Queen of Egypt in his arms," Stephen laughs, his mouth now void of the cheese.

Ezekiel grins. "Yes. One of the logs broke and tipped the barge. Cleopatra fell right into your grandfather's strong arms. He said she had laughter in her eyes. Anyway, he quickly got her back up on the barge, and the procession continued with him forgotten."

"But he wasn't forgotten, was he, Father? Cleopatra ordered that he be rewarded with his freedom."

"Yes, but he did not accept it."

"Grandfather did not take any reward for himself, did he?" Stephen finally says. "He gave away his reward."

3 ~ ARMS OF DANGER

Ezekiel becomes quiet. He looks out over the railing.

He watches the helmsman. He watches the crew swabbing the deck. Then back to the rolling waves. He touches the ring on his finger and moves it back and forth. His father's ring that he had made for Ezekiel those long years before.

"He sacrificed his freedom for me, Son. I had always lived up in the forests with my mother and father. My father told them, 'Educate my son.' "

"And that is how you became a scribe. Isn't that right, Father?"

"Yes, that is how I learned to be a scribe. After that, he was sent to work on the docks so I could visit him on weekends."

"And that is when he taught you the blacksmith trade," Stephen adds.

"He always said, to get along in the world, a man needs to know how to use both his brain and his hands."

"Move out of the way!" One of the sailors steps close to Tullia. He drips water from the brush in his hand onto her tunic.

"I said move. We gotta get this deck cleaned before the captain gives us a good lashing."

Ezekiel puts his arm around his wife's shoulder, standing between her and the sailor.

"Hey, Orontes, get away from the passengers," the quartermaster shouts at the swabbie.

"But, sir."

"We were just getting ready to check on my mule," Ezekiel says.

They walk over to the stalls on the opposite side of the ship. Ezekiel takes some of the barley off the mule's back and feeds it to the animal.

Tullia sees a small keg and sits on it while her husband and son sit on the deck in front of the stall.

For a long time, they do not talk. Their thoughts are caught by the waves swishing up against the hull and travel back and forth between emotions.

Stephen stands and walks over to his father's four scribes.

He sits cross-legged in front of them, puts his chin on his chest, and sleeps.

"Huh?"

Stephen wakes up and walks back to the railing where the deck had been swabbed earlier. He watches the waves go on in endless repetition in silence, and sits alone a while, napping sometimes.

"I am proud of you, Son," Ezekiel says when Stephen returns to the mule's stall. "I know you are struggling inside. You are handling it like a man."

Mid-afternoon.

"Okay, everyone," Tullia announces when she arrives with a basket of food near the mule's stall. "Bring your mats to sit on and we shall refresh our bodies and minds with food and prayer."

The seven gather around the array of cheese, bread, dried figs and pistachios. Each has his own skin of wine and another skin of fresh water.

After eating, Stephen naps again. Then walks around a while. *Is Abraham dead yet? Oh, God. Make it all go away.*

Each has brought along a scroll of something to read on the trip. They read a while, think a while, talk to each other about what they have just read or would like to read. Then the routine starts all over again.

Stephen takes the mule for a walk around the deck. On his way back to the stall, he calls up to the helmsman. "When do you think we will arrive in Tarsus?"

"About daybreak," comes the reply.

The sun descends, the sky growing gold and red, then disappears. It is night. The night is warm. Ezekiel and Tullia decide to spend the night by the stall near their son.

All is quiet and peaceful except for the lap, lap, lap of the meandering waves as they gently carry the ship to what used to be home—Tarsus.

Sliver of a moon. Stars. Night breeze. Quiet. Peace.

The stars make their way across the sky as the passengers dream of a better life.

A bell rings on the hour to indicate beginnings and endings of watches, thanks to the clever invention of the sand-filled hourglass by a certain Alexandrian over a century earlier.

Not much talking now. Not much going on. Just sentries sitting or standing or marching all alone on a deck in a great big sea while everyone else sleeps and dreams.

"Huh? What was that?"

"Ahhh!"

The sentry hears his comrade in pain and rushes to him. Just as he arrives, another arrow flies through the air and catches him in the back.

The helmsman hears the cries and the tumbling of bodies and grabs the copper rod and rings the bell fast and hard.

They hear the familiar booming voice of the captain as he rushes out through his cabin hatch to join the helmsman.

"Battle stations! Battle stations! We're being attacked! Battle stations!"

The bell continues to ring, but by now can hardly be heard over the shouting. The quartermaster opens the hatch to the orlop deck below and jumps down rather than take the ladder. Shortly, sailors are scrambling up top.

"Father, wake up," Stephen shouts in the darkness.

The mule neighs, rises up on his hind legs, and comes down hard on the wooden hull.

"I am awake. Where is your mother?"

"I am right here," Tullia says. "What's happening?"

"Probably pirates."

"What can we do? Where can we hide?"

"Watch out!"

A fireball flies over the deck and lodges in the bottom of a sail. A sailor pulls out his knife, climbs up the mast partway, and cuts the lower part of the sail loose. It burns itself out on the deck.

"Father, take Mother below," Stephen shouts. "I will try to protect you. Hurry."

The three make their way crawling in the direction of the burning sail that has landed near the hatch.

Pounding of footsteps shakes the deck. Stephen stands and pushes a sailor out of the path of his parents.

Once they disappear down the ladder, Stephen looks for something he can do to help defend the ship.

He is knocked backward. He hears the cracking and crunching of wood and a boom. The ship tips on its starboard side, taking friend and enemy sailors alike with it toward the treacherous waves.

Stephen is rammed into a board, he knows not from where, and grabs hold of it. Will he go down with it, or will it be his salvation?

Just as he reaches the water, the ship rights itself, and he slides in the other direction, then stops against a fallen mast.

By now, the pirates have boarded the *Marmore Viridi* with torches in one hand and swords in the other. Some use the torches to find their way to hidden treasure and others as weapons against assaults.

More pounding on the deck of boots and bare feet. More shouting of attackers and the condemned.

Stephen looks around for something he can use to defend himself. He feels around for iron tools he can throw at them. Or loose chain links. Why can he not find something? Anything?

Men assaulting and being assaulted. Men killing and dying. Shouts. Screams. Commands. Then an unfamiliar voice from up on the bridge.

"Stop! Stop where you are. I have your captain. If you want your captain to live, you will not resist."

A little at a time, men stop moving and stand in place. A little at a time, the killing and dying, the shouting and screaming stop.

"Now, then," the strange but booming voice announces, "we do not want to hurt you. Well, we do want to hurt you because you are rich, and we are not. But what we really want is your cargo." He pauses for his words to take effect.

"If you help us bring your famous green marble up and to our ship, we will not kill your captain. And we will not kill any more of you men than we already have. The sooner you give me your marble, the sooner I will back my ship away from yours and be on my way."

Stephen is shoved toward the hatch. He turns around to see if he recognizes the culprit but is cuffed in the head and shoved again. Once at the hatch, he half steps and half shimmies down the ladder

Now in the orlop deck, Stephen looks around for his parents and hopes he cannot see them. He cannot.

He and the others are pushed down yet another hatch to the next deck—the bilge where the green marble is stored.

Torches are attached to the bulkhead. Stephen and the others know what must be done. He takes hold of one slab of marble while a man across from him takes hold of the other side. They scoot around, wondering what to do with it. They hand it over to two men who had been behind them. A relay is formed.

Once again, Stephen and the other man grab hold of a heavy slab of green marble, scoot around, and hand it over to the next two men.

The process is repeated over and over through the night. They hear three bells.

They keep working. Stephen is strong. His arm muscles have grown hard by hammering hot, glowing chunks of iron into flat sheets.

They hear four bells.

On the men work. Grabbing, shuffling, handing over, back for more. The pile of green marble grows smaller. Stephen is used to hard work, but the hours of heavy lifting ravage his back.

Five bells.

He grabs the next piece, but his grip is insufficient. The marble slips and lands on his foot. He cringes and looks around at his taskmaster. He knows he cannot stop. Despite the blood and possible broken bones, he stands back up and resumes his tasks.

Before six bells are rung, the last of the green marble is handed over.

Stephen and the other men collapse onto the deck, their muscles burning, their arms scratched, their backs numb, and Stephen's foot sending lightening up from his now blackened toes.

Smells from body permeate the air, and for the first time, Stephen notices. He does not care. He leans his head back against the bulkhead and closes his eyes.

"Get up there," he hears. He notices light coming in from the hatch above and knows morning has arrived. The morning when life was supposed to begin anew in Tarsus where he had been born, his father had been born, and his grandfather had spent most of his life as a slave.

He closes his eyes again, and a foot lands in his side. Get up, you rat. Get top side. Now!"

Stephen stands so fast, he momentarily forgets his wounded and now swelled foot. He tumbles, but straightens again and hobbles on one foot toward the hatch. He arrives at the ladder and is not sure how he is going to climb it.

"When I push you up, put your knee on the runner."

The voice is familiar. It is Secundus with the long arms and legs. "I will jump up behind you and give you another boost. Got it?"

Stephen turns to thank him but is jabbed in the shoulder. "Get going."

How he manages to be on the main deck again, Stephen is not sure. Rigging and supplies are scattered everywhere. The foremast has been broken.

Though all the men he sees look exhausted, all are standing and looking toward the bridge. He and Secundus are some of the last ones to arrive. When they line up with the others, they hear the same booming voice of the pirate leader.

He is not as tall as his voice had given the impression in the dark, but tall enough. His hair is almost blonde but matted and tangled. He is dressed as a Hellenistic aristocrat, though his clothes show more wear than an aristocrat would allow to happen.

"My name is Anicetus, in case anyone asks you," he announces. "You may think I am too young to be captain of my ship, but there are circumstances you do not deserve to know.

"As soon as my men and I are back on my ship, I will pull it out. You should probably be ready with some sort of reinforcement for the hole I will be leaving in your hull.

"In case you are thinking of retaliation, you need to know who you are dealing with. I presently have my abode in Pontus, but my people are Clitae. Perhaps you have heard of us. My grandfather led our people in the Taurus Mountains and managed to evade foreign Roman rule for decades." He pauses.

"I do not want the people of Tarsus to be alerted to the misfortune you have experienced out here because that is where I am going. I will have the pleasure of selling your marvelous green marble there. I promised the rich of Tarsus—there are many of them—the very best, and they are expecting me to keep my promise." He looks over the crew.

"I do not care what happens to you from here on, though I secretly wish for you to survive long enough to spread the word that you came up against Anicetus and were too weak to rebuff me. So, go ahead and spread a little fear around. It will you a little good. It will do me a lot of good."

The pirate leader hears a flute and looks over at his ship.

"Ah, my first mate is calling. Things must be ready for us to take our leave."

With that, Anicetus leaps down from the bridge, crosses over to the copper-covered bow of his own ship still protruding into the side of the *Marmore Viridi,* leaps onto his ship and gives the order for his crew to fix rudder and begin backing out.

As soon as they begin, the captain of *the Marmore Viridi* shouts orders for reinforcements to be put in place immediately. The quartermaster orders sails to be hauled down to help fill the gap.

Stephen takes this chance to look around. He sees that the stalls of the animals are all empty.

He wants to look for his parents, despite his injured foot. He looks around for a stick he can lean on to work his way back to the hatch leading to the orlop deck.

"You'll never make it," Trophimus says. "Justus has just gone down to look for them. I am sure they are fine."

Stephen turns to look at Trophimus with his broad reassuring smile. He falls in the process.

Trophimus helps him up and sits on the deck with Stephen. "May as well stay here. Nowhere else to go."

They look over at the gash in the ship being reinforced. Beyond that is the pirate ship making its way north toward Tarsus.

"Where to, Captain?" they hear the helmsman ask.

"We have one good sail left. I think we can make it to Soli Pompiiapolis. We will have to winter there."

"Stephen! Are you all right?" It is Ezekiel.

Stephen turns toward the soft voice and twists his injured foot though he is seated. He cringes, and his mother kneels at his side.

"Oh, what did they do to you? Let me look at your foot."

"It was my fault, Mother. I lost my grip and dropped a big slab of marble. But I cannot walk on it. Ouch!"

"You have broken two toes. It will be a while before you walk on that foot," Tullia says. She tears some strips off the bottom of her long tunic and wraps them securely around Stephen's foot.

"What about Achaius?" Ezekiel asks. "Has anyone seen Achaius?"

"Well, look at that," Justus says with a grin. "He's over supervising the work on the hull. Isn't that just like him? Always bossing people."

"Now that we are all accounted for, Tullia and I have a decision to make," Ezekiel says. "We cannot go back home to Tarsus. We cannot return to Antioch. Jerusalem may not work because five of you are Greek by heritage, and they are very prejudiced against those not of Jewish blood." He looks at his wife.

"Come, Tullia. Let us walk and try not to trip on the rubble. Where can we possibly go?"

4 ~ DESTINATION UNKNOWN

Stephen watches as his parents make their way toward the stern, away from as much activity as possible.

He sees his father take small steps to accommodate his petite wife, put his arm around her, and hold her close while watching the deck for rubble to avoid.

The breeze teases the wispy gray hairs of his 68-year-old father, and Stephen is amazed at their enduring love with his mother being thirty years her husband's junior.

The two stop at the rail and look out over the waves, then turn to face each other. One talks, then the other. Neither tries to override the other. They point in the direction of Tarsus to the north sometimes, of Antioch to the west sometimes, at Stephen sometimes, and sometimes toward the northeast.

Their conversation grows animated, then stops. They stare at the waves without saying anything more, then begin anew to discuss and weigh options.

"So, where do you think we're going to end up?" Secundus asks, pulling his long legs in so he doesn't trip a busy sailor rushing by.

"Where ever they take us, it will not be boring," Justus says.

"Maybe to the end of the earth," Trophimus says with a toothy grin.

Stephen closes his eyes and hopes to sleep so the pain will go away.

"Well, we have made our decision," Ezekiel says.

Stephen opens his eyes and looks up at his parents.

"We are going to Rome," Tullia says.

"Rome?" Justus asks. "Mighty Rome?"

"My father lived there a long time," Tullia says, brushing

back a curly wisp of black hair from her eyes.

"He did?" Trophimus asks.

"Oh, yes," Stephen responds. "I had a famous grandfather."

"You said your grandfather was a slave."

"Not that grandfather. My other one. My mother's father. He was famous."

"What did he do?"

"Let us save that for later," Ezekiel says. "There is too much going on up here. Let us just rest and hope the damaged hull will be sealed well enough we can be underway and dock somewhere safe before dark."

Ezekiel's words are just out of his mouth when they hear the captain up on the bridge.

"Left rudder, helmsman. Take us to Soli Pompiiapolis."

The rest of the afternoon, Stephen watches as the ship's crew tosses useless pieces of wood overboard, throws broken tools and equipment of iron in one barrel, of copper in another, and of bronze in another.

The quartermaster inspects the only remaining sail at intervals of one hour by the sand glass.

The crew thins, and Stephen assumes the rest are below trying to get some sleep after being up all night.

"Father."

"Yes, Son."

"Do you think Abraham is dead yet?"

"Probably so, Son. Probably so."

Tears return to his young eyes and flow down to his sparse black beard. His shoulders shake. He sobs aloud. Emotions he had held back during the previous day's and night's turmoil rush out like the waters of a broken dam.

His mother reaches over and takes his hand. He squeezes her hand tight.

"Oh, Abraham. If you hadn't pushed them so much." His voice grows hoarse. "We needed you," he half screeches, and half growls with his changing voice. "You had so many plans for us. Oh, Abraham."

He lets loose of his instinct to act like a man, leans his head on his father's shoulder, and his father pats him on the cheek.

After a while—he does not know how long that while is—Stephen realizes he is lying prone on the deck. He returns to his sleep. He dreams he and Abraham are praying to Jehovah at the foot of Tyche's statue. She melts and turns into the River Orontes.

Bells clanging. Seagulls squawking.

Stephen opens his eyes and sees the one sail has been taken down. How could he have slept through the noise of preparing the ship to dock?

He sits up and cringes, having forgotten his injured foot.

"Looks like we made it to Soli Pompiiapolis," his father says.

"They had emergency oars on board, and every crewman not needed elsewhere was below rowing." It is Achaius. "And we made it before dark."

Ezekiel squats near his son. "Here is a crutch I salvaged from the wood being thrown overboard. Can you stand on your good foot? Here, let me help you."

The younger and older men struggle to stand.

"Ah-ow," Stephen groans. "It hurts when I stand up."

"Young sir, if you are in favor of it," Achaius says, "I can carry you on my back. The sooner you are off the ship, the sooner you can sit somewhere on the dock and let your foot rest."

"I will do anything to make this foot stop hurting."

Ezekiel and Tullia lead the way down the gangplank with the other five following. Once on the dock, they stop to let their legs adjust to solid ground and check out their new surroundings.

"What now?" Justus asks.

"That looks like a good place for Stephen and I to rest," Tullia says. She points in the direction of a bench at the bottom of a cliff at the far end of the dock and away from the warehouses.

"Let me down, Achaius," Stephen says. "I need to get used to this crutch. I can walk with Mother over there."

"The rest of us will check around among the other ships to find one heading for Rome."

Stephen tries not to cringe when Achaius sets him on his feet. He forces a smile at his father, then makes his way toward the bench with his mother.

"Now that we are onshore, we can look for an apothecary to give you something for your pain," Tullia says.

They arrive at the bench, and Tullia puts his injured foot in her lap to elevate it and ease the pain. They look out over the water and watch the red of the sunset to their right.

"Mother, I am all mixed up," Stephen says after a time of silence. "Abraham was just trying to stop people from bowing to Tyche's statue. He was doing the right thing. He had other plans too. Now he's dead. Like Abraham."

"I have no answers for you, Son. Where do we draw the line? How far do we go before we destroy the very thing we want to accomplish?"

Silence.

"My father was a peaceful man, so I have no experience in such things," Tullia says. "Perhaps your father can answer your question for you."

"Hey there!"

Stephen and Tullia look in the direction of the stranger's voice.

A man approaches wearing a short tunic of red linen, high leather boots also dyed red, and a long matching cape of leather with the animal's fur left on the edges.

"Winter will be upon us in another month. You two look like you are expecting summer to linger."

"Well, come to think of it, there is a chill here that we did not have down in, down in, well, where we came from."

"Mother," Stephen whispers, "we do not know that man. Do not encourage him."

"He is well dressed," Tullia replies. "He certainly is not a beggar or bandit," she whispers back, still smiling at the stranger.

The stranger stops two man-lengths from the two on the bench. "I did not mean to startle you. But you looked a little lost and in need of a man's protection. A beautiful woman with an injured husband must be careful. These rough sailors around here may just try to do away with the husband and whisk you off to serve his pleasures."

Stephen takes his foot down off his mother's lap and stands. "Pardon me, sir, but you will leave us this instant," he says, gritting his teeth both to hide his pain and show dominance. "We do not need or desire your sympathies, warnings, or anything else you have to say. So, leave. I mean it. Leave."

"Ha, ha. I like that in a man. Protector of his beloved."

"First of all, she is not..."

"Excuse me, sir," Tullia interrupts. "I think he is right. May you have a good day. Goodbye."

"Well, if you need anything, my name is Pyrrhus. I am captain of the *Servus Marya*—Slave of the Seas. We will be leaving for Crete in three days. It's still summer down there."

"Go, I said," Stephen growls in the deepest manly voice he can muster. "Besides, I see my, my uh, servants coming now."

Captain Pyrrhus looks toward five men walking in his direction, smiles, turns, and walks away.

"Who was that?" Ezekiel asks, his brow hovering over

squinting eyes.

"Oh, just a man," Tullia says.

"And he'd better stay away from us," Stephen adds.

Ezekiel stares a moment at the man, then back at his wife and son. He and the others squat in front of the bench.

"So, which ship will be taking us to Rome?" Tullia asks.

"I am afraid it is too late in the season," Ezekiel replies. "Every ship is either on its way to Antioch to winter at the harbor there or is staying here."

"What are we going to do? Spend the winter here in Pompeiiapolis?" Tullia asks. "If we could only get as far as Athens, we would be halfway to Rome. That would be better than here."

"One man I talked to said the port is not yet full, and there will be more ships docking here," Secundus says, moving to a sitting position and crossing his long legs in front of him.

"Achaius," Ezekiel says, standing and reaching for his belt, which doubles as a money pouch. He pulls out a silver coin. "Go into the city and find a hostel. This should be enough for two rooms."

"All four of us will go so your family can be alone a while," Trophimus says. He winks and shows his toothy smile.

"Go fast. It is almost dark. Too dangerous down here at night."

Ezekiel looks back at his wife and son. Instead of squatting again, he pulls out the long knife he and every other traveler carries with him, spreads his legs wide, crosses his arms, and holds the blade so it can be seen even from behind him.

"What if we have to winter here?" Tullia asks.

"When I was walking along the docks, I looked up the hill toward the city and saw a statue to Asklepion, god of medicine and healing. I wouldn't want to go to his temple to get Stephen's foot looked at, but it is a sign there should be many apothecaries and physicians here."

"An apothecary shop should serve our needs," Tullia says.

"Come on," Ezekiel says after a few moments. 'It's getting too dark down here. Let us go up into the city, buy a torch, and find a safer place to wait. It shouldn't take them long to find a hostel for us."

"Good idea, Father," Stephen says, remembering the unwanted sea captain.

He stands with the aid of his crutch and makes his way up the hill to the city, grunting now and then.

Just as they approach the colonnade with its statues on

either side of the walkway, they hear Justus.

"We were just coming to get you. Here is a torch for you. Now follow us. We found a grand hostel for everyone, and are told the food they serve is wonderful."

The rest of the evening is pleasant. Everyone eats, is refreshed, then goes to their room for the remainder of the night.

The following day, Ezekiel and his four employees go back down to the docks to watch for ships coming in for a temporary stop before going on to Rome.

While his wife and son wait, they purchase cayenne to make a tea for Stephen's pain, and evening primrose oil to put on his foot for the swelling.

Ezekiel and the others do not return to the hostel until dark. Tullia and Stephen are in their room, waiting for the others to arrive so they can have their evening meal together.

"Ships are coming in," Ezekiel explains to his family, sitting on the side of the bed, his feet on the floor mat Stephen is sitting on. "But they are either staying here or heading south away from the coming winter."

"What are we going to do if we are stranded here for the winter?" Tullia asks.

"I can find work as a scribe, and Stephen can find a locksmith to work for."

"But it's too dangerous for us here," Tullia objects. "We're at the foot of the Taurus mountains, and too close to the Clitae mountain men."

"And too close to Anicetus," Stephen adds. "That pirate won't let us live to tell that he stole the green marble."

"Tomorrow is another day. I still have enough silver to stay here a few more days, then rent a room in one of the *insulae* for the winter."

The following morning at dawn, Ezekiel and his men meet to return to the waterfront.

"I want to go with you, Father," Stephen says.

"Your foot looks a lot better, but broken bones do not heal overnight. Stay here and guard your mother. I am depending on you, Son."

During the day, Stephen goes with his mother to the market, where she asks around for a scribe booth. They are in luck. One is not too far from their hostel. She purchases one of the smaller scrolls for something to read while waiting for a ship bound for Athens to arrive in port.

They return to the hostel, Tullia reads, and Stephen falls asleep on his floor mat at the foot of his parents' bed.

Stephen wakens with the shadows of late afternoon.

"Mother, I am curious about the Asclepius cult here," Stephen says. "While you read, I think I will stroll over to their temple."

"Just walk past it, Stephen. Do not stop and talk to anyone," Tullia warns.

"Oh, I won't talk to any of their priests."

"Anyone, Stephen. Do not talk to anyone."

Stephen takes his crutch and heads out the door and onto the street. He hobbles in the direction of the temple to Asclepius. When he nears it, he notices a park across the main entrance and hobbles over to one of the benches.

A man in a long white tunic and blue toga walks by.

"Uh, sir," Stephen says. "Do you come to this temple very often?

"I suppose I do, young man," the stranger in the aristocratic toga replies.

"What is it like inside?"

"It's a typical temple, except it has a *hospitium* in a courtyard adjoining it in the back. The priests watch over the sick there and pray over them."

"Does it work?" Stephen asks. "I mean, praying to a false god. Does it work?"

The stranger lowers his eyes, frowns, and twists his mouth.

"Young man, those are blasphemous words. Of course, it works. Asclepius is one of the greatest gods in existence. Who are you?"

Stephen stands. "Uh, my mother and I are just visiting from Tarsus. We're leaving tonight on a ship bound for Athens."

"Then, I suggest you go get your mother and board that ship for Athens immediately."

"Yes, sir," Stephen says, holding tight to his crutch and hurrying away from the temple. He feels the toga man's eyes on him as he goes.

Back at the hostel, Stephen says nothing to his mother.

Just before dark, Ezekiel and the others return. They eat an enjoyable evening meal provided by the inn keeper's wife, while Ezekiel explains the events of the day.

"Ships still coming in. A few left heading south, but we do not want to go that direction. We need to go west. There was one more ship down there. A mate on it said they were leaving tomorrow morning."

They return to their room for the night and, in their own thoughts, pray for Jehovah to send them a ship bound for Athens. A miracle.

Banging on the door.

Banging of fists. And of wood. And of metal.

Shouting.

Ezekiel sits up in bed. He hurries to the door, but no one is there. Still, in his nightshirt, he slips down the hall in the direction of the noise. It comes from the main gate into the hostel. Trophimus comes out into the hall and follows Ezekiel.

The hostel owner goes to the front gate.

"Where are the blasphemers of Asclepius? One of them walks with a crutch. We have orders from the high priest for their execution."

Ezekiel turns around in the hall and almost runs into Trophimus.

"Quick. Is there a back gate? Get us out of here!"

He runs to his room. "Hurry. Get up. Someone is after us. Grab your clothes. We must go right now."

Ezekiel hears Achaius out in the hall. "Uh, if you are looking for a crippled man, I think there is one down that other hall. Hurry before he escapes."

In the moment of time, Achaius has bought them, Ezekiel's family stumbles out of their room and follows Trophimus to a back gate toward the stables.

"We're safe here long enough to throw some street clothes on, then we've got to move again," Ezekiel says in an urgent whisper.

Justus has slept in his street clothes like the other scribes. He stands guard at the stall Ezekiel's family is hiding in.

Trophimus is still at the back gate leading out of the hostel.

Soon Achaius appears. "Hurry. Where is Secundus?"

"He has gone ahead of us to draw attention to himself and avert any night patrols along the way," Justus whispers.

Ezekiel and his family leave their stall. Justus leads the way, followed by Trophimus and Achaius. They work their way down the hill toward the docks.

"What are we going to do?" Tullia asks, hanging on to her husband's arm.

"There is one ship down there leaving first thing in the morning."

"Where to?"

"It doesn't matter. Let us just hope whoever is on guard duty will let us on board now."

"What if he doesn't?" Stephen asks.

5 ~ TRAPPED

*T*he seven work their way in the dark down to the docks.

Justus, always fast on his feet, runs ahead toward the only ship available to rescue their group.

Stephen now sees him standing at the foot of a gangplank, the ship lit up with torches for night safety. Whoever he is talking to disappears, then returns. He is nodding his head and grinning.

Moments later, Justus runs back to Ezekiel. "We're in luck. The captain is willing to take us on board tonight. The mate said his captain was more than happy to accommodate us. Wasn't that hospitable of him?"

Ezekiel thanks Jehovah, the only true God, and takes his family to the ship.

Just before they arrive at the gangplank, Tullia stops and stares.

"Oh, I do not think this is the wisest choice."

"Huh? What is it, Mother?" Stephen asks.

He looks in the direction she is pointing.

He reads the name of the ship. *Servus Marya.*

"No!" Stephen declares.

Ezekiel turns and looks at his wife and son. "What do you mean, no?"

"We cannot go on that ship, Father. We met the captain. I do not trust him. I think Mother has had second thoughts about him too."

"Did he threaten you? Is that who you were talking to when you were waiting for me at that bench?"

"Yes, Father. I had to make him leave. I threatened him."

"What did he do? What did he say?"

"It wasn't anything he did or said. I just got a feeling. You know how people get strange feelings about someone? That is what happened to me."

"Tullia," Ezekiel says, turning to his wife. "It won't take long for the temple guards to find us. We've got to get on board this ship. It is our only chance to survive."

"Yes. Of course, you are right, dear. We need to board this ship. Besides, he said it is going where the winter will be a lot warmer than it is here."

"God will protect us—if we need protecting, that is."

Ezekiel steps onto the gangplank first, followed by Tullia and then his son. His scribes follow the family.

Onboard, the mate on guard tells them they can spend the night down in the orlop deck. He gives them a small lamp to take with them.

Once below, they set down the few belongings they had been able to grab up in the hurry of escape. Soon, the hatch above them is slammed shut. Stephen thinks he hears a lock.

They lie back, using their ever-diminishing packs as pillows, and try to sleep.

Shortly, they hear scraping of a bar. The hatch above them is opened. It is morning.

They notice the ship swaying back and forth and know they are on the open sea.

"C'm on up," the sailor says. "If you're hungry, the cap'n said to share the crew's food with you. Do not know why. It's going to take us five days to get there, and food doesn't stay good forever."

The four scribes scale the ladder first. Tullia goes next, supported from behind by her husband. Last, Stephen.

On the main deck, they are pleased to feel a warm breeze.

"You said it will take us five days to arrive," young Justus asks the sailor, always in a hurry to know things. "Where are we going?"

"Crete. The balmy island of Crete." He forms a large grin. "You are going to love it there. In fact, you may never leave." The sailor adds.

"I do not like him, Father," Stephen says. "I do not trust him either."

"You are just too suspicious," Secundus says, leaning against the bulkhead near the hatch, stretching his long legs and relieving them from the night's cramped sleeping arrangement.

The sailor leads them to a small barrel. "Your food for the

five days is in there. If it's moldy, scrape the stuff off. If it's mushy, eat it anyway. If maggots are in it, consider them an extra treat and eat them too."

He walks away, still grinning.

Achaius opens the top of the barrel.

The seven sit in a circle around it.

"Well, I am the smallest, so will not need much," Tullia says.

"I think the best thing for us to do is divide it up now, and you can wrap your share in whatever you brought with you," Ezekiel says. "If not, you'll have to think of something on your own.

"Here, Stephen," he says. "Quit watching the sailors and take your share of the food."

"I do not trust them. They keep staring at us and grinning."

"Well, we are here now. At least we are safe from whoever it was that you stirred up in the city. Let us take a walk, Stephen. You and I need to talk."

Ezekiel and Stephen step over to a railing. They look out over the waves.

"Okay, Son. Tell me what happened. Who were those men, and why were they after you?"

"How do you know they were after me?" Stephen replies. "Maybe they were after Justus or Secundus or..."

Ezekiel's eyes darken, and his brow furrows over them. "Because they said they were after a man on crutches."

Stephen sees his father's expression and looks away. He holds on to the rail, and his knuckles turn white.

Ezekiel waits.

His son presses his lips together, squints, and takes a deep breath.

Still, Ezekiel waits.

"Father," he says with unmanly tears appearing in his eyes. "Why doesn't Jehovah protect us? I was declaring him as the only true God. I did not know the man was the high priest of Asclepius. I was just doing my duty as a good Jew. I was just trying to do what was right. I was just trying to save the man's soul. I was just trying to show him he was wrong. I was just trying... I was just trying... Oh, Father. I am so mixed up. I am sorry, Father. But I was just trying..."

Ezekiel puts his hand on his son's shoulder. "I guessed as much. You have always been outspoken like your grandfather."

"I wish I wasn't like my grandfather. And like Abraham. I wish I did not want to make people listen to the truth. I wish I knew how to keep my mouth shut, Father."

"I heard your grandfather say that very thing many a time, Son. And probably Abraham thought it many a time on his cross."

"Are you going to punish me, Father? I deserve it. I deserve for you to punish me. Take my part of the food away. Beat me. Cut my tongue out. Do whatever you want. I am a bad son. I am a bad..."

Stephen sinks to the deck, his shoulders shaking, his head touching the boards.

Ezekiel moves around to the other side of Stephen. Tullia joins him. Together, they hide their son from the stares of the curious sailors and of the scribes. Their son still has mourning to work through.

The remainder of the day is spent with the three seated in the same spot. The scribes leave them alone.

Tullia pulls out the small scroll she had purchased back in Pompiiapolis and reads it.

That night, they are escorted back to the orlop deck, and the hatch closed, barred, and locked above them.

Morning. Another day. A new day. This time, all seven sit together.

"So, you have a famous grandfather," Justus says, remembering an interrupted conversation nearly a week earlier on the other ship.

Stephen grins. "Yessiree. Tell them, Mother. Tell them about your famous father."

"Well," Tullia begins with a twinkle in her eyes, "my father was Athenodorus. He was ten years younger than my future father-in-law."

"That was my other grandfather, Stephen. He died the year I was born, so I was named after him. Go ahead, Mother."

"My father was born in a village not far from Tarsus and was educated in the city. When he was grown, he began tutoring the children of rich, influential families. One of his students was Octavian."

"Not *the* Octavian," Secundus asks, pulling his hand through his thick hair.

"I am afraid so," Tullia grins. "The Octavian himself before he was called Augustus."

"Octavian sometimes had a temper, and my grandfather used to make him recite the alphabet before responding to whatever made him mad. Isn't that so, Mother?"

"That is so, and I make you do the same thing, do not it?"

"You sure do. And it works."

"To continue, when Octavian was nineteen years old, his great uncle, Julius Caesar, was assassinated, and the family sent for Octavian to return to Rome."

"And, of course, my grandfather went with him to continue being his teacher and mentor."

"Does your father still live in Rome?" Achaius asks.

"No. But I was born there," Tullia responds. "Then, when I was eighteen, my father decided to return to Tarsus. Octavian was Augustus Caesar by then and no longer needed or had time for my father."

"Hey, you!"

The group turns toward the quartermaster. Stephen's heart jumps into his throat.

"Yes, you men still swabbing the deck. You lazy good-for-nothings. I need you to throw a net overboard and snag a swordfish for the captain. He is in the mood for swordfish for his dinner tonight. Snap to it!"

A pail of water is dumped onto the deck, some of its contents running over to Stephen. He jumps up, but not in time. "Oh, well, I am wet now. May as well sit back down in it," he says, grabbing at his still painful foot.

"Let us have a little something to eat," Ezekiel says. "We've got three days to go before our arrival in Crete. We should be able to eat a little each day."

"I've got some moldy bread. Better eat it now before the fuzz gets worse," Trophimus says. He presses it together into a ball, pops it into his mouth, and swallows without chewing. "That wasn't so bad."

He goes over to a rain barrel and scoops his hand into it to get a drink of water to wash down his meal.

The others eat their allotment in similar fashion.

"Okay now, Mistress. Tell us some more about your famous father," Justus says. "He did not die as soon as he got back to Tarsus, did he?"

"Oh, no. He still had important work to do. He had learned that the city was being governed by Boethus, who was keeping most of the treasury intended for public use for his own luxuries.

"Caesar gave my father authority to do what was necessary, so my father exiled Boethus and helped write a new constitution for the city of Tarsus. Strabo himself wrote of this."

"Then what did he do?" Justus asks.

"Oh, did a little writing until his crippled hands could no longer control a quill."

"But something else happened during that time," Ezekiel says, walking over to the group from the rail.

"What was that, Master?" Justus asks.

"She met me!"

"But you were a slave then, weren't you?"

"Yes, I was. But I was hired to take her father's dictation whenever he wanted to write a letter. And he wrote a lot of letters."

"When I first met Ezekiel, he was so handsome and smart. I have to admit I fell in love with him almost from his first words to me," Tullia says.

"What were his first words to you?" Justus asks.

"Do you know where I can find more papyrus for your father's letters?"

"Those were his first words to you?" Trophimus says with his toothy smile.

"You men just do not understand a woman's heart. It wasn't what he said. It was how he said it."

"So, how did your famous father take to you falling in love with his slave?"

"Oh, I did not tell him. Besides, there was that age difference."

"Yeah," Stephen adds. "My father is thirty years older than my mother."

"Huh?"

"Son, you did not have to tell that part," Tullia says, grinning. "Well, now, you know. But our age difference made no difference to me."

"So, what happened next?" Secundus asks.

"After a year, when I was nineteen years old, we secretly married."

"But not before I converted her to Judaism," Ezekiel says. "I had a lot of work to do because of all the gods she was taught to believe in."

"He was so logical," Tullia says, taking her husband's hand and looking into his gray eyes, "I had no trouble understanding there had to be just one God, and he was the creator of all."

"Then you had me," Stephen announces.

"Not right away. I did not have you until I was twenty-one."

"That is when Grandfather Athenodorus discovered you

had married my father."

"Was he ever mad," Ezekiel says. "He sold me."

"Ha! But we fooled him. I had some money saved up, and I am the one who bought him," Tullia says.

"Well, when her father realized he was not going to get rid of me, and after Stephen was born, he announced, 'No grandson of mine is going to be a slave.'"

"So, he gave you your freedom?" Justus asks.

"Indeed, he did. And it's a good thing he did so because he died when Stephen was two years old."

"So, that is how you came to be a freedman," Achaius says. "I always wondered but never had the courage to ask. But why did you name your son Stephen?"

"Because my father died the year Stephen was born. Tullia hadn't delivered yet, and he asked me on his death bed if I would name my son after him. I told him I would be honored to."

"Hey, you over there. It's time to get in your hole."

Stephen recognizes the voice of the sailor who apparently is in charge of them.

"But the sun hasn't gone down yet," Stephen objects.

"Be quiet, Son," Ezekiel whispers. "Yes, sir," he says, rising. "Come, everyone. It is time to rest. Tomorrow we will be closer to Crete, where I was told the breeze is always warm. Come, everyone."

"Yeah, you keep believing that," the sailor says.

The seven go below, and the hatch is slammed shut. Once again, they hear the sliding of a bar and clanging of a lock.

Morning comes. They hear heavy footsteps overhead, but no one comes for them.

"What's going on up there?" Stephen yells.

They can see slivers of sun through the boards above them. But no one opens the hatch and lets them out. They wait. It never comes. Their freedom.

Another night.

"Father, what is going to happen to us?"

"I do not know, Son. We must keep praying."

"Father."

"What, Son?"

"I do not want to die."

6 ~ UNSUSPECTING

During the long hours, the silence is broken only by the squeaking of rats and heavy footsteps overhead.

"What's that?" Stephen says, grabbing hold of his father's arm in the dark.

"I do not think it was pirates again, if that is what you are thinking, Son. The pitch of the ship was too gradual."

"Probably a storm coming up," Achaius says.

"Maybe that is why they kept us down here all day," Justus adds.

Over the following hours, the ship lists one way, then the other. The sound of footsteps overhead is replaced with the fast pounding of rain.

To keep from sliding every time the ship lists, they feel around for a beam supporting the deck overhead and hang on to it. They do not sleep.

"Do you think Jehovah is punishing them?" Stephen asks.

"For what?" Ezekiel replies.

"I do not know. For what they are about to do to us."

"And what is that?"

"I do not know. But we're not at Crete yet. Maybe they will throw us overboard."

"Why?"

"Father, I do not know. I just do not know. But I do not trust the captain of this ship."

"We haven't even seen him, Son."

"We will. And when we do, we will regret coming on board this death trap."

"That is enough, Son. You will cease talking like that," Ezekiel responds in the dark.

"Let us sing a song," Tullia suggests. "One of the psalms of

David I used to sing to you when you were a baby."

"As the deer pants one?"

"Yes, that is the one. Now sing with me."

She sings, but her lyrical soprano voice is hardly heard over the pounding of the waves on the ship.

Pounding and rolling and wondering.

In the bleak darkness, Stephen's mind reels.

Will we die down here?

Is this the end of my life?

Is this all there is?

It's my fault. All my fault.

It stops. As suddenly as it had begun, the listing stops, and the roaring dies away. Pounding of footsteps above resumes.

Then they hear the rattling of the lock and scraping of the bar overhead. They look up and are blinded by the early morning sun as it streams down on them.

"Sorry, everyone," the sailor says. "It's safe to come out now. It's going to be a great day. A great day indeed." His smile is broader than usual.

The seven scale the ladder and head for their normal sitting spot. Stephen stares at the sailor before taking his usual seat on the deck. And wonders. *Why is he so happy? It was just a storm. Is there more?*

The quartermaster walks over to them. He stands straight and tall. He does not smile.

"The captain is requesting your presence this evening in his cabin. He wishes you to sup with him."

With that, he returns to the bridge to watch over the crew cleaning up after the storm. The scowl never leaves his face.

"You will like it in Rome," Tullia says. "I was just a teenager when I left there. But I loved all the activity, especially the entourage whenever a senator traveled here and there around the city. The senators loved the attention. And imports from all over the world—peacocks, pearls, silk—you name it."

"I am sure Rome will be all that, dear," Ezekiel says. "But more amazing is how Jerusalem has rebuilt itself. Just one hundred years ago, Pompey destroyed much of Jerusalem. And look at it now."

"I've never seen Jerusalem, Father," Stephen says.

"You know what I mean. Besides, maybe my scribe school will do so well in Rome, we can begin going to all three of the Jewish festivals. Jerusalem, Jerusalem. It has risen to be one of the grandest cities of the world. And the magnificent white temple Herod the Great—with all his faults—built for us."

Ezekiel stares into the distance. His hands come up as though drawing what he sees.

"There it is. On the highest point of Jerusalem—Mount Moriah. It can be seen for *milles* around in all its splendor."

He drops his hands and drops his gaze. "But it is not enough. Your grandfather, Stephen, dreamed of the Jerusalem he had known as a youth being brought back to the glory days of Solomon."

Silence.

"Perhaps we can serve as ambassadors in Rome," Ezekiel continues. "Perhaps we can convert many to Judaism, and they will want to move there. And Jehovah's very name will be magnified before the pagan Gentiles. And they will give up their false gods with their statues and temples. That was your grandfather's dream, Stephen. Where ever we go, we shall proclaim his name."

Silence.

"But, Father, the more we act, the less we accomplish. Look at what happened to Abraham for speaking out. Look what happened to all of us because I was dumb enough to speak out at that seaport. I am all mixed up."

"Someone said we will be in Crete by tomorrow morning," Tullia says with an exaggerated smile. "They apparently have such mild winters there, we can consider it a kind of vacation. Then we will be all rested up in the Spring and ready to complete our move to Rome." She sighs.

"But we are a sight. What will the people of Crete think of us? We lost most of our possessions when our mule was thrown overboard after that pirate rammed our ship. And we lost more when we had to rush out of Pompiiapolis. I only have one change of clothes left, and both have become tattered. And I am so dirty from that awful place they make us sleep in. And..."

"Do not worry, dear," Ezekiel says. "I have enough money left to rent us a room on Crete and for you to buy some clothes. Do not cry. Tullia. Do not cry."

"Yes, Mother. Everything on Crete will be sunny and bright and clean. You'll see, Mother."

Mid-afternoon comes. "Folks, it's time for you to go for a little swim."

"Huh?"

"What?"

"No!"

"You cannot do that to us. We paid full passage," Stephen objects. "I won't do it. You cannot make us. You are devils."

"Up, everyone," the sailor says. "These are my orders. You can either jump into the water or lower yourself by a rope."

Ezekiel stands and helps Tullia up. His four scribes stand.

"Come on, Stephen. Postponing it will not make it any easier."

"But we did not do anything," he objects. "I won't go."

Tullia stoops and takes Stephen's hand. "Come, Son. We will do it together. I will be on one side of you and your father on the other. Between the three of us, I think we will be able to float for a long time. You will see. Jehovah will give us strength."

"But we're nearly a full day from Crete. We cannot float that long."

"Come, dear. Your father and I will help you."

Stephen looks up into his mother's eyes and allows her to bring him to his feet, holding his hand. He looks over at his father. Ezekiel takes his other hand.

"We do not have all day. Now get down there in the water," the sailor bellows. "Now!"

The four scribes lead the way. One by one, they jump feet first into the brine. Tullia, Stephen, and Ezekiel walk slowly to the edge of the ship, where the chain has been removed for entering and exiting.

"Are you ready, Son?" Ezekiel asks.

Before Stephen can reply, they are airborne. Then in the water. Down, down, down. Kicking. Holding their breath. Trying not to let go of each other. Down, down.

Then the reversal. They begin to rise. Kicking. Holding on. Not breathing. Reaching, Straining. Hoping.

Now breathing.

Stephen looks around. The ship is far above them. The four scribes are swimming what Stephen assumes is south. Ezekiel and Tullia are treading water and being brave for their son. The son they would give their life for.

"All right," they hear above them. "Do not go so far away."

"You just want to watch us die!" Stephen calls up to them, water seeping into his throat and the salt in it burning.

"When you are done," the sailor bellows from far above, "I have lowered a rope ladder for you to come back on board."

"Huh? What is he talking about?" Stephen asks his

parents.

"Ha, ha, ha. He sent us down here to take a bath," Tullia responds.

"I have to admit, we'd gotten pretty smelly," Ezekiel responds. "Ha, ha, ha."

"Well, run your fingers through your hair, Son, and make sure all the visitors are shaken out," Tullia urges.

"And under your arms. It can get stinky under there," Ezekiel adds, treading water with the others.

"All right, down there. That is enough. Come back on board."

Tullia is the first to reach the rope ladder. She pulls her weight up with her arms, but cannot do so far enough for her feet to reach the bottom rung.

"Sir," Ezekiel calls up to the rough sailor. "My wife is not strong enough. Can you send down a basket for her? She is not a large woman. Surely you have a basket she can be pulled back on board in."

"Wait here," the sailor growls. Momentarily, he returns with a basket. He ties a long rope on it and lowers it to Tullia.

Stephen holds it still while continuing to tread water, and Ezekiel helps her climb in, though she must do so headfirst.

"How graceful of me," Tullia says when she is seated.

"Okay, haul her up!" Ezekiel announces.

In a while, all seven are back on board, laughing and dripping seawater on the deck.

"All right. Walk around until you are dry," the sailor orders.

"Yes, sir," Stephen says, smiling at their guardian sailor for the first time.

Just as the sun begins to turn red in preparation for descending below the horizon, the sailor returns with a smaller basket.

"Your clothes are in there."

"Clothes?" Tullia asks, still smiling.

"You did not think you could eat with the captain looking and smelling like you did, did you?"

"I suppose not," she responds.

After the men don their fresh clothes, they form a circle around Tullia with their backs to her to provide privacy.

"Okay, everyone, you can quit protecting my honor. I am presentable," she says.

"Oh, sweetheart, you look wonderful. What is your tunic made of?" Ezekiel asks.

"I believe this is silk. Gold silk. And you men do not look so bad yourself. All your tunics are short, but that is okay. The air is already much warmer than it was up north. But you are all dressed alike. Even your sandals are the same. No imagination, that captain," she says.

They hear a voice from up on the bridge. "You will follow me," the quartermaster bellows, still scowling.

The seven stifle their grins and take the steps to the bridge. Behind the helmsman is a door which everyone knows leads to the captain's cabin. The quartermaster opens the hatch for them, and they file in.

As soon as Stephen sees the captain, he stiffens. He grabs his mother's hand.

"I know, Son. I do not think I trust him either," she whispers.

"Ah. At last, we meet again," Captain Pyrrhus says in his suave voice.

He steps up to Tullia and takes her hand. "You, my lovely one, shall sit on my right."

He looks over at Stephen, who is glaring at him. "Oh, well, the husband can sit on my left."

Ezekiel clears his throat. "Sir, I am her husband. This is our son."

The captain stops and stares at the other men, then back at Ezekiel. "How could you have been so lucky? Oh, I know. You have a lot of money and bought her affections. Well, that I can appreciate."

"It wasn't like that," Stephen interjects. Both parents glare at him, and he says no more.

The captain looks over at the quartermaster. "Tell the steward we are ready."

With that, the quartermaster leaves, and Captain Pyrrhus seats himself in a fine chair made of green marble. The others seat themselves on wooden benches.

Soon the steward arrives with his helpers. Trays are brought in of a strange meat which the captain identifies as swordfish. "My favorite."

A second tray contain slices of fresh apples and cooked apples, dried figs, and dried grapes.

A third tray contains an assortment of cheeses.

A fourth tray contains bread and bowls of yogurt and of raisin sauce for dipping.

Finally, a sailor arrives with a large pitcher of wine.

"Ha, ha! Do you like our feast? It is a feast of celebration. We will be in Crete by tomorrow morning."

"I think I and my scribes will be setting up business somewhere to make our services available to whoever wants a deed or other document drawn up, or a book copied, or whatever they desire." Ezekiel waits for approval.

"Indeed, I believe you will be busier than you dream using your skills. And will your, uh, son, be scribing with you?"

"No, captain. He is a locksmith. My father was a blacksmith and taught me the trade along with scribing. I, in turn, taught it to him. Then, when we moved from Tarsus when my father-in-law freed me...freed me...freed me to pursue my talents elsewhere, I apprenticed my twelve-year-old son to a locksmith."

"My master died just last year," Stephen adds, "and the family let me have his tools so I could continue his business."

"So, we have scribes and a locksmith. Fine. Fine. And you, my lovely, what can you do?"

Ezekiel stands, glaring. But before he can say anything, the captain offers him some fried apples. "They are delicious. We bring the apples onboard green, and as they ripen, I eat them. Do sit and enjoy my delicacies."

Ezekiel reseats himself, but his eyes do not leave his wife.

"As I was saying," Captain Pyrrhus continues, "what are your skills, dear?"

"Well, sir, I can read, write, and cipher numbers quite well," she says, smiling and blinking her eyes as a shy maiden would.

"But hostessing. I would imagine hostessing would be your greatest talent, my lovely."

The captain glances over at Ezekiel, once again glaring at him.

"You leave my mother alone," Stephen announces.

Pyrrhus smiles. "Oh, so protective. That is good. That is wise in the kind of world we live in. Good for you. Keep your woman protected. Now, who all needs more wine?"

The dinner progresses until everyone is satisfied.

"I play the lyre. Would you like to hear a song? It is a song of Crete. You will love it," the captain says.

His dinner guests smile at their host, and he sings them his song.

"This next one is a little slower. It is perfect for a beautiful woman to dance by."

"My wife does not dance," Ezekiel announces, once again

glaring.

"Of course, she doesn't. I was just saying. Well, here is the tune anyway. As I play, you can imagine her dancing in front of you."

A knock on the cabin hatch.

"Sir," the quartermaster says. "I hate to interrupt, but the helmsman would like you to double-check his directions. The stars are out."

"The time has gone by with such delightful company, I almost forgot. Certainly. Tell the helmsman I will be out as soon as my friends leave."

The hatch is held open for the seven. The last one to leave is Trophimus.

"Oh, and you do not have to give the clothes back. They are yours to keep. I do trust you will wear them when we disembark at Crete tomorrow morning. Everyone will be impressed."

Now back in the orlop deck and sufficiently locked in, they talk.

"What is he up to?" Stephen asks.

"Master, you are imagining too much," Justus says. "He is just a nice fellow. That is all."

In the blackness, Stephen feels his mother's hand touch his, and his father put his arm across his shoulder.

"Do not worry, Son. We will have a good winter and be well settled in Rome within six months. You'll see."

Stephen detects worry in his mother's voice.

Jehovah, do not let us be killed on Crete.

7 ~ THE SURPRISE

"**H**ey, everyone, today's your big day," the guardian sailor says as he opens the hatch above their heads.

They stretch and make their way up the ladder and onto the main deck. They look out over the waves and see land.

"Is that Crete?" Stephen asks.

"Yes, my boy, it is." The voice is of Captain Pyrrhus. "The storm blew us off course a little, so we are not going to be able to winter in the Balo Lagoon. Too bad, too. It is at the west end of the island and much closer to Rome."

"So, where are we docking?" Achaius asks, taking it upon himself to speak for the others, as is often his habit.

"We are going to Amyklaion Harbor," he calls down from the bridge. "The great palace at Phaistos is there. It is my second favorite spot on the island. The ancient palace is not exactly used as a palace anymore. It has many other uses."

The seven line up along the rail of the forecastle and watch the island draw closer.

Bells ring. Sailors man their landing stations.

"Weigh anchor!"

"Man the lanyards."

"Unfurl sails!"

"Ready to cast the howser!"

"Right rudder!"

Looking past the bowsprit and the figurehead of some goddess Stephen does not recognize, he thinks he can detect the palace high on a hill overlooking the harbor. It is dark, a surprise to him since the houses and warehouses are white or the color of peaches.

At last, they feel a jerk. The ship has nudged the dock. Sailors cast howsers along the pier until the ship is parallel to it.

They jump onto the dock and wrap the howsers tight around the pilings.

The chain is taken away from the exit, and the gangplank lowered.

Tullia smiles and runs her hands down her new gold silk tunic to straighten any wrinkles. She pats her hair, which she has tied in a knot on top of her head, to make sure no strands have worked their way loose.

"Shall we?" she says to the others.

They hear the captain. "Follow me, friends. Crete is going to be full of surprises for you."

Tullia leads the way onto the dock, smiling.

Ezekiel follows close behind. Then Stephen. Finally, the four scribes.

"Now, what?" she asks, turning to the captain.

"Now, I sell you."

"What?"

"Huh?"

"What are you saying?"

"You traitor you!" Stephen shouts. "I should have never trusted you. I hate you!"

Seven sailors walk up behind the new arrivals and chain their hands behind their back.

"The slave trade here is the best in the world. I have made millions off specimens like you. Buyers come here from everywhere."

"You devil!" Ezekiel bellows.

"Why, thank you," Captain Pyrrhus replies. "Of course, I cannot sell you today. You will have to wait a day or two, so I can advertise you. And you, my lovely," he adds, leering at Tullia, "will bring one of the highest prices I have ever charged. Men from everywhere will compete with each other to have you."

Ezekiel and Stephen simultaneously lunge at the captain. They are grabbed from behind by their chains and shoved to the dock. The captain steps over to Ezekiel and slams his foot down on his back.

"I am going to give you a day to say goodbye to your wife. Then, you will never see her again."

Captain Pyrrhus laughs his hearty laugh and walks away.

The sailor jerks Ezekiel up and runs a long rope around the neck of each of the seven until he reaches the person in front.

"March."

"Where?" Stephen asks. His parents glare at him.

"Shut up and march up that hill."

A horseman appears. The sailor hands the loose end of the rope up to the horseman.

"Do not pull them too fast. They need their clothes to be decent when we get them on the auction block."

With that, the horseman works his way slowly up the hill leading to the dark palace.

"Father, will I never see you and Mother again?" Stephen blubbers.

"Be strong, Son. Be strong," Ezekiel replies.

"Shut up back there," the horseman barks.

Stephen puts his mind in limbo. He can no longer allow himself to think.

The unwanted, unmanly tears that have flowed so freely since the crucifixion of his best friend, Abraham, invade again. One month ago, a normal life for a normal young man. Nothing normal since. Nor will it ever be again and forevermore.

No more mother. No more father. No more familiar neighborhood. No more Ahab or Abraham. No more anything but an existence that is no existence at all.

Walking.

Walking and stumbling and getting back up again.

Toward the palace. The dark palace. The palace that will swallow him up like a monster.

Arriving at the palace, the horseman dismounts and walks toward a guard at a door half underground and half above.

"Where do you want them, Babatunde?"

"I will take over from here. You go on back down to the docks in case another shipload of them arrives today."

The tall Nubian guard takes the end of the rope, jerks it, and Tullia steps forward, almost tripping.

He leads them inside the bowels of the palace. He pauses to grab a torch off the wall and takes them down a long, dark corridor. At the far end, he speaks to another guard.

"They're yours as soon as you open the gate," Babatunde says.

A gate rattles. The second guard unwinds the rope from around Tullia's neck and pushes her inside. He does the same with all seven, then slams the gate closed.

The clanging of the metal bars echoes back up the corridor they had just come from.

"So, you found another goon to add to your collection, eh?"

"Shut up!" their new guard shouts.

To their surprise, the cell is supplied with benches all the way around.

"I guess they do not want us to get our clothes dirty before selling us," Trophimus says.

They hear the second guard walk a few steps away, then stop.

"He must have a guard station nearby," Secundus says.

"Well, we're not going anywhere now. We may as well sit," Achaius says.

"Are you okay, sweetheart?" Ezekiel asks. He takes his wife into his arms. He notices Stephen watching them in the dim torchlight and extends his arm to include him in his embrace.

They break away and sit together on the bench closest to the gate.

"Well, I've been in worse situations," Ezekiel finally says.

"When was that?" Tullia asks.

"Well, not me. But my father was."

They are quiet for a long time.

They hear footsteps coming down the dark corridor toward them.

"They cannot be ready for us yet," Tullia says. "He hasn't had time to advertise us yet."

The footsteps stop, and a large tray is set on the floor just outside the bars.

"Dinner."

The footsteps disappear back up the corridor.

Justus steps over to the tray and reaches through the bars to retrieve whatever has been left for them to eat.

"Well, not bad, considering everything. Let me see. They gave us bread and some sort of stew. I guess they want to keep us fattened up kind of like the captain did last night."

Justus distributes the food, and they eat in silence.

There is not much talk the rest of the day. Ezekiel hears his parents whisper at length. He is curious what they have so much to talk about when all hope of freedom is lost.

Perhaps they are saying goodbye to each other.

"Uh, kind sir," he finally hears his mother say to the guard. "My name is Tullia. What's yours?"

"Huh?"

"I said, my name is Tullia. What is your name?"

"Well, uh, my name is Draco."

"That is a fine name," Tullia replies. "It is Latin for Dragon, isn't it?"

"How did you know that?" the voice in the shadows asks.

"I know the Latin language. More and more people are speaking it. In another lifetime, it will be the language of everyone in the world—well of every educated person in the world."

Tullia switches from speaking Greek to speaking Latin. "Do you read very much?"

"Yes, ma'am. I try to."

"If you can read, what are you doing in this job?"

"Ma'am, I am only twenty years old. I am working my way up through the ranks. As soon as I can afford a horse, I plan to be an equestrian. Equestrians get a lot of respect in Caesar's army."

"You're not working for the Romans right now?"

"No, ma'am. I am covering for a friend who is sick. I do not much like this job, but he is my friend, and friends help each other out whenever they need it."

"You sound like a fine young man," Tullia continues. "So, are you reading anything special right now? I mean, about medicine or mathematics, oratory or philosophy?"

"Posidonius. He wrote about everything."

"Are you sure you are who you claim to be?" Tullia asks. "Only the wealthiest of families are given such education as you seem to have."

"Well, okay. I am not in the Roman army. But I did make friends with the guard I am substituting for. I chose him because I wanted to do an experiment. I wanted to see how people act before their lives are sold away."

"Oh, my," Tullia responds.

"You are an enigma to me, ma'am," he continues. "You do not act normal."

"Well, then, I shall stop talking. By the way, how long is your shift?"

"Just got here. I will be here all night."

"Will you be back?"

"Yes, my friend agreed for me to take his place for a fortnight."

"In that case, wake me before you leave."

"I will, ma'am."

"Mother," Stephen says when she sits back between her husband and son, "this will be our last night together. I want to stay awake all night, but it's so hard."

"Son, there may be a way for us to reverse our destiny for the good. Pray to Jehovah tonight that he will make a new path for us. Pray hard, Stephen."

The night is not long enough. Suddenly, Stephen realizes he had dropped off in mid-sentence, praying to Jehovah, and he is just now waking up.

"Is it morning?" he whispers to his father. "Where is Mother?"

"Kind sir," he hears his mother say. "Draco, are you still here?'

"Yes, ma'am. I am still here."

"I am not sure where on Crete we are. Could you tell me just where Phaistos is?"

"Well, we are about a *mille* from the Libyan Sea to the south, and four *milles* from Gortyn to the east."

"Is Gortyn a big city?"

"Yes, ma'am. It is the Roman provincial capital of Creta Cyrenica. They made the island of Crete part of the province of Cyrenica in northern Africanus."

"I see. Well, I suppose you are leaving soon."

"As soon as my replacement arrives."

"Come over here. There is something special I want to give you."

Draco steps over to the bars of the cell gate with a torch.

Tullia has a small scroll in her hand.

"What's that?"

"Open it and see."

The guard puts his torch on the wall and unrolls the scroll. He reads.

"This is signed by Athenodorus himself, ma'am."

"Yes, Athenodorus was a student of Posidonius whose works you have been reading. Take this to your governor."

"Proconsul Governor Blasius?"

"Yes. Hand it to him personally and to no one else."

"First, he is preparing to attack an outlaw on the mainland. Second, I do not think he will consent to see me. He never heard of me."

"Tell him it is an urgent message from the daughter of Atherodorus."

"He was your father?"

"Yes. Tell him I and my family and my scribes are being imprisoned here and are due to be sold as slaves tomorrow by

Captain Pyrrhus."

"Oh, yes. Captain Pyrrhus, one of the meanest pirates coming out of Crete. Suave and mean."

"Tell him where Pyrrhus has his ship. An early win in his campaign against outlaws will go well with Caesar."

"You know Caesar too?" Draco asks.

They hear the echo of footsteps coming down the dark corridor.

"There is my replacement."

"Go quickly. You do not have a horse, but you are young. You should be in Gortyn by noon."

The footsteps are close.

"Hurry," Tullia urges.

"Reporting for duty," the day guard says.

Draco turns, salutes the day guard, does not look back at Tullia, and walks with quick steps toward the outside door.

The day guard shakes the iron gate to make sure it is still secure, then takes his place on a bench where Draco had just spent the night.

"Mother, what were you talking about to that guard?" Stephen asks.

"You shouldn't be fraternizing with those men," Ezekiel says. "Stop talking to them. I forbid it."

There is enough light from the torch on the corridor wall, they can tell Tullia is smiling.

"What are you up to, sweetheart?" Ezekiel asks.

"Ohhh, nothing."

"Mother, stop teasing us. This is going to be our last day together. These are our last hours together," Stephen says, annoyed at his mother's glibness.

She does not respond.

"Mother, do you remember when I was five years old and climbed into that vat? I was so scared."

"Yes, Son, I remember. Once you were in, you couldn't get out."

"Well, that is what I feel like now. Trapped. Which is exactly what we are."

"Silence."

"And all because I couldn't keep my mouth shut. I had to brag on Jehovah and how much better he is than make-believe gods. I had to go and make them mad. Big me. Now little me. Invisible me. Me that is going to be sold as a slave tomorrow and never see my family again. Why?"

Stephen stands in the dim shadows, puts hands on his head, and turns in place.

"Oh, shut up, Stephen," Justus says.

"Stephen," Ezekiel says. "sit."

"Grandfather spoke out when Pompey took Jerusalem. Why shouldn't I?" Stephen asks, standing still.

"You are, indeed, like your grandfather," Ezekiel says. "And look what it... Well, nothing. Just sit and be quiet."

"Yes, I know what it got him. Slavery. Just like now."

"Shhhh."

Waiting resumes. Waiting for what they do not want. Waiting for the dreaded impossible to become possible. Waiting for an unasked-for-doom. Or was it?

If they had not run away, the priests would have killed them. If they had not boarded that ship, the priests would have found and killed them.

They did escape. But escape one web only to be trapped in another. From black widow to tarantula. From killer waves to killer maelstrom. Nowhere to turn. Nowhere to go. No up anymore. Just down. Down, down to doom.

Footsteps. Is it noon already?

Tullia quickly steps over to the barred gate and says one last prayer.

It is Draco with the tray. He bends to set it on the floor outside their cell. Tullia bends also.

"There is a small boat waiting for you at the far end of the pier," he whispers. "It has branches over it, but I left a strand of red rope to mark it for you."

"How many will it hold?" Tullia asks in low tones.

"Four."

"No. It must hold eight."

"Impossible."

"Hey, what are you two whispering about over there. Leave the tray and go," the day guard says.

Draco stands. "It's just me. The guy who delivers the food is sick. Well, I will be back at dark to begin my shift."

Without looking at Tullia, he turns and makes his way back up the corridor.

She reaches through the bars and brings seven bowls through into the cell, then reaches back for the seven pieces of flatbread for sopping.

"What did he say?" Stephen asks his mother, whispering.

"He said they have a boat for us to escape in, but I told him it wasn't large enough. It must hold eight people."

"You said what? Mother!"

Stephen catches his father's eye and says no more.

They eat in silence.

Stephen eats half of his and throws the remainder of his bread into the bowl. He stands and walks in place in circles.

"Mother. Thank you."

"For what?" Tullia asks.

"For reminding me to stop being so selfish. But it's hard, Mother. It sometimes is so hard."

"I know, Son. It takes determination to stand for right when it would be easier to follow wrong."

He looks over at his father's four scribes. "Forgive me."

"For what?" Secundus asks, running his hand through his thick hair.

"Well, nothing. Just forgive me."

"You make it easy," Trophimus says with his toothy grin. "We do not know what we're forgiving you for, so consider yourself forgiven."

"You may not know, but I do." Stephen pauses. "Life gets too mixed up sometimes."

"You can say that," Justus says.

After more pacing, Stephen re-seats himself. The waiting resumes. The quiet waiting. Only this time, there is hope. A tiny flame of hope. Just an ember. Will it ever be more than that?

Sitting. Waiting. Hoping. Not hoping. Struggling. Will they ever see each other again? Will God rescue them, after all? Did God approve of defending him after all?

Footsteps finally. The new shift is about to begin. Draco appears. He does not look toward the cell.

"You're late," the day guard says.

"Sorry. It won't happen again. It will never happen again. I promise you that."

"Well, it had better not."

With that, the day guard walks up the corridor and to the outside.

Tullia, Ezekiel, and Stephen step to the bars. The other four have not been told the plan.

"Well?" Tullia asks.

"I was able to find a boat that holds twelve. It is at the far end of the pier."

"How will we get out of here?" Ezekiel asks. "We saw all

kinds of people in the courtyard of the palace when we came. I do not see how we can ever escape. It's useless."

8 ~ DANGER BETWEEN HERE & THERE

"While I was at the governor's estate, I found the archives and asked if there was a diagram of this palace. There was, and I found a door right on the other side of the table where I sit to guard you.

"It has been painted over and not in a long time, and we may not be able to get it open. But we can try."

"Thank you, Draco," Tullia says. "I will make sure you are well rewarded. I do not know how, but I keep my promises."

Draco takes out his keys and unlocks the cell door.

Ezekiel's four scribes stand. "What is going on here?" Achaius asks, balling his fists, his brows lowered above his dark eyes. "It's night, isn't it? Have they decided to kill us instead?"

Stephen turns toward Achaius. "He is setting us free. My mother arranged it. Did not you, Mother?"

"Okay, who is the strongest among you?" Draco asks.

"Stephen," everyone says in unison.

"Not me. I am the skinniest one of all of you."

"But the muscles you built up blacksmithing, Son. You definitely are the strongest. Now, go help the man."

Stephen grins and walks through the cell door out to the corridor.

"Okay, see if you can pull that door open," Draco says.

Stephen struts over to the door and grabs the wrought-iron pull with both hands. The pull is long and only two fingers wide. It has been flattened, but enough has not been that it can be taken hold of. Stephen tugs. His young muscles strain. The door does not budge.

"It may be sealed. I cannot make much noise down here without attracting attention," Draco says.

"If you have a cloth, place it over the edge of the door and tap with the handle of your sword," Stephen says. "Work your way around."

Draco looks at Ezekiel, who nods. "Do what he says. He's our expert on locking things up."

The group waits while Draco taps around the edges of the door to loosen whatever may be holding it. He steps back.

Stephen takes hold of the door pull with both hands and once again tugs at it. His shoulders lean back. His feet dig into the dirt floor. He grits his teeth. The veins on his forehead protrude. He grunts. The door does not budge.

"Justus, why do not you men take a turn?"

One by one, the four scribes grip and tug at the door pull. It does not move.

"Hey, what was that?" he mutters as the last man gives up. "I heard something."

"Shhhh, everyone," Draco urges. "What did you hear, Stephen? That is your name, isn't it? Stephen?"

"Hold your torch down here," Stephen replies.

"Looks like we have loosened rust around the lock."

"There's a lock in the door?" Draco asks.

"See if one of your keys works," Stephen says, shifting to one side.

Draco inserts every one of his keys on his wrought-iron ring. None of them work.

"Hand me your keys," Stephen says.

Draco looks over at Ezekiel.

"Do what the lad says. He is young, but he is also an expert locksmith."

Draco hands the keys to Stephen. He takes one and inserts it in the hole."

"That is my smallest key. It won't work in that large hole," Draco insists.

"Shhh. I am concentrating," Stephen whispers.

He gouges the small key one way, then another. He holds his ear close to the mechanism. He does it again. And again."

"What..."

"Shhh."

Again, he twists the key around in the large hole. He stands, smiling.

"Okay, Father. It's your turn. Open the door."

"Ezekiel grins at his son, knowing what he has done. He steps over to the door, takes the door pull with one hand, and the door opens.

"How'd you do that?" Draco asks Ezekiel, still whispering.

"I told you. My son is a genius locksmith."

"Hey, what's going on down there?" The voice at the other end of the dark corridor booms and echoes.

"That is my boss," Draco says. "Hurry."

Stephen is first through the door and out into the cool night. He looks up in the moonless sky and decides where the white seagulls are coming from. He runs in that direction and soon realizes he is on an incline.

He does not look back but hears the scuffling of feet running through the underbrush right behind him. He runs, dodging young palms still growing close to the ground. He trips on an occasional rock protruding from the soil. He zig-zags and takes each step as though his life depends on it.

Running. Running from slavery and hopelessness and a living death. Running for...for freedom. But where? It does not matter. Run. Keep running.

Stephen hears the water lapping against the seashore. He sees ships lined up along the docks, each one lit up with torches and guarded. He does not know whether the boat is to his left or his right. He turns left.

Running now through the sand and rocks. Running and looking for the boat. The small boat of hope.

He sees bushes ahead. He runs to them and grabs them. They are stuck to the ground. Wrong place.

He runs to another clump of undergrowth. Again, he grabs. Again, he is rebuffed by roots deep in the soil.

On down the beach. Hurrying. Running. Testing. Searching. Relentless searching for hope and escape and life.

He tries yet another clump of undergrowth. The first branch comes loose. He tosses it aside. He pulls another branch off and another.

"Here. Let me help you." It is Justus.

Together, the two youths uncover a boat.

Draco arrives. "There are twelve sets of oars inside. Everyone in."

"Draco? What are you doing here?"

"Never mind that. We were discovered. Hurry."

Tullia and the others climb into the boat. Stephen and Draco stay out and push it away from the shore. Once it is afloat, they too climb aboard.

They look back toward the shore and see torches all along

the docks from one end of the ships lined up for the winter to the other end.

They hear shouting. "Halt!"

They hear arrows flying through the air.

"Stay along the coastline," Draco says in a loud whisper. "But hurry."

The seven men pull on the oars as Tullia, sitting in the front of the boat, taps on the bench in a rhythm to synchronize their efforts.

When the lights from the dock disappear, they see ahead of them more lights.

"Oh, no."

"That is Gortyn ahead of us. Let us head out into the sea now. Look at the north star up there. Head south," Draco says in a loud whisper, knowing the waves will carry his voice far.

The men row. Tullia taps. All night they row. Tullia sometimes sings one of David's psalms to help keep the rhythm. The others join her to help them stay awake.

They row until they think their arms will fall off, and row some more.

Freedom. Row for freedom. Row for everything that is good in the world. Row to escape everything that is bad in the world. Keep on rowing. Keep rowing and rowing.

Do not listen to the aches and cramps. Do not listen to a body that screams to stop and rest. Do not listen to whatever interferes with freedom.

Gray appears in the eastern sky.

"Okay, guys. Let us stop," Draco says, no longer whispering. "We began rowing around the fourth hour of the night. I figured it would take you about fifteen hours to get there. We have rowed about nine hours, so we should arrive about the time the sun is highest in the sky.

"I have a couple questions for you," Ezekiel responds, rubbing his aching muscles. "Why are you here? And where is there?"

As the sun lightens up the world, Stephen and the others see that Draco is thinner than he seemed in the shadows of the dungeon and corridor. He is thin, has reddish-brown hair and no beard. He seems to be a little older than Stephen and a little younger than Justus.

"I am here," Draco explains, "because after the last of you left, I realized I was about to be caught helping you escape. Of course, that would have meant I would be sold as a slave in your place, or killed by slow death for costing your owner a fortune. So, I had to escape with you.

"As to your second question, there is Libya. Crete is about two hundred *milles* from Libya, the closest to the southern end of the island."

"But that is in the opposite direction we want to go," Tullia says. "Not that we do not appreciate your assistance, but wouldn't Athens be just as close for us?"

"Yes, pretty much the same. But, remember, we were on the southern end of the island, and we would have had to go around it to the northern point closest to Greece. That would have added another hundred and fifty *milles*.

"My wife and I are most grateful for what you did for us. All of us," Ezekiel interjects.

"Yes, yes," everyone says, almost in unison.

"Well, I guess we have rested long enough," Stephen says. "We need to get to—where did you say we were going? Oh, yes, Libya. How good is the food there?"

"Hold on, Son. You are younger than the rest of us. We older ones need to rest a little longer."

"I stashed some food onboard for us. There is a basket tucked under the front bench where Tullia is sitting."

Tullia looks under her bench and pulls out the promised basket. "Oh, Draco. We owe you so much. Let me see here," she says, almost giddy.

She takes the lid off and sees an assortment of cheese, bread, and dried figs. She divides them among everyone.

"Under my seat is a jug of water. I do not know how long it will last, but it's all I could carry."

Draco passes around the jug, and everyone takes a swig. Everyone but Tullia. Stephen holds the heavy jug for her while she takes a sip.

"Well, I guess we had better be on our way. As we draw closer, head to the left of the land jutting out into the sea the most. We do not want to get blown into the inviting harbor there and get caught in the treacherous sands of Syrta. The north wind is strong there. Sailors go in and never come out."

Tullia clears her throat and begins tapping the bench beside her in rhythm. The men stuff the remainder of their allotment of food in their mouth and begin rowing. Once Tullia is confident they are through eating, she begins singing another of David's psalms, and the others join in with her.

The sun is now red in the east as it makes its appearance on the new day. New and fresh and warm and full of freedom.
The Lord's my shepherd.
Beat.
I shall not hunger.
Beat.
He leads me to still waters.
Beat.
He makes me lie down.
Beat.
The sun is now yellow and bright and welcoming.

As they row, the sun brings more warmth. Then heat.

Tullia looks toward the back to her husband. His face is red, breathing hard.

"Dear, you need to stop and let the young men take us the rest of the way," she calls back to him.

"I am old, but not that old, Tullia. I do my share."

"Well, how about taking every other stroke then, Father?" Stephen says, calling over his shoulder.

On they row to Tullia's beat. Singing sometimes. Sometimes not. Thinking. Trying not to think. In a daze. A dream world. A world of waves with more churning bubbles all the time.

An hour. Another. Another. Ah, freedom. Sweet, sweet freedom.

"I see land ahead," Draco announces. "Let us stop and pass the water jug around."

"And have some more cheese and bread," Tullia announces.

"We ate it all," Stephen says.

"You just think we did. I was devious and kept back enough for everyone to have another couple bites. Here you go, everyone."

She stands, and the boat teeters a moment. When it steadies, she passes the food back to everyone.

After everyone has had their break, Draco makes another announcement. "It is going to take us another hour or two to reach the shore. Even staying to the left away from the harbor will be dangerous for its own reasons. We will have to slow way down and pick our way through the underwater rocks."

"I can watch for them if you men can continue to row in synchronization," Tullia says. "The water is clear and easy to see through."

"We won't be rowing much longer," Draco says.

Tullia stands and leans on the bow of their boat. "We seem to be safe so far," she calls back after a while. "No, wait. I think I see one. Veer to your right."

Stephen, seated closest to her, calls out, "Veer to your right, men."

They slow the boat and work it to the right, then back left again, so they do not go off course.

Little by little now. A hand span at a time.

"There's another one," Tullia shouts.

This time she holds out her left arm, and the men veer to the left.

Progress still slow. Slow and easy and steady.

"Veer right," she shouts, holding out her right arm.

Slower now. Veering right, then back on course.

"Veer left! No farther left. Farther. Okay, now, right."

Ezekiel stands in place so he can see into the clear waters off Libya. He holds out his oar and pushes it farther from the rock they just circumvented. He watches still. Now the rock on the left. He plunges his oar into the water and jabs at the rock to keep the aft part of the boat from sliding into it.

Slow. Steady. Veer left. Veer right. Left again. Right again. Zig zagging toward freedom.

They are close enough to see a few ships—though not many—tied up along shore. Ships he surmises that approach Libya from Egypt to the East.

I wonder what it will be like here in Libya, Stephen thinks. *Well, whatever it's like, we won't be here long. Just for the winter. Then on to Rome, where maybe we will be famous.*

He notices fishermen washing their nets along part of the shore, apparently after a night of fishing. *I wonder what kind of fish they eat here.*

"Left. Farther left. Farther."

The noise of the surf picks up. Waves. Incoming waves. Waves pounding in to shore. And into the rocks between them and safety.

"Now, right. Now left. Right. There are too many!"

Stephen hears it. The scraping along the bottom of their boat. They all hear it.

"What'll we do?" Tullia turns and shouts.

The boat begins to fill with water. Ezekiel climbs between the men and stumbles over the seats to get to the front of the boat and his wife.

He grabs her hand. He turns and grabs Stephen's hand.

"We've done this before. We can do it again."

With that, the three jump into the cold water and hope they do not hit a rock.

9 ~ NEW HORIZON

"**T**he undercurrent! It's grabbing me," Tullia shouts over the breakers.

Stephen swims around to her other side and takes her other hand.

They spot a rock jutting out of the surf and lunge for it.

"The rocks are so close together," Ezekiel shouts above the roar of the surf. "Let us try to make it from rock to rock."

Tullia lets go of the rock, and the two larger and stronger men strain to half swim and half tread water to get to the next rock with their wife and mother between them.

"Grab hold of it, Tullia," Ezekiel shouts.

She does, and the two men on each side of her do the same. They look around to find a rock to head for next.

"There's one over there on your side, Father," Stephen shouts. The men signal each other with their eyes.

"Let go, Mother."

They lunge in the direction of the next rock swimming with one hand and hanging on to petite Tullia with the other. They reach the rock, and Tullia lets go of their hands to grab hold.

"It must be a *mille* to the shore, Father. This is going to take us the rest of the day."

"Then, we take the rest of the day!" Ezekiel shouts. "There's a rock over on your side."

Once again. Letting go of safety and lunging for survival.

The rocks are rough and slippery and hard to cling to, especially by Tullia, who is petite everywhere, including her arms.

"Father!"

"Do not' talk. Keep swimming."

They lunge once again to temporary safety.

"Father!"

"What?"

Stephen pants. He can see the strain in his father's reddened eyes. He can tell, despite the surf blowing up on them, that his father is weeping.

"Father! Jehovah will be our strength and lift us up."

"Yes, Son. Jehovah will."

The men signal each other once more and lunge for the next rock.

And the next one.

And the next.

"I've got to stop, Son. I cannot, I cannot keep..."

"Father, why do not you and Mother hang on here," he shouts over the surf, "while I try to find help."

"There is no help out here, Son," Ezekiel shouts back. "The rocks and waves are too high to see us from shore."

Stephen pretends he does not hear and breaks away from his parents. He no longer treads water. He puts his feet back and kicks. His strong blacksmith's arms reach and reach and reach.

The waves hit him in the face, but he swims. Swims darting between the treacherous rocks. Swims despite the roar. Instead, he hears angels. The angels are whistling. Strange angels.

He sees red. Why is he seeing red? And green. Yellow? Blue? Is he already to shore? Where is the shore? Where is the warm, dry sand? Where is safety?

Two huge hands reach down for him. He looks up. A face with freckles, a big flat nose, green eyes, and surrounded by a mane of red hair smiles at him. "Here, let me help you up."

"No!"

"What do you mean, no?" He shouts, flipping his side pigtail out of the way.

"My parents. My father is old. My mother is small. They are both weak. Find them. I am okay. Find my parents." Stephen's voice is frantic.

Despite the noise of the waves hitting the rocks and the shore, the red-haired man understands and turns his small boat north into the underwater field of rocks.

Stephen resumes swimming. Reaching and clawing. Reaching and clawing. Closer to the shore. Closer to safety.

He sees a narrow inlet and swims toward it. There is a narrow strip of land with a lighthouse on his left and another strip of land on his right.

He swims through the inlet, and it opens up into a small protected harbor with several ship docks.

Jehovah! Help my parents!

He feels sand against his knees and stops swimming. He stands and wades the rest of the way to shore. He collapses on the beach.

Jehovah! My parents. Jehovah. My parents. Do not rest. Cannot rest. Go back. Go back.

Stephen stands and looks out over the water. He sucks in air, his heart races, he realizes he is cold. He wades back in. Just as he does, he sees the small boat with three people in it. He wades out a little farther and grabs the bow. He tugs at it to get his parents to shore before they disappear.

He hears laughter. A laughter he has not heard before.

"Ha, ha, ha! You're safe now! Ha, ha, ha!"

Tullia reaches for her son with his strong blacksmith arms, and he lifts her out of the boat. He carries her as he would a child.

The strange red-haired man with a pigtail on each side of his head wades behind him, his bulging arm around the shoulder of Ezekiel.

They reach the shore. They reach the sand and the warmth and the dryness and safety. And freedom.

Stephen sets his mother onto the sand and turns to reach out for his father. The two men kneel and the three huddle and embrace.

Ezekiel raises his gray head, and with the gravelly voice of a man who has done much aging in the near past, says, "Thank you" to the sparse white clouds above.

Tears of joy for all three. Tears of relief. Of release. Of survival.

Silence.

A giggle.

"What's so funny, Tullia?" Ezekiel asks, releasing his hold on her and leaning back.

"We look a sight. Here he gave us these fine clothes, and we go and ruin them. Ha! We showed ole Captain Pyrrhus, after all, did not we?"

"We sure did, Mother," Stephen says, now also leaning back, grinning.

Ezekiel and Stephen turn and sit on either side of Tullia and lie down in the sand, laughing.

Ezekiel toys with the ring his father had made for him. "It goes around and never ends. It will remind you of God's protection," his father had said.

A few moments later, Ezekiel sits up. "Where's the man? The one who rescued us. Where is he?"

He looks around and sees a red-haired man sitting on a small boat now turned upside down and watching them while stroking his red beard.

"Oh, there you are." Ezekiel struggles to stand. Still stooped, he takes a few steps to their rescuer. He holds out his hand, and the stranger takes his hand and forearm. "How can I thank you, friend?"

Before the stranger can reply, Ezekiel looks down and sees his belt is missing. "I am afraid I have lost all our money to the seas, kind sir. But I will repay you somehow someday."

"We have a wicked *labhare* around here. But, no need for that. Other people have rescued me plenty of times. Consider this me paying them back."

"Well, okay. But what is a *labhare*?"

"Sea, my friend. *Labhare* is Berber for sea.

"Now, did I tell you my name? Of course, I did not. My name is Ezekiel."

He feels his wife clutch his hand, just now joining him. "This is my sweetheart, my wife, Tullia."

Stephen joins them. "And I am Stephen, their only begotten son."

"May I assume you are Jewish? Both of you men have beards. That is often a sign. Is it so for you, or do you just like beards?"

"Yes and yes," Ezekiel replies.

"And the most obvious is that you, sir, have the name of a Jewish hero, the prophet Ezekiel."

"Then, you are right again. We are Jewish."

"Well, a double welcome to you. My name is Simon, I too am Jewish, and I live up beyond that cliff in Cyrene."

"Is that where we are? Cyrene?" Stephen asks.

"Cyrene is the name of both my city and this Roman province. Well, we call the province Cyrenica. Actually, we are in Apollonia. I was down here fishing."

Simon pauses and looks behind Stephen's family.

"Uh oh," he says, standing. "Do you have any enemies? Looks like they have caught up with you."

Stephen and Ezekiel immediately turn and look behind them.

Coming out of the water and headed in their direction are five men. They look angry.

"How did you get here before us?" Achaius asks, catching his breath.

Ezekiel trudges toward them, still regaining his strength. "Welcome to dry land, friends."

"Well, that is a relief," Simon mutters.

Stephen laughs. "These are my father's employees. Over here, men!"

Achaius, Trophimus, Secundus, Justus, and Draco stumble over, still dripping from the water and collapse in the sand.

"When you catch your breath, there is someone we want you to meet," Ezekiel says.

Justus, the youngest, rolls over onto his back first, then sits up. "Come on, men. Our boss has someone he wants us to meet."

The others struggle up, and Ezekiel leads them over to Simon.

"This man, my friends, is Simon of Cyrene. That is where we are now. He saved Tullia and me. Brought us in the rest of the way to shore in that small boat. Knew where all the rocks were."

Justus stands and holds out his hand to Simon. Simon takes his hand and forearm.

"The rest of you men, stay where you are," Simon urges. "You can shake my hand later."

He looks at the group. "Once everyone is rested enough, I want to take you home with me. Hungry? Of course, you're hungry. We will stop in the market first."

Simon takes a basket he had slid under his boat when he tipped it upside down. It smells fishy. He hails a young man passing by. "See that warehouse? Here is a bronze coin for you to take my boat up there. I have a berth for it."

Ezekiel watches the young man walk up the hill. "We're ready, Simon, when you are. If your home is too small for all of us, we can stay down here by the warehouses."

"And sleep where? Doesn't look like any of you have any money; no one is wearing a money belt. Go home with me. We will figure out where everyone will sleep when we get there. Now, let us walk over to the market."

Simon leads everyone past warehouses and granaries. On a little higher land, they walk past a public basilica on the right. To their far left is a large amphitheater. Between the two is the market. Simon leads them to a booth selling bread, and buys enough for everyone, along with a full wineskin.

"Let us sit over here on this sandy spot while you eat and get more strength back. Tullia, you will love my wife. Her name is Abelia, and she has the most beautiful long black hair. We were just married last year."

"I am sure she is a delightful young lady," Tullia assures.

"While everyone waits, I am going to get my horse. It is stabled right over here."

Once more, the eight wait, grateful for another opportunity to rest, and even more grateful for the food and freedom.

"I wonder if I will be able to find work here over the winter," Stephen says.

"Cities served by seaport cities are usually big, so you probably will not have any trouble finding a locksmith to work for," Tullia says.

Simon returns and has a blanket over his arm.

"Tullia, that silk dress you are wearing is pretty thin and torn. Why do not you put this blanket around you in this wind?"

He turns toward Ezekiel. "Okay, you and your wife ride on the horse. The rest of us will walk. The city of Cyrene is about five *milles* up that cliff. We should be home in a couple hours."

Ezekiel does not argue. He climbs onto the horse, and Tullia is helped up by Simon. She sits in front of her husband.

Once they are at the top of the cliff, they are in a forest of trees. Ezekiel holds the reins of the horse loosely, assuming the horse knows its own way home. The others walk beside and behind the horse.

They work their way through the trees until they thin out. In front of them is a valley, and within the valley is a grand city.

"Well, everyone," Simon pronounces, "This is Cyrene."

He leads them through the North Gate and the market. Then, on their right is a park and temple to Apollo. On their left is a decorative fountain. They walk past the park and to a residential section.

Simon leads them down one of the streets, stops in front of a gate, and knocks on it. "Abelia, I am home," he calls out.

They hear scraping of a bar and squeaking of hinges.

"Remind me to make a lock for you," Stephen tells their host.

The gate is opened. Abelia has the long black hair praised by Simon, a round face, large dark eyes, and a bow mouth.

"Welcome home, my darling," she says, reaching for Simon. He embraces her briefly.

"These are my new friends, or I should say our new guests. They are going to spend the night with us as long as they need.

"Welcome to our *tittarte*. It is small, but adequate for us for now.

"Stop talking Berber with our friends, Simon," she says, her hand on her hips and a grin on her round face.

"Abelia is expecting to deliver any day now," Simon explains. He turns and helps Tullia down from the horse. "Abelia, this is Tullia. I think she is cold."

"Come with me, Tullia. I have a tunic that will fit you. Then you won't need to wear that blanket around you."

The women disappear, and Ezekiel slides off the horse.

"Everyone, our house is not very large, but our courtyard should be large enough for all of you to sleep in. We have goat hair cloth, which we use to shade the courtyard in the summers. We will lay that out on the ground for you.

"You are lucky you came at the beginning of winter. You would probably have trouble adjusting to our summer heat without gradually getting used to it. You can use the horse's blankets and the blanket Tullia has been using. I put three blankets on the horse, so you have four in total. Will that be sufficient?"

"That will be fine," Ezekiel says, squatting next to the outer wall and leaning his back against it.

We shall have our evening meal soon, then it will be dark. I know you are exhausted," Simon says.

Shortly, Abelia returns with Tullia. The men smile when they see her dressed in a tunic of many colors and designs.

The ladies step over to the goat-hair-shaded kitchen corner of the courtyard. Abelia puts bread that has risen into her oven, gets more flour out, and forms flatbread to bake after the rolls are done. She takes cheese from a basket and dried grapes from a vat.

By now, Simon's company has dropped off to sleep leaning up against his outer wall.

"I hate to disturb everyone, but our evening meal is prepared," Simon announces with his deep voice. "Come, let us thank Jehovah for saving you so we can have more friends, and for providing bread and cheese to share with you."

Tullia stands and helps Abelia put the food on trays and pass it around to the men. She and Tullia sit just beyond the kitchen corner of the courtyard.

"Did your husband say you just married last year?" Tullia asks as they eat.

Abelia looks over at her husband, and he winks. "Yes, and he has been a good husband. I was stuck here with no one when he came into my life.

"Oh? What happened?"

"My brother, Tryphena, and I were born in Lystra up in Anatolia. He enlisted in the military, and I traveled with the men to make sure my brother was well fed and taken care of after battles, as did several other sisters, wives, daughters, and mothers. He enlisted late and already had a wife, Eunice, but she had to stay home with their young son, Timothy."

"What was his job with the army?" Secundus asks.

"He was a sword maker. He was very good at it and was in demand for his skills all the time."

"Ah, a blacksmith like me," Stephen says.

"You make swords too?"

"No, but I had a little experience with them when I was ten and eleven years old. My father showed me how. He learned from his father. But now I make locks. It's a long story how things changed like that."

"You said you were stranded here," Trophimus says to Abelia.

"Yes. My brother suffered several scorpion bites all at once. He stepped in a nest of them. He was a big man, but their bite was too poisonous. He died two days later. So now, here I was in a relatively strange country far from home up in Anatolia at the other end of the Great Sea.

"How did you meet Simon?" Secundus asks.

"Well, that is rather complicated. Simon, dear, how much do you want to tell?"

"If it's a secret," Achaius says, "you should not tell us."

"Can I depend on my new friends to keep my secret?"

"Of course," Ezekiel responds. "But we do not wish to pressure you."

"Perhaps you should know who you are associating with. You may change your mind."

"That bad?" Justus asks.

"Depends on whose side you are on. The Romans consider our leader bad. The Berbers are fully behind our leader. We do not want foreigners coming in and taking over our country."

"Who are the Berbers?"

"I guess you could say we are the original people of Libya. We've been here probably a thousand years. Remind me to take you to the caves some time to show you our ancestors' drawings. Anyway, the Berbers are in favor of what is going on and who is leading it."

Everyone remains quiet, unsure how much to probe into the man's secret.

"Well, the fact is, I was in the revolutionary militia of TacFarinas. The Romans call him TacFarinas the Outlaw."

MAP 2 OF CYRENE

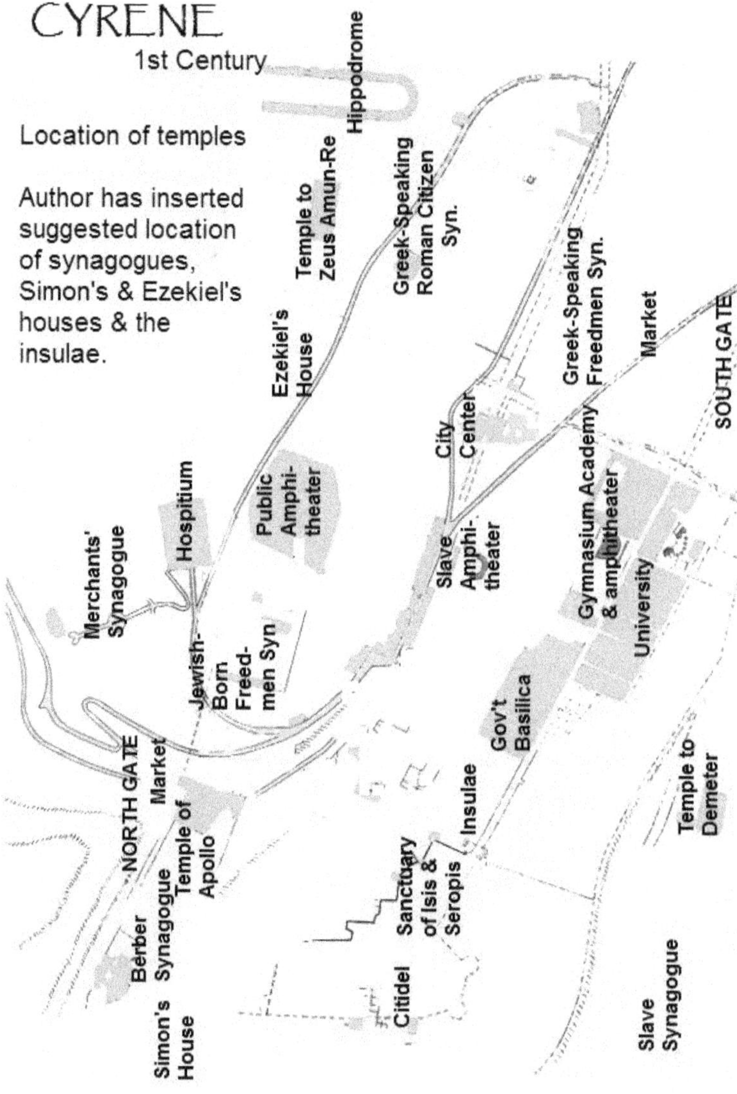

10 ~ STARTING OVER

"You were an outlaw?" Stephen asks with a large grin.

"Be quiet," Ezekiel urges, his eyes shooting arrows at the young man.

"No, that is okay," Simon intercedes. "You need to know this. TacFarinas is our hero. He had been in the Roman army, so knew their tactics. He deserted to come home and help his people run the Romans off our land.

"We only have the seacoast with plains and hills that can sustain crops. The farther south we go, the more desert there is. We call it the Great SaHara. It is so hot, nothing can grow in it, including people."

Simon looks over at Abelia for approval of the joke she has heard him tell a hundred times.

"The Romans came and took our land, forcing our tribes south into the desert," he continues. "We couldn't live like that.

"We have over a hundred tribes in Libya, and TacFarinas is a member of our largest one, the Musulamii Tribe.

"What tribe do you belong to?" Secundus asks, partly to keep himself awake to hear the story of a real outlaw.

"I belong to the Nasamonian Tribe. We are a large tribe that stretches from southern Cyrenica across to part of the Great Syrtis Gulf. I lived close to where TacFarinas was assembling his militia.

"So, anyway, when people realized he could help us run the Romans out of our country, we rallied to him from everywhere. I was twenty at the time and decided to join him. I went with him on raids up and down the coast from the territory of my tribe all the way over to Tunisia."

"Is Tunisia very far away?" Trophimus asks.

"Hundreds of *milles*. By the way, did you like my horse, Ezekiel?"

"I suppose I did. He got us here."

"He's a Barb by breed. You notice I did not have a saddle. Always rode it barebacked. Controlled it with my knees. We would rush into a Roman encampment, throw our javelins at lightning speed, then rush back out. We were so fast, they hardly knew we had been there and gone except for the damage we left behind."

"Dear," Abelia interrupts, standing, "our company is tired."

"Okay, I will tell you how Abelia and I met. Then we will leave you alone," Simon says.

"I fought with TacFarinas for five years. One day we raided a fortress and thought we'd forced them all to run away. But when we went to help ourselves to their food and anything else we wanted to take from the Romans, I saw Abelia hiding behind some crates, scared to death."

"I was not scared to death, I will have you know," Abelia says. "I was hiding because I'd heard how mean you Berbers were."

"Same thing," Simon says. "Well, I laid down my javelin and walked over to her out of curiosity. When she stood up, my heart jumped, and I immediately fell in love."

"Simon, these people want to go to sleep."

"Okay, so I took her back to our camp with me. Since her brother had recently died, and I immediately fell in love with her, I decided to marry her. TacFarinas forbade marriage, so I ran away with her."

"And that is how we ended up in Cyrene," Abelia says.

"Why did not you take her to your tribe?" Stephen asks.

"I was such a prized warrior, I knew TacFarinas would come after me, and Nasamonia would be the first place he'd look."

Abelia walks over to her husband. "Okay. Okay, prize warrior," she says, tugging at his colorful sleeve. "Now, we will see if anyone will remember a word you said tomorrow morning."

"Ezekiel and Tullia, we have a small room with a bed in it for you. You will sleep easier in there," Simon says. "Follow us."

When they fall asleep, the eight travelers—including the deserter from Crete—now know they will waken still free and once again in charge of their own destiny. The night passes like the blink of an eye. But it is a night of peace and tranquility.

Stephen wakes up to humming. His mother's familiar humming. She is happy once again. How sweet it sounds to his ear.

He opens his eyes and realizes the covers have been stolen off him by Draco at his side. "Ha!" he says aloud. "So, just because you freed us from prison, and helped us escape slavery for the rest of our miserable lives, and rounded up a boat and food, and were our guide all the way across the Great Sea, you think you can just reach over and grab my side of the covers!"

Stephen jumps up, straddles Draco, and throws the covers off him. "Now, how do you like that?"

Draco opens his eyes, but not before forming a large grin, and lunges at Stephen's ankles. Stephen falls onto Secundus, who grunts and turns over to go back to sleep. Draco jumps up just in time for Justus on the other side of him to grab him by the hem of his tunic and stick his knee in his back.

Ezekiel walks out into the courtyard. "I see I have my boys back. Plus one," he laughs.

"They need to grow up," Achaius grumbles. "Right Trophimus?"

"Right," Trophimus replies, throwing his crumpled-up cover onto his senior.

"Everyone!" Abelia calls out, standing with her hands on her hips. "If you have that much energy in you, I have all kinds of chores for you to do for me."

Stephen crawls over to his mother, stands, bows, and says, "We will behave. We promise," barely able to get it out before laughing again.

"What's this, I hear?" Simon says, coming in through the gate.

"My eight children have come back to life," Ezekiel says, still grinning.

"So, it seems," Simon says. "Well, I have been down at the market by the North Gate talking to a papyrus and ink merchant, and a couple of our blacksmiths."

"After you eat a bit, I want to take Ezekiel and Stephen back to the market with me."

"The rest of you can help me lay out that goat hair fabric and sow some of the panels together for our shade next summer."

Achaius looks over at Ezekiel with eyes that beg for rescue.

"It will do you good, men," Ezekiel says. "You need to get used to sitting all day again."

The meal over, Simon leads the way to the northern market.

"Hey! What's going on?"

They hear shouting from the third aisle of booths.

"Never!" they hear.

"That is what you think."

"You do not belong here."

"I belong just as much as you do."

"That will never happen."

"I am not budging."

"Get back there where you belong."

"I belong where I want to be. And this is where I want to be."

They hear cracking of wood, and a loud thud on the ground.

"That is what you can do with your booth. Now move."

They turn the corner just in time to see two merchants scuffling in the aisle.

A third merchant circles behind them and grabs two pieces of pottery. He throws them to the ground.

"Hey, you cannot do that!"

Another merchant moves in. He grabs a post holding up a shelf and works it loose until the shelf falls, breaking all the pottery on it.

"Stop that!"

Another—whether merchant or customer, it is uncertain—grabs at the front counter, moving it back and forth. Still, another grabs the other end, and they both work it until the nails loosen. The strongest one lifts it, and throws it into the aisle.

"No. Stop! My wife made them."

Someone steps into the remains of the booth and slides all the pottery off another shelf. They teeter, then fall to the ground and break.

"No! You cannot!"

Two more push on the back wall of the booth until it falls flat.

"So, you thought you could just set up your booth here where the civilized people are!"

"You think you're somebody, but you are nobody. You're just an animal. You dirty Jew."

"No! I am a good person. I obey the Law of Moses and..."

"Ha, ha, ha, ha!"

With that, everyone walks away, leaving the Jewish merchant sitting amidst what earlier in the morning had been his booth with some of the finest pottery in Cyrene.

Simon steps over to the man. "Joshua, let me help you."

Joshua stands. "Help me what? They have ruined all the pottery it took my wife three months to make and paint. It's gone. All gone. Ruined. I am ruined."

"Perhaps your old place is still available in the back."

"The back row where none of the customers ever go? It isn't fair."

"Do I ever know it," Simon says. "I fought for the freedom of all Berbers, pagan Gentiles, and Jews. I fought to get rid of the Romans and their settlers."

"It should be against the law to treat us like that."

"It is against the law," Simon replies. "But, they do not enforce it."

Stephen walks forward and looks through the rubble. He turns toward the merchant. "Sir, I do not think this jar broke. Maybe there are others."

"Yes, let my son and I help you," Ezekiel says.

Big Simon picks up the counter, supports it on his head, and carries it to the back row.

The merchant follows him, seeing but not seeing. Blindly, he follows Simon back to where he belongs.

Stephen hands the two unbroken jars to his father, picks up one of the poles with his strong blacksmith's hands, and balances it on his shoulder. He follows Simon.

When they are done setting up Joshua's booth in the back, Simon excuses himself to go back home.

"My wife has bought some beautiful pottery from you," Simon says. "I will bring some of them so you can at least show off what you can offer your customers. Yours is some of the finest in all of Cyrenica."

"Sir," Ezekiel says. "I want to offer the services of a scribe to your city. If I can share your booth with you until you can bring in more inventory of pottery, I would pay you after my first order."

Joshua stares at Ezekiel.

"May I introduce myself? I am Ezekiel, and this is my son Stephen. We are proud to call ourselves Jews. We are proud you are our brother."

"Ezekiel, you are new here. You would be better off going to another city. The prejudice against Jews here is rampant. It is out of control. You will never be able to make a living here."

"We will only be here for the winter. Then we are moving on to Rome. We just need to sustain ourselves for a few months, then we will be gone."

"Why would you want to go to Rome? There is nothing there for a Jew. Why do not you go to Jerusalem?"

"It is a long story. It is our desire to do this, and that includes wintering in Cyrene."

"Well, okay, if you want to share my booth for the winter until my wife and I replenish my supply of pottery, I welcome you."

The two men shake hands and forearms.

"I guess I should introduce you to the other Jews in the back row where no customers come."

Joshua starts down the row with Ezekiel at his side and Stephen following them, not saying anything.

"Ezekiel, may I introduce you to Ebron. He is our baker."

"I make the best baklava in the world," Ebron laughs. He holds out a piece of the sticky sweet morsel to Stephen's mouth.

Stephen opens his lips and takes the bite. He smiles. "Very nice," Stephen says.

"Next, we have Eben. I know it will be hard for you to keep Ebron and Eben straight at first, but eventually, you will learn."

Ezekiel notices Joshua's returning smile.

"Eben is our butcher. His grown sons hunt the game up in the mountains between us and the SaHara, and he sells it to us the same day or first thing the next day. Well, and he serves the sheep and goat herders also."

Joshua leads Ezekiel and Stephen to the next booth. "This is Midyan. He is a tanner. He takes the hides off the meat Eben's sons hunt down and tans them, so they are nice and soft and easy to work with.

"And guess what is on the other side of Midyan?" Joshua asks.

"A tailor, of course," Ezekiel guesses.

"Yes, the boot, sandal, pouch, and saddle maker. He has a double booth because he does so much and has several helpers."

Joshua looks over at Stephen.

"Doesn't your son feel very well?"

Ezekiel looks back at his son, glares at him, and smiles at Joshua. "Maybe he did not get enough sleep last night. We just arrived from... Well, we just arrived yesterday.

"I guess I need to take him back to Simon's house. Oh, on our way, do you know where I can purchase some papyrus?"

"The only papyrus is sold in the front row, of course. And they double the price we Jews must pay. They make it very difficult for us to live here. Which is what they want. They want us to leave so the Romans can take over the rest of Cyrene and Libya."

Ezekiel notices Joshua beginning to revert to his earlier depression. "Well, I, for one, will be proud to set up business next to you. Now, I need to get my son home."

Ezekiel turns and walks next to Stephen as they work their way through the various aisles of the market.

"What is wrong with you, Son?"

"It's not worth it."

"Spending the winter here? We have no choice."

"Not that, Father. It's not worth speaking out for Jehovah. No one wants to hear it. It cost Joshua his business, or cost most of it. It cost grandfather his freedom. It cost Abraham his life. It cost our whole family our home and almost our freedom. Where will it end? When will it end?"

"There has always been prejudice in the world, Son. We must be strong and bear it. In the end, our persecutors will respect us."

"No, they won't, Father. They will never respect us."

"Then, they will at least respect Jehovah, the only true God."

"No, Father. Look around. Everywhere we go, people who believe in many gods are in the majority. We who believe in the one true God are in the minority. They do not want to know the truth. They never will, Father."

Father and son are out of the market now and working their way past the fountain on their left and the park and temple to Apollo on their right.

They enter the residential neighborhood and finally arrive at Simon's house. They knock on the gate and are let in.

"Well, how was your trip to the market?" Tullia asks, leaving her seat where Abelia has been showing her how to do colorful Berber whipstitching.

Stephen mutters "Fine" and goes to a corner where he sits, knees up, leans back his head, and closes his eyes.

"What's wrong with our son?" Tullia asks.

"He has become ashamed of who we are, who he is."

"Oh. Well, let me try talking to him."

Tullia steps over to the corner and sits next to her son.

"You know, before I was converted to be a Jew, I believed what I had been told about them. I heard all Jews were stubborn, stiff-necked, greedy, and those long beards made them look dirty."

Stephen does not open his eyes. She continues.

"Then I met your father—the kindest, most intelligent man I had ever met—outside of my father, of course."

She looks over at Stephen, and though his eyes are still closed, she thinks she sees him form a slight smile.

"My father always believed that, if someone believed something hard enough and dedicated his life to making it come true, it will happen."

Stephen's eyes remain closed.

"Someday, Jerusalem will be great again. Someday, Jerusalem and all her people will be respected throughout the world as they were in Solomon's time. We have to keep believing and working toward that goal."

Stephen opens his eyes, stands, and looks down. "Excuse me, Mother. I am going for a walk."

Stephen heads back to the market and wanders among the aisles. He leaves and wanders through other parts of the city seeing public buildings and temples, grand in their marble. He pauses by one of the public basilica and sees a man struggling with an outside door lock.

"Here, let me help you with that lock. I know something about them. Do you have the key?"

"Yes," the stranger says, holding it out.

Stephen takes it, looks at it, squeezes it with his strong hands, and hands it back to the stranger. "Try it now," he says.

The man puts the key in the lock and unlocks the door.

"What did you do, young man?"

"It was bent. I just unbent it."

"Well, we could certainly use a good locksmith in this city. Here is a bronze coin for your trouble."

Stephen takes the money and walks back to one of the booths he had passed earlier. He gives the barber his coin and sits in the customer chair.

Half an hour later, he emerges and walks to the blacksmith's shop at the end of the second row of the market.

"Hello, my name is Stephanus, and I am a locksmith. Would you be interested in my services, at least for the winter?"

The blacksmith looks at Stephen with his high cheekbones, straight nose, ample lips, and clean-cut square jaw.

"I think I could use a fine young man like you. What was your name again? Stephanus? My name is Ovidius."

11 ~ UNIVERSITY ELITE

Stephen spends the rest of the day with Ovidius. They get along well. Ovidius does tell Stephen he will have to build his own forge, however, because his is always in use. Ovidius says they will be sharing work and selling space, but their businesses will be separate.

Stephen builds a smaller forge. It takes him a week.

A month has passed. Everyone is settled in their new jobs, and Ezekiel has just been able to rent a three-room apartment in one of the *insulae* near the market. It is on the fourth floor, which Ezekiel does not like since arthritis is settling in his knees. But he likes the price.

Tullia is down in the courtyard where tenants are allowed to share ovens for cooking and a well.

Stephen struts into the courtyard and only acknowledges his mother with a nod. He stands in the middle among the women and raises one hand.

"Something must be done," he pronounces.

No one but his mother looks up.

"The streets are littered far more here than they were in Antioch up in Syria. Yes, littered. This cannot continue."

He swings around in place and raises his other hand.

"Citizens of this city must rise and demand the government eliminate the problem!"

His mother smiles.

He pivots and points to one of the ladies. "Did you know there is sickness in the air around places where people dump their body wastes?"

The woman giggles.

He turns and walks over to one of the other women. "Did you know the food that is thrown out into the gutter attracts animals that can bite us?"

The woman looks up at him, shrugs her shoulder, grins, and returns to her work.

"Ladies and gentlemen," Stephen continues, "something must be done about the attack on this city by the uncaring!"

"Son, come over here," Tullia says. "I think we need to talk."

Stephen obeys and sits on the cobblestones next to his mother's oven. He watches her knead bread for the evening meal.

"Son, you have been working for the blacksmith for a month now. How are things going for you?"

"Fine, Mother. I like Ovidius."

"But you told me you only have enough orders for locks, hinges, and door pulls to keep you occupied half a day."

"Yes, but Ovidius pays me to help him with all his orders. I am learning to handle larger pieces now."

"We are only here for the winter, and this *insulae* is good enough for us. Your father and his scribes are doing well enough to pay for our keep and save some for ship passage next spring."

"I was worried about that since Jews are only allowed to put their booths up in the back row of the market."

"My point, Son, is, well, have you thought about attending the university while we're here? It is one of the finest universities in the world in the same class as those in Rome, Athens, Alexandria, and Tarsus."

"I do not know, Mother," Stephen says, his mind now completely off the plight of Cyrene's streets.

"I just thought you were pleased for me to be a locksmith."

"Oh, we are pleased with you. And your grandfather would be mightily pleased if he were here." She splits the dough into small sections to set on a flat rock.

"But..."

"But my father, your other grandfather, would want you to have more. He would want you to have an education in philosophy. Also, science and medicine."

She stops and smiles.

"And, of course, your father would be pleased. He has been teaching you what he knows all these years. He has taught you writing, vocabulary, and mathematics."

"And a hard taskmaster he has been," Stephen says with a slight grin.

"You are beginning to show a gift of oratory. Why, you held those women spellbound during your sewage speech?"

"Well, they weren't exactly spellbound, Mother." *They hardly knew I was here.* He smiles, anyway.

Silence. Tullia gives him time to think this through.

"You know," Stephen continues, "I haven't seen Draco in a while. He returned to the university after we got here. I think he must live there on the campus. Do you think I should go see him?"

Tullia slides the flat rock into the oven and looks directly at her son.

"Actually, he came by to see you this afternoon. He did not go by your shop?"

"No."

"Then, you should go over to the university and find him. You need to talk to him about entering the university. You turned eighteen last week. It is a perfect age for this."

"I wonder if Ovidius would mind if I weren't around half a day each day," Stephen muses. "Well, I shall go to the university tomorrow and try to find Draco. I certainly do miss him. You know, he's not that much older than me."

The rest of the evening goes by in slow motion for Stephen. He tolerates Ezekiel and his four scribes with their stories about documents and wills they are drawing up for the citizens of Cyrene, especially the Jewish citizens.

He goes to bed early in hopes it will hasten the new day.

Morning. He goes to work at the blacksmith shop at the end of the second row in the North Gate Market.

Once he has fired up his forge and raised its intensity with his bellows, he begins his work. He pounds the piece of steel sufficient for a door hinge, dips the hot ore into his barrel of water, and sets it on his anvil. Still holding his tongs, he clears his throat.

"Uh, sir, has my work been satisfactory?"

"Of course, Stephanus."

"Well, would it be okay if I, uh…"

"Just say it, Stephanus."

"I am thinking of attending the university."

"Oh. I see. How much time would it take?"

"Well, I think I would like to learn philosophy and oratory first. I do not know what else they offer."

Stephen waits for his employer to respond. When he does not, Stephen continues. "Would it be possible for me to walk over there when I am through with these two locks?"

"Go on ahead, Stephanus. As long as your order is completed before you leave."

When the sun is high in the sky, Stephen leaves the shop and heads up the street. He passes the fountain on his right as well as a temple to Dionysus. To his far left is the amphitheater. He continues to walk along the columned street. When he comes to the smaller theater at the slave market, he shutters.

Jehovah God, be with the poor souls being sold there. Give them strength, and someday give back to them their freedom.

He turns right and sees ahead of him three buildings lined up side by side with another theater attached to one of them. They are all the city's gymnasium academy for the physical and mental exercise of younger lads. All buildings have columns along the front.

He hears cheering coming from the theater. *Is that how they react to philosophers here? He must be famous. Maybe from Athens or Rome.*

Stephen walks between those buildings to a long building behind the three. It is majestic in its architecture with columns all along the front portico. On the walkway leading to the front entrance are statues on each side of great scientists and philosophers who have taught at the university in years and centuries past. He wonders at being the only person in sight.

The double doors into the building are covered with copper. He briefly admires the brass locksets, door pulls, and hinges.

Once inside, he wishes he had gone home and washed and put on a clean tunic first.

Too late for that now.

The floor is of polished green marble. Columns supporting the second floor are of pink granite. Between each column in a rounded niche with an urn of varying colors and shapes on display.

"May I help you?"

Stephen looks toward the sound of the voice and walks over to the alabaster counter with a stately chair behind it. The young man behind looks to be about the same age as Draco. He has black wavy hair slicked down with oil and is ample around his waist.

"I am interested in enrolling in the university."

"Who are your parents?"

"Ezekiel and Tullia of Tarsus."

"The Tarsus part is good, but that is all. I am sorry, but there are no openings for you here. For one thing, your father is Jewish. I assume your mother is as well, and that you are."

"Stephen, is that you?" Stephen turns and smiles upon hearing Draco's voice.

"Humph. Stephen. How quaint."

Turning back to the young man behind the counter, he says, "My name is Stephanus, and I too am of Tarsus the great philosophy center of Anatolia."

"Stephen, come with me. Do not pay any attention to Cato." Draco takes hold of Stephen's arm and directs him to a door over to one side. "What brings you here, Stephen?"

"It's Stephanus, Draco. Stephanus," Stephen whispers.

"Oh. Okay, Stephanus, what brings you here?"

"You came by my apartment yesterday, Mother said."

"That I did. They are having games among the students at the gymnasium academy's theater, and I thought you might like some diversion."

"When are they?"

"Right now. I am late, or I would have missed you. How lucky is that? Come. We will cut through the lecture rooms wing. It will be closer.

They go through the side door, down a long corridor, then out a back exit.

Cheering again.

"This will be fun. Have you had any training in the sports, Steph... Stephanus?"

"Simon—you remember Simon, who rescued us—has been teaching me to throw the javelin. He says I am a natural with my strong arms."

"Then, you will have to enter the javelin-throwing competition one of these days."

They enter the theater and climb to the top of the benches. When they are seated, they can see across and down to the waters of the Libyan Sea.

For the rest of the afternoon, they cheer for their favorites in foot racing, boxing, wrestling, and camel racing.

"Most races are held over at the hippodrome," Draco says, "but competition among students is held here."

By the time the games are over, it is nearly dark.

"You said you would like to enroll at the university," Draco says, "but it is too late now. Can you come tomorrow? I usually have the afternoon off to do my private study."

"Yes, I believe I can. It will be about the time I arrived today," Stephen says.

"By the way, Stephanus, when did you shave off your

beard?"

"At the same time, I decided my life would be easier if I were Stephanus."

"I understand. Well, when you return tomorrow, just go through the left door over there and look for me. That wing is the library. On the other side of the library is a combination of dormitory and study rooms."

When Stephen returns home to the *insulae*, he tells his parents about the events of the day. He says nothing about the comment by the man in the front lobby.

The following day after completing his work at the blacksmith shop, Stephen walks past the fountain, past the temple to Dionysus, and turns right before the slave market and theater. He enters one of the city's two bathhouses, this one at the far end of a government basilica. After washing, he dons a clean tunic, puts his dirty one in a shoulder pack where he also has a couple small scrolls, a jar of blackener, a stylus and a pen.

Satisfied with his preparations, he walks to the university and enters the same building as the day before with the double copper doors.

He hears the same voice behind the alabaster counter as the day before but pays no heed.

"I said, come here," the voice repeats.

Stephen turns, stares at the pudgy young man a moment, then decides not to cause trouble. He walks over to the counter.

"I thought I told you yesterday you were not wanted here."

"No, you did not exactly say that."

"Well, I am saying it now. No Jews are allowed in this university."

"Sir, I have money from my father, who is both a scribe and a teacher of scribes."

"That does not make you a non-Jew. Now, you must leave."

"I am afraid I cannot do that."

"Do you defy me?" the young man says, now standing.

"I defy no one. I come in peace. I do not wish any problems here. I only want to study. I have the money for tuition."

"Do you know who I am?"

"I do not believe you have introduced yourself yet, sir," Stephen replies.

"I am Cato, son of Rabannas, censor over the entire province of Cretan-Cyrenica. He has powers to arrest you and your family for breaking the laws of Rome and civilization."

"Oh, there you are, Stephanus." Draco walks over to his friend and takes his arm.

"Cato, leave him alone. You are nothing but a bully. You have no authority here."

"Well, my father does."

"You are a student like everyone else. If I were you, I would quit harassing our visitors and study your mathematics before you fail completely."

With that, Draco leads Stephen out of the lobby and back out the double front doors.

"Good riddance to both of you," Cato shouts after them.

"Stephanus, do you realize who these men are whose statues you passed on your way here?"

"No, I did not recognize them. Maybe one I did, but not the others."

The largest statue is of Aristippus. He was the founder of our university over three centuries ago. He was born here, went to Athens, where he studied under Socrates almost until he committed suicide by command. He loved luxury and fleshly indulgences, so was just the opposite of stoic Socrates. But, he had a positive attitude and was always calm. One time he went to a dinner and was insulted by being told to sit in the lowest seat. He replied, 'you wish to dignify the seat?'. Ha, ha."

Stephen stares at the full-length marble statue.

"Over here is Callimachus of Musalamii and Battus tribes," Draco says. "He claimed to be a direct descendant of the first Greek king of Cyrene, Battus I. Back then, everyone was copying Homer's method of writing long epic poems. He was in favor of short poems that were to the point. He used to say, 'Drive your wagons on untrodden fields.'

"His poems were indeed interesting. His favorite was in the form of a question regarding things people did that were not normal. 'Why on Paros do worshippers of the Charities use neither flutes nor crowns?' 'Why at Argos is a month named for lambs?' 'Why at Leucas does the image of Artemis have a mortar on her head?'

"How many poems did he write? I must find a copy of his book and read it," Stephen says.

"Oh, there are many books. The man wrote 800 poems. Ha, ha."

Draco lets Stephen look at the bust a little longer, then leads him to the next statue.

"This is Theodorus, who lived even before our founder lived.

At this time, all the coast along here from Egypt to Tunisia was known as Africana. Now only Tunisia is called Africana.

"He was a philosopher and a mathematician. He decided that the square roots of non-square numbers up to seventeen are irrational. If you love mathematics, I shall leave it up to you to argue his point. However, he was admired by Plato, and Plato eventually came here to Cyrene to study under Theodorus."

"I thought I told you to leave." It is the familiar voice of Cato.

"Talk all you want, Cato. Stephanus is my friend, and he stays."

"I do not want to cause any trouble," Stephanus whispers to Draco. I've had enough of trouble."

"He will leave you alone. He is just a coward and a bully. Now, here is the next one, who, to me, turned the world upside down—Eratosthenes. He lived a couple hundred years ago. Born right here in Cyrene like the others. You're not going to believe this, but he calculated the circumference of the earth, the tilt of the earth..."

"The earth tilts?" Stephen laughs.

"That is what he said. Plus, he calculated the distance of the earth to the sun. He is the reason we count 365 days in a year with an extra day every four years. Plus..."

Stephen holds his hand up to the top of his head and grins. "All that?"

"And more," Draco continues. "He drew the first map of the world. Annnnd, on top of that, he actually criticized Aristotle for dividing humanity into Greeks and barbarians."

"Was he stoic or hedonist?"

"He was stoic. He was taught the philosophy by the founder, Zeno."

"Now I have heard of Zeno. My grandfather used to speak of Zeno often. Or at least that is what I was told. My grandfather died two years after I was born. My father loves mathematics. I cannot wait until I get home to tell him about Eratosthenes measuring the earth."

"Hey, you!"

Stephen turns and sees two Roman legionnaires marching in his direction.

"Are you the son of Ezekiel? You must leave. You are not allowed on these premises. You must leave."

Draco steps in front of Stephen.

"I am a student here, and I say he stays. He has every right to be here."

"This man is a Jew and not allowed on the premises," one of the legionnaires repeats.

"Who said?" Draco asks.

"This order was made by Most Excellent Rabannas, Censor of Cretan Cyrenica. We have chains and a prison awaiting you if you do not go quietly."

12 ~ RICH AND POWERFUL

*S*tephen turns away from Draco and the statues and steps between the two legionnaires.

As Stephen walks, he struggles to maintain his composure and keep his knees from buckling.

What now? First, the market. Now the university. Should I push Father to move to another city? Perhaps one down the coast toward Simon's tribe where the cities are not so important?

But there will be no universities there. If I hadn't run into Draco, who is trying to get me to enroll, it might have been different. If Draco hadn't spoken with Mother, the matter probably would not have come up.

How dare I dream the impossible? How dare I dream that I could someday actually be like my grandfather—educated and sought after by the elite of the Roman world?

Two choices I have: Stop the dream or be imprisoned. Then what? Another threat of slavery? If I run away, will there be a threat of execution? Oh, Abraham. I am so mixed up.

Once they arrive at the amphitheater beside the gymnasium academy, the legionnaires turn about-face and walk away from Stephen.

Stephen walks over to the entrance into the empty amphitheater. It is not locked. He wanders in, and the cheering of the day before echo in his memory. He climbs the steps to the top tier of benches, turns, and sits.

He looks out beyond the cliff and down to the beach and ships. He remembers. Remembers the rocks keeping them from safety. He remembers the bars in the cell on Crete, keeping them from safety. He remembers ships, the storms, the pirates. He remembers Abraham, his very best friend.

Stephen bows his head, resting it in his hands. His shoulders shake. He sobs alone.

Oh, Abraham. Oh, Jehovah. Why does everyone hate us? It was never that way in Tarsus. What has happened to the world?

When Stephen raises his head and opens his eyes, it is dark. He feels his way down the steps, leaves the arena, turns left, passes the baths, the government basilica, and arrives at the *insulae*.

He walks up the steps to the fourth floor and opens the door into the three-room apartment.

"Welcome, Son. How was..." Ezekiel stops and stares, as do Tullia and the four scribes who work for Ezekiel.

Stephen sits on the floor where they are assembled around a table.

"They rejected me."

"They did what? They cannot reject you," Ezekiel says. "I gave you good money for tuition."

"Father, we're Jews. They hate Jews here."

Ezekiel does not answer.

"Well, I am going to the university tomorrow and convince them you are one of the finest students they will ever have," Tullia says.

"Mother, they have had world-famous teachers there. You are not going to convince them of anything."

Tullia's dark eyes flash.

"Just let it be. I will go back to working full time at the blacksmith shop."

"No, I will not let it be," she pronounces. "They are going to hear from me, and when I am done, they will wish they had never turned you down."

"Mother..."

"Son, she has made up her mind," Ezekiel says. "You cannot win."

"He will win! Because I will win," Tullia adds.

Justus, by now, is hiding a snicker behind his hand. Secundus has both hands on the top of his bushy hair and is staring at the ceiling. Trophimus is glowing with a toothy smile. Achaius is quietly dipping his bread into Stephen's raisin sauce.

Stephen only eats when his mother urges him to, which is not much since she early gave up. Ezekiel leads the family in evening prayers.

"Let us end our day by singing one of David's psalms," Tullia says. Stephen does not join in.

Sleep is fitful that night. Stephen dreams he is on board the slave ship. A storm comes up, the ship turns into a giant scroll, and the wind carries the scroll into the sky, only to be dropped and drowned.

Morning comes. Stephen dons his work tunic and heads down to the courtyard where he knows his mother is baking bread for now and for a mid-day respite.

"Good morning, Son," she says without looking up. I will not ask you how you slept."

"Thank you for that," he replies.

"Now, I want you to take another fresh tunic, your scrolls and writing supplies with you this morning."

"No, Mother. I am asking you not to go there and stir up trouble."

"Things cannot be any more troublesome for you over there than they are."

"You will only make things worse. I do not mean to be disrespectful, but they have the power to make us leave not only Cyrene, but the entire province of Cretan Cyrenica. Then where can we go? It's winter. We cannot go by sea anywhere. They will make sure any city we try to settle in here in Libya will run us off. We will be forced to go down to the Great SaHara, and from what I hear, we will never survive in that desert. So just stay home, Mother. Please."

Tullia does not look up. She pulls her bread from the oven and transfers the fresh rolls to a basket. She stands.

"You forget I attended university myself before I met your father. I know what I am doing. Now come along. We shall break our fast."

An hour later, Stephen is at the blacksmith shop.

"I guess I will be working for you full time after all."

"The university too expensive for you, Stephanus?"

"I do not really want to talk about it," Stephen says, making a fire in his forge. He speaks no more the rest of the morning. Just before pulling out one of his mother's rolls for his respite, he hears it. The familiar deep voice.

"Sir!"

Stephen and Ovidius look up. The same two legionnaires that had escorted him off the university campus the day before are back.

"Are you talking to me or Stephanus?"

"The young man. Stephanus," one of them growls.

"But I left peacefully," Stephen objects. "I promised you I would never return, and I keep my promises, sirs."

"Come with us."

"No. Do not arrest me."

"You are being summoned by Most Excellent Rabannas. Whether you are arrested is up to him. Now, come."

Stephen looks over at Ovidius, who shrugs his shoulders. "Go," he says.

Stephen takes off his heavy leather apron and leg and arm protectors to keep the sparks from burning him and lays them aside. He picks up his shoulder pouch, and steps between the two legionnaires.

Oh, Jehovah God. I did not mean to make trouble. Help me. Help my family. Oh, Jehovah God.

They walk past the fountain and march into the columned-on-all-four-sides government basilica. Once inside, he sees his mother.

The two guards leave, and Stephen walks over to where his mother is seated.

"Mother, what's going on?"

I have been sitting here all morning. They have given every excuse they can think of, but I told them I was not budging.".

"But, Mother..."

"Finally, a clerk came out with a note from Most Excellent Rabannas, demanding to know what I wanted. I wrote my answer on the same tablet. Moments later, the clerk was rushing down the corridor, then back here with two legionnaires. I told them where you were, and I expected you to be here within the hour. And safe."

"What did you tell Rabannas?"

Tullia grins. "I told him I was a personal friend of Augustus Caesar."

"Mother. You cannot do that!" Stephen declares, walking in place in a circle with his hands on top of his head.

"I can, and I did."

"But..."

"Now, brush off the front of your tunic. Here, I brought a basket with a wet cloth in it. Wipe your hands and face with it. We are about to make ole Rabannas want to bow at your feet."

Stephen obeys, then sits next to his mother, his hands unsteady. Moments later, the nearby door opens.

"Madam, his Most Excellent Rabannas is able to see you now. Come right this way." He holds the door open for Tullia.

Tullia and Stephen stand. The clerk eyes Stephen. "Not him."

"If he stays, I stay," she declares, her chin held high.

"Come in! Come in!"

The voice is deep and coming from inside the room. Tullia enters with Stephen at her side.

The man before them is wearing a green toga connected at his shoulder by a large ruby. His tunic is blue, adorned with a heavy chain of gold with a ruby pendant. He wears a band of gold on his nearly bald head and has rings on most of his fingers.

"Forgive my clerk. I am afraid he misunderstood your name when you first arrived. He will be severely punished for his impudence."

They hear the door close behind them and fast footsteps out in the corridor.

"Uh, you, my lady, I recognize. But I do not believe I recognize this young man."

"This, your excellency, is my son, Stephanus."

Timothy stifles a smile that says, "Thank you, Mother."

"But I do not understand. I thought only the friend of Augustus was here."

"Your excellency, he is the grandson of the none other than Athenodorus."

"The Athenodorus? The famed philosopher and leader of Tarsus?"

"Yes, the Athenodorus," Tullia says, maintaining her straight posture, her dark eyes watching every movement of the provincial magistrate.

"I remember when your university tried to steal my father away from the university in Tarsus."

"Really? That must have been before my time."

"He was busy rewriting the constitution of Tarsus and taking over its leadership. But back to Augustus."

"Ah, yes, Augustus. We of the Roman world have been granted grace by the gods to have such a great Caesar. Yes, great indeed."

"He is only five years older than I, and we played together as children many times. Later, when his great uncle, Julius Caesar, was assassinated, he was recalled to Rome, and of course, our family went with him. My father was his most trusted advisor."

"Such an honor for me to be host to such a great woman.

But now about your son."

"Yes, that is what I came to discuss. I am sure this matter can be straightened out."

"Well, it is our understanding that he is Jewish. Although I have high regard for all Jews, their education is rather—what shall I call it?—limited. I understand you married a Jew by birth."

"Yes, Ezekiel."

"Well, as you know, the Jews are practically atheists."

"If you mean believing in one God instead of myriads, you are correct in your assessment."

"And your young men study only your own law—named after some man who used to live in Egypt—and they never study mathematics, geography, astrology, or any of the other sciences. In fact, he only knows how to read and write in the Hebrew language. Your son, madam, is not ready for our university, I am afraid. You have no idea how it pains me to say this. But, if he wants to gain a little more exposure to the other realms of education, then perhaps he can attend the academy gymnasium for young lads."

Tullia stands, her dark eyes flashing arrows. "Sir, you are impudent, insolent, and uninformed. My son is highly proficient in mathematics. And his writings and reading proficiency is impeccable in Hebrew, Aramaic, Greek, and Latin."

"Yes, ma'am," the magistrate replies.

"Do not interrupt me, sir. My son is also excellent in throwing the javelin, the discus, the shotput, and is an excellent marksman with the battle-ax."

"Yes, ma'am. I did not mean to interrupt."

"Aaaand, he is an excellent horseman."

Stephen's eyes dart toward his mother with her last point. Then he remembers the lessons Simon had given him on his African Barb.

Silence.

"Uh, madam," the magistrate says at last, "I believe your son must take after your Anatolian side of the family. We sometimes forget that not all Jews were born that way. Did you become a Jew?"

"Yes, I did. And it is a religion I am proud to belong to."

"Well, if your son believes he can blend in without causing any..."

The magistrate stops. Tullia glares at him. "Causing any what?"

"Well, misunderstandings. Under the present

circumstance, we will welcome him into our university. He may begin next month.”

Tullia, who had reseated herself, stands once again. “Not next month, not next week. He begins now.”

“Uh, that is what I meant to say. Now, if you will wait one moment, I will write out this notification to be given to the headmaster.”

“You will not!” Tullia pronounces. “Your son has unduly humiliated my son. Your legionnaires have unduly humiliated my son. You will walk with us over to the university and personally announce him in a lecture hall or library or where ever there are the most academicians.”

“What a delightful idea, madam,” the magistrate says, forcing a smile. “I will be honored. Shall we go?”

Centor Rabannas steps to the door and opens it. He walks out into the corridor, followed by Tullia and Stephen. He rushes through the outer door, down the steps, and turns right. He walks briskly past the gymnasium academy of the younger boys, and to the university. He hurries between the statues of famous Cyrenians of centuries long past, and up the steps onto the portico. Tullia and Stephen rush to keep up with him.

He goes through the double copper doors, across the marble lobby, and into the library. Tullia and Stephen step through the library door just as he begins his speech.

Everyone in the room stands at attention.

He holds up his arms and calls out, “Attention, everyone. Attention, everyone. Our newest student is Stephanus of Tarsus.”

With that, he turns and leaves. The students stand in place.

Silence.

“Welcome, Stephanus!” It is Draco. He walks up to Stephen and pats him on the back, then turns toward the others in the room.

“Everyone, this is my friend, Stephanus. And this is his mother.”

The students snicker.

Tullia steps forward, but Draco takes hold of her arm.

“Stephanus’ mother is the daughter of the famous Athenodorus. Studying his works is required here. A fine stoic philosopher and tutor of Augustus Caesar himself. His mother has been in the presence of Augustus on many an occasion. She is also admired and respected by the governor of Cretan

Cyrenica."

Draco waits for his words to sink in. The students and teachers scattered around the library, shuffle and smile at each other.

"And, on top of all this, *Stephanus* is the finest javelin thrower in all of Cyrene. You will want him on your team."

"Hurrah!" The students raise their arms in celebration.

Draco turns to Stephen. "I guess that means you have been accepted. Welcome."

"And that means I have dinner to begin if my family is going to eat tonight," Tullia says. "Oh, and you are welcome to come home with Stephanus to sup with us tonight."

Tullia reaches up and leans her son down to her lips. "It looks like we won't be going to Rome after all," she whispers.

Stephen straights up and grins at his mother.

Tullia winks at her son, turns, and leaves.

Draco draws closer to Stephen.

"What happened?"

"It was my mother."

"I should have known. She is something else. Remind me to never say anything bad about you in front of her."

Stephen laughs. "You're safe with me."

"Will you be staying in the dormitory?"

"No, I do not think I will need to. After all, we live just a few blocks from here."

"Well, let me show you around the library. Over there are the books of history. Come. I want to show you a book I came across just yesterday. All the way from Parthia. Written in your Hebrew language, I believe."

They walk over to the history section, and Draco looks among the scrolls, some of parchment, and some of papyrus.

"Here it is. It has some drawings in it. Can you tell what it is about?"

Stephen unrolls the first part of the scroll. "It was written by the emperor of old Persia's personal advisor, a prophet and philosopher by the name of Daniel."

"See there? I knew you would know."

"You will pay for this."

Stephen and Draco spin around and see Cato standing two man-lengths from them.

"You, Stephanus, or whatever your name is, son of Ezekiel, the Jew, will be sorry you ever came back."

13 ~ WHO IS MY ENEMY?

"**F**ather, we have been here six weeks and have attended all the synagogues," Stephen says one afternoon late in the week. We attended the Greek-Speaking Synagogue for Roman citizens at Mother's urging, but they did not accept us, even though Mother was born a Roman citizen, and you inherited citizenship when you married her.

"We attended the Berber Synagogue with Simon but did not understand much of what they were saying. We attended the Greek-Speaking Freedmen Synagogue by the North Gate and the Jewish-Born Freedmen Synagogue by the South Gate. We've attended them all."

"And you think it is time we choose a synagogue to go to all the time," Ezekiel replies.

"Yes."

"There is one more we have not attended."

"Not the Slave Synagogue."

"Why not? Do you believe we are above slaves? Haven't you been looked down on enough in your life to know what it feels like? Remember, you and I were both born into slavery. Never forget that, Son."

"Yes, Father." Stephen looks down at the floor, not liking the reminder.

According to Roman custom, at midnight, the Sabbath begins. The family rises at dawn and gathers in the front room of the apartment.

Tullia does not go to the ovens in the courtyard below. On this day of rest, she has bread, cheese, dried and fresh fruit in a basket in the corner.

Ezekiel's family and his four Greek scribe converts gather

around the basket on a large mat. The food is placed in the middle. Ezekiel leads them in a benediction. They eat. At the end of the meal, he leads them in a prayer of thanksgiving.

After the remainders of the food are put back in the basket and the mat taken up, they descend the four flights of stairs to the ground floor and head out for the Synagogue of the Slaves.

There is no easy way to get to it. They turn right and walk past the government basilica and bathhouse, the gymnasium academy, through the market, and out the South Gate. They circle around the way they came, but on the other side of the Cyrenian wall. They pass the temple to Demeter and finally arrive at the Synagogue of Slaves.

They are some of the last to arrive. They bring a shawl up to their head out of respect and enter through a flimsy wooden door. Tullia, who has dressed in her plainest tunic, enters and sits on the women's side. Ezekiel leads the other men to sit toward the back of the men's side.

People look around at the strangers and whisper to each other.

"Who are they?"

"Who is that?"

"They're not one of us."

"Are they spies?"

Stephen notices they are all speaking Greek, and wonders about the Jewish-born slaves.

The rabbi stands. He does not wear the normal white linen tunic with blue robe and turban. His hair is gray, and everyone grows silent out of respect.

He steps up to the podium. A replica of the Ark is behind him facing Jerusalem. The Ark is actually just an unadorned wooden box. Inside are supposed to be scrolls of the Torah, though they are absent. Above the ark is a board with the Hebrew words scratched into it:

Know Before Whom You Stand

Normally, on either side of the ark are cubicles holding the psalms and the prophecies. The cubicles are there but are empty.

The rabbi walks behind the center table with a copy of the Torah opened before him. He reads a prophecy of Malachi about the long-ago-promised Messiah, their Savior.

See, I will send my messenger

who will prepare the way before me.
Then suddenly, the Lord you are seeking will come.

Ezekiel realizes he is not reading at all. The scroll has no words.

After reciting the chosen Torah passage, a man on the front row stands and recites one of the Ten Commandments. Another, this time on the third row, stands and recites the next commandment. One by one, they stand until all ten are recited.

Silent prayer.

One of the women begins a chant. The rest of the congregation joins in.

More silent prayer.

A member stands and recites some of Solomon's proverbs, probably his favorites.

The rabbi leads a final prayer. The service is over.

When everyone stands to leave, most look toward Ezekiel and company still standing by their bench. Ezekiel steps out into the aisle and holds out his hand to the rabbi.

"I am Ezekiel, son of Stephen, a young lawyer at the time Pompey took over Jerusalem. He was taken as a slave first to Rome, then Germanicus, then Britannia, and finally to Tarsus in Anatolia." He takes his son's arm. "I was born in slavery, as was my son, Stephen."

"What brings you to Cyrene?" the rabbi asks, still not smiling.

"I was given my freedom sixteen years ago. I was trained to be a scribe and retain that occupation." He turns to Justus, Secundus, Trophimus, and Achaius.

"I used to run a scribe school. These men helped me teach. They are Greek Jews."

The rabbi looks at the four beardless Greeks and the beardless Stephen and scowls.

"We would like to supply you with copies of the Torah. Five of us should be able to have them completed by mid-winter. We will work very hard to get them done for you and your congregation as soon as possible."

The rabbi smiles.

"May I introduce myself? I am Rabbi Obadiah. We have no way of paying you."

"We do not ask for pay. We just ask for your friendship. We Jews need each other in this city."

"I suppose so."

"When did the persecution begin?"

"It started way back when Ptolemy VI ruled us a hundred years ago. But it has gotten worse in the last two years since Blasius was made governor of the province with orders to destroy that outlaw hero of the Berbers, TacFarinas. That Blasius is a mean one and doesn't care who he's mean to."

"There you are, my dear. May I introduce my wife to you? Tullia."

"I think we need to be going now, so the rabbi may have his noon respite," Tullia says.

The rabbi smiles and embraces Ezekiel, kissing him on each cheek.

"Uh, sir, where do the Jewish-born slaves meet?" Stephen asks.

"They meet here. We share the building. They should begin arriving soon, so we need to be on our way to give them their turn."

"I did not realize the slaves met under such poor circumstances," Stephen says as they walk back toward their apartment in the *insulae*."

"I am sure some have very good jobs, but their masters do not give them anything for their worship of just one God," Ezekiel explains. "Most people call us atheists."

"That is not true," Stephen replies. "We believe in God."

They walk through the South Gate and back into Cyrene proper.

"Well, one God is not enough for them," his father replies. "So, next week, where would you like to attend synagogue? Here or go back to one of the others?"

"Uh, since Mother is a Roman Citizen by birth, perhaps if we returned to the Greek-Speaking Synagogue and arrived early enough, they could meet and talk with us and would accept us better this time. And your employees are Greek. I think we just arrived too late and left too soon. Let us try there."

"Are you sure that is what you want to do?" Tullia asks.

"Well, I think I am sure."

The remainder of the Sabbath is spent in leisure, though part of that time is spent taking turns reading from the prophet Isaiah.

"I sure wish our Messiah, our Savior, would come," Stephen declares. He stands and hits the wall. "We need him to save the world from so much meanness and tyranny." He raises his hands. "What is he waiting for?" He raises his arms. "God has been promising he would come for thousands of years." He folds his arms. "I just do not understand." And he reseats himself on the wooden floor.

Silence for a while. Silence and meditating.

"How is school going?" Secundus asks.

"I like it a lot. Would you like to see me orate on something?"

"I think we just did," Trophimus laughs.

"You remind me of my father, your namesake," Ezekiel says. "He was trained to be a lawyer, you know. I think you inherited his gift."

"If only Cato would leave me alone," Stephen says, standing back up and looking out their small fourth-story window down at the city.

"Oh, yes. Cato the spoiled son of the provincial censor," Tullia replies.

"He taunts me about being a Jew."

"Son, you cannot control him. You can only control yourself," Ezekiel responds. "Stand tall, Son. Stand tall."

"Are you working on any interesting locks?" Justus asks.

"Well, I have this idea for a new kind of lock. It is impenetrable," Stephen says.

Evening comes, the family eats the remainder of the food Tullia had prepared the day before the Sabbath and retires for the rest of the night.

The next morning, Stephen heads for work. Much to his father's disappointment, he no longer walks to the market with him.

"No, offense, Father," he had said. "But, if I am going to make a decent wage in Cyrene and help pay for my tuition, I need to work in front of the market, not at the back where the Jews are forced to go."

Through the week, both at the blacksmith shop and the university, Stephen thinks about his father, allowing him to choose which synagogue the family should identify themselves with.

I wonder why he's letting me decide. Well, I would prefer the Greek-Speaking Synagogue. I really think, if we give them another chance, we would be accepted there. Please, Jehovah God, help us be accepted by the Greek-Speaking Synagogue for Roman Citizens.

The week is about to end. Ovidius knows Stephen does not work on the Sabbath or the day following. Ovidius has never questioned Stephen why since Stephen technically has his own business of locksmithing, and they are sharing a booth. Any extra work Stephen does for Ovidius is Stephan's choice.

Stephen arrives back at the apartment on the fourth floor of the *insulae.* Soon after, Trophimus arrives with disturbing news.

"I was talking with Rabbi Amias today when I was shopping for more blackener. I told him we were all planning to attend his Greek-Speaking Synagogue tomorrow."

"Did you tell him we were looking forward to it?" Stephen asks.

"I did not get a chance. He said Achaius, Secundus, Justus, and I were welcome to come back. And your mother, of course. And maybe you since you do not look like one of those uneducated Israelites. But your father he was unsure about."

Trophimus looks over at his employer. "I am truly sorry. I just thought you would like to know what he said. He did not say you couldn't attend, but, well…"

"No!" Stephen, who had been standing in the doorway, slams the door into their apartment. "No! He is educated. More educated than a lot of them. Just because he dresses like what they consider uneducated… No! They cannot do that."

He paces around the room. "We're going anyway."

"It's okay, Son," Ezekiel says. "We are to endure persecution without fighting back."

"Who said?"

"Did Elijah fight back? Did Isaiah or Jeremiah fight back? Did Hosea fight back? No. And we shall not either. And that is final."

Stephen sits on a cushion on the floor with his knees up and puts his head in his hands.

"I am so mixed up, Father."

"So, choose which synagogue we should return to tomorrow."

"Well, I guess one of the Freedmen synagogues. Let us go to the Greek-Speaking Freedmen Synagogue."

The following morning, the seven assemble in the front room of their apartment, eat the food prepared the day before, don their prayer shawls, and walk down the four flights of stairs.

They turn right and walk past the baths, government basilica, gymnasium academy, and theater. They turn left just before the market and arrive at the Greek-Speaking Freedmen Synagogue.

Though not large, it is opulent. It has columns along a front portico, and wide marble steps leading up to it. Just as they approach, a doorman opens the way for them.

Stephen has made sure everyone arrived a little early so a few people can greet them and get to know them better. They stay in the back behind the doorman. They wait as worshippers enter, and smile.

Some glance their way. Others do not. Some smile, but hurry on. Some glare at Ezekiel, then notice Tullia and smile. No words are spoken. As the regulars enter, they find each other and speak briefly, but warmly.

The rabbi stands and walks to the podium, so Ezekiel's group finds seats and sits in the back.

The Ark behind the rabbi is a chest covered in copper with the image of an angel over it. The plaque above the ark—Know Before Whom You Stand—is of copper with raised lettering. The ornate cubicles on either side of the ark are full of scrolls, enough for all the Torah and a few of the Prophets.

He stands behind the adorned table facing the congregation. properly dressed in the white tunic, blue robe, and blue turban.

The congregation rises, he raises his hands and offers the benediction. Immediately the congregation reseats itself.

"I know it was hard for you to break away from your friends," he says, looking down at the regular members, "but we must begin our worship. We are known for our friendliness, but now we must concentrate on our Lord."

He turns one end of the Torah scroll on the table, then announces for a brother to come read the passage for the day.

That done, a chanticleer mounts the podium and leads the congregation in five psalms of David. He seats himself, and a bent, gray-haired man comes forward to lead a prayer, his hands pointed heavenward.

The rabbi speaks of God and of the Messiah coming someday, then closes the service with a final prayer of his own.

Ezekiel's family is one of the first to go out onto the grand portico. They stand to one side, ready to be greeted. The congregation intermingles with sounds of laughter and happiness everywhere except in the direction of Ezekiel's family.

When the crowd thins out, the rabbi approaches them.

"Haven't I seen you here before?" he asks with a smile.

"Why, yes. We are deciding which synagogue to become a

part of while we are here in Cyrene. My name is Ezekiel."

"Greetings, Ezekiel. My name is Rabbi Solomus. And who do you have with you?"

"I have my wife and son, and four employees with me. Some have Roman backgrounds and some Jewish, though all are Jewish in beliefs, followers of Moses."

The rabbi eyes Ezekiel's beard. "You must be very orthodox. Where is your phylactery?" He grins when he says it.

"We only wear it during special prayer," Ezekiel replies.

"I see. You know there is another freedmen congregation in the city. That congregation is much more orthodox than we are. I assume you lead your family in the orthodox ways. I fear we even have a Sadducee among us who does not believe in life after death. I am sure you will feel more comfortable worshipping with the Jewish-Born Freedmen."

With that, the rabbi proceeds to the steps and leaves.

Stephen looks around. No one is left but them. The door to the synagogue has been closed and locked. He presses his lips together and grits his teeth. He clenches his fists. He looks away from his family to make sure he does not release an emotion he dreads.

14 ~ CHANGE OF STRATEGY

It is midweek. Everyone has just finished their evening meal. Tullia is down at the courtyard well, cleaning up. Justus and Secundus are playing a game of *patteia*, using dark stones at one end of the board and light stones at the other end. Trophimus and Achaius are debating whether the great poet, Horace, a Roman citizen, was the son of a freedman.

Stephen has a clay tablet in his lap, taking notes with a stylus to a scroll his philosophy instructor has assign to be analyzed.

"You are really liking the university," Ezekiel says. "Your mother and I are proud of you."

Stephen looks up, leans back against the wall with a broad grin, and stares at the unadorned wood ceiling.

"Father, do you think a Jew will ever be able to become a magistrate here in Cyrene? Well, you know, if he is also a Roman citizen?"

Ezekiel smiles. "Where did that come from? You're a long way from that."

"Yes, I know. I know. But, if we did stay, and if I became so respected at the university, I was asked to be one of the instructors..."

"You certainly have become ambitious, boy," Ezekiel replies, emphasizing "boy."

"You're not going to talk me out of it, Father."

"Out of what? You're a visitor from Syria on your way to Rome. Oh, wait. You do not think you can try to hold public office in Rome when we get there."

"No, of course not. But do we really have to go to Rome? I mean, I know they have a university there, but I am getting used to this one, and the instructors are beginning to like me."

"What about Cato?"

"Draco says no one pays any attention to him."

"But you are still Jewish."

"I know. I know. But, if the Jewish community backed me up..."

"None of us are allowed to vote, even if we did stay here."

"Even if we are Roman citizens through Mother?"

"Here in Cyrenica, I doubt they would let even citizens vote if they were Jewish."

"Mother, what do you think? Do you think a day might come when I could try to run for a public office?"

"Ha, ha. I think you inherited some of my father. He became a philosopher in his own right, tutored the future Augustus Caesar, and ran the government of Tarsus for a while."

"But, do you think I could do it here, Mother?"

"You have not even graduated yet. Besides, we will be leaving in another three months. Four at the most," Ezekiel says.

"Son, you are a Jew," Ezekiel continues. "You cannot change that. And there will always be people like Cato and his father who hate Jews."

"Well, there doesn't have to be. Up until a hundred years ago, our people were not persecuted here. I just learned that in a history class yesterday. Maybe we Jews could become respected again. It happened before. It could happen again."

"What's this about running for magistrate of Cyrene?" It is Justus with a large grin on his face.

"So, you won your game with Secundus," Stephen replies.

"And now you want to win an election. Well, go for it."

"Even if I am a Jew?"

"Especially then."

Sabbath arrives two days later.

"I am glad we're going to the Jewish-Born Freedmen Synagogue after all," Stephen announces. "We can help elevate their status in Cyrene. After all, we—well, I—have leadership blood in me. Yes, Jehovah God knew best."

They leave the *insulae*, and instead of turning right as they had done to go to the Greek-Speaking and Slave Synagogues, they turn left. They walk past the temple to Dionysus and the fountain. They turn right in the direction of the *hospitium*. Before they go that far, they arrive at the Jewish-Born Freedmen Synagogue.

The building is fashioned after the temple in Jerusalem with four columns and a double door in the middle.

When they enter, instead of the marble walls of the Greek-Speaking Freedmen Synagogue, the walls are covered with cedar brought down from the Jebel Akhdar Mountains behind the city, in imitation of the cedar lining in much of the temple and in Solomon's famous palace.

Tullia walks over to the women's section. Ezekiel leads his men to the third row of the men's section.

They see before them the Ark, not as large as the other Arks in the other synagogues, but covered with pure gold like the original ark of Moses. They do not have angels on the lid—even though Moses did—for fear the pagan Gentiles may see it and conclude they are worshipping graven images.

The podium is high. The sign overhead—**Know Before Whom You Stand**—has been printed in Hebrew on a large but wide scroll that has been secured to the wall. On either side of the Ark are nineteen cubicles, all filled with scrolls covering all the Law, Poetry, and Prophets of the Lord God of Israel. The thirty-ninth scroll is on the ornate table made in the shape of the alter of unleavened bread in the Jerusalem temple with four horns—one on each corner—and all covered with gold.

Rabbi Levi stands. He wears the white linen tunic and blue turban. Instead of the blue robe, he wears a long apron-like ephod of blue, purple, gold, and scarlet. He refrains from wearing the breastplate of twelve precious stones representing the twelve Tribes of Israel, only allowed to the high priest.

When he stands and raises his arms heavenward, the congregation stands. He pronounces a benediction that includes promises to keep each of the Ten Commandments, which he itemizes.

When he says the "amen," he and the congregation bow with their heads to the floor where they pray in silence.

They hear a chanticleer begin a psalm, and everyone rises to join in the song. After two songs, an elder rises and asks that the sacrifices be made.

He holds out a large basket, and one by one the members file by to place their weekly contribution therein.

The rabbi stands once again and reads one of the prophets—Micah—predicting the Messiah being born in Bethlehem someday. He elucidates on the prophecy, and members of the congregation periodically nod in approval or say a sacred amen.

The service is over. The rabbi steps immediately over to

Ezekiel.

"I believe you were here once before. My name is Rabbi Levi."

"Yes, we were here a few weeks ago, and I do remember your name," Ezekiel replies. "Although there are many synagogues in Cyrene to choose from, we would like to be part of yours."

Ezekiel puts his hand on Stephen's shoulder. This is my son." He motions for the others and announces, "These are Greek Jews, and you will find them dedicated to the Law and the Prophets. Oh, and here comes my lovely wife, Tullia."

The Rabbi smiles at them all, but only embraces Ezekiel.

"Welcome."

"I had a scribe school over in Syria. These four young men assisted me in teaching the craft. All are skilled in copying the sacred scriptures."

"Oh? Well, in that case," Rabbi Levi says, "we are going to have a meeting this week about obtaining newer copies of our scriptures—especially the Torah—because the edges of the papyrus are beginning to wear. Would you care to join us?"

"Indeed, we would," Stephen says.

Rabbi Levi looks at Stephen momentarily, then back at Ezekiel. He embraces the old man and kisses him on each cheek.

"Oh," the rabbi says, looking around. "It seems most of the congregation has left while we were talking."

He walks toward the outer door, followed by Ezekiel. They part on the street.

"Things could not have turned out better," Stephen says. "They accepted us and are even looking to us for leadership."

"They are not, Stephen," Ezekiel says. "Stop that. Just stop that. We are going to blend into this congregation and help when asked."

Three days go by.

"Tullia, we will be back in a few hours," Ezekiel announces at the apartment door. "The meeting Rabbi Levi invited us to is this evening."

The six men with torches do not take long to arrive at the synagogue with petite Tullia not with them. They douse their torches and walk in. The meeting room is empty.

"What's going on here?" Stephen says. "Where is everyone? We have been tricked."

"Slow down, Son," Ezekiel says. "I see light at the bottom of that door over there. They may be meeting in the room used by the schoolboys during the day."

Ezekiel leads them and knocks on the door.

"Hello there, Ezekiel," one of the men says upon opening it for them. "I am Benjamin. This is Shamgar, and this is Meshek. Be seated. I guess we are ready for our meeting to begin."

Rabbi Levi leads them in a benediction, also asking Jehovah God's blessings on their meeting.

"Now," the rabbi begins, "we need to replace our copies of the Torah as soon as possible. Tattered copies show disrespect to the only true God."

"Uh, brothers," Stephen begins, standing. "my father—as well as Achaius, Trophimus, Secundus, and Justus— are more than willing to provide you your copies. Currently, they are making copies for the Slave Synagogue, but..."

"For who?"

"Uh, the Slave Synagogue."

"Why?"

"Because they had no copies."

"Well, we would hope you would give us some kind of priority."

"Well." Stephen looks over at his father and sits down.

"I believe we will be able to start on yours tomorrow. Then, perhaps, we can work on theirs and yours at the same time," Ezekiel says.

"Oh," the rabbi responds. "Oh. Fine. Fine."

"If I may add a little something," Stephen says, standing again.

"Go ahead, young man," Rabbi Levi says.

"It occurred to me that, if we offer to upgrade the pavement on the street out here in front of our building and in front of the buildings on either side of us, the magistrates might look to us for leadership in upgrading the other streets of our grand city."

Rabbi Levi glares at Stephen. Ezekiel pulls at Stephen's sleeve to get him to sit. Trophimus puts his hand up to his mouth to stifle a grin, as do the other three scribes. Benjamin's eyebrows furrow over darkening eyes, Shamgar hits his fist on the table they are sitting around, and Meshak leans forward as though ready to attack.

Ezekiel stands. "Uh, brothers, it is time for us to leave. We will begin on the synagogue's Torah copying tomorrow. Peace be with you all."

With that, Ezekiel pushes at Stephen to walk ahead of him while his scribes follow close. They shut the door and hurry across the congregational meeting room, grabbing their unlit torches by the door.

Behind them, they hear, "Who does he think he is?"

Out on the street, Ezekiel slams his knuckles into the back of Stephen's head, then slaps him.

"Are you out of your mind?"

"What did I do?"

"You insulted them. It's their synagogue, not yours. It's their city, not yours."

"But I thought... I was just trying to show initiative. You know, leadership."

"When they want your initiative and leadership, they will ask for it."

"Well, maybe I did move a little fast for them."

"You are not to bring that outlandish idea up to them again."

"Never?"

"Never. And may we live long enough to get out of Cyrene and go to Rome."

Tullia opens the door when she hears the men's heavy feet on the wooden steps. She refrains from saying anything to her husband or son. She looks over at the others, and Achaius whispers, "Do not ask."

The following day, one of the Jews who had given Stephen an order for new pulls for his house doors comes by the shop and cancels it. The following day, another Jew stops by and cancels his order.

The Sabbath arrives. The joviality of the previous week is gone while they break their fast.

They walk out of the *insulae* and turn left. They pass the temple to Dionysus. At the fountain, they turn right and arrive at the Jewish-Born Freedmen Synagogue. They arrive at the last moment, and all sit in the back row.

Rabbi Levi stands and raises his arms heavenward to pronounce the benediction. With the amen, everyone bows his head to the floor until the chanticleer begins. The service continues in its predictable format.

At the end of his sermon, Rabbi Levi says, "I have an announcement, everyone."

When Stephen sees how serious the man is, he hangs on to his seat. *Uh, oh. They are going to excommunicate us. And it will be my fault.*

"We have been blessed by Ezekiel, our newest member. He

was master of a scribe school in Syria and has brought his teachers with him. They have kindly consented to copy the Torah for us on brand new papyrus. They expect to be able to present them to us by the next new moon. Jehovah God has surely blessed us with their presence. Everyone be sure to tell them thank you after we dismiss."

Stephen smiles and nudges his father. Ezekiel glares at his son.

Once on their way home, Stephen announces, "See there, Father. They weren't insulted. They are happy to have us."

"No. They are punishing us for you trying to take over. We must drop the scrolls for the slaves and give them priority, or we will lose face. Well, lose face more than what we already have."

"Oh. I will help."

A new week begins. Stephen is repentant. He puts up a sign. Ovidius reads it.

"What are you doing, Stephanus? Take that sign down."

"Why? It will be good for business."

"To give a discount to all Jews? You will ruin our business. Take it down."

Stephen takes the sign down, and before going over to the university for his oratory class, he walks through the market.

I have to find some way to raise the reputation of the Jews in this city.

He slows at a tapestry booth, stares a moment, then moves on.

My grandfather, Stephen, probably would have risen to a seat on the Sanhedrin. My other grandfather taught Augustus, then led the city of Tarsus. It's in my blood.

He slows at a basket booth but continues on.

The Jews need me. This city needs me. I can lead them both to greatness.

He slows at a booth selling sign sheets made of copper.

"Yes, we emboss whatever the customer wants on his sign," the shop keeper says.

"What kinds of things do people want on their signs?" Stephen asks.

"Some want their family name or their occupation on theirs with the intention of hanging it on their outer gate. Some veterans want the military insignia of whatever legion they served with. Some want the name of a god embossed to put somewhere in their house to invoke the protection of that god. Some...."

"Oh, I get it. Very nice. I like that idea. Thank you, sir."

Stephen leaves in a hurry. When he arrives at the university, he pulls his supplies from his assigned cubicle and goes to his class.

"Stephen," the instructor says after lecturing a while, "are you taking notes to my lecture on your tablet? You other students should follow his example. It impresses me, and you do want to impress me."

Stephen grins and puts his clay tablet and stylus away. He had been caught.

The following day at work, he pulls out the largest block of iron he has. He heats his forge and raises the temperature with his bellows. The rest of the day, he alternately heats the piece to white heat, pounds it to make it flatter, heats it again, hammers it again, and repeats the process again and again.

"What are you doing, Stephanus?" Ovidius asks.

"Making something to present to the city," Stephen grunts between slamming down his hammer onto the anvil.

By the end of the day, he has a flat plate of iron two handbreadths high and six handbreadths wide.

The next day. Stephen takes out some copper he had saved for special decorative items. He pounds it until it is in a thin sheet. Pleased with himself, he sets it aside and walks to the university.

On the third morning, he takes his sharpest iron tool and cuts the copper in strips. Then he reheats the copper, one strip at a time, just hot enough that he can bend it.

A little at a time, he forms his design until it is completed.

Pleased, he sets it aside to go to his afternoon classes. When they are over, he returns to his shop instead of going straight home.

He lights a torch and surveys his plaque.

Perfect. Jehovah God has been with me. This should solve all our problems.

Stephen takes off his heavy leather apron, and his arm and leg protectors, puts the iron plaque with the copper design on it under his arm, and walks in the darkness toward the government basilica. When he sees no one is looking, he sets his plaque in front of one of the two columns closest to the front door. He smiles and returns home.

The next morning, he hurries to the city center. When he nears the government basilica, he sees Jews and Romans shouting at each other. His excellency Rabannas stands on the portico holding the plaque.

"Who brought this here?" he shouts.

"How dare it be said the Jews and Romans are brothers!" someone in the crowd shouts.

"Never! Never will we be brothers!"

"The Romans are power-hungry."

"No, the Jews are."

"The Jews are uneducated."

"The Romans are uncivilized."

"The Jews are atheists."

"We are not, we worship the only true God."

"You blaspheme our gods!"

Then the fist fighting.

Merchants in the market and students at the university-run out onto the street to join in.

15 ~ FAILURE

It has been two days since the riot. Stephen is still missing.

"Where could he be?" Tullia asks, dabbing her reddened eyes.

"Thank you for coming, Simon," she continues. "It seems as though the only time we see you is when we need something."

"We will find him. Do not worry, Tullia," Simon says.

"I have searched several times through the North Gate Market," Justus says. "And Secundus has searched through the South Gate Market just as much."

"I have searched the docks down in Apollonia, but with no luck," Simon says.

"I have searched the university," Trophimus says, "and Achaius has searched the gymnasium academy."

"What about the synagogues?" Tullia asks.

"Good idea," Ezekiel says. "We will divide up and check in all six synagogues."

Late in the afternoon, the men return to the fourth-floor *insulae* apartment.

"It is too late to search any further tonight," Ezekiel says. He embraces his wife. "He is eighteen years old and strong. He will be fine."

"What if he isn't? What if he was caught in the riot, killed, and his bo...."

Tullia breaks into tears again and buries her face in Ezekiel's tunic.

"I have another idea, Tullia," Simon says. "I will be back tomorrow, and we can all go together. Try to sleep. We will all pray."

"Will he be cold tonight?" Tullia whispers.

"Shhh."

The next morning, Simon knocks on their door. The men are ready to go.

"Grab your robes. And bring weapons."

"Knives?" Justus asks.

"Yes, knives will be fine."

"Where are you going that you need knives?" Tullia cries.

"Just for wild animals, Tullia. Not for wild people. I think this time, we will find him."

"Where?"

"While I was teaching him to ride my horse, we went up into the mountains a little way. I will bet he is there. I remember when I was doing it because my son, Alexander, was born at that time."

He smiles at Tullia. "By tonight, your son will be safe at home, and you will be spoiling him with some of your famous stew."

Tullia hands her husband a basket of food, a skin of water, and a blanket. Ezekiel embraces her, and the men leave.

"Over to my house first, men. I have horses for all of us and an extra one for Stephen."

They arrive and see there are no saddles on the horses.

"They would buck you off if you put a saddle on them. They've never experienced it. Just hang on to the reins, and remember, they are sensitive to the touch of your knee. That is where they get your directions."

Simon leads the way. They go out the North Gate and circle around the city wall to head up into the mountains to the south.

They pass a vineyard. "Oh, by the way," Simon calls over to Ezekiel. "My wife received an inheritance from her brother, enough for me to quit fishing and have my own vineyard. It's right over there on our left."

"That is great," Ezekiel replies, trying to smile at his friend.

"My son, Alexander, will inherit my vineyard someday."

It does not take them long to arrive at the tree line. They ride single file. At last, they see a steep ridge ahead of them. Simon stops.

"Okay, there are caves all along here. Tie your horses up. We need to do this on foot."

The men dismount.

"This ridge ends a *mille* in each direction. When you get to the end, come back here."

The men divide up with the scribes going left while Ezekiel and Simon go right.

"Stephen!"

"Stephen!"

"Do you hear us, Stephen?"

"Come out, Stephen!"

"Stephen, everything is okay!"

"Stephen, come out."

"Please, Stephen!"

Two hours pass.

"We may as well go back," Ezekiel says, sitting on a rock. "I wish you had been right. I wish to God you had been right. I do not know what to do, Simon. I just do not know what to do. It's my fault. I pushed him one way too hard, and I guess Tullia pushed him the other way too hard. What are we going to do, Simon? What are we going to do?"

"Come on, friend," Simon says. "Let us go back. We will think of something. Maybe he came home on his own and will greet us at the door. Come, my friend."

Simon helps Ezekiel up and takes slow steps with him.

"You know, I am sixty-nine years old, Simon. My time on earth..."

"Let us work on one problem at a time, my friend."

"Father?"

"Huh?"

The two men stop and look around.

"Father?"

They look up at the top of the ridge.

"Father?"

"Son? Is that you?"

The young man rushes down the precipice, half running, sometimes scooting, sometimes tumbling.

Ezekiel hobbles in the direction of his son, trying to run, his arms outstretched.

Stephen picks himself up at the bottom of the ridge and runs toward his father.

They embrace for a long time.

"Father," Stephen whispers. "Do not cry. I am okay."

They draw apart from each other. "Son, your mother and I have not slept since you disappeared. Why did you do this to us?"

Stephen sits on the ground. His father and Simon sit across from him.

Shame.

Confusion.

"Father, every time I try to stand up for Jehovah God, it ends in disaster. Nothing I try works. I am cursed. Why, Father?"

Stephen scoots close to his father, lays his head on the old man's shoulder, and sobs.

Ezekiel toys with the ring his father had made him when he was but a boy—the forever circle to remind him God would forever keep him safe.

Simon stands and walks toward the waiting horses.

"I do not know, my son. I wish I did."

Stephen continues to sob.

"Your mother has always said you were destined for greatness. I sometimes thought so too."

"I cannot even do one thing right," Stephen says, raising his head and running his sleeve across his reddened nose.

"Every time I try to defend Jehovah God, I end up betraying him."

"Jehovah knows you love him. You love him with a depth I do not even think I have."

"Then why does everything always turn out wrong. Even worse than it was?"

"Son, I am beginning to get cold. I think the sun will be down soon. Let us go home."

The two stand and walk with arms across each other's shoulders.

Slowly they walk. Not knowing what else to say. Not knowing what else to do. Now knowing, even, what to pray for.

"There they are!" Justus shouts.

"Bring their horses to them. Quick," Simon shouts.

Achaius arrives with their two horses.

"My father and I will ride together," Stephen says.

Stephen helps his father up, then mounts the Barb behind him.

Once again, Simon leads the way. They arrive back at Simon's house just when the sun begins to turn red.

Stephen slides off the horse, then his father does. Once again, arms across shoulders, father and son walk together. They walk toward home. Alone together.

The others stay behind.

They arrive at the *insulae,* and Stephen stops. "Father, what am I going to tell Mother? I am so ashamed."

"She loves you, Son. Nothing can ever happen to make her

stop loving you. Right now, all she wants is for you to be home and safe again."

Ezekiel leads the way up the four flights of stairs. As they progress, he climbs slower. Just as they reach the top, a door opens, and Tullia rushes out to the landing, her arms outstretched.

She and Stephen embrace. She rocks him back and forth, and he lets her. She lays her head on his chest and weeps.

"If we do not go inside where I can get off these old feet of mine, I am going to sit right here on the steps for the rest of the night."

Tullia takes one hand, Stephen takes his other. The three enter the apartment together and close the door.

"Did your father feed you?" Tullia asks.

"Mother, I am sorry that I..."

She puts a finger on his lips.

"Shhh. You're home and safe, and that is all that matters. Now is the time for me to return to spoiling you. Here is your favorite cheese."

Stephen takes the food and stuffs it in his mouth.

"You were hungry. Weren't there any berries up there?"

"A few blackberries. And I saw a vineyard once, but it was too much in the open."

Ezekiel presses his lips together in a slight smile and nods to an invisible Simon. *My son kept your vineyard protected.*

Soon there is silence in the little fourth-floor apartment. Sleep comes. And with it peace. A peace they do not understand.

Morning.

"Well, Son, may I make a suggestion?" Ezekiel says. "You do not have to take it. But, if you want to at least hear it..."

"I do not know what I am doing anymore. Tell me."

"Go to work this morning. Say a jovial hello to everyone you meet on the street as you go. Hold your head high. When you arrive, whistle, put on your leather apron, fire up your forge, and go back to work. Keep your normal schedule. In the afternoon, go on over to the university. Hold your head high. Greet everyone with a smile. Whistle. Pretend the riot never happened, and you never disappeared. They will follow your lead."

"Do you really think it will work, Father?"

"What a marvelous idea," Tullia says. "Of course, it will work. Isn't your father the smartest man we ever knew?"

"Even smarter than your father?"

"Smarter than both of your grandfathers," Tullia says.

"Take his advice. He is right. You will see."

Stephen stands and takes a deep breath. "This is it," he says, and opens the door.

"God go with you, Son. God go with you."

Stephen forces a smile once he gets out onto the street. He turns left and passes the temple to Dionysus. He waves at the priests standing on their portico. He holds his head high and smiles at the passersby. He strolls past the fountain, whistling and waving at people. "Isn't it a great day?" he says.

He enters the market, walks to the second aisle, and to the end. He enters the shop, greets Ovidius with a large grin, puts on his heavy leather apron, and fires up his forge.

"I wonder if it will rain today," he muses.

Ovidius eyes the young man, takes his cue, smiles, and returns to his own work.

Evening arrives. Stephen leaves the university and walks home, still greeting everyone with a cheerful smile. No longer is it a forced smile. It is genuine.

Days go by. Ezekiel's four scribes have rented an apartment of their own in the same *insulae* in order to give the family privacy.

At home, Stephen alternates between peace and confusion. Sometimes he paces, and sometimes he sits on his floor cushion, his head leaned back against the wall, his eyes closed.

Sabbath comes. *Well, Son, it is time to go. You can face them with your head held high.*

"I am not going, Father."

"What?"

Tullia kneels next to her son. "No. You have to go with us."

"Mother, Father, just let me do this."

"Do what?"

"I am going to stay home and worship in private. The early prophets did sometimes. Remember all that time Elijah stayed hidden in a cave?"

"No, stand up, Son," Ezekiel says.

Tullia looks up at her husband and stands. "He has to work this out for himself," she whispers.

Stephen is left alone. He pulls out the scroll he has been helping to copy for one of the synagogues—he does not know which one will get it—and reads.

My God, my God, why have you forsaken me?

He reads the psalm aloud. He reads how David's heart has a talk with his soul.

Be still, my soul. You will yet worship.

After reading the psalm and thinking about it, he chants it. He stands, holds his hands upward, and pronounces his benediction. He slumps to the floor and bends his head all the way down in obeisance to his God.

He pulls out a few coins and sets them aside. *I will give them to the beggar over by the North Gate.*

He reads another scripture. This one written by Zechariah the prophet about the promised Messiah, the promised Savior to come someday as king on earth.

The Lord shall be king over all the earth.
Then there shall be only one God.

Stephen chants it, ponders it, stands and orates about it, and prays.

The door to the apartment opens. His parents have returned.

"You would have been proud of me, Son," Ezekiel says, walking over to Stephen, who has reseated himself. "I told the rabbi and the others in the committee that they get their scrolls of the Torah after we have delivered the promised scrolls to the Slave Synagogue."

Stephen smiles at his father. "Yes, I am proud of you."

Another week goes by. Once again, on the Sabbath, Stephen says he will stay home and worship alone. Once again, his parents relent.

The following day, the first day of the week, even though Stephen never goes to work or to the university on that day, he is gone all day.

He returns in time to eat the evening meal with his parents.

Tullia rises to take up the remaining food and the dishes.

"Mother, sit back down. I have made a decision."

Tullia reseats herself and looks at her husband. Ezekiel takes her hand.

"Father. Mother. I have decided the only way the cause of God is going to be advanced here is to be like Queen Esther. I am going to follow her example."

"What do you mean, Son?" Tullia asks.

"She kept her identity as a Jew secret for many years. Yet she continued to pray and fast and worship in private. She continued in her faith. She lived with a powerful emperor, and he always loved and respected her. God blessed the Persian Empire because of her. And, as a result, when her people needed her, she was able to obtain the blessings of her emperor husband who sided with her and protected the Jews."

Stephen's parents watch him in silence.

"Do not worry. I am not going to leave Judaism. What I am going to do is start a secret synagogue. We will rent an apartment in the *insulae* to meet in. From now on, I will be Stephanus to everyone, including you, while in public.

I will live as a Roman citizen, which I am. I will work as a Roman and study as a Roman. I will continue to look like a Roman, dress like a Roman, eat like a Roman. In public, I will speak in either Latin or Greek. I will be all things Roman in public. In private, I will be all things Jewish."

"But..."

"This secret congregation will be able to accomplish more for the advancement of Judaism, working secretly, silently, and peacefully." He pauses.

"The Jews in Babylon were looked down on and persecuted just like we are here. But, by working in secret, Esther accomplished more in the long run for her people than if she had done so publicly. So, when the perfect time came, all was ready, and the Jews were elevated to mutual respect because of Esther. Perhaps here too someday the persecution will end."

"But, Son, who? Who will join you?"

16 ~ THE ESTHER QUEST

*E*zekiel stands and paces a few moments, running his gnarled hand through his gray beard. Stephen gives his father the same courtesy of waiting for him as Ezekiel had done for him on many an occasion in the past. After a little while, the old man reseats himself across from Stephen.

"Some have already joined." Stephen continues. "Yesterday, I went around to several Jewish friends who I thought felt the same as I do. They all agreed this was the best way to advance Judaism."

"Who?"

"Well, Achaius, Trophimus, Secundus, and Justus to start with."

Ezekiel squints and tilts his head. "Them?

"They felt out of place in the Freedmen's Synagogues because they had never been slaves. They felt out of place at the Greek-Speaking Synagogue too because the brothers there were arrogant and not interested in anyone but themselves."

"Oh, I see," Ezekiel says.

"Any others?" Tullia asks.

"Yes, Draco. He was a member of the Greek-Speaking Synagogue. And Benjamin, a member of the Jewish-Born Synagogue. We even had a woman from the Greek-Speaking Synagogue, a widow named Patrice. And a man from the Slave Synagogue—Jonas—joined us. And Carpus."

"Have you met together yet?"

"No, tomorrow we plan to meet in Achaius' apartment up on the fifth floor. We will each contribute enough to rent an apartment for six months. Justus said there is an apartment available on the top floor—the sixth floor."

"Well, if you want to remain secret, you won't have

neighbors climbing the stairs outside your door who might hear you singing," Tullia says.

"Mother, we will whisper our songs. And, at the same meeting, we will begin planning our strategy to spread the Word of God in a good way around Cyrene."

"You already tried it, Son," Tullia says. "It just caused a riot."

Stephen sighs and puts his head in his hands. Momentarily, he looks up, and his mother pats him on the hand. "I should not have brought it up," she says.

"We will think of something." His eyes are moist. "With all our minds and hearts working together, we will come up with some workable methods. Surely Jehovah God will be our help and strength."

He puts his head down on his raised knees and hugs them.

"Won't he, Father? Won't he be our help and strength?"

"Yes, Son," Ezekiel whispers. "He will. Because of your good heart, he will."

The next morning, Stephen prepares to go to work. Just as he opens the door to leave, he pauses and turns around.

"Oh, Mother, would it be okay if you would prepare some bread and yogurt dip and some fresh grapes and dates for us to eat at our secret synagogue after we worship? I will buy the food."

Tullia steps over to her son and takes hold of both arms. "I would be pleased to, Stephen," she says.

"No, not Stephen. Stephanus."

"Okay, Stephanus," she replies, grinning.

Two days later, after dark, the new congregation meets in the sixth-floor apartment rented in the name of Achaius. They pray for wisdom. They take turns suggesting what things to try.

"First off," Carpus says, "I need to explain why I am here. If you visited my synagogue of Greek-Speaking Freedmen, you were probably told there was a Sadducee in their midst. They were talking about me. They claim I do not believe in life after death. That is not true. I have been suggesting we give food to beggars, regardless of their beliefs. That made them mad, and they began trying to discredit me. I hope our group will reach out to the beggars."

"I will help you, the Widow Patrice says."

"We need a secret word or secret mark so that, as we grow, we will be able to recognize each other," Jonas says.

"What about the temple candlestick with one of the

branches missing?" Secundus suggests.

"What about a scroll with a crown on top to represent God as our only king?" Trophimus suggests.

"What about *harot,* which is backward for Torah?" Benjamin suggests.

"What about *sesom* which is backward for Moses?" Carpus suggests.

"I like that last one," Benjamin says.

"Me too," Stephanus says.

Everyone nods their head.

"Then *sesom* is our secret word, whether drawn or said. Now, what will our first project be?"

"I would like to suggest we put pieces of the Ten Commandments under stones that are likely to be moved aside and moved," Achaius suggests.

"That is a good idea," Justus says. "We could slip them in cracks between clay bricks in people's outer walls," Jonas says.

"And under merchandise on counters in the market," Patrice says.

Stephen laughs. "I think we all have ideas where to hide them so they will be discovered and read when we're not around. We could do a lot of it at night. So, why do not each of us write out the Ten Commandments on Papyrus, clay tablets, parchment—whatever we can—and secretly distribute them at night on our own?"

"Good idea," Secundus says. "That way, no one is burdened with it all."

"Is there anything else? Have we given you enough money, Achaius, to rent that top-floor apartment?"

"Yes, Stephanus, it is sufficient for six months. It will be ready for us by Sabbath, which is two days away."

The following night, Stephen sits in the room he now has to himself and writes out the Ten Commandments on small pieces of papyrus he had bought earlier in the day.

"I will be late coming home from work tonight," he tells his mother the next morning.

Evening arrives. Stephen has his pieces of the Ten Commandments stuffed in a leather shoulder pouch. As soon as it is dark, he works his way around the city to places he had spied out on his way to the university at noon.

Though now dark, he knows where everything is. The stars are all the light he needs or wants.

He walks over to the bathhouse, looks up and down the

street to see if anyone might spot him, then enters. He goes over to the men's changing room and leaves a copy of the Commandments. Out in the corridor, he gets an idea and slips over to the women's changing room. He slides a copy under their door.

He walks back to the exit and hears, "Hey, you! What are you doing in here at night? You are not allowed!"

Hearing the voice of the night watchman, he flings open the door to the bathhouse and runs out in the direction of the gymnasium academy where he hides behind a Juniper tree. He watches as the night watchman rushes out onto the street and looks both ways, then gives up and goes back inside.

Whew. That was close. I did not know they had guards at the bathhouse at night. Where to next?

Stephen looks toward the gymnasium academy with its small square building, small amphitheater, and large building on the other side.

He walks over to the smaller building. *I will bet this is their dormitory. Hmmm. Where should I leave their copies? Hmmm.*

No one is around to see the twinkle in his eye. He sneaks around the back of the building to where he had seen a back door. He tries the latch, and it is not locked. He looks around both ways to see if anyone has spotted him by starlight.

Convinced no one has, he cracks the door a little. The hinges do not squeak. He opens it a little farther and a little farther until he can squeeze his thin frame inside.

He waits for his eyes to adjust and sees rows of beds. He kneels on all fours and moves forward a hand span at a time. The floor is made of marble, so is smooth and easy to slide on. He makes his way to the first bed and slips a piece of the Ten Commandments under it. He works his way in silence to the next one. And the next.

He reaches the far end of the room, and someone stirs. He turns around to see what is happening. He holds his breath. He prays not to be caught.

Someone stands, walks to a small wing where he hears water in a clay pot. Soon, the boy returns to his bed.

Stephen waits until he believes the boy is asleep again. On his way back, he builds up his courage and slips a piece of the Ten Commandments under the foot end of his mattress. The boy stirs but does not waken.

Little by little back down the row to the rear door, Stephen works his way. When he arrives, he raises up to aa crouch and hears a noise behind him. He does not know if it is snoring or someone growling at him. He reaches for the latch, pulls the door open a hand span at a time, and slips out into the night air.

Unsure whether someone will follow him out in the next moment, he stands stooping, works his way a couple man-lengths from the rear door, and lies flat on the ground, his body pressed up against the foundation of the building. He waits. He hears no footsteps. He looks around and props up on his knees. He looks around again.

He stands and runs to the end of the building next to the amphitheater. He looks up in the sky and decides it is not too late, then sprints over to the other structure. He eases through one of the entrances leading to the arena itself.

Should I proceed? It is completely black. The magnitude of the structure has blocked out even the starlight. He hugs the wall and takes small steps, knowing he could fall into an unexpected pit if he is not careful.

A sound. A sound of scraping. Stephen stops and listens. The scraping sound comes closer.

I cannot be caught. I must be free to keep spreading the words of Moses so the pagans will learn.

He turns in the direction from which he had come and works his way back, one small step at a time, until he reaches the outer edge and can see stars again.

Perhaps I should stop for the night. If I get caught, my work will be over.

Rather than return home the way he had come, Stephen works his way behind the gymnasium academy and the university until he arrives at the city wall. He works along the wall until he comes to the edge of the citadel. He knows the *insulae* is on the other side of the citadel.

He slips over to the *insulae,* enters through the front door, and climbs the four flights of stairs until he arrives at his apartment.

Once inside and safe, he sits on his cushion near a low table where a candle has not quite burned itself out yet.

"You okay, Son?"

"Yes, Father," Stephen says.

"Be very quiet. Your mother is asleep. You do not want her to worry."

"Father, did you ever have to sneak around to do something good?"

Ezekiel sits on his cushion opposite Stephen.

"Did I? Did I? Of course, I did. How do you think your mother and I were able to see each other alone that year after they arrived back from Rome?"

Stephen smiles. "It's hard to realize you were courting Mother."

"Sometimes we met by a fountain or behind an arbor, or in the shadows of a veranda. We had to be creative."

"Ha, ha. Did you ever get caught?"

"Of course, I did. They punished me by making me go down to the docks and stay with my father for a week. Well, my father liked that, and he was able to teach me more blacksmithing, though not much. He was in his eighties, and they did not make him work anymore. But he gave me plenty of advice."

"Sabbath is in two days, Father. Are you and Mother planning to join us in our secret synagogue?"

"No. I would rather be a Daniel than an Esther. You know. He was openly a Jew."

"He was sentenced to death by the lions."

"Yes, but God protected him, and he survived."

"Well, I guess someone has to keep an eye on the Jewish-borns in this city. Not that they will ever veer from staying to themselves and not spreading the word in a positive way about Moses."

"Okay, Son. I am going back to bed."

Two days later, after breaking their fast, Stephen walks to the door of the apartment.

"Wait here, Stephanus," Tullia says with a wink.

He pauses, and she brings him a basket from the corner. "Here is the bread, some fresh grapes, and some dates—enough for twelve of you."

"Thank you, Mother."

With that, he heads up the steps two more flights until he is on the sixth and top floor. He tries the pull on the door, and it opens.

Most of the others have arrived. The Widow Patrice has not yet, nor has Draco.

"From now on, we will have to keep it locked," Achaius says when he sees Stephen.

"Tomorrow, I will work all day to make my best and most complicated lock, and enough keys for all ten of us."

"Better make eleven," the Widow Patrice says, having

arrived shortly after Stephen.

Patrice walks in with another woman. Whereas Patrice is very tall, the other woman is very short.

"This is my best friend, Judith. She was widowed when her husband was cutting trees for their master, a bear attacked, and..."

The Widow Judith brings a kerchief up to her eyes.

"Oh, I am sorry. It is such a painful memory," Patrice says, looking at the others. "Let us go sit over there."

"But I do not know what to do," she says to Patrice.

Patrice looks at the others. "Judith has been a worshipper of Apollo most of her life. Nothing is helping her with her loneliness. She wants to find out if Judaism can help fill that void."

"Welcome," each one says with a smile. "We are your friends."

Patrice notices cushions have been brought for everyone to sit on and are arranged in a circle. She leads Judith to two of them.

Not long after, the last member, Draco, arrives. He, too, has brought a friend.

"Brothers and sisters, this is my friend, Cadmus."

"Cadmus?" Stephen says. "I had no idea... Everyone, Cadmus is a fellow student at the university."

"Is that you, Stephanus? Cato has been telling everyone you are Jewish. I guess he was right, though not everyone believed him."

Stephen looks over at Draco and smiles but says nothing.

"I have been worshipping Zeus," Cadmus says, "because I wanted the god who was over all the other gods. But Draco has been telling me there is a God more powerful than Zeus. I want to know about him."

Draco sees there are no cushions left. Just then, Achaius, who had slipped away earlier, comes from the other room with four more cushions, "In case we have more visitors."

They sit in a circle, men and women together. The men take turns praying and chanting David's psalms and reciting scripture.

Stephen notices a difference in their prayers from those he had so often heard in the synagogues. Prayers for their pagan neighbors. Prayers for the priests of Zeus, at one of the finest architecturally perfect temples in the Roman Empire. They pray for the priests at the temple to Demeter. The priests and priestesses at the temple to Dionysus. And for the priests at the

Sanctuary of Apollo.

They chant another psalm. Someone recites a scripture. They pray again and find themselves praying for Governor Blasius and Censor Rabannas and all the magistrates. Then they pray for the Roman cohort stationed in the citadel.

More psalms and scriptures. More prayer. This time for TacFarinas and his gang treated like outlaws by the Roman army and heroes by the people native to Libya.

"Before we adjourn, we need to discuss what we have done this week to spread God's Word and what we plan to do next week."

"Well, Stephanus," Draco says, "I went over to the gymnasium academy amphitheater two nights ago, and..."

"That was you?" Stephen says. "Ha. I was there too. You scared me so much I did not know if you were an animal, a guard, or what. But I left, and fast."

"That scraping noise was you, Stephanus?"

The secret synagogue exchanges experiences on spreading the Ten Commandments around the city. "May the pagan Gentiles realize Judaism gives society dignity, hope, and an unselfish God who actually loves them."

The guests remain silent. Stephen notices and abruptly stands.

"Uh, I think our time is up. We need to discuss family matters at another meeting. My mother sent up to us this basket of food."

He steps to the corner where he had set the basket and spreads the food out in the middle of the circle but on the floor. "Someone remind me to bring a small table for us before we meet next time."

They eat and several stand, ready to leave.

"Shall we have a meeting next...uh....at the same, uh, time and, uh, place we met last time?" he asks. The other original members nod in agreement.

Four days later, they meet again, this time in the top-floor room, which serves as their synagogue.

"There were some things we forgot to decide on," Achaius says when the original ten are all present.

"Yes," Benjamin says. "When do we trust visitors enough to tell them the secret word?"

"And just how much should we know about someone before showing them our secret meeting place on the Sabbath?" Justus asks.

"And how do we protect ourselves from spies?"

Back and forth with ideas, none of which are agreed on by everyone.

"We would have to be mind readers to protect our synagogue completely," Trophimus finally says.

"Then the only solution I can see is that every time one of us wants to bring someone new, we let the others know ahead of time. A couple of us will break off and go with him to start a new synagogue."

"Stephanus, what are you saying?" Justus asks.

"I am saying that the city may end up with many secret synagogues, and we will not know who or where we all are. It's the only way we can stay secret and safe from harm."

"How will people know we have helped someone in need, Stephanus?" Patrice asks. "Leave a note for the person we helped?"

"Exactly," Stephen says. "I see no other way to escape being arrested and jailed or even worse. We must stay free to keep spreading the word."

17 ~ THE DEBATE

"**I**t's about time you visit my home," Simon tells Ezekiel. Alexander is nearly a year old."

Simon steps back, so Ezekiel, Tullia, and Stephen can enter. They look around.

"I see you've expanded your courtyard. How did you do that?"

"Ha, ha. I was lucky. My neighbor put his house up for sale, I bought it, and I tore down the wall between us. Now, little Alexander can have his room, and I can have a wine press for my vineyard. You remember my vineyard, do not you?"

"Yes, you showed us the day you helped us find our son."

"How are you these days, Stephen?"

"No, it is Stephanus now," Ezekiel says. "He wants us to call him Stephanus. Well, it seems we may not be going to Rome."

Simon looks over at the nineteen-year-old with a smile and crooked tip of his head. Sounds like you are working hard to blend in with the Romans."

"Sir, it is no offense to the local Berbers. But I am attending the university and..."

"I understand, Stephanus. Everyone, have a seat. You do not have to explain. Oh, here is Alexander now."

A boy toddles out to the courtyard giggling, followed close by Abelia.

"Cannot catch! Cannot catch!" the boy announces between giggles. Thereupon, he wobbles and sits on the cobblestone.

Abelia whisks him up and swings him around in her arms.

"Well, hello there, Tullia," she says when she notices their visitors.

"He seems to be walking early," Tullia replies. "Stephen, uh

Stephanus, did not walk until he was nearly two years old."

"Mother, that is embarrassing," Stephen says.

"Has anyone served you any refreshment? Allow me to bring you some grape juice fresh from our vineyard," Abelia says, her pleasing round face embraced with a smile.

Tullia joins Abelia, and soon both woman have returned with goblets of fresh juice.

"Come, Tullia," Abelia says. "Let me show you the copper bowl I bought last week."

The women leave, and Simon shifts his attention back to Ezekiel and Stephen.

"So, how is the university? You know, you are lucky to get in, being Jewish."

Stephen grins. "Ha. If you only knew. My mother is one to be feared when she makes up her mind to something."

Simon looks over at Ezekiel, who only grins and shrugs his shoulders.

"Well, Steph...Stephanus. What are you studying right now?"

"I have been studying oratory. But now our instructor wants us to learn to debate."

"A worthy goal, young man," Simon says. "So, have you participated in any debates yet? How did you do?"

"No, sir. But I am preparing for one. The opposition declares there are a multitude of gods. I propose there is only one God."

"I have been warning Stephanus that this could create a lot of problems for him," Ezekiel tells Simon.

"Father, I am a lot smarter than Cato."

"You're debating the son of the provincial censor, Rabannas?" Simon asks. "That is dangerous in and of itself. You do not oppose that man. He can be mean."

Both Ezekiel and Stephen chuckle.

"What? What am I missing?" Simon asks.

"You have not seen my mother stand up to him."

"That petite woman? He's twice her size."

"Are you talking about me?" Tullia asks, walking back out to the courtyard with Abelia carrying Alexander.

"We were just saying it is dangerous for Stephanus to be debating the existence of one God or many gods."

"Oh, indeed, it can be. But I am sure Stephanus can handle it and stay out of trouble with the local priests and their followers," Tullia says, winking at her son.

"Ya, ya, ya, ya, ya," Alexander says, pounding on Stephanus' knees.

"Ha. Look at that. My son is going to grow up to be a famous debater like Stephanus," Simon pronounces.

"Well, we must be going," Ezekiel says, standing.

"Yes, our son has a debate to prepare for," Tullia says.

"Thank you for the fresh grape juice," Stephen says, "and letting us enjoy your little Alexander."

The following morning back on the fourth floor of the *insulae*, Stephen dresses in his best tunic. His normally flighty hair is slicked down with aromatic oil.

"If he ever backs you into a corner, just smile, shake your head as though he has no mind, turn your back on him momentarily. Then by the time you are back in place, you will have thought of a rebuttal."

"Where did you learn to do that, Mother?" Stephen asks.

"Your grandfather used to do it all the time when debating the Tarsus magistrates. Well, actually, he also taught the method to Augustus. Now go."

Ezekiel walks into the room. "Not going to work today?"

"No. The debate is this morning. I will make up for it tomorrow."

Stephen takes a deep breath and lets it out hard.

Ezekiel holds out his hand, and the two men clasps hands and forearms. "You will do fine."

With his nervous energy, Stephen skips down the four flights of stairs and steps out into the fresh spring air. All the way to the university, he alternates between going over his points and counterpoints and praying.

He walks between the statues of famous Cyrenian philosophers and salutes ole long-nosed Aristippus, founder of the university three centuries earlier.

When he enters the library where the debate was scheduled to be, no one is present.

Stephen stops hard and looks around. His stomach churns, his head swirls.

What's going on here? Was it a trap? Are they going to rush out and attack and kill me? What's...

"Ah, Stephanus. There you are." It is Draco. "So many people showed up for the debate, we have moved it to the amphitheater beside the gymnasium academy. Come. Everyone is waiting."

Stephen forces a quick smile as he comprehends he is not in trouble and follows Draco.

They arrive at the smaller of the three amphitheaters in the city, and Draco steps aside for Stephen to walk out onto the arena floor.

Cheering mixed with booing.

When he arrives at the center, Cato and the moderator, their debate instructor, greet him.

"By the end of this debate, Jew, you are going to wish you had never been born."

"By the end of this debate, son of mankind, you will be glad you were born," Stephen says with a smile.

The moderator steps between the two young men.

"You know the rules," Diogenes begins. "I introduce each topic with a resolution, and you either oppose it or affirm it. The audience is allowed to respond with clapping, stomping their feet, hooting, or cheering. You must wait for them to cease before proceeding.

The moderator turns toward the audience and raises both arms high.

The crowd gradually notices and grows silent.

"Let the debate begin!" he declares, whereupon the audience applauds.

When the sound dies down, Moderator Diogenes announces the first round: "Affirmed: Only one God makes all the rules while many gods leave it up to mankind to live the way they wish."

Cato steps forward and raises his left hand as he had been shown in his oratory class.

"I declare to you, ladies and gentlemen, that no god has a right to tell us what to do. The gods do not care what we do as long as we do not disturb them. They have their own lives to live. They live in peace with each other and expect mankind to do the same."

Clapping and cheering in the audience.

Cato steps back. Stephen steps forward and raises his right hand.

"If there is only one God, he, of course, is the one who created us. Like any artisan, he knows what is best for his gold, his pottery, his tapestry. As our creator, God knows what things will hurt us and what things will make us beautiful. He becomes angry when we do things that ultimately hurt us. His rules are like any father's rules: To help us live the best life possible and make it beautiful."

Some clapping, some booing. Stephen steps back.

The Moderator Diogenes stays in place. "Affirmed: Only one God is selfish and makes people spend their life trying to please only him."

Cato steps forward and raises his left hand.

"Ladies and gentlemen. The gods are not selfish. They share the glory with each other. They do not try to destroy each other because one has more worshippers than another. This, then, makes their worshippers open-minded toward each other's chosen patron god."

Cato steps back. Stephen steps forward and raises his right hand.

"The one God did not create us just so he will have people to worship him as some erroneous claim. He created us because he wanted children to love. He wants to share his glory with us. The multitude of gods is confusing. God is not a God of confusion but of love, especially for us."

Cheering, hooting. Stephen steps back.

Moderator Diogenes makes his statement. "Affirmed: Only one God cannot provide us with all the wisdom and talents mankind needs and desires."

Cato steps forward and raises his left hand.

"Ladies and Gentlemen. It is not possible for one God to know and handle it all. Each god must specialize so they can bestow on their own devotees a special manifestation of their wisdom and talents. This is the best way and only way."

Cato steps back. Stephen steps forward and raises his right hand.

"If the one God is capable of creating the entire universe with the sun and earth and all the animals and peoples, do you not think he is capable of bestowing upon us part of his wisdom and ability to create?"

Silence in the audience.

Stephen steps back.

Now Moderator Diogenes. "Affirmed: Only one God stifles religious depth."

Cato steps forward and raises his left hand.

"Ladies and Gentlemen: Every god is different. One god is worshipped one way, another is another way. With this method, everyone can choose his own preferred way of worshipping. Choice is good."

Cato steps back. Stephen steps forward and raises his right

hand.

"When we worship, who are we worshipping? Ourselves. To choose our own way of worshipping is just that. Then we make ourselves gods."

Booing. Foot stomping. Cheering.

Stephen steps back. The moderator makes his last declaration. "Affirmed: There is not just one truth. There are many truths."

Cato steps forward and raises his left hand.

"Ladies and gentlemen, it is narrow-minded to say there is only one truth. What egotism. What arrogance. What vanity. If everyone said the sky is blue, we would be cheated, for the sky is also crimson and gold and every color in between."

Cato steps back. Stephen steps forward and raises his right hand.

"If I tell my mathematics professor, I am going to solve the problems my own way, I am saying there is more than one truth. If Cato says there are four people standing here before you, that is his truth. But it is also confusion. There must always be one truth in order to have perfect harmony, order, and peace."

Hissing and cheering.

Stephen steps back. Moderator Diogenes announces, "We will now allow both sides to make a final statement."

Cato steps forward and raises both hands. "Without many gods, we would not have Apollos and his wisdom, Demeter and her fertility, Dionysus, and his free love and joviality, Zeus, and his supremacy."

Stephen steps forward and stands next to Cato, who has stayed in place. He raises both hands.

"Was Pharaoh Akhenaten of Thebes wrong to believe in one God? Is King Phraates of Parthia wrong to believe in one God? Was Joseph, *Comita Tributa* of all Egypt, wrong to believe in one God? Was our own Theodorus of Cyrene—falsely called the atheist philosopher—wrong to reject all the gods and believe in only one God?"

The audience rises and cheers, raising their own hands in the air. The cheering continues longer than Stephen can keep his arms in the air.

Briefly, his mind flashes back to Abraham with his arms nailed above his head. In a flash, he returns to the present and walks forward toward the crowd.

Cato follows him, scoots in front of him, and puts out his foot. When Stephen trips and falls, Cato laughs. He backs off and looks at the audience.

"See your mighty hero? Not so smart now, is he? He is a nothing. A nobody. Do not believe a word he says. He is a liar and a thief. Some day when I prove it, you will wish you had voted for me."

Cato turns and walks back over to Stephen, now on his knees. He kicks him in the back so that Stephen returns to the dirt floor of the arena, then keeps walking.

"You will pay for this, Jew Stephen." He turns around, puts both hands on his hips and glares as Stephen returns to his feet.

"The moderator wouldn't let me bring up the fact that you are nothing but a Jew. That is okay. Everyone knows you are worse than a Jew. Someday I am going to destroy you."

With that, Cato walks out the amphitheater without again looking back. At the same time, the audience on the tiered concrete benches are pouring onto the amphitheater floor in Stephen's direction.

Two of the men grab his legs.

"No! No! I am not your enemy!" he shouts.

Now he is elevated above the crowd. His legs sit on the shoulders of a big man who hangs on to his feet. The crowd cheers still.

Stephen smiles again. *I am a hero. They're ready to hear directly about the God of Moses and my God. They do not want to hurt me anymore. I am a hero.*

When the crowd becomes bored, they let Stephen down and gradually leave.

Only he and the moderator are left. "Stephanus, you surprised me. First, your timing was impeccable: You waited until your final statement to throw your spear. It hit right on target. Brilliant. Did I teach you that?"

Stephen smiles but does not reply.

"And, second," the moderator continues, "you chose the unpopular side of the issue. When I proposed it to my oratory class, I did not believe anyone would oppose all the gods openly. You do know all the priests in the city are probably meeting right now to figure out a way to destroy you."

"Well," Stephen says, "they won't get a chance if Cato gets to me first."

"Although I do not agree with your premise, I must insist that protocol be kept. I will talk to Cato."

A stone falls at Stephen's feet. They look up and see Cato

standing six man-lengths away.

"I will destroy you, Stephanus. If it is the last thing I ever do on earth, I will destroy you."

18 ~ KIDNAPPED

It has been two months, and the temple priests have not given Stephen a hard time," Ezekiel tells his wife as they eat their evening meal.

"Well, after you presented their high priests with a copy of one of my father's writings along with my signature, how could they turn you down?"

"I guess my grandfather was more famous than I thought," Stephen says, popping a piece of flatbread dipped in yogurt in his mouth.

"And let us hope he stays famous," Tullia adds.

Silence.

"It's time we move," Ezekiel says. "I have saved up enough to buy a house on the other side of the city."

"So, it sounds like you have definitely made up your mind to stay in Cyrene," Tullia says with a smile. "But, isn't it expensive over there?"

"Abner, the tapestry merchant in the booth down a little way from mine, has decided to move to Jerusalem. He is tired of being considered uneducated and a subclass resident of the city. We are not even allowed to vote."

Stephen stares at his father but says nothing.

"Isn't it too soon?" Tullia asks. "Do you have enough money saved up?"

"I think I do. Anyway, he has told several people about it. I think we should check it out. Tomorrow is the Sabbath. We will go the following day."

The day after Sabbath, Stephen walks up the *insulae* steps to the top floor and takes his key out. He unlocks the door and enters. He spreads seven pillows out in a circle. Soon, Achaius arrives. They are all that is left of their original organized the previous year. They had decided to trust each other's judgment when they brought someone new to their worship. It has worked for them.

One by one, the other five arrive. Their arrivals are staggered, so anyone watching the door to the *insulae* from across the street would not become suspicious of whole groups arriving together.

Their worship has not changed much. They still whisper their songs in case someone is out in the corridor, ready to go up on the roof to spread out clothes to dry or sit in the sunshine. They do not use incense; it would attract attention also. They now have their own Torah, thanks to the hard work of Achaius and Stephanus.

The one thing that has changed is how often they read prophecies of a coming Messiah, the King of the world.

Exchanging experiences of getting parts of the Law of Moses distributed around the city at night has now become part of their worship too.

They end their worship with a special prayer for the other secret synagogues scattered throughout the city. Though they do not know where the others are meeting, the worshippers know they are all worshipping at the same time and blessing each other at the same time.

"I wonder when it will be time to expose ourselves as Queen Esther did," Achaius muses.

"I suppose we will know when the time comes. Until then, we will worship, spread the word to pagan Gentiles secretly, and help the poor secretly."

The following day, Ezekiel leads his small family to the other side of town. They find the house with the Acacia gate. They knock, and Abner, the tapestry merchant, slides the bar out of the way and opens the gate for them.

"Welcome, Ezekiel. I thought you'd be the first to see my house, but the butcher beat you to it."

"So, I am the second?"

"Yes, come in. Your wife will like the oven my wife uses. You'll like the extra room I have. I use it to store my tapestries in, but you could use it as a place to do your writing. In fact, the courtyard is large enough, you could start up your scribe school again."

Ezekiel puts his hand over a smiling face and says, "Hmmmm."

"Fifty thousand *sesterces*. That is what I want for the house," Abner says. "I have set the price the lowest I can and have passage to Jerusalem and money to rent a house when we arrive."

"Well, I guess we will have to go home and think about it. We thank you for your time. You have a fine home."

When the three are out on the street, Stephen stops his father.

"I have some money. How much are you short?"

"I cannot let you do that, Son," Ezekiel replies.

"I live here too. And when I get married…"

"You're getting married?" Tullia asks.

"No, of course not. But someday, I will. And I'd like to continue living with you so our children will be able to know their grandparents. I never got that chance."

Silence.

Ezekiel walks a little way down the street. Stephen and his mother hang back.

Ezekiel stops and turns around. He arrives halfway back to them, then stops again. Then goes again.

"Well, okay. But I will pay you back someday."

"No, you won't, Father."

"Yes, I will, and that is final."

"Yes, sir."

"Why do not you walk around the North Gate Market a while. I will hurry home and get the money. I should be back within the hour."

As promised, Stephen returns about the time his parents arrive at a booth selling silver jewelry.

"Here, Father." He hands Ezekiel a money pouch full of thick silver coins. "And someday when I am old, you can pay me back," the young man says with a grin.

An hour later, Ezekiel, Tullia, and Stephen walk out of their new house, the deed signed and sealed.

With the money in hand, Abner takes his wares from the shelves of his booth and adds them to the household goods he has piled onto his wagon. He says goodbye to the other Jewish merchants in the last row of the North Market and heads out the North Gate.

Two weeks later, after Ezekiel's family settles in, they are eating their fast-breaking meal together in their new home.

"We have been invited to Alexander's second birthday celebration, his official weaning," Tullia announces.

"When?" Ezekiel asks

"Three days from now. Actually, in early evening. It's perfect. It will give me time to make the boy a tunic. I have some blue left over from the tunic I made you last winter."

The third day arrives, and as the sun begins its descent below the horizon, Ezekiel and Stephen pull out their torches to use on their way home, and Tullia puts the small tunic in a basket.

Simon's house is much farther away than it had been from the *insulae*. When they arrive at the Greek-Speaking Synagogue for Roman Citizens, they turn right. They walk past the largest of the three amphitheaters in Cyrene and attached bathhouse.

Eventually, they arrive at the Jewish-Born Freedmen's Synagogue and turn left. They walk to the fountain and turn right.

"Woah," Stephen says as he dodges out of the way of a Berber horseman with a bundle resting on the neck of his Barb. Ezekiel pushes Tullia out of the way just in time to avoid being trampled.

"What's the hurry?" Stephen calls after the horseman.

Ezekiel, who now walks with a cane, shakes it at the man, though knowing he cannot see or hear them.

"You all right?" Ezekiel asks his wife.

"She runs her hand down her tunic and looks up. "I guess I am," she says, picking up the basket with the two-year-old boy's birthday tunic in it. "They should outlaw horses going that fast on the city streets."

"I am sure there is a law against it," Stephen says.

They pass the Berber Synagogue and finally arrive at Simon's house. Ezekiel knocks on the gate, and they hear scraping of the security bar on the other side.

Abelia, pregnant with child number two, opens the gate for them.

Stephen notices a clay tablet on the ground outside the gate and picks it up. "Here," he says to Abelia. "It is addressed to you. I guess the message is on the other side."

Abelia thanks Stephen and welcomes her other guests. "Come in and join in the celebration," she says as Simon comes down from the roof with the men and joins her.

"Everyone!" she calls out. "Meet our three special friends. They came here a year ago, all the way from Antioch in Syria. Welcome them."

Three men greet Ezekiel. "This is my son, Stephanus."

Tullia walks over to the four women seated on separate

benches in the courtyard, some with a child on their lap.

"This is Tullia, everyone. Tullia, this is Delylah, Liba, Nissa, and Zilpah.

"Ha, ha, I can catch you."

Liba calls out. "You children stop running around."

Abelia joins the women on a bench next to Tullia.

"What's that in your hand, Abelia?" Nissa asks.

"Oh, I almost forgot. Excuse me a moment while I see what the tablet about."

She sits.

Silence.

Screaming.

"Nooo! Nooo!"

Abelia cries out, "Where's Alexander? Where's my baby. Where's Alexander?"

"I thought he was with the children playing in your storeroom," Delylah says.

"I did too," Zilpah says.

Abelia ducks into the storeroom. "Alexander, come out from behind where ever you are hiding. Alexander. Alexander!"

She rushes out of the room just as Simon arrives from the other side of the courtyard. "What is it?"

"It's Alexander. I cannot find him."

Simon turns and calls out. "Alexander. Alexander. Come out this instant. This is not funny, Alexander. Do you hear me?"

"The last time I saw him," Kehath says, "was just before we went up on the roof. He was playing next to the wall where your wine press is."

Abelia stands as though paralyzed in the middle of the courtyard screaming

Everyone scatters throughout the house and courtyard.

"Alexander. Alexander! You came come out now. Alexander."

When they return to where the children had been playing around their mothers' feet, Abelia is collapsed on the cobblestone, her head on one of the benches. Simon knees beside her and puts his arm around her.

"We will find him. He must have climbed up on something and scaled our wall. Give us a few moments to check outside. He is little. He could not have gone far."

The big man stands and signals for the men to follow him out to the street.

"There is a field behind my house. He might have gone that way."

The men scatter, looking first on the street, then in the field behind Simon's house.

The sun is now completely down. They return to the house.

"Get the torches, Abelia," he calls out as they come in through the gate."

Abelia continues slumped on the ground. Simon kneels next to her again. "It won't do any good," she whispers, sniffing and dabbing her eyes. "You cannot see far enough."

"We've got to try, sweetheart," Simon reassures. He stands and steps over to his storeroom, where his torches are piled.

"Simon, stop," Ezekiel says, taking the man's arm. "Stop. We cannot search at night."

"What if an animal gets him?" Simon shouts, at last showing his hidden emotions.

"Come to think of it," Stephen says. "Father, do not you remember that horseman that almost ran over us on the way here?"

"Yes, I do," Ezekiel says, turning his full attention to his son. "Do you think..."

"Simon," Stephen continues, "he was wearing a short tunic of red and brown stripes, with a cape flowing behind him of maybe red and dark blue. I am not sure, but I do remember the red."

"Oh, no."

"And he had some kind of sash around his head that flowed way out behind him."

Simon rushes back to his wife. "Just what did the message say? Where is it?"

She hands the tablet up to him.

Simon reads it and grits his teeth. He slams his fist onto a wooden table nearby and breaks it. He swings around and stares at a sky that is oblivious of the tragedy that is going on below.

"TacFaranis," Simon sneers.

"Who?"

"TacFaranis!" He shouts it this time. "Those are his colors—red, blue and brown. He has kidnapped my son. He says, if I do not report to duty with him, I will never see Alexander again. He says I am a deserter.

"I've got to go after him. He has had two hours' head start. How am I going to catch him? I have to catch him. I have to bring my son back. I've got to free my son."

"That man is too strong for you," Cheber says. "Let us go

with you."

"No, I have to do this alone. I am the one he wants."

Simon rushes to a chest at the far end of the courtyard in the section he had bought from his neighbor. He pulls out a tunic and cape that are red, brown and blue, and a long sash that is red.

He puts them on over the tunic he is already wearing and ties the headband at the back of his head. Next, he pulls out leather sandals with long straps. He crisscrosses the straps up his leg to his knee. Last, he pulls out his wide curved sword.

With heavy, broad steps, he walks back to his wife. He kneels. "I will get our son back, *yammasse*. I do not know how long it will take, but I will get him back. I promise."

Abelia lays her wet cheek on his arm, looks up at her husband, and whispers, "Please. Please."

Simon stands and marches to a door at the far end of his house. He opens it to the stables. He chooses his fastest horse, throws a harness over its head, mounts it, and rides out into the street and west in the direction of the Syrtis Gulf.

Tullia spends the night with Abelia. Ezekiel and Stephen stay to guard her in case TacFarinas sends more of his men to kidnap Simon's wife to make sure he does not desert again.

A few nights later, when Simon has not returned home, they decide to take Abelia home with them.

"What if he returns, and I am not here?" she asks.

"I will write him a note on that piece of clay over there where the vat has broken," Stephen says, "and lay it on one of your benches."

They leave Simon's house and walk beside the Berber Synagogue. They walk to the fountain and turn left. They progress to the Jewish-Born Freedmen's Synagogue and the *hospitium*, and turn right. They pass the large amphitheater and bathhouses. At the Greek-Speaking Synagogue, they turn left and arrive at Ezekiel's house.

Stephen lets her have his room for privacy.

"The weather is warming up fast," he says. "I've been wanting to sleep up on the roof anyway."

Days go by. A week. Two. Three. At the beginning of the fourth week, Stephen makes his announcement.

"I am going after him."

"You cannot do that," Ezekiel says. "You do not know the way."

"I can go to the government basilica and see if Blasius is there. If he isn't, I will go to the citadel. Someone will be able to tell me where TacFarinas' encampment is."

"They'll never let you close," Ezekiel warns. "You will end up with an arrow through your chest."

"Abelia," Stephen says in response. "Did your husband store more than one uniform?"

"Yes. There were two uniforms in that chest. But there was only one sword."

"That is okay. While I am at the citadel I will try to buy a javelin from them. I am best with the javelin. Then, I will go by your house and pull his other uniform out. I will spend the night there so I can leave at dawn tomorrow."

"But, you do not know where TacFarinas is."

"While I am at the government basilica, I will find out."

Abelia looks at Tullia. "I cannot let him do this."

"You have lost a husband and son—at least temporarily. I shall let my son try to rescue them."

"As a father, I do not want him to go," Ezekiel says. "But, as a friend to the one who saved our lives, I do. This is our chance to at least partly repay him."

"If I can blend in with the other Berbers at the camp," Stephen explains, "maybe I can find out where Simon and your son are. I am sure they'll escape at night. Your husband knows that wilderness as good or better than any of the outlaws. He will be able to guide us even in the darkness."

Tullia hurries to the goat-hair covered corner of their courtyard and gathers up all her bread, cheese, and figs to put in a leather pouch for Stephen. The petite woman returns to where Stephen is waiting for her.

"Here you are. Did you fill your water skins?"

"I filled four of them, Mother."

"Good. Now bend over and let me kiss you on that clean-shaven cheek."

"Son," Ezekiel says, joining them, "What if they figure out you are a spy?"

19 ~ THE DISGUISE

*T*he shadows of evening are moving in fast over the city of Cyrene when Stephen arrives at Simon's house. He uses the key he had kept when he had given Simon a new lock soon after settling in Cyrene.

He slips in, slides the bar across the gate to keep it secure during the night, and props up the javelin he had purchased. He hurries over to Simon's chest in the added part of his house and opens it.

He pulls out the other uniform and puts on the short tunic, the cape, the high-top sandals. He ties the red sash on, then realizes it cannot hide his short, Roman-style hair.

He sees his mother's basket with Alexander's blue birthday tunic in it. He pulls it out and stares at it a moment. *This is silly but worth a try.*

He tries the tunic on his head and sees that it fits. *Those outlaws will never figure out what it was really made for,* he tells himself with a grin. He ties the long red sash from Simon's chest over the blue tunic on Stephen's head, now turned turban.

I guess I can stop shaving and hope my beard grows enough the Berbers think I am one of them. Well, my skin isn't as dark, but well...

He looks up at the sky and imagines the stars as the eyes of God.

"Jehovah God, Simon is a good man. I guess TacFarinas knows this, and that is why he wants him back. Help me find them. Help Simon find his son and then escape with him. But, what if he did try to escape, was caught, and is now being held prisoner with guards around him? What if they have killed his little Alexander to punish Simon for trying to escape? What if I cannot find them? So many what-ifs."

Stephen picks up his pouch of food and four water skins and goes to the stables. He puts bridle and reins on the horse he had trained with and notices a large leather pouch for the horse to drink from. With no saddle, he attaches that to the bridle.

"I wonder if he has a small tent here?" he says aloud to the Barb. He looks around the stable and finds one, along with a rug, blanket, and small bow drill for making fires. He sees a strap for the rump of the horse and loads the tent, rug and blanket, and a supply of barley wheat for the horse. Last, he attaches his food and water skins to them by cords.

"Sorry, friend, to make you wear them all night. But I will not have time come morning to do this."

Stephen returns inside Simon's home and over to the outside gate, where he takes the javelin he had propped up there. He goes up on the roof so he can stand watch the rest of the night and be ready to leave at daylight.

He surveys the city for a long time. He strains to keep his eyes open and alert to any new dangers down on the street.

It is daylight. He is angry that he had fallen asleep. The sun is higher in the sky than he had intended for his departure out of the city.

He rushes down the stairs, unbars the front gate, goes out, locks the gate, hurries around to the outer gate into the stable, mounts his horse, and guides it at a walking pace through the early streets of Cyrene.

Stephen takes off his headband and birthday-tunic-turban, so he does not attract attention. He works his way past the Berber Synagogue on his right and the sanctuary and temple of Apollo on his left. He guides Simon's horse through the market, out the North Gate, and turns left at the Roman road that leads to the Syrtis Gulf.

It will take him longer to go this way, but he realizes he does not have the knowledge or skills to take the shortcut through the desert.

By mid-afternoon, he is at Naucidai at the coast. He stays outside the city and turns south. Just before dark, he sees Ptolemais ahead. He stops and takes the supplies and reins off his Barb. He spreads out his rug and tent, gives his Barb water and food, builds a small fire with Simon's bow drill, eats, and falls asleep, praying he will waken just before dawn.

When the sky is still gray with the new morning, Stephen rises and resumes his quest to help Simon free his son.

He is pleased with the stamina of his Barb and is able to reach Teuchira, then Hadrianapolis, before the sun is completely down. The third day he passes by Berneice and Tritonis. He is in the lands of the Barcite Tribe.

The fourth, fifth, and sixth days, he passes by six more cities along the Syrtis coast of Libya on the edge of the Asbytae tribal lands.

At this point, he takes out his blue tunic-turban and long red headband and puts them on, tying the headband on the back of his head so that it flows behind him as far as the horse's tail.

It takes him another day to pass through the coastal lands of the Macatutae Tribe and into the much larger lands of the Nasamones Tribe, the one Simon belongs to.

Here he sees the Wadi Hamim. His water skins were emptied the night before. He leads his horse to the dry wadi but digs down until he hits water, the remains of which had flowed through the wadi during the previous rain. He takes some water into his cupped hand for himself, then lets the Barb drink all he wants. He drinks once more, then fills the water skins.

Stephen now travels west again and knows he is in the disputed territory TacFarinas dares try to wrench back from the hands of the Roman occupiers. It is nearly dark. He camps for the night.

Morning comes. It has taken Stephen a week to progress this far. He wonders how long peace for him will last. He mounts his Barb and loosens his grip on the reins, letting the horse almost guide himself.

That night outside of the coastal city of Ara Philanorum, he sees ahead of him a stretch of mountains and knows on the other side of that narrow range is the beginning of the East Numidia territory, controlled mostly by the Garamantes Tribe.

Late on his tenth day out, he sees the magnificent Roman city of Lepis Magna ahead and knows he must stop hugging the coast and head south into the rugged, barren Atlas Mountains and the desert controlled by the Berbers and their leader, TacFarinas.

He spends one last night in Roman-controlled territory. With morning, he heads into the unknown. *Will I be able to find them? Jehovah, be my guide. And lead me to water when I need it.*

Although Stephen had noticed an occasional Berber pass him on the Roman highway skirting the outside of the coastal cities, he sees more now. Sometimes a family of Berbers.

Sometimes a farmer taking his wagon or cart of produce to market in the big city. Sometimes just riding alone. More and more, now, he sees the lone riders.

Though early spring, the weather is much hotter now. More like the heat of mid-summer up in Antioch and even Tarsus.

There is a strong northern breeze coming in off the gulf. But the farther he climbs into the mountains, the more the breezes of relief from the heat are blocked.

He rides higher into the mountains, up, down, twisting, turning. Searching. Nothing. Nothing to see but the mountains and the desert. Still twisting and turning. Wondering what will be around the next bend, over the next ridge, below in the next vale, at the top of the next incline. Searching.

Simon, where are you? Alexander? Do you have your Alexander yet? Have you escaped? Have they bound you and perhaps tied you to a stake for desertion when you married Abelia?

If they accepted your return as penance, why has little Alexander not been returned to his mother? What is going on? Where are you, Simon and Alexander? Where are you, TacFarinas? Where are you, Jehovah God? Be my strength and guide.

He has passed a dozen or so Berbers riding alone. They have not bothered him. He wonders why.

Time to do something. The next time Stephen passes a lone Berber rider, he looks around to see if he might have come from a side trail. He dismounts and leads his Barb while looking at the ground for hoof prints.

His hunch is right. He sees evidence of a seldom-used trail off to his right, farther into the range. He follows it a while and pauses. He looks around in the near and far distance for evidence of a camp.

He hears a whiz and feels a sharp pain in his lower leg. He looks down and sees the arrow. He clasps his leg.

"Stop where you are!"

There on the trail where he had just been, is a Roman equestrian. He is dressed in a short tunic with leather armor, high-topped sandals, and brass helmet. His horse looks Frisian and is unadorned but carries the Roman four-horned saddle on its back.

"State your business, Berber. What are you doing on this side of the mountain? Spy!"

"Uh, sir," Stephen gasps, still holding both hands around his wounded lower leg.

"Do not speak."

The Roman equestrian leads his horse over to Stephen's.

"Dismount," he orders.

"I cannot," Stephen objects. I've got this..."

"Do not speak. Dismount."

Stephen slides off his horse.

The equestrian leans over and takes the reins from Stephen. He puts a noose around Stephen's neck.

"What? I did not do anything," Stephen objects, looking up in a panic. "Please, please," he begs, speaking Latin, the language of the Roman army.

"So, an educated Berber."

"I am not really... Help me."

"Do not speak."

The equestrian leads his and Stephen's horse in front of Stephen, and tugs on the rope around his neck.

"March."

Stephen has no choice but to leave the arrow in his calf and straighten up enough he can walk.

They backtrack a way, then head down a trail Stephen had not noticed before. They wind around until they come to a vale, the Roman encampment.

Stephen stumbles as the equestrian urges his horse into a trot. He pauses long enough for Stephen to stand again. When he resumes, Stephen runs to keep up, so he does not stumble and be dragged into the camp. He leaves behind on the ground, his blood.

They pass two legionnaire guards, standing at attention with javelins. On each side of the guards is a low fence of rocks with javelins wedged between them facing up.

The equestrian leads Stephen to a large leather tent surrounded by many smaller tents able to hold perhaps ten men each.

The two legionnaire guards on either side of the tent opening cross javelins.

"I bring a Berber prisoner," he tells them. "Call the centurion out."

Stephen leans down and grasps the calf of his leg again. He grits his teeth, both in pain and fear. He hears a sound and jumps. He falls to the ground, still grasping his lower leg. He looks around behind him, his eyes jumping from one legionnaire to another. His breathing comes fast. He tries to control the trembling. And the bleeding.

One of the guards goes inside the tent. Moments later, he returns. The centurion is behind him. He is a large man with black hair. He wears a brass helmet with red plume. He carries on his arm a red cape.

"What have we here, equestrian?"

"Sir, a Berber spy."

"I would say a wounded Berber spy. Did he try to escape? Well, take the noose off him. He won't get far if he tries to escape here. Then bring him to me."

One of the guards forces Stephen to his feet and leads him inside the tent. "Stand," he orders, then leaves.

By the time Stephen is inside, the centurion has taken off his helmet and sat in a low-backed gilded chair behind a table. He throws his red cape onto the table.

"That thing is hot. Why they want us to wear a cape in this heat is...well, I guess we need it to display our rank."

Trying not to show his pain, Stephen looks around and is surprised at the opulence of the tent. Ornate rugs are scattered throughout. No evidence of the bare ground is seen anywhere. Brass lamps are hung from each tent pole. He sees baskets on the floor with scrolls in some.

"Excuse me, but if you're through evaluating my tent, tell me what your leader TacFarinas is up to. Then I won't let my legionnaires have you for some of their version of fun."

"Sir, uh...."

"Lost your camp, huh? You must be from one of the other tribes. Let me guess. The Musulammi Tribe? The Gaetuli or Maurii Tribe?"

"Uh, no, sir. I was looking for someone."

"You speak Latin. An educated Berber. Well, isn't that something?"

With no breeze at all inside the tent and with the pain in his leg sharpening, Stephen's perspiration beads on his forehead and drips down into his eyes, stinging them with their saltiness.

"Take that thing off your head. What is it, anyway?"

Stephen reaches up and takes the red sash and blue tunic-turban off his head, wiping his forehead in the process. He stares at the centurion, not knowing how he will react to his real identity.

The centurion stares, stands, and walks around his table. He circles Stephen with his short hair and new beard.

"You're not a Berber at all. What are you? And who? And why are you up in these dangerous and god-forsaken mountains dressed like that?"

The centurion returns to his chair. "Well? I am waiting."

What do I say? I thought only Berbers were up here. What do I tell this Roman?

"This is your last chance to explain yourself. After this, I hand you over to my blood-thirsty legionnaires with nothing to do. Maybe add a few more arrows to your collection."

"Uh, sir, you are right. I am not a Berber," Stephen says, trying to keep his voice steady. "But I have a friend who is. He is a good man. He used to fight for TacFarinas, but deserted him to get married and settle down in Cyrene far from the fighting."

"And you are a citizen of Cyrene."

"Kind of."

"What does kind of mean?"

Stephen takes a deep breath and bites his lip. "I was born in Tarsus of Anatolia and most recently lived in Antioch of Syria."

"Go on. I am not going to harm you and put any more arrows in you as long as you keep talking and keep my interest," the centurion says.

"Well, he—my friend, Simon—was a good horseman, what Romans call an equestrian. Apparently, TacFarinas is getting desperate. Maybe men are deserting him. I do not know."

"This is getting more and more interesting," the centurion replies, leaning on the arm of his chair.

"His name is Simon and..."

"Good, good. I like names. Go on."

"...and he has a son two years ago who he named Alexander."

The centurion stands. "Ha. Named his son after Alexander the Great, I see. Kind of tells you what he thinks of TacFarinas. Excuse my interruption. Go on."

"One of TacFarinas' men came into the city over a fortnight ago and kidnapped little Alexander. He left a note behind that he would not see his son again unless he came back to fight for the Berbers."

"And, of course, he went."

"Yes, he went. But the baby was never returned to his mother, and we have not heard from Simon."

"And, you have decided one inexperienced young man like you in a strange land full of desert and mountains and scorpions, and outlaws is going to rescue them."

"Kind of like that, sir."

The centurion shifts to the other arm of the chair. He stares at Stephen.

Stephen waits.

"You know, we could use you as bait."

"Bait, sir?"

The centurion stands and walks closer to Stephen. He turns and paces. He looks back over at Stephen and smiles. He puts his hand on his clean-shaven chin and strokes it. He shakes his head back and forth with a grin.

"The gods must be with us, after all."

He stops in front of Stephen. "Do you know what that TacFarinas has put us through? For nearly ten years…"

"That long?" Stephen blurts, then bites his tongue.

"For nearly ten years, we have been after him. Did you know he used to be one of us? Fought as an auxiliary in the Roman army and learned our tactics. Anyway, we have been after him for ten years. Caesar sent Camillus down here to get him under control. Couldn't do it."

Stephen holds his tongue.

"So, he sent Apronius, and he failed too. Slippery man, that TacFarinas. Finally, he sent Blasius down here to go after him. I like Blasius. He'll get the job done."

Stephen presses his lips together, trying to control the pain

"Ole TacFarinas is usually in the Atlas Mountains. We're in the eastern edge of the range searching for him. He will not escape us forever."

Stephen faints.

"Guards!"

Both legionnaires at the entrance into the tent rush in and stand at attention.

"Go get the *medicus*. We cannot afford to lose this man. He is going to be very valuable."

Both guards leave. The big centurion lifts Stephen and takes him over to his bed.

Moments later, Stephen opens his eyes.

He remembers his pain, he remembers where he is, and looks up into the face of the centurion.

"By the way," the centurion says, "My name is Theophilus. Theophilus of Berea up in Greece."

20 ~ PRISONER

"**T**his is the plan. We give your horse back to you, and you continue as you were when we caught you. The only difference is that I will be your prisoner."

Stephen stares at Theophilus, squinting.

"Oh, I will not really be your prisoner. Anyway, you will lead me on my horse. I will look like I am disarmed, but will have hidden weapons on me."

Centurion Theophilus walks away from Stephen toward his table and back again. His grin is broader.

"They won't know my identity, but I will be in uniform, so they will know my rank. Of course, we will go in a cool part of the day, so I do not drench my uniform."

Theophilus walks away again, arrives at the front of his table, and swings around. "Ah-ha. This is going to be so good," he says, slapping his hand on his thigh. He leans on the table and crosses his bulky arms.

"We will, of course, be followed by my archers. Behind them will be my equestrians. But they will have orders to stay unseen until the Berbers show themselves. What a plan. The gods have certainly smiled upon us."

Stephen tries in vain to will the pain away. "But, there is only one G…"

The tent flap opens.

"There you are, Gaius. My friend here seems to have an arrow in his leg."

The *medicus* steps over to Stephen and kneels to examine his wound.

"I will get that arrow out of you as soon as one of the legionnaires gets you over to my *hospitium*," he says.

"Gaius, how long do you think it will be before he can ride perhaps a full day?"

"That I cannot tell you. He looks pretty healthy. Thin but muscular. What do you do for a living, young man?"

"Well," Stephen says between shocks of pain, "I am... I am a...a locksmith."

"Oh, a blacksmith. That explains the muscles. Got to have a lot of strength to hold the sledgehammer in one hand and slam it down on the hot metal enough to flatten it. Well, let us get you over to my tent. Guard!"

Medicus Gaius stands and steps toward Centurion Theophilus. "I should know better tomorrow when he'll be able to ride. I would think not more than two days."

The two days go by fast for Stephen. On the second day, he makes use of the cane brought to him by a medical apprentice and makes his way to the *hospitium* tent flap. "Tell Centurion Theophilus I want to see him."

The guard faces Stephen. "You do not send for the commander of a Roman camp. You go to him, but he does not come to you."

"Then tell him I refuse to go. I refuse to go to him, and I refuse to go with him to capture the Berber leader."

"You are signing your death warrant then," the guard says as he leaves for the centurion's tent.

A standoff ensues.

On the fourth day, two guards arrive at the *hospitium* tent, set Stephen on a bench, then pick up the bench between them. They carry him to the centurion's tent.

Centurion Theophilus is behind his table, reading a parchment scroll. When the guards set Stephen's bench in front of the table, Theophilus stares at him.

"So, you refuse to save your life."

The resolve Stephen had intended to have melts as he sees the big centurion with a clearer head.

"Sir," he says with a voice not as strong as he had intended, "I came here to save the life of my friend. He is a good man. He saved my life as well as the lives of my mother and father and the scribes who work for my father."

"Your father has scribes?" Theophilus says, dropping the scroll and giving Stephen his full attention.

"I do not even know your name. What is it?"

"Stephanus, sir."

"You told me you were from Antioch and Tarsus. Who are

your parents?"

"My father is Ezekiel, freedman, and master of a scribe school in Antioch."

"And your mother?"

"My mother is Tullia, daughter of Athenodorus."

"Which Athenodorus?"

"The Athenodorus."

"The Athenodorus? Tutor of Augustus Caesar?"

"Yes, sir. He is my grandfather."

"So, you have one famous Roman philosopher grandfather and one slave grandfather."

Theophilus slaps his thigh and laughs.

"You are more entertaining than a javelin-throwing contest. I do not suppose you... Oh, never mind. So, you have a Berber friend named Simon, who saved your family's life and the life of the scribes your father employs. Did I get it straight?"

"Yes, sir. Sir, I must find a way to locate my friend and his baby."

"Yes, yes. Alexander. Well, I do not know what I can do to help you. We know TacFarinas is in these mountains somewhere, but the range is hundreds of *milles* long."

"Sir, may I suggest one thing."

"Since you are the grandson of Athenodorus, yes, you may make a suggestion."

"Sir, if I lead you as a supposed prisoner and TacFarinas' men see me and take me to their camp, would you keep your men from harming any of the Berbers until I can search the camp?"

"Your chances of finding your friend there are very slim, young man."

"I know. But I promised his wife I would try. And with the help of the one God, J..."

"You believe in only one god? How quaint. Never heard of such a rash idea. Why, that is close to being an atheist. Are you an atheist? I hope not."

"No, I am not an atheist. I believe in the one God—Jehovah—who created all things and loves all of mankind with his whole heart."

"Hmmm. A god with a heart. That is new."

"Sir. About my request."

"Okay. I will order my archers to send their first volley of arrows over the heads of the Berbers. Then the second volley—if they will stop running toward us—at their feet. Of course, I cannot guarantee all of them will stop running. But that is the best I can do."

"Then your equestrians will ride in and surround the camp so they cannot escape."

"You are one smart young man," Theophilus says. "I could use someone like you. Are you married? Of course, you're not. Too young to marry. Have you thought of a career in the Roman army? You're smart."

"No, sir. When can we leave, sir?"

"Ha. I like that. So, you can walk after all."

"With a cane, I can. I think I will be okay on my horse. And I do not think I will need it to walk with in a day or two."

"Good. Then we leave in the morning. Guard!" he calls out.

The legionnaire at the flap of the commander's tent enters.

"Send for my prefect."

Centurion Theophilus turns back to Stephen.

"My prefect will get things organized. We will leave just at daybreak tomorrow."

"Yes, sir. Thank you, sir."

Stephen returns to the *hospitium* tent and falls asleep, praying for the safety of Simon and Alexander.

He hears the horn of the *cornicen* and jumps out of his cot, momentarily forgetting his injured leg. He flinches, puts on his blue tunic-turban, ties his long red sash behind his head, grabs the javelin that had been returned to him, and hobbles out into the cool morning. He sees his Barb tied up to the tent post with its bridle and reins already on it. Two of his water skins are attached to the reins.

He uses his good leg for leverage to swing his injured leg up onto the horse and uses his strong arms to help lift his weight.

Just as he settles on the Barb, Centurion Theophilus arrives on his horse in full uniform. He hands the reins to Stephen.

"I have a dagger, some darts, and a few other secret weapons in the pouches of my saddle and slipped inside my uniform. Shall we be going? I certainly hope they capture us before the sun gets too hot. I will melt under this full uniform."

Stephen takes the centurion's horse's reins and pauses. "Thank you, sir. I hope we both get what we are looking for."

Stephen passes through the entrance into the camp and back up the trail the way he had come. After some little time, he notices dried blood on the ground, part red and part black. He says nothing, but knows he is not too far from where he had turned off the main trail.

He turns back onto the main trail and rides farther up into the Atlas Mountains. The ride is slow as the horses work to not slip on the gravelly passage.

The trail winds and twists. It turns upward toward a low peak, then down into a vale. Around, up, down, this way, that way. The sun rises higher and higher.

Stephen's eyes dart back and forth to both sides. He strains to see what should not be there. He spies movement of a desert animal and jerks to a stop. He watches, then urges his Barb to continue.

His jaw is set. He squeezes his lips together, then licks them. His gut knots. He listens for something besides the wind. Or is it wind? He stops. Listening more carefully. Listening and wondering. And watching.

Something red catches his eye. There. Then not there. But still red. It appears. Disappears. Stephen slows his Barb to a hesitating walk. Step, pause. Step, pause.

The red comes into full view. It stops. Stephen stops.

It begins.

Stephen raises his hand. He dares not speak and betray his ignorance of the Berber language.

The rider comes closer. He smiles. He raises his hand to Stephen and approaches him. The stranger rides over to Theophilus and stops his Barb. He takes out his sword and pokes Theophilus in the side. Theophilus looks straight ahead.

The rider goes to the other side of the prisoner and pokes him there. He rides even with Stephen and says, *"Talafssa! Talafssa!"* while pointing at the prisoner.

Stephen does not understand the Berber word for snake. But the stranger is smiling with so many teeth showing, he reminds Stephen of Trophimus.

Stephen shows a broad smile of his own and gestures that they go back the way the stranger had come from. The stranger agrees and leads the way.

They zig-zag down toward a vale. As they draw closer, the Berber raises his hand. He lets out a whoop of triumph.

The Berber camp of TacFarinas comes into view. The men in the camp stare up at the threesome.

The stranger lets out another whoop of victory, and the others in the vale answer him with their own whoop.

Stephen notices almost the same arrangement in

TacFarinas' camp as in the Roman camp. He sees a big, dark man come out of the largest tent in the camp and stand by the flap looking up.

Now on level ground again, the stranger leads Stephen and his Roman prisoner to the man in the middle.

The Berber militiamen congratulate Stephen, or he assumes that is what they are saying. One of the militiamen grabs at Theophilus hard enough, he falls from his horse onto the ground. The big man grunts but says nothing.

Stephen knows his deception can only last a little longer until they figure out he does not understand their language. He raises both hands and shouts out as loud as he can in Hebrew, "Praise be Jehovah God, the creator of heaven and earth!"

The Berber militiamen stop what they are doing and stare at Stephen, wondering what celestial language he is speaking.

Once again, Stephen raises his arms and bellows in Hebrew, "Praise be Jehovah God, creator of the universe and everything in it!"

"And praise him forevermore," he hears in the distance, also in Hebrew.

Stephen looks in the direction of the voice.

A Berber militiaman rides up to the ones surrounding the Roman prisoner.

He says something in the Berber language to the commander of the camp. The commander replies, and the militiaman on the horse replies with a salute. He then draws close to Stephen and whispers in Hebrew, "Follow me, and stop SMILING."

He rides around to where Theophilus is on the ground and orders something Stephen does not understand. Two of the militiamen boost Theophilus back up onto his horse.

Stephen follows the man on the horse to a tent in the far back of the camp. Two large, burly Berbers stand on either side of a smaller tent that is leather, but badly tattered and torn. He tells Stephen in Hebrew to take his prisoner inside. All three dismount and enter the tent.

The flap is closed, and Simon opens wide his arms. "Stephen, my young friend." He embraces Stephen, kissing both cheeks, then draws back. "How did you find me?"

"I do not know, Simon," but I am equally glad to see you," Stephen replies in Greek. "Well, I must say Jehovah guided me."

"And who is this?" Simon asks, lowering his brow and staring with his dark eyes at Theophilus.

"Oh, this is my friend, Theophilus," Stephen says.

Simon steps back and draws the sword Stephen had seen him pull out of his storage chest in Cyrene.

"No, Simon," Stephen says.

Simon stares at Stephen. "What is going on?"

"This is Theophilus, centurion of the cohort I was captured and taken to."

"You were captured? I am more confused than ever," Simon says, still having not put his sword away.

"Well, let us just say I agreed to be used as bait to draw out TacFarinas' militiamen in exchange for saving your life."

Shouting in the camp.

"We're being attacked!" Simon shouts.

"It's my archers," Theophilus explains. "They will shoot over the heads of your men to get their attention,   then will shoot at their feet to get them to stand still long enough for my equestrians to move in and surround the camp."

Simon opens the tent flap. Theophilus grabs his arm and pulls the flap back in place. "Stay in here with us," he urges. "They will not kill anyone without my command. Now, to keep you safe," Theophilus continues, "you will have to become my prisoner. That will keep your Berbers from getting suspicious and satisfy my legionnaires."

"Have you found your son?" Stephen asks.

Simon lowers his sword and stares off into a distance. Moments later, he looks back at Stephen, his eyes red. "No. I think he is here. Sometimes I hear a small voice, and I think it is Alexander. I am almost sure it is his voice, but it is muffled so much, I am not completely sure, and I cannot tell where it came from."

"As we empty the camp and take these outlaws prisoner to our camp," Theophilus says, "we will watch for him."

Simon stands. "They will kill him. If they know his whereabouts are about to be discovered, they will kill my son. They could be doing it right now."

Theophilus grabs Simon's sword and rushes out of the prison tent. He mounts his horse and gallops to the center of the camp.

He raises Simon's sword high, sees the *cornecin*, and bellows, "Sound attention!"

The *cornecin* raises his horn with the stem circling his chest, and blows the signal.

Without waiting for anyone to fall to, he bellows, "Search the tents. Quickly. Disarm everyone first, then look for a child. A small child. *Tempore duplo! Tempore duplo!*"

Inside the prison tent, Stephen and Simon hear the command. "He said it in Latin," Simon tells Stephen. "I do not understand Latin."

"He told them to find Alexander."

Simon slips out of the tent, and Stephen pulls him back in. They listen. They hear shouts and clanging of dropped weapons and more shouts. They do not hear the voice of a child.

Simon's shoulders shake, and he sucks in a breath.

"Be strong, my friend. If Jehovah led me to you out in this wilderness, he will protect little Alexander until we can find him."

They hear a horse approaching and rush through the tent flap.

"I am sorry, sir," Theophilus says in Greek. "They found no child."

"At least let me look around behind the tents to see where they buried him. Give me that," Simon pleads, his eyes red.

"Go ahead. My men are shackling the outlaws now. Wait for them to leave camp. Then, I need Stephen to bring you back to my camp. I need to interrogate you."

Simon stares at the big man on the horse. Finally, "Yes, sir. I understand."

"Will you let him go free after that?" Stephen asks. "You promised."

"We will see how the interrogation goes."

"You promised, sir. You promised to help me find Simon to take him back home if I allowed you to bait me."

Theophilus smiles. "If I allowed you to be the bait," he corrects. He turns his attention back to his men, clicks his tongue, and rides away.

Stephen and Simon watch as the Romans take Simon's comrades away.

"They only wanted to be free," Simon says. "That is all any of us wanted. Why couldn't the Romans see that and leave Libya alone?"

"The Romans are like that. They are too strong. They will win in the end," Stephen replies in a soft voice.

When the last of the Romans and Berbers leave the camp, Stephen and Simon go out of the prisoner tent and begin their search. Stephen searches behind the tents while Simon goes inside each one to search for signs his son was buried in one of them.

After a long while, Stephen walks toward Simon, now seated cross-legged in the middle of the camp. His eyes are looking, but Stephen knows they are not seeing.

"I found nothing, Stephen."

"I found nothing, either."

"His body must have been left out for the animals." He looks up at Stephen. "I am not going with you to the Roman camp."

"But, Simon, it's a good sign. He could still be alive. Someone may have hidden him in a basket or something before they were searched. They may have taken him with them to the Roman camp."

Simon shakes his head. "Oh, God, what did I do so wrong?"

"No, Simon, do not be discouraged. Jehovah guided me to you. He will guide us to Alexander now. Alexander is still alive. We must believe that."

21 ~ ENDLESS SEARCH

Stephen and Simon arrive at the Roman camp riding their Barb horses. Stephen, now well recognized by most of the legionnaires, is easily allowed in. He and Simon ride to the centurion's tent in the center.

When they enter, they see Theophilus at his writing-table speaking with someone standing nearby who they assume is an aide.

"I am indeed glad to see you for several reasons," Theophilus says. "First in importance, Simon, did you find your child? By your demeanor, should I surmise that you did not?"

The big Roman centurion steps over to equally big Berber Simon and puts his hand on his shoulder. "Be strong, my friend. Perhaps your one God has other plans for you."

Simon's "Yes, sir" is not with any enthusiasm.

"Under the circumstances, I must admit I am a little surprised you kept your promise to return to me. You did not have to, you know. You Berbers know these mountains like I know my own hands and feet. Perhaps you came for a reward, Stephanus?"

"Not at all, sir," Stephen replies.

"Well, Rome has reason to rejoice anyway. We have captured TacFarinas, and the war is over."

"Sir," Simon says, "I have no more reason to stay with TacFarinas' militia. Whoever took my son has killed him out of spite."

"You said 'whoever' took your son. Do you mean it was not TacFarinas? Then, who did we capture?"

"If you will make the one you think is him to stand in front of your prison tent, I will look from here where he will not notice me. I will tell you who you have. They betrayed me. Now I betray them."

"Excellent idea." The centurion turns to his aide. "Make it happen."

The aide leaves, and Theophilus invites the two men to sit in two gilded chairs in front of his writing desk, then reseats himself.

"I am truly sorry, Simon. I never married—the Roman military frowns on it—so never had children. So, I can only imagine what you are going through."

"My wife is pregnant again and due any day. She may have had it by now. But that child will never be able to replace my little Alexander."

The aide arrives. "The prisoner is standing outside now, sir."

The three step out and look toward the far end of the camp where the prison tent is.

"Do you know who he is, Simon?"

"Yes, that is TacFarinas' brother."

"Well, better than nothing. Come back inside now."

The men resettle in their chairs.

"Is there anything I need to know to help put this revolution down?"

"Your horses. Get Libyan Barb horses. They are much faster and can handle the heat better."

"Well, I will have to check into that. Anything else?"

"The only way TacFarinas will ever stop is if he is dead."

"Yes, we assumed that. Well, if there is nothing else, I would like you to share my dinner with me tonight."

"Then, I need to go home tomorrow."

"Yes. Yes. Well, I shall see you just before the sun goes down then."

Stephen and Simon walk around the camp. They stop at the blacksmith, and Stephen becomes engrossed in a discussion with him.

"I need to be alone. I think I will just wander down the rows of tents while you to talk your business," Simon says.

Stephen and the military blacksmith discuss qualities of iron and where they are mined. They discuss tin and bronze. They discuss working with copper and gold.

"Stop that man!"

"Stop him!"

"I've got him, Stephen. I've got him!"

By instinct, Stephen runs in the direction of the

commotion. His pulse races. His mind jumps from one possible action to another. Roman legionnaires rush after Simon.

Stephen runs to get his horse. He slides up onto it and urges it in Simon's direction. When he arrives, Simon hands the child up to Stephen.

"Go!" he bellows.

The pursuers draw closer.

"Not without you!"

The noise of shouting grows as more legionnaires join in the pursuit, assuming Simon is a Berber escapee.

"Go!"

"No!"

Stephen's horse panics at the growing noise. Stephen pulls in on the reins, then lets go of them. He leans, reaches his strong arm down, and Simon grabs it.

The first legionnaire arrives and grabs at Simon.

Stephen yanks his arm up and Simon with it, his leg swinging up and around the horse's rump.

Stephen kicks the legionnaire and turns the horse toward the front guards. His knees punch the Libyan Barb, and it breaks out into a gallop and lightning speed.

More legionnaires. Now javelins thrown at the escapees. Now arrows.

Ducking. Dodging. Galloping in a zig-zag.

The men crouch on the back of their Barb and continue to charge toward escape and freedom and a doomed quest fulfilled after all.

The guards, not knowing what is going on, cross spears to block the escapees' only way out.

Stephen veers the horse and heads for the rocks with a wall of spears jabbing up from them like a front-line army. Closer, they draw toward the sharp points. Closer. Almost upon them.

Still, the Barb runs. Runs like a rushing mighty river down a desert wadi during a storm.

Now jumping. Now leaping. Now in the air. Wind blowing through the mane. Nostrils flaring, eyes bulging, breath labored, and defiant. Charging. Charging like a jaguar leaping from a boulder toward its prey.

They are over the wall. On they go. Away from the enemy. The enemy that had stolen a child. The heartless enemy. The enemy of everything that is good and pure and innocent.

Galloping. Over rocks. Up a mountain trail away from the camp in the vale. Up and toward jagged peaks Climbing. Twisting around and around with the trail. Down, then back up. Zig zagging.

Away from the enemy. Toward freedom and happiness once again. Away from death. Toward life.

Stephen slows the Barb into a trot, then a walk. Then pulls on the reins for it to stop.

Simon slides off and reaches both arms up. Stephen hands little Alexander to the arms his father, then climbs down himself.

"*Passe. Passe.*"

Father and son united at last. Clinging to each other. Laughing. Crying.

"*Passe*, hurting me."

Simon draws back when he realizes he is squeezing his son so hard and, for the first time in two fortnights, looks into the lovely face of his two-year-old son.

"Hey, doesn't Uncle Stephen get a hug?"

Simon lets Alexander lean over far enough to hug Stephen, but does not let go of him.

"That is enough for now, you two," Simon says, still laughing and still crying. He sees a boulder and sits on it with his son.

"Oh, no," Stephen says.

Simon looks at Stephen and his heart races. He stands and looks the way they had come, then back at Stephen. "What?"

"Blood on his belly."

Simon takes little Alexander's hand and steps over to the horse, still panting hard and with white lathery sweat all over its body.

"Oh, no."

"Here is my sash," Stephen says, untying it from his head and laying it under the horse, so the ends are easily reached from both sides.

"No, you need that in case we run into more of my people. You do not look Berber enough without it. We can use mine."

"We left in such a hurry, we do not have any supplies except this waterskin I had attached to the reins."

"Look around for a Tamarisk bush."

"What's it look like?"

"It looks like the only bush that grows up here in this rocky desert."

Simon picks up Alexander in his arms and looks in one direction, then another.

"Is this one?"

Stephen approaches Simon, showing him a spindly branch with spiny leaves and purple flowers.

"Yes. We do not have water to spare, so gather up all the flowers that you can and come lay them on my headband. It will stop the bleeding almost instantly and get that gash started on its way healing."

"Well, if you say it will work," Stephen replies.

"Do not you know anything about medicine?" Simon adds.

"No, I guess I do not," Stephen says. "But they have lectures on medicine at the university. Do you think I should start attending them when we return to Cyrene?"

"Definitely."

When the sash is covered with the purple flowers, Simon sets Alexander down, and each man takes one end of the headband. With care, they draw it up until it touches the Barb's belly.

The Barb neighs. Stephen reaches up and calms the horse with his free hand. They tie the ends together on the back of the horse.

"Okay, Alexander. *Passe* can pick you up again. Alexander? Alexander?"

Both Stephen and Simon look in all directions, terror in their eyes.

"Alexander!"

"Alexander!"

"Hi, *Passe*."

Simon runs toward his son and lifts him into his protective arms.

"You scared me. Where were you?"

"Playing with the rope under the pretty flowers."

"Rope? What rope?"

Stephen goes back over to the bush and sees a snake.

"Let us get out of here," he says with as calm a voice as he can.

Stephen takes the reins of the Barb and leads it away from the bush and snake. When he is confident the snake preferred the beauty of its surroundings, he mounts the horse, Simon hands Alexander up to cling to Stephen's back, then he too mounts.

Once again, on the trail toward home. A home that is far away, but now is reachable.

"Uh, you are taking us north toward the Syrtis Gulf," Simon objects.

"That is the way I came," Stephen replies.

"Then you do not want to return that way. Besides, I know a closer way. A short cut through the desert you went around."

"No. We are not going into any desert. I do not understand deserts," Stephen objects, calling over his shoulder.

"Yes, we are. I am a Berber, and you are not. I know my own land, and you do not. In fact, I can speak Berber, and you cannot."

"What's that have to do with it?"

"Nothing," Simon says with a grin. "I just thought I'd throw that bit in."

"Ha, ha. I will get back at you for that. Just you wait. So, if you are so smart, which desert are we going through, and where is it? The only one I have heard much about is the SaHara, and I certainly do not want to challenge the largest desert in the world—even larger than the deserts of Parthia."

"We are going northeast and into my tribal Nasamonian territory. I know where the oases are. But first, we've got to get out of these mountains. After that, we will be okay."

"So, we should be out of these mountains by tomorrow?" Stephen replies.

"Not tomorrow or the next day. If we're lucky, we will be out of them in five days."

Stephen stops the Barb for a rest and turns around.

"We cannot last that long, Simon. We only have this one water skin for the three of us. Plus, we may be meeting Roman soldiers and Berber soldiers both."

"Pray a lot, my friend. Pray a lot."

The men slide to the ground and check the Barb.

"Well, the blood hasn't seeped through the sash. I think we got the flow stopped," Simon says.

"Still, let us walk a while and give it a rest. We can walk nearly as fast as it can with all the fallen rocks to contend with."

"*Passe*. Thirsty. *Passe*. Thirsty."

Simon looks at Stephen. Without saying anything, Stephen takes the water skin, hands it to Simon, and looks at little Alexander.

"Sure, little one. This water is especially for you."

Alexander slurps on the spigot. Simon replaces the stopper and hands it back to Stephen.

"You may as well take some for yourself. We need to keep his *Passe* fit to care for his son."

"No, I do not need any water yet. I will tell you when I do," Simon replies.

"Well, why do not I follow with the horse," Stephen says. "You lead the way. Oh, and we need to give it a name."

"Do not have to. He's my horse. I named him *Nmare*."

"What kind of name is that?"

"Do not make fun of it. If *Nmare* hears you, he may bite you and chew you up. It means tiger. He is as fast as a tiger chasing a gazelle."

The rest of the day, they work their way northeast out of the mountains, though sometimes it is impossible to go in any certain direction.

One step at a time, twisting and winding when necessary, watching the sun, determining its approach with the horizon, and deciding which way is northeast.

"*Yisse*," Alexander says sometimes, leaning toward *Nmare*.

Simon sets his son on the back of *Nmare* and lets him ride a while.

"*Yisse*. Does that mean horse?"

"Did I ever tell you how smart you are? At least sometimes?" Simon replies.

"You are certainly in a good mood, friend," Stephen says, "and, of course, you should be. Indeed, you should."

They walk on, sometimes on gravel that has cracked off a cliff and tumbled down to a new resting place. Sometimes on rare sandy places. Sometimes they must go around large boulders.

"How is your leg, Stephen?"

"It's okay. The *medicus* put some honey with purple things in it onto my leg, and it has healed faster than I expected. I suppose those purple things were Tamarisk."

"Yes, I suppose so."

"*Passe*, thirsty," Alexander says, leaning toward his father.

"It gets dark fast in the mountains," Simon says. "I see three boulders bunched together over there. If there is space between them, maybe we can spend the night protected from the animals and the night air."

Without saying anything, Stephen leads *Nmare* to the boulders, takes down the waterskin, and hands it to Simon. "He needs it more than I do," he says.

"Thank you, my friend."

They settle in between the boulders. Alexander cuddles up to his father and immediately falls asleep. Stephen becomes cold, and his leg hurts in the cool night air. He falls asleep dreaming of building a hot forge large enough for ten blacksmiths. The roar of the flames reminds him of a desert mountain wolf, and its howl fills the night.

Morning of the second day.

The two men stand and stretch.

"Alexander. Where is Alexander?"

Stephen and Simon both hurry out of the shelter of the boulders.

"Alexander!"

"I right here," a small voice calls out with a giggle.

They look in the direction of Alexander's voice and see him sitting on a rock in front of *Nmare,* feeding him Tamarisk branches.

"Where did you get those?" Stephen asks with a grin.

"You scared me to death, Alexander," Simon says. He rushes over to his son and lays his hand on the boy's shoulders. "You must promise me you will never leave your *Passe* again without my permission. Do you understand?"

Alexander puts stubby hands up to his eyes and begins to cry. "I sorry, *Passe.* I sorry."

Simon puts the boy's head on his big chest and whispers, "I am sorry too, Son. I was just so scared."

"Here is some water for you," Stephen says, holding the water skin for Alexander.

"You need to take a drink, Simon. I did."

Simon obeys.

The two men pour some in their cupped hand and give it to *Nmare.* They do it twice.

The three climb back on to the Barb and proceed northeast once again out of the eastern range of the Atlas Mountains.

Once again, turning and winding. Once again, stepping over stones in the way and kicking those they do not see.

Thinking about family, knowing they are worried. Knowing they are praying the men are still alive. Knowing they are praying, especially for Alexander to be found alive and safe.

Stones and dryness. A blue sky with no clouds. A brown earth with no food. No water.

When is it going to end? Stephen thinks to himself. *We're never going to get out of this. We're lost.*

Wandering and hoping they know where they are going. Wandering and knowing at least Jehovah God knows where they are.

The sun is warm already. The air grows from warm to hot. Hard to keep going. Hard to breathe up here and in the heat.

When the sun is high in the sky, they stop. Alexander gets his sip of water. *Nmare* gets his four cupped hands of water. The men do not take any.

They rest, they nap. They hear *Nmare* whinny and stomp the ground. Jumping up, they see a snake. Stephen picks up rocks. Simon too. They throw the rocks at the snake. Over and over, they throw the rocks. The snake is dead.

Stephen keeps throwing them and throwing them and throwing them.

"Stop!" Simon says. He reaches over to Stephen's hands and pulls the rocks out of them.

Stephen slumps to the ground, his head in his hands.

"We're not going to get out of here, are we?"

22 ~ THE WILDERNESS

"**C**ome, my friend," Simon says. "Didn't I save you from the endless sea? Now I am going to save you from the endless wilderness."

Stephen looks up at Simon.

"Am I not a Berber? Am I not a conqueror of Romans and outlaws? Am I not the finder of sons?"

Alexander lets go of his father's hand, reaches over to Stephen, and hugs his neck. "C'mon, Unkee Stephen. C'mon. Git up."

Stephen looks into the eyes of the child, then up at Simon. Simon reaches down his hand. Stephen takes it.

They return to the horse, set Alexander on it, and spend the rest of the day walking on each side of the Barb. They say nothing more.

As the sun sets, they stop. Alexander has laid his head over and slept on the Barb most of the afternoon.

Simon wakes his son and takes him off *Nmare*.

Alexander puts his chubby hands up to his eyes and cries.

"What's the matter, Son?" Simon asks.

"Hungry. Al'xer hungry. *Yammasse*. I want my *Yammasse*."

Simon's eyes become moist, and he hugs his child close. "Oh, my son. Your *yammassee* is at home waiting for you. She is fixing your most favorite food."

Alexander stops crying and looks at his father. "Can we go there now? Can we go see my *yammasse* now and eat my most favit food? I hungry."

Simon quickly holds out his son for Stephen to take, turns away and walks over to a boulder. He lays his head down on the stone and sobs, hope nearing exhaustion.

Stephen sets Alexander down and walks him in the other direction.

"Do you know what Tammarisk is? Can you say Tammarisk?'

"Tamisk," Alexander repeats.

"That is right. We are going to look for some because it is so yummy."

"Yummy, like what, Unkee Stephen?"

"Yummy, like honey."

"I like honey, Unkee Stephen. Does the Tamisk have water too? I am thirsty."

Stephen stops. "Oh, look. I think I see some Tammarisk right over there. Now do not run to it. We do not want to meet any wiggly ropes."

They go to the bush, and Stephen plucks off the flowers. "Here. These are for you. Eat 'em right up. Pick some yourself if you want to. Aren't they yummy?"

"Thank you, Stephen," Simon says behind them.

Stephen stands and looks at Simon. "I understand. I know. He looks down at Alexander. "He is eating his fill and should sleep well tonight. Let us go get some water now."

"How much do we have left?" Simon asks.

"I think enough for all of us to have a drink, *Nmare* to have two hands full, and one last sip for Alexander in the morning."

They find a place offering some shelter and sit.

"By the way, Simon. If Alexander needs a change of clothes, I've got another tunic for him. Made for his birthday by my mother."

"Well, it isn't here, so it's not going to help."

"Oh, but it is here." Stephen takes off his blue head covering and holds it up."

"Oh, Stephen. Is that what you've been wearing? No wonder it looked so silly."

"It worked, didn't It?"

Smiles turn solemn, thoughts drift, and they fall asleep. Stephen dreams he is climbing a Tamarisk and throwing purple flowers down to the ground until the rocks themselves become flowers.

Morning of the third day.

When they wake, Stephen and Simon look at each other and take a deep breath.

"Well, I guess this is it," Simon says.

"Yes."

Alexander wakes up.

"Can I have some water now? And a pretty flower to eat?"

"Come with me," Stephen says. "There is a special drink of water just waiting for you on *Nmare*. Then your *Passe* will bring you a few purple flowers to eat."

He takes the boy by the hand, leads him to the Barb, reaches for the water skin, hopes what is left has not evaporated during the night, takes the stopper off, and kneels before Alexander.

"Here you are, big boy."

Alexander takes his drink. "Now one for you, Unkee Stephen, one for *Passe,* and one for *Nmare.*"

"We will take ours later. Why do not we give some to *Nmare* right now?"

Stephen steps over to the Barb, lifts its head, and tips the water skin nozzle into his mouth. The horse chews on it a moment, then drops its head back, the container now empty.

Stephen bends over to check the horse's belly wound. The sash is still in place. But it is soaked and yellowish.

"Jehovah God. He was so brave. Heal him. Let us take him home again."

"Here you are, Son. There were no purple flowers today. But I brought you something else."

"Yup. I ate them allll up yest'day."

"Well, *Passe* pulled and tugged and yanked and finally found a root for you to suck on. Now, the way you do it, you put it in your mouth and let it soak so it gets so soft you can swallow it. Won't that be fun?"

"Okay, *Passe*." He does not smile. The men do not either.

They take the horse's reins and resume their journey from the highlands of treachery toward the lowlands of comfort and family and happiness again.

One step at a time. One step. Another step. Another.

Do not think about it. Do not think about the torn clothes. Do not think about the empty bellies. Sunburns. Cracking lips.

Think about home. Think about happy friends and the love of family. Think about going and doing and being.

"I think we're going down now, do not you, Simon?"

"What? Oh, yes. Yes. We are headed down now."

The sun beats on them, and the air grows hotter.

They walk on, saying nothing.

"What was that?" Stephen says, stopping in his tracks.

Simon's eyes jerk in every direction. "What? Where?"

"Straight ahead."

They see a red sash.

Simon calls on his inner strength and straightens up.

"Stay here. Hide Alexander."

Simon forms a broad smile and walks sure-footed and confident forward toward the red sash.

The Berber comes into sight, riding a Barb. He stops when he sees Simon, smiles and greets him.

Nmare whinnies, Simon looks toward it, then back at the stranger. They talk a little longer, and Simon points in a direction away from Stephen and Alexander.

The stranger turns toward his left and disappears on the other side of the ridge.

Simon returns to Stephen. "He was on his way to join up with the Berber militia. I told him they had been captured, but there might be another hideout to the south."

"What about water? And a little food?"

"He had three water skins but said he needed them for himself. If I had brought up food, he would have detected weakness. Berbers do not respect weakness. He would have taken my horse and then killed me."

"Well, I guess we need to be on our way."

"Not yet. He may think twice and realize how bad my clothes look, and double back out of curiosity. We had better go back to where you were hiding for a while. Just where were you hiding?"

"Oh, Alexander and I found a cave."

"A cave out of this heat. How lucky. May I join you?"

They enter it and are soon asleep.

"Okay, nap over. Onward we go." It is Stephen.

As the sun descends, Alexander begins to whimper. It is a soft, weak whimper.

"What is it, Son?" Simon asks, wishing he had not given a chance for the boy to say it.

"I thirsty. Can I have a drink?"

Simon looks at Stephen. "If only I could give him my tears to drink," he whispers in such a low tone Stephen can hardly understand.

Stephen takes a deep breath and kneels. "Uh, would you like to play a game, Alexander?" Stephen asks.

"No, I thirsty. Do not want games. Want water."

"This game is about water. Now, do you know how to lick?

Show me with your tongue you know how to lick."

Alexander looks toward Stephen, sticks out his little tongue, and pretends to lick."

"Very good. Now, I am going to turn my back to you. Then something magical will happen. When I turn around, there will be water in the palm of my hand. The trick is for you to lick it up so fast it disappears. If you do not, there won't be more."

Alexander smiles. "Okay."

Stephen turns his back, holds his hand under his mouth, and brings it around to Alexander. "This is special water. It's bubbly. See? That is just for you."

Alexander licks what is in Stephen's hand. Stephen turns his back, and they repeat the process. When Stephen is unsure he can produce much more saliva, he takes Alexander into his arms.

"Now, wasn't that fun?"

"I guess so, Unkee Stephen."

Simon, having watched the process, rushes out of the cave and dashes behind a boulder. Stephen can hear his sobs.

"Hey, Alexander," Stephen shouts. "Would you like to learn a really loud song?"

"What kind of song?"

"About sheep. You know what sheep are."

"Oh, Unkee Stephen. I know. I am smart."

"Of course, you are. Now sing loud.

The Lord's my shepherd.
He'll never let me thirst.
He leads me.
He guides me.

The last line is sung also by Simon, who grabs his son up and embraces him while forcing a smile.

They hear whinnying.

"*Nmare* is calling us," Simon says, his eyes wide with pretend excitement. "I guess we'd better get going."

Stephen takes the reins of the Barb, Simon sets Alexander on its back and holds on to him as they work their way out of the relentless barren mountains.

The sun continues to beat down on them. The air hot and heavy. Their steps grow shorter. Their legs tremble. They do not admit it to one another.

One step.
Then another.
And another.
Struggling.
Surviving.
On they go.
No strength any longer to talk.
No need any longer to talk.
Just keep stepping.
And keep stepping.
Away from danger. Toward…
Nmare stumbles.
"I guess we need to stop," Stephen says.
They find what shelter they can, Alexander snuggles up to his father. In their exhaustion, they fall asleep.
Morning the fourth day.
Alexander nudges his father awake.
"Huh? What? Oh, there you are, Alexander. And how is the best and strongest son in the whole wide world this fine morning?"
Alexander tugs on what is left of his father's tunic.
"*Nmare* sick, *Passe*. *Nmare* sick."
Stephen, now awake also, joins Simon as they step over to the Barb.
They stare. *Nmare* is on his side. Simon steps around and checks his breathing. He looks up at Stephen.
"He gave his life for us."
Stephen says nothing. He takes Alexander's hand.
Simon pats the side of *Nmare's* nose, strokes his mane, and puts his head down close to the animal's.
"You knew you could not make that jump, did not you? You did it anyway. You loved me that much. *Nmare.* I will never forget you."
He stands, tears running down his cheek into his red beard. "Goodbye, my friend. Goodbye."
Simon takes Alexander into his arms, and they work their way northeast.
"Al'xer will wipe your tears, *Passe*."
"Yes, Son. Wipe *Passe's* tears."
They stumble on. One step at a time. Over rocks, gravel, whatever is before them. On through an uncaring wilderness that mocks them.
The heat returns. Their tongues are swollen, their lips cracked. The tips of their fingers cracked. Their sandals barely

hanging on. Stephen has had to discard one of his when the straps were torn completely off. His foot bleeds.

They cannot stop. Alexander is so young. For Alexander, they cannot stop.

On they go in a race between life and death. In a race that ends only when little Alexander is held in the arms of his mother.

"Oh, Abelia. My love. Thank you for the life you have given me. And for Alexander. And for..." Simon stops and looks at Stephen.

So hard to talk now. Throat dry. Breathing hard. Lips cracked. Still, he needs to.

"What if my daughter has been born? I will bet...she has. Abelia was...was going to name her after...her mother."

They continue walking. "I do not remember...her mother's name. Well, maybe she will...name her Tullia. She loves...your mother."

"Everyone loves my mother," Stephen replies. "I think...even ole...Censor Rabannas kind of...does." They stumble on.

"Look!"

"What?"

"The valley. See it? We're almost...out of the mountains. We did it, Simon. We did it!"

"We did it, *Passe*," Alexander says, joining in the fun that he does not understand. "We did it."

"Are you through eating...the Tamarisk root...I gave you to eat...yesterday? I have another...one for you. It tastes just like...honey."

"No, *Passe*. It was yucky. You give me something else to eat."

"We're almost...to the valley. The desert down there...will have food for...us."

"It will?" Stephen asks with a grin.

"Let us pray...it will."

The men try to hurry their steps but stumble all the more.

Stephen trips and falls. Simon turns and helps him up.

They stumble down the rest of the way out of the mountain.

Simon trips. Stephen grabs him.

The sun. Always the sun. Hot and relentless. Eating the life out of them.

Stephen shouts at the ground while shaking his fist at the sky. "You will not win, sun!" Softer now. "You will...not win. We will not let…you." Almost in a whisper now. "Jehovah God will not…let you."

Alexander thrusts his chubby fists skyward. "Al'xer won't let you," he declares.

"Oh, my son. You are going to…grow up and do great…things. You are so…strong."

"I am going to be as big as you, *Passe*."

"Indeed, you will."

They hurry on. Hurry in their minds, though their bodies cannot. Life being sucked out of their bodies. Slowly dying.

Sunburn ravages them. Cracks in their skin. Swelling. Eyes that barely focus anymore. Ears that refuse to listen to the deadly silence only broken by the rolling and tumbling of the ever-present rocks.

Feet barely scooting now.

Knees buckling.

Back bent.

Gagging in their effort to take another stifling breath.

"There it is…Simon," Stephen whispers. "We're closer."

Simon does not respond. Alexander is now on his back, clinging to his father as Simon clings to hope.

"Well, I am ten years younger…younger…than you, and I am tired…of all this…laziness. I am going to run…run ahead of both of you…and plant my feet flat on…on the desert."

"I never saw…anyone so anxious to…enter a desert," Simon calls after him with his hoarse voice.

Simon stops. He sits.

"*Passe* tired again?"

"Yes, *Passe,* tired again. Sit next to me…and watch Uncle Stephen…act like a kid."

Simon watches, and through eyes that give him only blurred vision, he sees Stephen reach the floor of the desert and throw himself flat onto it.

Stephen turns and waves for them to join him.

Simon stands. "I guess we need…to join him before…before he turns into a…sand dune, Son."

He stumbles forward.

"What's a sand dune, *Passe*?"

"You will find out soon…enough, Son. Soon enough."

Stephen returns up the steep final ridge of the mountain and helps Simon and Alexander down.

"Ha, ha," he croaks. "Ughhh. Isn't this great? No more gravel…and boulders."

"No more hiding places...either," Simon says.

"Huh?"

"Oh, nothing."

"Are we home now, *Passe*?" Alexander says.

"No, we have a long...a long way before we get...get home. But we are...are closer."

They find northeast and resume their journey home.

The sun is hotter now. Their clothes so tattered, parts of the fabric fall off with hardly any urging.

Walking and walking.

Plodding.

Trudging.

One dragged step. Another one. Another.

On they go with no other thought than home and getting Alexander back to his mother and safety.

The sun begins its descent for the day. They do not notice. They have collapsed.

Day five.

"Passe. Wake up *Passe*. Get up. Get up. I am thirsty, *Passe*."

Stephen and Alexander raise their heads out of the sand and look around.

"I'm thirsty. Make Unkee Stephen play his game with me."

Simon stares at Stephen but says nothing.

"Come to Uncle Stephen. We will...ughhh...play our game. But I am afraid...Uncle Stephen may not...be able to play...the drinking game...ughhh...much longer."

Simon watches. As he does, he becomes nauseated. "What kind of father...ughhh...am I?" he mutters.

"Okay. Game over. Ughhh...We have to start walking...walking again so we can...can get you home to your...ughhh...mother."

Stephen takes Alexander by the hand and begins walking. Alexander has no trouble keeping up with the men whose feet now drag from one step to another.

"Do you have a mother, Unkee Stephen?"

"Ughhh...Yes."

"Is she pretty as my *yammasse*?"

"Almost. And guess what?" Your *yammasse* and...ughhh my *yammasse* are...friends, just like we...ugh...are friends."

"I like that," Alexander says.

"Passe, would you hold me? I do not feel so good."

On they walk. And on.

"What's...ugh...that?" Simon asks.

"What's...what?"

"I think...I think...ughhh...it's a Peyote cactus. It...ughhh...has water in it."

Simon lunges forward. He falls just as he reaches it. He looks over at Stephen, panicked.

"I have...nothing to cut...ughhh...it open with. I have nothing! I cannot get to...ughhh...the water. I cannot get to...ughhh...the water. I cannot."

The men collapse in front of the cactus.

"*Passe.* Wake up. Wake up, *Passe.*"

"Is this your *Passe*?"

Alexander looks up.

"And this is Unkee Stephen," he tells the stranger.

"Then we shall take them home with us. Welcome to Nassamonia."

23 ~ HOME

"**I** am going back to my own house," Abelia announces to Tullia a week after baby Rufus is born.

"No, you're not. You are not strong enough yet."

"I have to," Abelia says, drawing her month-old infant to her breast. She shakes her head back and forth in slow motion, her lips tremble, and once again, the tears flow freely.

"I have to be there. What if they return, and I am not?"

"You are exhausted," Tullia replies. "You hardly sleep. When you are awake, you pace. You hardly eat anything. That is not good for you or your baby."

"I must stand watch. I must send my strength to them somehow."

"Here, let me take your baby a while," Tullia replies. "You are exhausted."

Abelia steps into the room that had been Stephen's and picks up clothing. She puts them in a basket and walks out to the courtyard.

"Ezekiel," Tullia calls toward the workroom he has set up with his scrolls and writing supplies. "Come help me explain to Abelia she cannot go home alone."

Ezekiel walks out to the courtyard.

"What's this about Abelia going home?"

"Ezekiel, do not try to stop me. I must go. I should not have left in the first place. It has been two months. I cannot stand it."

Ezekiel looks over at his wife. "Well, what are you waiting for? Collect our clothes and any fresh food you have on hand, and let us go to her home."

"What about your writing?" Tullia replies.

"What about it? I will take what I need with us."

"But..."

"Abelia is ready. So, give her baby back to her while you pack."

Tullia pauses. "Maybe she is right," she replies, handing the baby back to Abelia and walking toward their room.

Ezekiel steps over to Abelia and puts his hands on her shoulders. "Libya is a big, big place. It is going to take time. They are okay. I promise."

Abelia looks at the seventy-year-old man. She manages a weak smile. "Thank you," she says with trembling lips.

An hour later, they are at Simon's and Abelia's house. By now, the baby is back asleep. Abelia goes into the room she and Simon sleep in and lays Rufus on the low bed made up mostly of two large cushions on the floor.

She returns to the courtyard where Ezekiel is already hanging the black goat hair awning from one outer wall to another to help block the hot winds that come from the SaHara below.

She sits. She folds her hands. She looks around. She stands and walks to her kitchen area, where they are lucky enough to have their own well. She pumps water, picks up her clean serving dishes, and washes them again.

Tullia walks over to Ezekiel when she is through putting their clothes in the room, normally Alexander's. She lays her head on his shoulder.

"What if Simon and Stephen never find little Alexander?" she whispers. "What if they do not return?"

"I do not know. I guess we will go on living," he responds.

Each day, they go through their routine of living. Each day they go through their charade. Sometimes they talk about it. Mostly they do not.

Ezekiel and Tullia waiting for their son's return. Abelia waiting for her husband's return. All waiting for the return of the boy child, their little Alexander.

Sometimes Abelia goes to the market, but not very often.

"Have you heard from Simon yet?"

"Do you think they kidnapped him?"

"Do you think they killed him?"

"Do you think little Alexander was sold to be raised as a slave?"

"Do you think he got out in the desert and died of thirst?"

"What do you think, Tullia?"

Questions. Their questions. Her questions. Questions that are impossible to understand because the answers are.

Each night they pray to the one true God, Jehovah. "Hear us, Lord," they cry out. Does God really hear? Does God really care? God, where are you?

A week. Two weeks. Hanging on and just existing. Hanging on to a faint hope. A hope that grows weaker and weaker and is about to die.

"What's that noise out on the street?" Tullia says one afternoon. "Do not they know they need to be inside where it is cool?"

The whooping and shouting continues. Whooping and shouting and the rattle of wheels on the cobblestone.

Pounding on the gate. Pounding and shouting.

"Leave us alone," Abelia sobs. "Go away."

The pounding continues. The shouting grows louder.

"Abelia!"

She looks up, looks around, then holds her baby closer, rocking back and forth, back and forth.

"Abelia!"

Dreaming. Dreaming in the middle of the day. Dreaming and hoping beyond hope. Existing. But not existing.

"Abelia!"

Her tears run down her sweet round face. She raises her eyes. "Oh, I cannot stand this, she cries out, then puts one wet cheek on her baby's.

"Abelia!"

The knocking and shouting and pounding. Go away. Go away and leave me alone to weep and mourn.

"Abelia!"

"Abelia, do not you hear that knocking?" Ezekiel says, coming out to the courtyard.

He goes to the gate, unbars it, and stares into the eyes of two men and a little boy.

Simon rushes past Ezekiel.

"Abelia!"

"Abelia!"

"Where are you, my Abelia?"

He looks over in the corner. The dream he had dreamed so many thousands of times over the past three months becomes reality.

Abelia stands. She stares. Her lips part, she gasps, her eyes squint, her knees tremble.

Simon rushes to her and folds her within his big arms.

"Oh, my beloved, my sweet, my own Abelia," he whispers. "How I have longed for this moment."

Something is not right.

He steps back, his eyes widen. "Our baby? Our baby was born? Did you name her after your mother?"

"Another son," she almost squeaks, trying to find her voice. She clears her throat. "We named him Rufus after your father."

She hands their baby over to Simon. For the first time, he stares into the eyes of his baby and rocks it.

"Thank you," he whispers, looking back at her.

"No! No! No!" she screams, realizing Simon is alone.

Simon takes hold of her arm. "What is it? What is it, my sweet? I will protect you."

"Alexander. He is dead."

"That is where you are wrong," Stephen says, having greeted his parents and watched his friend's homecoming.

Stephen walks over to Abelia and puts her hand in Alexander's chubby little hand.

"Here is your *yammasse*, Alexander. Just like we promised."

With his free hand, Alexander reaches up to his mother.

"*Yammasse. Yammasse!*"

Abelia kneels. She embraces her son and rocks back and forth, spilling new tears on his cheek.

"*Yammasse*, hurting me. *Yammasse*, hurting me."

Abelia loosens her grip and pulls back to look at him with eyes still wet with tears.

"My, look how my little boy has grown," she manages. The tears return, the embrace returns. The flame of hope reaches to the sky.

Ezekiel steps over to Simon and shakes his hand. "Welcome home, my boy."

Tullia, standing beside her husband, reaches up to embrace Simon, the one who had saved their lives less than a year earlier.

"Welcome home, Simon. We must be going now. We need to take our son home. I am sure we will be hearing many a tale over the next few weeks. But for now, you need to be alone with your family."

Simon squeezes Tullia back, then releases his hold. She takes his face in both her hands, looking up at him. "God kept you safe," she whispers, her lips trembling.

"Yes, he did," Simon replies.

"And someone needs to fatten you men up," Ezekiel says.

Stephen walks over to the outer gate. His parents join him, and they step out into the street to go home.

"Oh, I forgot our clothes," Ezekiel says.

"I did not. They're right here in this basket."

"But, your scrolls."

"I have them, Mother," Stephen says.

"You have lost weight," Tullia says, looking up at him as they walk."

"Yes, I suppose I have." He pauses. He snickers. "You should have seen me a week ago."

"You were worse?"

"Oh, yeah. We stayed with Simon's uncle so we could get our strength back, and his aunt could fatten us up a little."

"You're limping," Ezekiel says, stepping to Stephen's other side.

"Oh, that? That was an arrow."

"An arrow? What happened?" Tullia asks.

"Too much to tell you out here on the street. By the way, what is all the excitement over at the Zeus Temple?

"Planning the Olympic games."

Stephen stops. "Cyrene has the Olympic games now?"

"Well, not the big official one. But they do have tryouts here once a year to filter out our young men so they can send the best to Olympia."

"Sounds like fun," Stephen says, resuming his walk home.

"Do not think further upon it," Tullia says. "I know that look. You are not participating. You are too weak. Besides, the contestants are all naked."

"Well, Mother, I have time to rebuild plenty of strength, and I heard they make allowances for objectors if they are good enough."

"Here we are home again," Ezekiel says. "I do not suppose you still have the key to our lock."

"No, I do not suppose so," Stephen replies as his father pulls out his key and opens their gate.

Stephen walks in, stands in the middle of their courtyard, raises his arms heavenward, and lets out a yelp.

"I guess that means you're glad to be home. I should think so," Tullia says. "You must be hungry. You were always hungry. I shall leave you two men to tell stories while I go to the market for some cheese, bread, and figs."

"How has the university been while I was gone? Has Cato taken over again?"

"I do not know, Son."

"Well, I have been thinking, Father. They have lectures in medicine. I was not interested in them before, but I am now. Simon taught me a lot while we were out..." he pauses. "Well, crossing the mountains."

"I think I have learned all the mathematics, philosophy, and oratory they can teach me. I had thought about discontinuing my education now. But, well, for my twentieth birthday, do you think I could attend their lectures on medicine?"

"Perhaps you need to check in with your partner, Ovidius, first."

"He's not exactly my partner. We share the same shop."

"At any rate, there has been more trouble in the market about Jews selling there at all. Some of the Gentile merchants think we should have our own market among our 'own people' as they call it."

"Oh, Father, that is so unnecessary."

"This city is growing more and more hostile to Jews."

"Well, since I am now Stephanus and I attend synagogue in secret, perhaps I will be able to stay with Ovidius and spread goodwill and do good works among the pagan Gentiles, so they will eventually learn to open their minds and hearts to Judaism."

"How much progress have you made thus far with your Esther Quest as you call it?" Ezekiel asks.

"Progress is slow, Father. But we will see results eventually."

"Changed your secret word so you can identify each other lately? When the wrong people find out and infiltrate you, you need to change it."

"You are right, Father."

"Ah, there weren't many people at the market this time of day," Tullia says, returning home. "The heat is getting nearly unbearable. I shall have a big meal for you in about an hour, Stephen. Simon's aunt did not do a very good job of fattening you up. Then, after we eat, you can tell us how you found Simon, how you found Alexander, and if they were together at the time or you had to find them separately."

Stephen eats what he can, tells a little about his venture, and falls asleep.

The following day, instead of turning right to work his way to the market and his shop at the far west end of the city, Stephen turns left and heads east.

The temple to Zeus-Amun Re is not too far from his house. It is the largest building he has ever seen, even in Antioch. He has heard it is larger even than the Pantheon in Rome. Something like over twenty man-lengths wide and nearly fifty man-lengths long. Each column holding up the gargantuan structure being more than a man-length thick.

He walks past it, staring in wonder, and comes to the hippodrome where the races take place. Stephen stares a moment at the hippodrome, then turns back around. He works his way back past the temple and his house. On the other side of his house is the largest of the three amphitheaters in the city. He passes the *hospitium,* turns left past the Jewish-Born Freedmen's Synagogue, and arrives at the market.

He walks to the second row where he shares shop space with Ovidius. Despite the heat, Ovidius is inside working. The protective and tightly-knit black goat hair he has spread over the roof and sides block part of the sun's piercing, unrelenting rays.

Ovidius looks up.

"So, you're back. Did you get the Berber's son?"

"You knew about it?" Stephen asks.

"Everyone knew about it. And everyone decided you were daft to go after them in that strange desert and those mountains, especially with TacFarinas lurking behind every boulder."

"Huh, well, I made it back, didn't I?"

"So, it seems."

Any excitement while I was gone?" he says, seating himself and resting after his walk.

"Oh, the Jews complaining. You know, the usual. They're never satisfied."

"Did anything come of it?"

"For them or us?"

"Either."

"A standoff. They're still in the back of the market. Makes no sense. They need a market to sell to their own kind." Ovidius pauses. "Well, they do have some good craftsman. Take that man, Ezekiel. Excellent hand. Everything he writes is clear and precise. Would hate to lose him, but wouldn't want to go among their kind if they started their own market."

"Hmmm."

"Well, I should say 'When they start their own market.' So, are you ready to go to work?"

"Yes, sir."

"Several people have come by wanting you to make locks for them. The government is even interested in you. So, I guess you'll have to quit the university so you can meet the demand for your skills."

"While I was gone, I realized my lack of knowledge of medicine," Stephen says, wiping his brow.

"More? You have learned mathematics, philosophy, and oratory. By the way, I was proud of you when you debated that spoiled what's his name—Cato. Anyway, you want to learn medicine now? Not thinking of becoming an apothecary, are you?"

"Not at all. But seems to me everyone should have a basic knowledge of medicine. That is the only thing I will be learning now. I am through with the others."

"So, you will be here more hours then. That is good. I kept a running list of people needing your locksmithing skills."

"Yes, thank you. As soon as I rest and get things under control here, I think I will go talk to that government representative you told me about. Who was he, anyway?"

"The Cyrenica provincial governor himself—Blasius."

"Well, I hope he doesn't start with a large order and doesn't want it filled fast. There is one other thing I think I want to do."

"What's that?"

"Enter the Cyrenian Olympics as a contender in the javelin throwing competition."

Ovidius sets his hot tongs back in his forge and scowls at Stephen. "You do not have energy or time for fool things like that."

"And maybe even the discus throwing competition."

"You are in no shape!"

24 ~ GAMES

A week passes.

"So, you want to train for the javelin throwing contests. You don't look healthy. I don't know. Well, are you willing to following my instructions, no matter what I tell you to do? If you're not, then I will not be your coach. So, which is it, young man?"

"I will obey your every command, sir."

Achilles eyes Stephen as though not sure how sincere this "every command" response was.

"I would not have taken you on, but I heard you went down in that desert and those ruthless Atlas Mountains to find your friend right in that outlaw, TacFarinas' territory. Anyone fool enough to pull something like that is fool enough to win this competition against known greats. But, of course, you'll have to fatten up some."

"Yes, sir," Stephen says. "What do you want me to start with?"

"Well, you do not need strength training. You get that with the sledgehammer," Achilles replies. "As long as you throw the javelin with the same arm, you will be fine. But you need to control that muscle. I want you to find something heavy, lie down, put one in each hand, and jerk it up and down over your head as fast as can."

Stephen thinks a moment. "Yes, sir. I know what I can use."

The next morning when Ovidius comes to the blacksmith shop, he hears grunting inside. He opens the door and stares.

"Stephanus. What do you think you are doing with those anvils?"

Unable to talk and lift the anvils at the same time, he sits up. "I am doing my jerking exercises. I jerk them up and down as fast as I can until I am too tired to do it anymore."

"Then I declare you tired," Ovidius says. "Now put those things back down where I had them."

Stephen stands, replaces the anvils, takes off his tunic, and puts on his thick cowhide apron, and arm and leg protectors.

"This is my first summer in your country. I am not used to the heat," Stephen says, working to get the fire going in his forge.

"The first summer is always the hardest for everyone, or so they say. I grew up here," Ovidius replies.

"When I was in the desert, the sand burned my foot."

"Yes, that sand can burn almost like fire, but why did it burn just one foot?"

"I lost just one sandal. Had to walk without it."

Silence.

"It's okay," Stephen continues. "I do not talk about everything that happened. At least we weren't in the SaHara. Nobody lives down there anyway."

"Yes, they do," Ovidius replies. "They live in underground cities."

"Oh."

"Here, everyone just quits working when the sun is highest in the sky. That is when you are at the university. Their walls are thick. It's a good place to be in the heat of the day. I suppose quite a few of your fellow students will be entering the Cyrene Olympics."

"Yes, a few. Cato has made himself a coach for discus throwing. A new student was gullible enough to hire him."

"I thought you and he did not get along. Especially since he lost to you in that debate."

"I do not think he gets along with anyone," Stephen says, then grows silent wondering in what way Cato will get his revenge. *He promised revenge*, he sighs to himself, *and someday he will get it.*

The forge hot enough for what Stephen wants to do, he takes hold of a block of iron in his left hand with his tongs and holds it in the fire until it turns white-hot. He takes it out of the fire, lays it on his anvil, picks up his heavy hammer, and slams it down on the iron over and over to flatten it enough to form a lock with it. Only, this time he quickens his blows.

Ovidius looks over at him and frowns. Stephen continues the quick blows until the iron needs to be reheated.

He puts the iron back in the fire with his tongs and leaves them there while he sits and rests.

"What in the world are you doing, Stephanus? You're going to wear yourself out, hammering that fast."

"Got to," Stephen replies. "My coach says I have to practice my jerks so I can thrust the javelin quicker. Well, rest over. Another twenty fast blows."

Ovidius shakes his head and mutters, "Young people."

The following day is the Sabbath. Despite his coach's warning to exercise every day, Stephen does not obey on the Sabbath. He does not tell the coach this. He does not tell anyone what he does on the Sabbath. To the pagan Gentiles, he just disappears on that day. It is too dangerous for them to know.

Survival. Judaism must survive. Worship in secret. If the unbelievers ever decide to destroy the synagogues, they will not be able to destroy Judaism. Secret worship. Keep it a secret. Like Queen Esther, the secret Jewish wife of an emperor. Keep it secret to survive. Good works in secret. Everything in secret. Survive.

After breaking his overnight fast with his parents, Stephen leaves their house and runs straight south across town to the *insulae* for the secret synagogue meeting. His coach had told him strong legs are necessary in javelin throwing, though not as necessary as in racing. He must go to the synagogue anyway. Why not run?

He goes to the top floor and stares at the door. He frowns. No lock. He pushes, and the door opens almost on its own. Empty. No one there.

He sucks in his breath. His brow furrows over his eyes. He squeezes his lips together. He walks to the back room of the apartment. Nothing. No one. He rushes out and bounds down the steps to the fifth-floor apartment of Achaius. He pounds on the door. Achaius opens it.

"Where are they? What has happened?" Stephen's eyes are wide, his face red. He stands before Achaius, shoulders bent forward as though lunging at an unseen enemy.

Achaius smiles and opens the door wider.

"Come in, Stephen. Forgive me for not warning you. I did not know you were back."

Stephen steps inside and sees eight people sitting on benches in a circle. He looks back at Achaius.

"We were discovered. One of us brought someone who feigned interest in our one God, but it was only to spy on us. We gave up the apartment and are meeting here now. Come in. We have a bench for you."

Stephen takes a deep breath and forces a smile that becomes easier as he receives the smiles of the others present.

"Yes, yes. We must stay secret to survive. Survival is key."

He seats himself and is quieter than he had been before his three-month absence. They understand when they speak of God's word as bread, knowing he must have gone without. Water too. How could he have survived?

They pray. A prayer of thanksgiving that Stephen has been given back to them to help lead the secret cause of their secret God. Tears often come to his eyes. They do not look away when it happens. They shed tears with him.

A prayer of thanksgiving also that their secret has been successfully protected. They exchange experiences of leaving pieces of scripture in strange places around the city for the pagan Gentiles to read and learn to love. They exchange experiences of doing good works and leaving notes telling the name of the secret group doing the favor. Surely the Esther Quest is working.

Stephen returns home. He sits in quiet the rest of the afternoon, only sometimes participating in his parents' conversations.

Remembering. Remembering when he had the privilege of saving the life of his friend in the desert who had saved his from the sea. Grateful but fearful. What if he had died instead?

The next day, Stephen runs south of the city to look for medicinal plants. Never again will he be caught not knowing how to survive. If it had not been for Simon...

Oh, that gives me an idea. Instead of returning home after his expedition, he goes to Simon's house. Abelia opens the gate, holding tiny Rufus in one arm.

"Oh, Stephen, it's you. Simon is at the orchard."

"I did not want to see Simon. Is Alexander here?"

"Unkee Stephen! Unkee Stephen!"

The two embrace. Stephen's eyes briefly fill with tears. He controls them, pulls back from Alexander, and says, "How would you like to play a game?"

"The water game was yucky," Alexander replies.

"Shhh, that is our little secret," he whispers. He stands and walks to the center of the courtyard with a big grin on his face.

"I helped you, now you can help me."

"Really, Unkee Stephen?"

Abelia watches then seats herself. "What are you up to, Stephen?"

"My javelin coach says I am strong in my arm but need to

build up my chest and back muscles too."

Stephen lies flat on his back with his hands directly above his head. "Come here, Alexander. I need you to sit on my hands."

Alexander giggles. He climbs onto Stephen's chest, turns around, and backs up to his hands.

Stephen grasps the toddler's hips. He thrusts him up in the air as far as he can reach, then back down to his chest. Then up again and down again.

"This is fun, Unkee Stephen," Alexander says, giggling even more.

Up in the air. Down again. Up. Down. Up Down. Faster. Faster. Up. Down. Up. Down.

"Okay, I've got to stop for a few moments. Then we will do it again."

Stephen jogs home.

"You're wearing yourself out," Tullia says, opening the gate for him. "You haven't built your strength back from your ordeal out there."

"That is what I am doing now. Well, you could feed me extra bread if you want. I have to be ready when the games begin in the cooler weather."

"You'll never make it to the cooler weather if you do not stop running in this heat. At least come under the goat hair canopy out of the direct sunlight.

"I am young, Mother. I can handle it."

He stares at his mother, remembering. She nods as though understanding, and says no more.

Smiling again, he arranges himself on his belly and pushes himself up. After a few warmups, he takes a deep breath, grunts, and jerks his body all the way off the floor. Up. Down. Up. Down. Three times.

"My coach is a hard man. He wants me to be able to do ten of these. Maybe I can work up to it."

By now, Ezekiel is seated on a bench under the canopy watching his son. "Oh, I wish I were young again," he says, wiping his sweaty forehead with the kerchief in his gnarling hands.

"Father, that tanner with the booth near yours at the market. Does he ever carry cowhides?"

"He probably does. Why do not you go over there and ask him?"

"Well, it's in the Jewish section and..."

Ezekiel shakes his head. "Okay, when it cools down a little, and I go back to work, I will ask him. How big do you want it?"

"Big enough to make a ball."

"I do indeed have a strange son. I will not ask you why."

"That is okay. I am going to fill it with heavy sand. Then I am going to bounce it against the wall as fast as I can. Hippocrates, a long time ago, said it will build up…"

"I know. Your javelin muscles."

Days go by. Four more months. Stephen feels nearly ready.

The weather is not so hot. The city of Cyrene gradually fills with fans of the games. The rich from Leptis Magna and Sebrata and Ptolomais and Carthage arrive from the west with their fancy tents. The rich from Alexandria and Memphis and Caesarea and Tyre arrive from the east, trying to outdo each other with the opulence of their tents and togas.

The rich are allowed to camp closest to the grand temple to Zeus Amun-Re. The poorer set up small black goat-hair tents or sleep under the sky.

The city fills with spectators and poets and entertainers. The city fills with athletes with their coaches and equipment and horses, and chariots.

Stephen works out with Coach Achilles more than ever. Achilles remains relentless.

He has learned from his apothecary lectures to drink tea made from *teelscin* for his aching muscles and *sotar* tea to build up his lungs, and to apply *tilult* ointment to strained muscles.

Lectures are dismissed at the university. Most of the students will be participating.

The festivities begin with a parade led by the high priest, then the lesser priests. Then the sacrifices to the god Zeus-Amun Re. One thousand sacrifices. Then the feasting to the honor and glory of Zeus-Amun Re.

Stephen disappears the day of sacrifices with Coach Achilles.

The priests are in full regalia, reigning supreme over the games dedicated to their god. The temple is adorned with sacrificial flowers. Athletes kneel at the statue of the father of all gods and pray to win.

The second day is at the hippodrome, built next to the temple. First, the sprint race. The runners speed across the full length of the hippodrome. Cheers. Boos. A laurel crown is awarded. A poet stands and recites the glories of their new hero.

The second race. Contestants run a full lap. Then another. Hurrahs. Hisses. Another laurel crown bestowed. Another hero with a poet ready to stand and declare the honors of the winner.

The third race. This time running seven laps. Not many make it the whole way. Clapping, Foot stomping. The laurel crown. A greater hero. A greater poet.

The final race of the day—runners wearing full armor. Two laps. Struggling. Straining. Surviving. Cheers. Roars from the crowd. Fans stand and welcome the final and greatest hero of the day. Laurel crown granted. The greatest poet of the day stands and, with bellowing voice, declares the glories of their warrior hero.

The day over, spectators scatter to small groups on the hillsides, empty lots, in the markets, at the taverns, along the streets. All retelling the adventures of the day and the poetry dedicated to them. Poetry that will be retold until the day they die.

Stephen knows his time of practicing is nearly over. Still, Coach Achilles pushes him. And pushes.

The second day is his day. The day of wrestling, boxing, and the pancratium of discus and javelin throwing.

Events of this day are held at the largest of the three amphitheaters in Cyrene, located on the other side of the temple to Zeus-Amun Re. He and a few others have been allowed to wear a small apron instead of participating naked.

He waits through the day, wishing his turn would come. Dreading. Anticipating. Wishing it were over, then not wanting it to ever end. Flexing muscles. Pacing. Jogging in place. Lifting two small anvils he had brought to stay limber and prepared.

The announcement is made. "All javelin throwers, report to the center of the arena." Coach Achilles pounds Stephen on both shoulders. "Go out there and show them who is the best."

Stephen watches the other contenders until it is his turn. He walks into his circle and plants his foot opposite his throwing arm. He takes hold of the javelin by the thong wound around the middle of the shaft. He pulls his arm back with his other arm pointing out to balance him. His legs and hips jut forward just right. He tightens his stomach muscles, flexes his back, and feels the core of his body strengthen.

He takes one last glance at the banners of Roman legions flying over the arena from the outer wall. He determines the direction and strength of the wind. He becomes one with the javelin.

Then the thrust. The javelin flies spiraling through the air. It hits in the center of his intended target—three man-lengths beyond any of the other contenders.

The spectators stand as one and roar their approval. Applause. Whistles. Hoots. Hurrahs.

Stephen steps out of his circle, turns to the fans, and raises his arms. In his moment of glorious victory, he turns around to hail his fans on every side of the amphitheater.

Stephen now turns in the direction of the judges to receive his hero's laurel crown. He notices stirring among the judges, many of whom are lecturers at the university. Another man, not a judge, is among them. They are whispering. They are not smiling.

He walks closer to them for the laurel-granting ceremony. As he does, he sees who the other man is: Cato. He stops. One of the judges stands. He is the head of the university. He makes his announcement.

"Stephanus, you stepped over the boundary of your circle. You have been disqualified. Your fine is that you may no longer attend the university. You are expelled."

25 ~ THE GUILD

"Ovidius, I did not step over the boundary."

"I heard it was Cato's birthday, and he convinced his father to disqualify you as his birthday gift. He said it in public. What could Censor Rabannas do?"

"Sometimes, life just isn't fair."

"You are right about that, Stephanus."

They return to their work in the blacksmith shop. After a while, they hear the bell at the front counter. Ovidius steps over to the centurion.

"May I help you?"

"Yes, I have a large order for locks. Do you think you can handle it?"

"Stephanus," Ovidius says over his shoulder. "This one is for you. It's a centurion."

Stephen immediately drops the yellow-hot slab of iron in the fire. *Theophilus?* He turns and does not recognize the man. He presses his lips together. *I wonder whatever happened to him.*

"I am Centurion Cronos. Governor Blasius has sent me here to order one hundred locks. That is to start with. He will be sending them to his fortresses and limes in Libya."

"My name is Stephanus. I thank you for the order. How soon do you need your hundred locks?"

"Now."

"Those I have on hand were specifically ordered by others. It will take time. I will work as fast as possible. I have been working five days a week, but will increase it to six."

"Why not seven?"

"I will look for people to hire if you can give me an advanced payment of perhaps twenty percent."

"Those were not in my orders. I will grant you a fortnight. No more."

Centurion Cronos does an about-face. He stops a few paces away and turns. "I will check on the advance payment."

Stephen walks back to Ovidius. "What am I going to do? How could such good news also be bad news?"

"Did not you learn logic at the university? Think, man."

Stephen steps over to his anvil, picks up one of the blocks of iron in his bin, throws it back, walks to the front counter, back to his forge, picks up his bellows, pumps it, sets it down, bends over and reties his sandal, pushes the hair out of his eyes, lifts the front counter, looks out to the street, comes back, and sits on a bench.

"I can find some apprentices, but there is no way I could teach them blacksmithing, then how to make locks. Just one skill would take them years to learn."

Ovidius walks over to his young colleague.

"Did he tell you how they want the locks to be made?"

"No." He stares at Ovidius and catches the older man's smile. He stands and hits his palm against his forehead.

"Of course. We smiths will work together. Okay," Stephen says, tapping each finger as he talks, "let me see now. There is Ianos, the coppersmith, Sethos who works with bronze, and even Nikon, the brass worker."

"And, of course, you and me," Ovidius adds.

"That is five of us. If I can teach all of you how to make the simplest lock, we would only have to make twenty locks each. Ovidius, you should have taught logic at the university."

As soon as Stephen blurts it out, he recalls the pain of his reputation having been smeared by his forever taunter, Cato. He clears his throat and takes a deep breath.

"Well, I think I will go see those men right now."

Late that afternoon, he returns to the blacksmith shop.

"Well, Stephanus, how did you do? Did you convince anyone to help with the order? Or need I ask? You look pretty happy."

"Ovidius, I was very surprised. They said, if I taught them how to make locks, they would make their share. But they want a percentage before they cut off their regular customers to make these for the Roman legion."

Stephen sits, leans his elbows on his knees and his chin in his hands. "Pray, Ovidius."

"Pray to which one?" Ovidius asks.

Stephen stares at the older man, realizes what he has said, and leaves out the back door.

The next morning, Centurion Cronos returns to the shop. "No."

"No, what?" Stephen asks. "No, the governor has decided not to order the locks? No, he's going to get someone else to make the locks? Or no..."

"No, he will not give you an advance."

"Then, no, I will not make them."

"Fine. I will go to the coppersmith. He will make them."

"No, he wants an advance also," Stephen responds.

"Then, I will go to the brass smith."

"You are out of luck. He will not, neither will the bronzesmith."

"How do you know all this?" the Centurion demands.

Stephen smiles. "Of course, you can go to the goldsmith or silversmith and pay fifty times more than you were planning to pay me."

"I shall return."

The centurion does an about-face and marches smartly away.

Stephen sees a boy playing on the street in front of the shop and walks out to him.

"Boy, here is a copper coin. Do you know where the brass, bronze, and coppersmiths have their shops? If you will go see all three and bringing them back with you, I will give you another copper coin."

Stephen sets up the hourglass and waits, pacing.

"Governor Blasius refuses to pay us an advance so we can buy our materials," Stephen tells the other smiths upon their arrival.

"What an opportunity we will be missing if we agree," Ianos, the coppersmith, says.

"It's everything or nothing," Nikon says.

"We could always go back about our business as it has always been, and forget the whole thing," Sethos says.

Silence. Thinking. Wondering. Pondering.

"What about a compromise?" Ovidius asks the others. "We ask for ten percent in advance."

"What does everyone think?" Stephen asks.

One by one, the men raise their hands in agreement.

"Well, I think two things just happened," Stephen

announces. "We have just had our first smith guild meeting, and we have joined forces to guarantee our demands are met."

Smiles all around.

"I guess we should have done this long ago," says Ianos.

Sethos stands. "Well, Stephanus, I have a feeling we are going to win this one. So, why do not you take one of your locks apart and show us how it is made."

"I can give you the rest of the afternoon," Nikon says. "And all of tomorrow."

The smiths return the following morning and resume learning how to make locks. Stephen shows them the most simple method.

At noon, they take a short respite with fresh figs and cheese, then return to work.

At mid-afternoon, Centurion Cronos returns. He sees Stephen with the other men working on locks. Stephen steps over to the front counter.

"You may have five percent advance," the centurion says.

"Fifteen percent," Stephen counters.

"Then, I go to..."

"You go to who?" Stephen says, smiling. "The silversmith? The goldsmith?"

"Fifteen percent."

By now, the other smiths have stopped working and turned to watch the negotiations.

Stephen looks over his shoulder at them and grins.

"No," the centurion says. "It must be five percent."

"What about a compromise? Ten percent."

Centurion Cronos glares at Stephen.

"No!" he bellows.

He makes an about-face and marches away. He stops, then turns. Everyone in the shop watches him.

"Very well," he says. "Ten percent. But if all hundred are not completed within a fortnight, we will withhold part of your pay."

The centurion leaves.

Stephen turns and flashes a smile at the other smiths.

"We did it. United, we did it. The smith guild is official. Now, we need to bring in the silversmith and goldsmith. Do not you think?"

"Let us worry about that later. How many more lessons do you think we will need to work on our own?"

"I'd say three more days," Stephen assures.

On the fourth day, Stephen does not report to the shop. It is the Sabbath.

He eats, then jogs over to the *insulae*. He arrives early and joins Achaius in welcoming the others. This time they have a visitor.

"This is Pandaros," Benjamin says. "He found one of the pieces of papyrus one of us left near his shop. He asked me if I knew anything about it because he was very impressed. Isn't that right, Pandaros?"

"Yes, indeed," Pandaros assures. "This is some of the most serene writing I have ever read. It is far superior to Socrates or Aristotle or any of the great philosophers."

"He understands we worship only the one God, Jehovah, do not you Pandaros?"

"At first, I thought it was strange to forsake all the other gods. But Benjamin explained it to me, and it all makes sense. I would be honored to be one of you."

"There is the circumcision ceremony," Achaius explains, "but after that, you will be officially Jewish. Your heart will be blessed, and Jehovah will be glorified. Let us all pray."

The group moves from their benches and prays, sometimes with their heads touching the floor and sometimes on their knees.

Their scripture reading is one of David's psalms.

I will establish the throne of David forever.
I will appoint his descendant my firstborn.
He will be the most exalted of the kings of the earth.

"If our Messiah would only come," Stephen says, "we would be free of foreign rulers. We would be free of oppression. He will rule the world."

"But I do have a prayer of thanksgiving," Stephen adds. "Jehovah God has sent a centurion my way and arranged for me to make enough locks, I may be able to open up my own shop. Praise be Jehovah."

As always, they end their service sharing experiences of planting the scriptures secretly in the night.

The next day, Stephen returns to the shop. He builds his fire in the forge, puts the bellows to it to intensify the heat, then selects a block of iron with his tongs.

"How dare you!" The voice behind Stephen is deep and growling like a mad dog. "How dare you," the voice repeats.

Stephen drops the tongs and turns around. Immediately a cold shiver runs up his spine, and he tightens his muscles.

A high priest stands at his counter, though which high priest Stephen is uncertain.

He has on a white tunic and crimson red toga. On his head is a cone-shaped tunic made with gold threads. He wears a pendant of gold on his chest in the shape of a thunderbolt, the symbol of the god of gods, Zeus.

"How dare you insult Zeus and his son, Vulcan."

"What are you talking about?" Stephen asks.

"Take him!"

The high priest steps aside and two underling priests raise the counter. They throw a sack over his eyes, tie his hands behind his back, and lead him out.

Ovidius, having witnessed the whole scene, is speechless. He knows no one will step forward to rescue Stephen. No one in the entire city of Cyrene dares defy the high priest of Zeus, who unofficially controls the city.

Stephen stumbles forward in his artificial darkness. Sweat streams off his face. His breaths come short. He struggles not to panic. The muscles in his shoulders tense and tighten, while the muscles in his legs grow weak.

His heart races. He grows dizzy. His lungs scream for air. His chest hurts.

Jehovah God. Help me. Oh, help me. Do not let me die.

He stumbles through the market. Instead of turning left toward the temple of Zeus, he is jerked around to the right.

Jehovah, I have only done good for your cause on earth. Please, do not forsake me.

He smells flowers. Only the Sanctuary of Apollo has such a strong scent of flowers and greenery. He is pushed forward until he stumbles and falls on something hard like marble.

Be my shield. Surround me with your protection. Jehovah God, let me live.

Stephen is taken up steps and through a gate. They stop, and the sack is taken off his head. He looks around at the grand columns. Before him is an imposing statue of Apollo.

"Well, here he is, Dialis," his superior growls. "As high priest of Apollo, you will take care of this situation."

"Indeed, I will, your worshipful Flamenus. You will be happy with the results."

The high priest of Zeus, father of Apollo, and his two lesser priests turn and leave.

Stephen fights to continue standing, despite the growing weakness in his knees. He is angry at the perspiration, still falling from his forehead into his eyes.

High Priest Dialis wears a tunic of pale blue with a darker blue toga. It is attached at his shoulder with a ruby on a gold strand. On his head is a cone-shaped turban similar to that of High Priest Flamenus, though somewhat smaller.

He motions his own priests forward, all wearing the same pale blue, but without the toga. Three stand on one side of Stephen and three on the other.

Stephen remember his father's words: "When in trouble, stand tall. Do not let them see your fear." He sets his jaw, raises his chin, and gazes at a nearby column.

"How dare you insult my master's brother."

"High priest Flamenus has a brother?" Stephen blurts out before catching himself.

"Silence! You mindless fool. My master is Apollo. His brother is Vulcan. They are sons of Zeus."

Stephen looks up. "I, I did not mean to, well, maybe I..."

"Silence!"

High Priest Dialis walks forward and stops just a handbreadth from Stephen, staring. Stephen looks down at the marble floor.

The high priest turns his back on Stephen. When he arrives at his throne, he seats himself.

"Not only are you a filthy Jew..."

"Who told you that? I am Stephanus."

"Not only are you a filthy Jew, but you have been caught blaspheming the great god, Vulcan.

"You do realize that Vulcan is the god of fire and everything good that comes from it. He is, therefore, the god of all smiths. That means he is your god."

"No, sir. I mean..."

"Silence!"

My temple is the only one allowed to form a guild of smiths. You have overstepped the bounds of the gods. They are angry. They must be pacified."

He looks at his priests. "Do what must be done."

Stephen is taken through a back exit from the temple through a pathway of flowers and to a smaller building. Inside the building, it is dark. A torch is lit. He sees chains on the wall.

"No!" Stephen cries out. "Please. I did not know. I did not

realize. Do not make me die."

His tunic is torn off. Two priests grab long rods. The first one slams onto his back.

"Ughhh."

The second one follows fast.

"Ughhh."

On they come. Beating. Beating. Beating.

Stephen cries out. "Abraham! Abraham!"

When he wakens, he is on the cold stone floor. His back is aflame. He looks around. His eyes adjust to the darkness. He sees no one.

He tries to raise himself with his arms. He cannot. He tries again.

I've got to get out of here. He tries again. He remembers the urging of Coach Achilles. He strains and pulls himself to his knees. He tries to block out the pain in his ribs and the fire in his back.

"Help me, Jehovah."

26 ~ GOODBYE

"**W**hat a way to spend your twenty-second birthday," Ezekiel says, watching Stephen lying on his front at home.

"Shhh," Tullia says. "Lie still, Son. I've got to finish putting this honey and *uzuar* on your back. When I am done, I've got a warm tea of Turmeric to help with the pain and to put you to sleep."

When she leaves the room, Ezekiel resumes his questions. "How did you get out of there?"

"I do not know, Father...It was dark, and a back door was open. I found...the wall around the sanctuary. I followed...it around until I found a gate. It is...never guarded. People use Apollo's...sanctuary as a park."

"They wanted you to pass the word around," Ezekiel says. "They used you as an example. I am sorry, Son. I am truly, truly sorry. You have a good heart. Well, it will be a few weeks before you can go back to your synagogue."

"Excuse me," Tullia says. "Achaius is here."

She steps aside. "Justus, Secundus, Trophimus, Draco, Carpus, and Benjamin are with me. Also, Jonas and Patrice. We are stunned at what happened to you, Stephen."

They crowd into Stephen's small room and stand along the wall.

"It's all over," Draco says, almost in a whisper.

Stephen raises up onto his elbows, his back ribs and flesh scream, and he lies back down. He groans, and crosses his arms in front of him, putting his chin on them so he can see.

"What's all over?"

"The secret synagogue meetings."

"What do you mean? No, they cannot be."

The eight men and one woman, along with Stephen, the original secret synagogue, are once more together again. They stare at Stephen. No one speaks for a long time.

Stephen turns his face to the wall. They can hear the sniffs. They can see his shoulders tremble. They watch as he shakes his head over and over, and listen as he mumbles, "No, no, no."

Ezekiel reaches over with his gnarled hand—the hand on which rests the ring his father had made him while still a child, the ring his father said was endless and would remind him of God's endless protection. He places his hand on Stephen's head.

"Son, you tried. God knows that. Jehovah God know you tried. You are one of the most devoted souls I have ever known."

"Maybe we did some good with our night ventures," Justus says. "Probably, we did."

"We grew for a while," Trophimus says.

"It was too hard to determine who was a spy and who was not," Secundus says.

"Sometimes a member started out honest, but gave in to a bribe when suspected by one of the pagan Gentiles," Justus says. "Their freedom in exchange for information."

Stephen turns his head to face his friends. "The Esther Quest. It worked for...Esther. She made known she...was a Jew at just the...right time and it helped...our people."

"Maybe now is that time," Ezekiel says.

"How? They beat me as an...example. Things are growing...worse for us now that...we have been discovered. Isn't that right...Father?"

"Perhaps not. God is ruling."

"I just wish he would...hurry up and come to earth and...rule as our king as he has been...promising so many centuries. What is he waiting for?"

"Until then, we must believe he knows what he is doing."

"What if things become...worse for our people now?"

"Maybe we should have done what we were doing, but with a public synagogue," Draco says. "Be public like Daniel instead of Esther. The pagans left the public synagogues alone."

"Well, I guess there...is no more Stephanus. I am just...Stephen again. May as well grow my...beard back." He pauses. "Though I did like...not having it, especially in this...hot climate."

He smiles. The others smile back.

"Will you be worshipping again with your mother and me

at the Jewish-Born Freedmen Synagogue?" Ezekiel asks.

"I will be," Benjamin says. "That is, if they will take me back."

"I am returning to the Greek-Speaking Synagogue for Roman Citizens," Draco says.

"What about you, Patrice?"

"Yes, I will be returning there also."

"I guess Justus, Secundus, Trophimus,, and I will be joining Draco," Achaius says.

"I will be going back to the Greek-Speaking Freedmen Synagogue," Carpus says.

"Father, would you be offended if I...return to the Greek-Speaking Freedman Synagogue? If they'll accept me...back, that is?"

"Whatever you decide, Son, is fine with your mother and I. You need to stop talking now and rest."

"I suppose I've been kicked...out of Ovidius' shop. I will have to set up a shop in...the back row with the other Jews. Do not know...if I can afford it, though."

"If you will stop talking and rest, you can have my booth, Son."

"What about your scribes?"

"We've opened up a school. Your father comes over sometimes to give us some prestige."

"I did not know that. Why did not...someone tell me?"

"You had a lot of other things on your mind. I was going to tell you soon," Ezekiel says.

The following Sabbath arrives. Stephen can sit up now, but still cannot put on a tunic, nor can he walk well.

"I do not know if my back broken ribs hurt worse than my front broken ribs," Stephen says. "But I still hurt all over."

"Try to stay still," Tullia urges.

Ezekiel and Tullia leave to go to their Jewish-Born Freedmen Synagogue. They close the gate, and Stephen sits in the sun of the courtyard.

He sits and stares in the quiet. He tries to worship.

He chants a psalm of David.

Many are they that hate me.
Those who hate me without reason
Outnumber the hairs of my head.

"You spoke this through David, Jehovah God. Who do you mean was hated? Who were you talking about? David? Me? Someone else?"

He prays, leans his head on a table next to his bench, and falls asleep halfway through.

"Oh, you're going to break your neck, sleeping with it all twisted like that," Tullia says three hours later.

Stephen opens his eyes. "How was it?" he groans.

"Well, a lot of people were upset, I must admit. But they will get over it," she says.

"Come, Tullia," Ezekiel interrupts. "We are hungry. And I need to get our son back to bed."

He helps Stephen to his feet and walks him toward his room.

"What did she mean, Father?" Stephen says in a groggy voice.

"Oh, nothing."

"Yes, she did," he says louder. "What did she mean?"

"Well, a few of the merchants have lost some of their customers. That is all."

"That is all? It's all my fault, Father."

Stephen shuffles back to his room. Ezekiel helps him. "Nothing is your fault, Son. Now I mean it. I never want to hear you say such a thing again. Your Esther project might have worked. You had a good heart."

"I guess you were right," Stephen says, reclining on his front, his chin on his folded arms. "I should have followed Daniel's example and done everything in the open."

Ezekiel leaves the room. Moments later, he and Tullia hear the wailing.

"No! No! Why, God? Why does everything I try turn out wrong? What's wrong with me, Jehovah God? All I ever did was love you. God, I am such a failure. How can I face everyone now?"

Stephen falls asleep and dreams he is sitting in a den of lions. The lions turn to doves and fly away.

Morning comes.

Stephen raises himself up with his strong arms, cringes at the pain, and swings his legs around until he is sitting on the side of his bed. He stands and stumbles over to his tunic.

"What are you doing?" Tullia says when he comes out to the courtyard. "Get back to bed."

"No, Mother. I need to know what happened in the market."

"It's too early. You will learn soon enough."

Stephen struggles into his tunic, leaves his sandals off, and stumbles out the gate.

"Go with him, Ezekiel," she says.

Stephen walks out and turns right in the direction of the market at the North Gate. He stumbles past the grand amphitheater where he won and lost his glory, and past the baths on the other side.

He stumbles past the Jewish-Born Freedmen's Synagogue, then stops to lean a shoulder on the outer wall. He tilts his head over and closes his eyes a moment. He opens them again and resumes walking.

He arrives at the market and straightens up as much as possible. He holds his head up, raises his chin as his father had always told him to do, focuses, and walks forward to the second aisle. He turns and walks to the end of it. He pauses and enters the blacksmith shop.

"I have been expecting you," Ovidius says in his familiar voice. It is still kind. "But, you know you cannot continue here."

"Yes, I know that," Stephen says.

"I have set your tools and supplies together. You will have to get help moving them out. I need you to be completely gone by the end of the week. By the time of your next Sabbath. You know, you should have told me the truth."

"I know," Stephen says. "But I thought... Oh, it matters not anymore."

He stares a moment at Ovidius. "Thank you for your friendship. I will never forget you."

"Nor I you," Ovidius laughs. "You were always full of surprises. But now we must part and pretend we do not know each other."

"Yes, sir."

Stephen stumbles over to his tools and picks up a few of them, then leaves.

Instead of returning home, he goes to the main aisle and shuffles to the back.

"There goes the trouble maker."

"There goes the cheater."

"Liar."

"Imposter."

Dirt is thrown in his eyes. He stumbles on. Someone throws green dates at him, and they meet their mark. He cringes in pain at the sharpness on his flesh.

He arrives at the last aisle. He walks past Joshua, the potter who turns his back on him.

He walks past Ebron, the baker. Ebron throws flour in his face.

Eben, the butcher, throws entrails at him.

He turns around before getting to the booth of Midyan, the tanner. And sees his father.

"Father, what are you doing here?"

"You did not think I would let you face this by yourself, did you?"

Ezekiel turns and holds his hands high above his head.

"Listen to me, Brothers," he bellows. "This is my son. How dare you treat him like this. He has done nothing to hurt you."

"He betrayed us."

"We're worse off than we were before you came. The Gentiles hate us even more than ever. Why did you have to move here?"

"Well, we are here, and we are not going anywhere. Now, I still have my booth, and my son is going to take it over. If any of you need a lock or hinges or pulls made for doors or chests of any size, he will make them for you at half price. As your brother, he will do this for you."

Ezekiel goes to his booth and unlocks the back room. "Sit here while I bring the rest of your things to you."

"Why, Father? They all hate me."

"They only think they do. By tomorrow, they will forget anything happened."

Ezekiel walks out to the middle of the aisle. He raises his hands over his head again. "Okay, now. Anyone who goes with me up to Stephen's former booth to bring his tools and equipment back here will receive one free copy of any one of the shorter prophets of the scriptures."

Ezekiel waits, and moments later, men walk out to stand with him. Within two hours, all Stephen's things have been transferred to his booth in the last row.

"Let us go home now, Son. You've had a big day. It's time to go back to bed."

They leave, Ezekiel relocks the back room, and hands the key to Stephen. Just before rounding the corner to head out of the market, Ezekiel turns and waves. "We will be seeing you in a week, friends."

The two men—one young and feeling foolish, one old and wishing he could undo all the pain his son has gone through the past two years—walk side by side home.

Tullia unbars the gate for them.

"Well, well. How did things go? Or should I ask?"

"It was a success, my love," Ezekiel says. "A success indeed."

Stephen smiles a weak smile at his father, then shuffles over to his room.

It is morning. Stephen has slept all night in his tunic. He walks to his door.

"Father, I believe my tunic is stuck to my back. Will you come help me unfasten it."

"Ha, ha! Our son wants me to unfasten his back. He must be better."

Five days pass. Stephen stays up a little longer each day.

A knock on the gate. It is Delylah, one of Simon's and Abelia's friends who had been at Alexander's weaning celebration the night he was kidnapped. She is crying.

Ezekiel opens it farther and steps back. "What is it, Delylah?"

"My husband. He has been arrested."

"For what?"

"For nothing. For stealing something he did not steal. For being a Jew."

"Where is he?" Stephen asks, coming out of his room.

"At the jail under the government basilica."

Stephen, walking better now, returns to his room, slips on his sandals, and takes something out of a basket near his bed. "Take me to him."

"There is nothing you can do for him. They won't listen to you. Especially you. Well, what I mean is..."

"Father, come with us."

Ezekiel walks up the street with his son and Delylah, the street heading north and south through the city. They arrive at the gymnasium academy of the young boys. Stephen pauses and looks a moment at the university behind it. They turn right and arrive at the jail.

"We would like to see our friend," Ezekiel tells the guard. "We are harmless. This is Delylah, Cheber's wife. This is my son, who is in very bad health. They are weaklings and no threat to you. I will stay out here since I am the strong one."

The legionnaire on duty looks old Ezekiel up and down, chuckles to himself, unlocks the door leading down to the dungeon, and explains, "He's at the end."

Stephen and Delylah take one of the torches off the wall and work their way down to the end of the cells.

"I am here, sweetheart," Delylah says, stirring her husband out of a restless slumber on the cold floor among the rats and slime.

"Okay, you keep talking. I have work to do," Stephen instructs.

Stephen pulls out the key and the long prong he had brought with him. He tries the key. It does not work.

"Stop watching me. Keep talking."

He stoops until he is kneeling, trying not to break open his wounds.

"Hold the torch down a little farther, and keep talking."

Stephen probes into the lock with his prong. He works it around. He listens. He returns the key to the lock. He stands. "Okay, you can leave now."

"What?"

"You can leave now. The cell door is unlocked. Now walk slowly so I can go ahead of you. My father and I will draw the guard away from the outside door and convince him to look in the opposite direction. Then you two slip out and go to Simon's house."

"Stephen, how can everyone be saying such awful things about you?" Delylah asks.

"Oh, here. Take my probe and key in case they search me."

Stephen slips them into Delylah's hands, takes the torch, and works his way toward the outer door. When he arrives, he opens the door just enough to get his father's attention. He winks, and his father smiles.

Stephen steps through the door, his back humped over.

"It's so damp down there, my back is worse. Would you like to see my back?"

"Yes, do look at his back. It is a sight to be seen. Come over here where the light is better. Yes, over here," Ezekiel urges. "Now, Stephen, lean over. Hang on to the wall, so you do not faint. This is going to hurt."

Ezekiel raises his son's tunic. "Look at what those thieves did to my son. They ought to be arrested."

"Well, we cannot be everywhere at once," the guard replies.

Ezekiel looks beyond the guard and sees Cheber and Delylah slip through the prison door and around the corner of the building.

"Something has to be done with the thieves around here," Stephen whimpers.

"Probably those Jews. They're nothing but trouble makers," the guard says. "There are going to be a lot more arrests."

Ezekiel leaves, holding Stephen's arm. Instead of going home, they turn left and walk past the Sanctuary of Isis, then the Berber Synagogue. They walk around behind it and knock on Simon's gate.

Simon opens it. When Stephen and his father enter, they see Kehath and his wife Liba and their children. Soon they realize Nebo and Nissa are there with their children. The women are crying.

Ezekiel stares at Simon.

"What's going on?" Stephen asks.

"Sit, Stephen. You need to rest," Abelia says. "Besides, we have something to tell you."

Stephen and Ezekiel take a seat on a bench together.

Simon sits across from them.

"We're leaving. We cannot handle all the prejudice here. They are prejudiced against both Berbers and Jews. It's just too much."

"Where will you go?"

"To Jerusalem," Simon announces. "We're moving to Jerusalem."

27 ~ CONFRONTATIONS

"**H**ave you changed your mind, Son? Would you like to attend the Jewish-Born Freedmen Synagogue with us this morning?" Ezekiel asks.

"Maybe another time. I feel a little more comfortable with the Greek-Speaking Freedmen. It is nothing against you and Mother, of course. Maybe I will go with you another time."

They leave out their gate together. Stephen's parents turn to the right, he turns to the left. He passes the Greek-Speaking Synagogue made up of Roman citizens. There, he turns right and walks until he arrives at the Greek-Speaking Freedmen Synagogue.

When he enters, he notices there are not as many present as there had been in his previous visit over a year earlier. There is a surge of whispering and turned heads. He seats himself on the back row. The whispering and turned heads continues.

Well, I may as well give them what they want. Worship has not begun, so he stands, steps back into the aisle, and walks up to the second row. He looks around at everyone staring at him, smiles, and reseats himself in the front.

Rabbi Solomus steps up to the podium, wearing his usual official white tunic with blue robe and turban. The copper-covered Ark with the image of an angel hovering over it sparkles in the morning sun streaming in from the two windows.

He raises his hands heavenward. On cue, the congregation rises. He pronounces the benediction, and the congregation reseats itself.

"Brother Usirus, will you kindly come forward and read our scripture for the day?"

The middle-aged man steps up to the podium and stands behind the ornate table upon which a scroll open to the psalms of

David rests. He reads.

The LORD says to my Lord:
"Sit at My right hand,
until I make Your enemies
a footstool for Your feet."

Rather than reseat himself, Usirus smiles at the congregation and says, "Who do you think the Lord was speaking to in this prophecy?"

A brother—Xexon—in the fourth row, rises. "I think he was speaking to David."

Agathon in the twelfth row rises. "I think he was speaking to David's father."

Stephen rises. "I think he was talking about the Messiah somehow. The Lord God was speaking to the divine Messiah. The Messiah's throne will be attached to God's throne somehow. Further..."

Usirus points at a brother in the sixth row. "You had something to say?

"Yes," Balios says. "Who are the enemies?"

Helios in the tenth row stands. "I think they were political enemies of David. You know. Like the enemies we Jews have here in Cyrene. If certain people had not turned hypocrite and pretended he was not a Jew and ended up getting us all into trouble..."

"That is not true," Carpus says from the back row.

Stephen turns around and sees his friend. They lock eyes briefly.

"That is not true," Carpus repeats, now standing. "He did more to advance the cause of Judaism than everyone in this room combined."

"Like what?" Balios demands.

"He was out every night hiding pieces of papyrus all around the city to be found the next day by the Gentiles."

"And just what was on those so-called pieces of papyrus?"

"Moses' Ten Commandments," Carpus states.

"I do not believe it," Xenon says. "You cannot squeeze all of them onto a tiny piece of parchment."

"And he prayed for all of you," Carpus continues. "Every time we were together, we prayed for you. Did it ever occur to you to pray for him?"

"Cannot believe anything a Sadducee unbeliever like Carpus says," Agathon interjects.

"Brothers, brothers, brothers," Rabbi Solomus says, scooting Brother Usirus away from the scripture table with his shoulder and hip. "Shall we sing?"

The service is over. Stephen holds out his hand to those sitting around him. They turn away from him. He watches as everyone leaves. Everyone but three—Stephen still in the front, Carpus still in the back, and Rabbi Solomus standing in the doorway with the key.

Stephen walks toward Carpus, and they embrace and kiss each other on both cheeks.

"Thank you, Carpus," Stephen says. "But, you did not need to defend me."

"Yes, I did. You are one of the most dedicated men I know. I really respect you, Stephen."

Stephen smiles. "You'd better watch out. People will call you a trouble-maker next."

"They already do."

"Uh, brothers. If you do not mind, I need to lock up and go home. My family is waiting, you understand."

Stephen and Carpus walk out, pass between the grand columns on the portico, and head down the street together.

"So, what are your plans, Stephanus?"

"Ha, ha. I am still Stephanus, am I?"

"Old habits, I guess. So, are you going to switch synagogues?"

"I think I will try it here a little longer. Who knows? Maybe I can turn them all into troublemakers. Ha, ha."

Over the following month, Stephen remains quiet during the synagogue service. Then a subject is brought up that pricks him too much to remain silent.

"Yes, what about the poor?" He stands and asks.

"We help the poor, and that is that," Xenon says.

"But which poor? Jews or Pagan Gentiles?"

"Jews, of course," Xenon replies.

"And which Jews? The ones born Jew? The Greek-speaking Jewish converts? The Greek-Speaking Jewish freedmen converts? The Jewish-born slaves? The Greek-Speaking Jewish slaves? Just which Jews?"

For the following month, he sits toward the back so he can control his instincts to say something and make everyone mad.

Two months later, the Rabbi speaks of going near and far

to convert others to Judaism.

"So, do we?" Stephen asks, unable to control himself longer.

"Do we what?" Helios asks back.

"Do we travel far to convert others to Judaism?"

"Not everyone can afford to go running around the world to convert Pagan Gentiles.," Usirus shoots back.

"How about here in Cyrene?"

"They would kill us," Agathon explains. "You of all people should know that."

"You could teach certain ones in secret," Stephen retorts.

"Uh, we already tried that," Carpus, sitting next to Stephen, whispers.

Stephen sits back on his bench and remains quiet for two more months.

"I am quite surprised you have lasted as long as you have in this congregation," Carpus says one day, stopping by Stephen's locksmith booth in the back Jewish row of the market.

Stephen grins. "Well, I do not like beards. They are too hot in this climate. If I shifted over to the Jewish-Born Freedmen Synagogue, they'd treat me even worse."

"Well, you could always join the slave synagogue."

"They may not want me," Stephen replies, slapping his friend on the shoulder.

"By the way, I reminded my parents recently that I am twenty-three years old and have never been to Jerusalem for any of the three main festivals. Simon has been there a year now. So, no more excuses."

"What did they say?" Carpus asks.

"They said, 'Then let us go.'"

"Just like that?"

"Just like that. Well, my father is seventy-four years old and admitted he'd like to go to Jerusalem before he dies."

"So, which festival do you think you'll go to? One of the spring ones or one of the autumn ones?"

"Spring. Definitely spring. Ha. Cannot wait to see ole Simon's face when we show up at his gate."

"Do you know where he lives?"

"Well, no. But we have three clues: First, he is in or around Jerusalem somewhere. Second, he is big and red-headed with two pigtails on the side of his head and wearing a Berber tunic full of bright colors. Third, he is probably working at a vineyard—either his own or someone else's. There cannot be that many vineyards around Jerusalem."

"Here we are at my house. Well, whenever you go, have a good trip," Carpus says, pounding Stephen on the back.

Stephen is at his own house shortly.

"Mother. Father. I think, if we go to Jerusalem this year, we should go in the spring—you know, for the Passover or Pentecost." He sits in the courtyard by their well.

"I prefer Passover," Ezekiel says. "It is the more solemn of the two spring festivals. Pentecost is more for celebrating spring and the harvest of winter crops. Besides, my old bones are not up to sleeping in a booth made of branches for a week."

Stephen is silent a moment. "This will be the first time any of us have been in Jerusalem since Grandfather was taken prisoner by Pompey's men when he was—well, I guess he was about my age."

"Close. He was twenty-one,"

"Am I like my Grandfather Stephen?"

"Oh, yes. He did not know when to not talk and ended up being a slave. You tend to do that. You are also like him because you have a quick mind."

"Besides, I've become a blacksmith like him." Stephen watches a bird land on their back wall, peep, and fly away. "I wonder what our life would have been like if he had not been made a slave the rest of his life."

Tullia walks from the kitchen end of the courtyard with a tray of figs and cheese for their mid-day respite. "Ha! You wouldn't have been born," she says.

"Oh, that is right. We—well, Grandfather—would have stayed in Jerusalem, and you lived in Tarsus up in Anatolia."

Stephen forms a large grin and slaps his knee. "I guess that proves even good things can come out of bad things. After two generations of slavery, you got me!"

"Come pick out which kind of cheese you want, Stephen."

Ezekiel disappears in his and Tullia's sleeping room. They hear coins dropping into a chest. He returns after a few moments.

"Uh, we may have to wait until next year to go," he says in a low voice. He sighs and grins. "Well, I have been approached by a couple of fathers wanting me to tutor their sons in scribing. They should be advanced as far as I can take them after a year. So, I think next year will be better."

The rest of the Sabbath, the family reads or sings or naps. Tullia has mending to do but leaves it undone since it is against the Law of Moses to work on the holy day.

That evening, as Tullia prepares a final meal for the day and Ezekiel is busy lighting the wall torches, Stephen slips into his room. He stays a few moments, comes out, notices his parents are still busy, and slips into his parents' sleeping room.

He comes out just as his father lights the last torch, and his mother brings out a tray of bread with a bowl of raisin sauce for everyone to dip it in. She catches him and winks.

"Uh, Father," Stephen says. "I thought you had plenty of money saved up."

"I did too, but I guess not."

"I hate to say it, but your eyesight isn't so good anymore," Tullia says. "Go back and check again. For me."

"Yes, Father. Go back and look again."

Stephen finishes up the last of the raisin sauce with the last of his bread and pops it into his mouth. By the time he is through chewing, they hear Ezekiel in the other room.

"Ha, ha, ha! Well, look at that," he says, walking back out to the courtyard. "I did count wrong. Jerusalem, get ready. We are going to join you this spring."

The following day, Stephen returns to work at his booth on the last row of the market.

"Any of you men going to Jerusalem this spring?" he asks as he manages to get the attention of one merchant or another. "Well, we're going this year."

"Then Jerusalem can keep you," Eben the butcher calls over to him.

Stephen pretends not to hear.

Around mid-day, Stephen sits on his bench, satisfied with a slab of copper he has finally flattened out enough to decorate iron hinges. He closes his eyes for a short rest.

"When can you close up your shop?" Ezekiel asks.

Stephen opens his eyes. "Father. When did you arrive?"

"Just now. When can you close up your shop?"

"For the night or the season?"

"For the season. I have bought fares for the three of us aboard the *Festum,* which leaves tomorrow for Joppa. Then it's just a day's walk from there to the holy city. The price goes up the closer to Passover it gets.

"Well, I will have to visit my customers and ask if they would be satisfied if I delivered their locks in two months," Stephen says, staring at the ground.

He slaps his knee. "Of course, I will be ready. They'll just have to keep using the bars on their gates to keep them safe until I return. Praise be to God. We're going to Jerusalem."

Stephen skips the rest of his nap and works until past dark to finish as many locks as possible before leaving. On his way home, he stops by the homes of the customers whose orders he had been unable to complete.

Some ask for a refund. He has a pouch of coins in his belt and pays them back.

He arrives at the gate of his home and knocks on it.

Tullia opens it for him. She brushes the hair out of her eyes. "There you are. We have so much to do, I may be up all night. Go to your room and pack what you need. Remember, we will have nothing to do on the ship, so you need to bring books, blank papyrus, or whatever you want to stay busy."

"Motherrr. You would think I've never been on a ship before." Stephen reaches down, tucks a strand of her hair back, and kisses his petite mother on the forehead.

"What do you need done? Let me help you," he says.

"Perhaps I was exaggerating. I think I am almost through. I spent all afternoon baking. Your father went to the market for me and bought all kinds of dried fruit for us—figs, dates, nuts, grapes. Hopefully, it will be enough to keep us from starving on the ship."

"Do not forget, I bought extra water skins for us," Ezekiel adds, joining them in the courtyard.

"Uh, Stephen, would you look in the storeroom for the three largest baskets. Each one of us can carry our own supply of food."

She pauses, the strand of hair falls back over one eye, she puts her hand on her head and turns in a circle. "Now, let me see. What else do I need to do?"

"Oh, uh, Stephen, bring me the wicker chest too for our clothes. You can carry it on your back. It has healed, and you are strong."

"What about your new embroidery project?" Stephen says.

"I am glad you reminded me. Hopefully, I can finish it on the ship. I was making it for Abelia—a Berber sleeveless outer tunic. Oh, and I need to make something for both their children."

Ezekiel walks up to his wife and takes hold of her hands. "Sweetheart, they will love us even if we do not clothe their children."

"I know. I know. But, when we go through the market by the North Gate to head down to Apollonia, if I happen to see enough cotton fabric for the two boys..."

"Ha, ha! That reminds me, Mother. I should get out that blue headcover I was wearing on my search for Simon and Alexander. It was actually... I guess you're not interested in that. Well, I am going to bed now."

He heads toward his room, stops in the doorway, and turns. "Will Simon ever be surprised to see us!"

28 ~ PROMISED LAND

*T*he ship *Festum* slips out of the harbor of Apollonia. Stephen looks past the city and to the top of the massive cliff behind it. Cyrene.

"What are you thinking?" Ezekiel asks, joining his son at the starboard rail.

"The city is confusing to me."

"You used to tell me often when you were younger that you were mixed up. It's been a while. What about Cyrene confuses you?"

"I do not know if I love it or hate it."

"Every city is like that. You loved Antioch because of learning the locksmith trade and having a lot of friends. But you hated what they did to Abraham."

"I still miss him, Father."

"I know you do."

"Do you think Jerusalem will be like that for me? I mean, will I love it and hate it both?"

"Hey, what are you doing here?"

Stephen and his father turn.

"Achaius! We could say the same about you," Ezekiel replies.

"Ever since you handed the school over to us and we are our own masters—not saying you were a bad master because you weren't—we have wanted to give ourselves time off to go to Jerusalem," Achaius explains. "So, what is it like? Have you ever been to the temple? We heard it is so high on a hill called Moriah, you have to take a precarious walkway across a deep chasm to get to it."

"Ha. We haven't been there either," Stephen says. "You say it has a hazardous walkway?"

"Did not say it was hazardous. It's just high. Oh, here come Trophimus, Secundus, and Justus. Look who I found," Achaius calls over to his approaching friends.

"Where are you going to be staying?" Ezekiel asks.

"We assume the city will be full of hostels," Trophimus says. "Would you like to join us?"

"We plan to see Simon as soon as we arrive."

"Good thinking," Secundus says. "He might have room for you at his house—unless, of course, he is living in an *insulae.*"

"Attention, everyone. Attention, everyone."

The passengers look toward the bridge.

"As you know, there are many treacherous rocks along this coast, and will be until we reach Alexandria." The captain stands next to the helmsman.

"My officer here is very good. But right now, he needs everyone to go over to the starboard side of the ship. In doing so, the port side will lift farther out of the water and farther away from any rocks that the last storm might have pushed closer to shore. Now, in case you do not know where the starboard side is, it is to my left and your right. The side closest to shore. Thank you for your cooperation."

"Ask me about those rocks," Stephen says to a stranger who has moved next to him. "I know all about them. First-hand knowl...."

"Son, come over here."

"But, Father."

"I need you right now."

Stephen joins his father. "What do you need?"

"I need you to think about what you are saying. Remember what saying the wrong things cost your grandfather."

"We're not being attacked. It's nothing like it."

"Think before you talk. Some things are better unsaid forever. Now, have you memorized David's eighth psalm yet?

> Oh Lord, our Lord,
> How majestic is your very name
> Throughout the earth.
> You have shown us your splendor
> Throughout the heavens.

"Isn't that better than what you were talking about just now?" Ezekiel says. "Continue on."

On the third day, the *Festum* docks at Paraetonium, the destination of some of the passengers. Others go ashore to do some sightseeing of an ancient Egyptian temple built there over a thousand years earlier.

"I am going to stay on board," Tullia says. "I am not used to the Berber form of embroidery. It is intricate. I have only six days left to finish it, plus two tunics for the boys, and a turban for Simon."

"A turban. You did not say anything about a turban," Ezekiel says.

"Well, I saw the perfect fabric for one when we passed through the market on our way to the ship. Now, go along, you two."

Ezekiel, his four former employees, and Stephen go ashore and find the market. They spend most of their time at booths that sell parchment, papyrus, and blackener. Achaius buys a small supply of everything, and they return to the *Festum.*

The next morning, the ship takes on new passengers and new cargo to be sold as it works its way off the shores of Israel and on to Lebanon and Syria.

Stephen remembers the exercises Coach Achilles had taught him plus beaten back and broken ribs and decides to see how well he can do them after all this time. He is disappointed, both because he has lost some of the strength he used to have and because he lost his title.

The older members of the party resume their reading or writing, their sewing or planning.

"What is the first thing you are going to do when we arrive?" Tullia asks her husband.

"Find Simon."

"Do not you want to see the grand world-renowned temple?"

"That is second. I am more practical than you. Always have been."

Tullia smiles at her husband, and he leans back to take a nap.

After two days sliding along the waters off the coast of Egypt, the serene boredom once again ends.

"Look!" Stephen announces, pointing at something protruding high above the water. "What is it?"

"Son, I believe it is a lighthouse," Ezekiel says.

The *Festum* slips past an island off the north shore of Egypt. Once at the lighthouse, it veers into a great harbor full of ships from all over the world. Closest to the mainland, they see a smaller harbor within the larger one. A great barge with red and gold sails seems to be preparing to leave its nest.

"Attention, everyone," they hear from the bridge. passengers turn toward the captain. "We are now in Alexandria, considered the third-largest city in the world. Tomorrow is the Sabbath for those of you who are Jews. In deference to you plus the fact it holds the largest library in the world, we will be leaving to proceed on our journey to Israel in two days. Enjoy your stay."

As the *Festum* works its way toward an available dock, Stephen notices a temple on his right. "It looks some like the temple we have in Cyrene to Isis. I wonder if it is. Probably."

Heavy footsteps across the main deck and the crew reports to work stations. Sails are unfurled. Hatches opened. Chains unraveled to let the anchor down. There is a tug and a bump.

"You do not need your chest do you, Tullia?" Ezekiel asks.

"No. I have already gone through it and have clothes with me for two days. I wonder what delights are in the market here. Better yet, I wonder what delights are in the library here. I fear we are going to have a problem pulling our son away from that library."

Mother and father glance over at Stephen, and he smiles, basking in their love and the new adventures before him.

They go onshore and check in at some booths along the waterfront. One booth has papyrus maps of the city. Ezekiel purchases one for them.

"Stephen, why do not you go on in the library and enjoy yourself while your mother and I rest in the gardens just beyond that amphitheater?"

"Gladly. But why do you need to rest? That is all you have been doing."

"We're old. That is why. Now, go."

Almost straight ahead, Stephen sees a grand staircase with statues of Rameses on either side. He ascends the broad majestic staircase, trying to look everywhere at once at the wonders. He walks across a grand portico with columned verandas on each side. He goes through a broad open gate. What he sees next is a courtyard the size of ten of his parents' houses. Gardens. Reflecting pools. Statues.

Two more flights of marble stairs and into the library itself. Inside, he stops and stares at the ceiling far above with scenes of the pharaohs doing what pharaohs do best—conquering.

Painted columns everywhere. A labyrinth of shelves. Tables. People rushing or wandering or sitting on alabaster benches musing on the wisdom of the ages.

He walks closer to one of the sections. Small cubicles along the walls full of scrolls and ladders to reach them. His mind races. Where to begin?

He turns in a circle and sees a large and high table facing the grand entryway.

"Excuse me, sir. But your library is so huge, I do not know where to begin."

"Ha. Everyone says that," the clerk says. "Here is a tablet showing you where each category of books is—history, mathematics, philosophy, oratory, medicine, navigation, geology, building, exploring—whatever is your delight."

"Do you have any books about the Jewish religion?"

"We have books about every religion in the world. Look at the tablet I gave you, and you will find what you are looking for. And sit at any table you like..."

Stephen finds several scrolls that look intriguing and takes them to a table.

"Son. It is nearly dark."

Stephen turns at the sound of his father's voice.

"Already? I just got here."

"You just got here five hours ago. Your mother and I have found a hostel in the Jewish sector of the city near the synagogue."

Stephen puts away his books and follows his father out.

"Father, you'll never guess what I read."

"After we settle in tonight, you can tell me all about it."

They leave out the south exit of the imposing library and head east down the street called Canopic. They pass a temple to Saturn on their left, and a gymnasium academy beyond that. They turn left again and walk three blocks. They are now in the Jewish Sector and back at the seashore.

"Mother, I found some of the writings of your father," Stephen says as he enters the room rented by his parents. "He really was famous, wasn't he? I was so proud, I bragged to the librarian about it. I do not think he believed me."

"You have inherited my father's brains and curiosity," Tullia replies.

"And my father's tongue," Ezekiel laughs.

"Also, would you believe, I found the Law of Moses, the history of the Jews, our poetry, and all our prophets? In two languages—Hebrew and Greek."

Stephen shifts from sitting on the floor with his knees up, to lying on his front with his chin propped up. "The librarian in that section of the library said the Greek version had been translated right here in Alexandria and was called the *Septuagint.* Ptolemy II actually sponsored translating the Torah three hundred years ago. I never knew that."

Stephen sits up again. "Our people must be very strong and very respected here in Alexandria." He is quiet a moment. "Not like in Cyrene."

He stares at his parents, who do not reply. He stares at the ceiling and down at his sleeping mat. The last thing they hear before falling asleep for the night is, "Why?".

"This is going to be a memorable day. I just know it," Ezekiel says, tapping his son in the ribs with his sandaled foot. "So, get up. Eat some fresh grapes, cucumbers, and dried fish your mother bought for us yesterday."

Stephen splashes water on his face and throws on a clean tunic.

"Here, this is something new I found in the market," Tullia says. "You put it under your arms to make you smell better. I guess Egyptians have stronger noses than the rest of us."

"What is it?"

"I think it's a mixture of vinegar and cinnamon. Give it a try."

"Let us be going now," Ezekiel says. "I am anxious to meet our Egyptian brothers."

They leave the hostel and walk east along the waterfront. They walk another block and see the sign.

"Oh. It wasn't what I was expecting," Ezekiel says.

"It's what I expected. The synagogues where ever we go are in the style of the local architecture. Egyptians do not build domes like Romans do, so their large buildings are full of columns to hold up the ceiling," Tullia explains. "Aren't they beautiful? The columns?"

They walk between columns inside the structure and see a long-narrow section down the middle with rows of benches stretching the length.

Most of the congregation has already assembled. Stephen and Ezekiel sit toward the back on the men's side, and Tullia does the same on the women's side. Ezekiel looks around and notices someone waving to him. It is Achaius sitting with Trophimus,

Secundus, and Justus.

A rabbi stands and walks up to the podium. It is typical with the replica of Moses' original ark, the sign overhead—Know Before Whom You Stand—the cubicles for the Torah, Poetry, and Prophets, and the special table upon which the scripture scroll of the day is already rolled out for the reader.

The rabbi opens the worship with a benediction. The congregation alternates between silent and spoken prayers, and chants of David's psalms led by their chanticleer.

The scripture for the day is read.

Hear, Oh Lord. Listen, Oh Lord.
I am groaning for you.
Heed my cries for help.
For you are my King
And my God.

The reader of the scripture ends with an amen. "Turn your attention now to Rabbi Apollos as he expounds the meaning of God's words through David."

Apollos stands. He is a thin man, though not emaciated. His hair is black and wiry. He has high cheekbones, full lips, a square face, and a close-cut beard. Stephen assumes a beard like that would be an effort to keep both Jews and Pagan Gentiles happy.

Apollos raises his right hand, reminding Stephen of his oratory lessons.

"Did you get that? Did you get what David was saying? Listen to it again, my brothers: *You are my King and my God.* His deep voice echoes between the columns.

"King of what and of who? God is King of heaven and earth. He is King of angels and mankind.

"Listen carefully, my friends. Since he is King of the earth, someday God will walk the earth with us."

He pauses while members of the congregation stir and whisper to each other.

He raises his left hand. "Impossible, you say? I say no. Nothing is impossible with God. Surely you remember Adam and Eve our common parents. They walked and talked with God in the Garden of Eden."

Once again, Apollos pauses. While he waits, his eyes sparkle as they shift around the room,e spreading his love over them all.

"If God can walk the earth with Adam and Eve, he can walk the earth with us. Brothers, someday God will return to earth and once again walk with us as our King."

Apollos stands still, smiles, presses his full lips together, nods in approval of what he himself has just said, and seats himself.

The chanticleer rises and leads a final chant followed by a final prayer.

Everyone rises to leave. The usual chatting among friends ensues. Tullia joins her husband and son as they work their way to the exit, but with many happy interruptions.

"Welcome, brothers. Are you visiting?"

"Welcome. Have we seen you here before?"

"Welcome. Are you moving here?"

"Welcome. Are you traveling by any chance to the Passover? My name is Apollos."

"Yes, we are," Stephen replies. "These are my parents, Ezekiel and Tullia of Tarsus, then Antioch, and now Cyrene.'"

"My, you are well-traveled. And to such prominent cities," Apollos replies. "I hope to see you again next Sabbath. If not, have safe travel to Jerusalem. I, too, am going, but there are always over a million of us invading the city, so the chances of us meeting there are slim. Please excuse me now. I must visit a sick widow. Peace be to you."

Stephen and his family amble back in the direction of their hostel.

"I really like it here," Stephen says. "Too bad, we do not live here."

The following day, they rise early, walk through a market set up just for the ships, and Tullia purchases enough food for her basket to keep the family fed two more days until they arrive in Pelusium.

After Pelusium, the *Festum* heads north. A day and a half later, they arrive at the harbor of Joppa.

The city rises straight up as if born out of the sea itself. It reigns like a giant turtle amidst minuscule crabs.

The crew rushes around the deck dousing the sails, weighing anchor, and casting dowsers to the pilings lining the pier.

"Ah, at last, we are in Israel," Ezekiel says while scooting out of the way of a busy sailor. "Son, go below and get your mother's wicker chest."

"I suppose we need to go on into the city," Tullia says. "Maybe someone will be selling maps so we can find our way to Jerusalem."

"I heard all we have to do is head along the highway going straight east," Stephen says. "The ship is full of Jews, so I just asked.

"Anyway," he continues, "about ten *milles* from here is Lydda. Some fifteen *milles* past that will be Emmaus. And fifteen *milles* on the other side of that is the grrrreat city of Jerrrrusalem."

As he says it, Stephen raises both arms in the air and looks up at the puffy white clouds overhead.

He stares a moment at the small, round clouds piled together like stones in a heap.

MAP 3

JERUSALEM
1st Century
Location of 6 public pools, Pilate's & HP's palaces, fortress, ramp up to temple & Solomon's porch.
Author has inserted suggested location of synagogues & residences of characters in this book.
Sheep Gate
Greek-Speaking Roman Synagogue
Greek-Speaking Freedmen Syn.
Pool of Bethesda
Simon's Insulae
Antonia Fortress
Draco's House
Stephen's Insulae
Philip's House
Pool of Amygadalon
The Temple
Solomon's Portico
Apostles' hostel-HQ
Flower Gate
Phasael's Tower
Hippicus' Tower
Mariamne's Tower
ramp up to temple
Royal Portico
High Priests' Palaces
Pilate's
Herod's Palace
Jewish-Born Synagogue
MOUNT ZION
Nicodemus' House
Gihon Spring (Pool)
Jewish-Born Freedmen Synagogue
CITY OF DAVID
Serpent's Pool
Lower Pool
Kidron Valley
Jewish-Born Synagogue
Siloam Pool

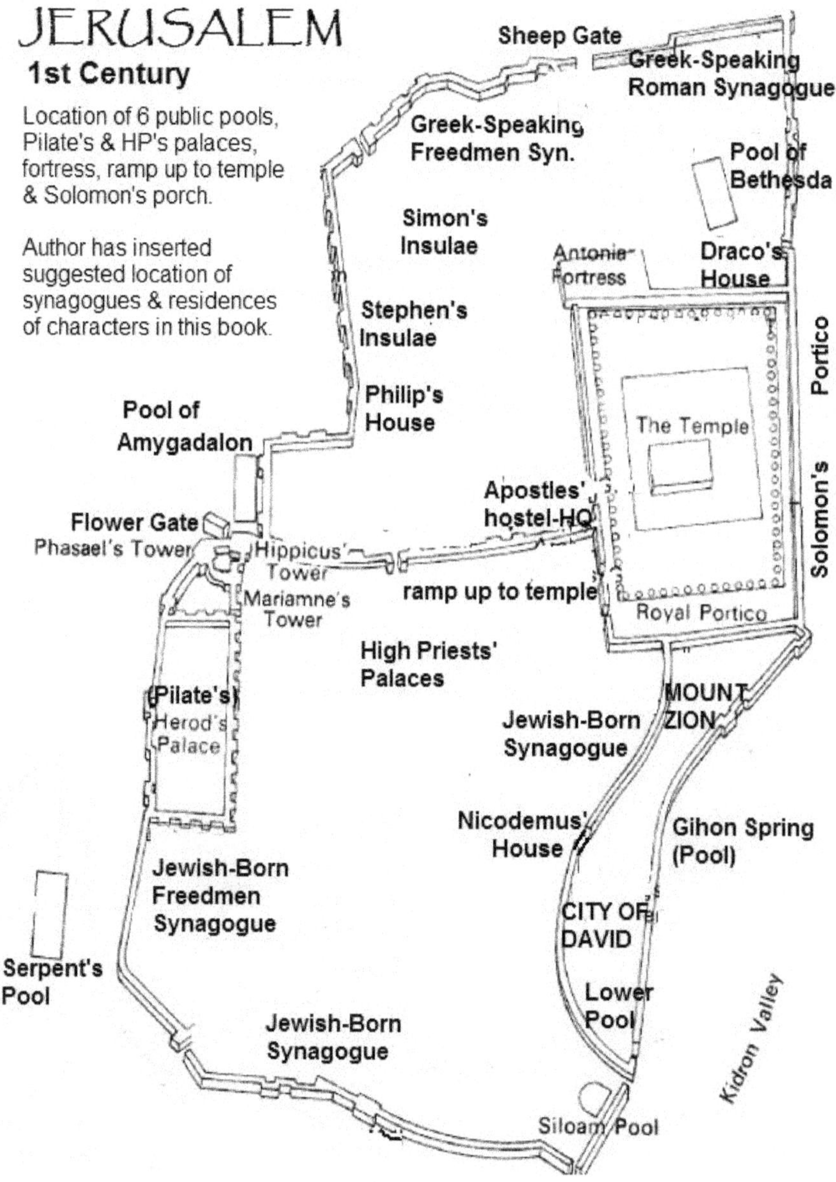

29 ~ JERUSALEM

"**A** week ago, we were in Cyrene of Libya where everyone hates Jews," Stephen says. "Have you noticed how happy everyone is on the road with us? We're almost to Jerusalem, where everyone loves Jews."

"No, Son, we are not almost there. We are there." Tullia points in the direction they are headed. "See, just above the horizon?"

"Those three towers?" Stephen asks.

"That has to be Jerusalem," Tullia answers.

They draw closer, walking gradually uphill. They see the three towers rise higher above the horizon. Then the top of the wall. At last, they see before them the full height of the great walls of Jerusalem.

"They must be ten or fifteen man-lengths high," Stephen surmises. He looks closer at the three towers, then to the right. "I wonder if this is a citadel and palace."

Another road from the south merges with theirs.

"What do you think, Father? Do you think this is the...Father? Father?"

Stephen and Tullia stop and look for Ezekiel. They see him standing still back where they had first come into full view of the city. Standing still and weeping.

"Sweetheart," Tullia says, walking back to her husband. "What is it?"

"Well, Father," Ezekiel says, gazing at the city before him, "you left Jerusalem nearly a hundred years ago as a young slave. We have returned home, Father, and we are free."

Ezekiel looks down at his family. They smile. Each takes one of his trembling hands, and they walk together into the holy city beside the towers.

"Did you see the name over the gate, Father? This is the Flower Gate."

"I can see why. Look at all the flowers on each side of the street. No grand columns like the other cities we have visited. Just God's own creation. Flowers." Tullia smiles.

Straight ahead is a long elevated ramp that leads to another wall high on a second hill.

"The temple," Ezekiel whispers. Looming over the walls is a tall building sparkling in the sun with its white marble. "We shall visit it tomorrow when we are fresh."

To their right is a palace in the older architecture. "I wonder if this is the palace built by the Maccabees," Tullia speculates. To their left are houses.

"Why do not we start looking for Simon in that area?" Tullia continues. "The part of the city where the old palace is looks very rich. Simon won't be living over there."

"You're probably right."

They turn left and watch the people passing them going both directions.

"Not as many beards in this part of the city," Stephen says. "I wonder if more Gentiles or Greek-Speaking Jews live over here."

"Sir," he says, stopping a man just passing them. "We are looking for Simon of Cyrene. He is Berber, so wears colorful embroidered clothes and has a pigtail on each side of his head."

"Uh, yes, I think we have a few people who fit that description. There are some *insulae*s straight ahead. Go past Fort Antonia on the right. Then you'll start seeing them. You will pass through our second wall and be in the most recent part of the city to be developed. Start with the *insulae*s."

"Thank you, sir," Ezekiel says.

As they walk north, they notice the walls to the Temple complex on their right continue all the way to the city's second wall, built after a second addition to the city.

They pass through that gate and see the *insulae*.

"Father, there are some benches here. Why do not you and mother wait while I ask around?"

Stephen proceeds alone and stops at every *insulae*. He knocks on the door of the bottom-floor apartment. It is not until he arrives at the fourth *insulae* that they acknowledge a Berber living in their building.

Stephen works his way up the inside stairs and knocks on both apartment doors at each landing. On the third floor, he knocks once again.

"Pardon me, but...Simon! We found you, Simon!"

"Who is it?" Stephen hears farther inside the room.

Without taking his eyes off Stephen, he calls over his shoulder, "Come quick, Abelia. Stephen is here in Jerusalem." He turns back to Stephen with a wide grin. "Where are your parents? Could they not come?"

"They're waiting for me down at the gate to this part of the city. I will run get them."

Half an hour later, Stephen, Ezekiel, and Tullia arrive back at Simon's apartment.

"Come in. Come in," Abelia says. "Please find a seat. You must be exhausted. Did you walk or take a ship?"

"And we want you to stay with us," Simon adds.

"Unkee Stephen!" Alexander rushes into the front room and charges at Stephen. "I am six years old now," he says, settling in on Stephen's lap.

"And who is this?" Tullia asks when another little boy pads into the room.

"This is our baby, Rufus," Abelia says.

"I not baby. I three," Rufus replies, lowering his brows in childish anger.

Simon picks up his younger son and sets him on his lap. "I guess you are here for the Passover celebrations."

"That we are," Ezekiel says.

"Then we families will enjoy the feast together. Last year at our first Passover, it was just the four of us. This year will be much better."

"Uh, Achaius, Trophimus, Secundus, and Justus are here somewhere. If we can find them..."

"Of course," Simon says. "We will have triple the blessings with your family and them at our table."

Abelia goes to the corner where she has a large basket and brings out bread, cheese, dried figs, and dates, which she places on a large tray. She pours yogurt out of a lidded jar, and into a bowl in the middle of the tray, then takes it all to a low table.

"Gather around, everyone," she says. "Simon will pronounce the blessing."

"I forgot how good your yogurt is, Abelia," Stephen says after the prayer, popping a large piece of dipped bread into his mouth.

"I made a large batch of flatbread this morning. A bird must have told me while I was down in the courtyard baking that we were going to have company. And delightful company. Oh, Tullia, I am so glad you came. I have been a little lonely for home.”

“Ha. She likes Cyrene so much, she has forgotten her home used to be Lystra up in Anatolia,” Simon responds. “I married the right woman, didn’t I?”

“But we thought you left because of the persecution of the Jews.”

Simon grows quiet a moment. “Well, yes, we did. But it wasn’t always like that. That new governor, Blasius, just made things worse. He also hates Berbers. He set up forts and limes all across our country to keep us Berbers under control. So, I was hit from both sides. Maybe things will be better when someone else takes over as governor.”

“Were you able to buy a vineyard?” Ezekiel asks.

“No, I am working mostly as a night watchman in someone else’s vineyard right now and saving up my money.”

“You did not sell your vineyard back in Cyrene when you left?”

“No. Hopefully, we can go back someday. Well, it is almost time for me to go to work. I will see you in the morning. I will take you over to see the temple as soon I return home. Then I will sleep a while and join you for supper.”

Stephen’s sleep that night is intermingled with thoughts of the grand temple. His last attempt at sleep is interrupted by a deep voice.

“Wake up if you are going with the rest of us to see the temple this morning.”

Stephen opens his eyes to see everyone staring at the pallet he had been given to sleep on in the middle of the room.

“Unkee!”

“Umph!” Alexander lands on Stephen’s chest. Rufus lands on his knees.

“Your mother and I have been baking honey cakes for your fast-breaking,” Abelia says.

Stephen struggles to his feet. Alexander hangs on to his neck. Rufus clings to his lower leg. He drags himself and them over to a table with pitcher and bowl of water. He splashes it on his face, pours a little on his head, double checks his hands, then wipes himself dry with a small towel.

Not fast enough, the morning meal is eaten, and everyone descends the stairs. Out on the street, they turn south toward the Flower Gate.

"I left the boys with a neighbor," Abelia says.

They work their way up the street that seems more crowded than the day before because of the increasing hordes of out-of-town Passover pilgrims.

"Across at this intersection is the high priest's palace," Simon explains.

"The high priest has a palace?"

"Ha, ha. You have not seen anything yet, Stephen," Simon responds, leading them to turn left.

"That is the old Hasmonean Palace, which I think High Priest Caiaphas has moved into."

"I thought you said that other palace belonged to the high priest."

"We have two."

"Two?"

"The old father-in-law, Ananus, who used to be the high priest, retains his title, and everyone lets him. Now ahead of us is a ramp that will take us all the way up to the temple complex," Simon continues.

When they arrive at the top of Mount Moriah and go through the temple gate, they see porticos all the way around the outer courtyard with great columns holding up the roof. People are milling around, bumping into each other, but not seeming to mind.

About how large is all this?" Ezekiel asks. "I had no idea it would be so large."

"The temple building itself and all the other buildings and courtyards covers the entire mountain top plus where Solomon used to have his palace. It is larger than the original City of David, the original part of Jerusalem when David settled here. The portico on the north side has been enclosed and made into rooms for priests and Levites who live here."

"Dear, do not bore them with so many details. We are on the west side, and the temple faces east. Let us walk around to the Song Gate Into the Treasury Courtyard that some call the Women's Courtyard. Anyway, we need to go on around to it."

"You have a Women's Courtyard?" Tullia asks. "We have our own Courtyard?"

"Anyone can use it. It's just called that because the women cannot go farther into the temple complex."

When they arrive at the gate, they ascend steps that are one and a half man-lengths high. They see Levites scattered around playing on lyres or singing or both. Some in the crowd notice, but most seem not to.

"The chamber in that corner is for Nazarites," Simon says. "They go in there to get their hair cut off to affirm their vow. The chamber in that corner is where the priests keep their sacred oil and incense, and the chamber in that corner is where the priests keep their supply of firewood."

"What's the chamber for in that corner?" Stephen asks.

"That is the Lepers' Chamber," Abelia explains. "They are unclean and cannot associate with the rest of us. So, the priests have made it possible for them to come here and worship in their own area."

Someone bumps Stephen in the shoulder. He looks around but does not see anyone familiar.

"It is just more crowded than usual right now," Simon explains. "It will get worse the closer we come to Passover Day."

"The temple building is more magnificent up close than I imagined," Ezekiel says. "All that white marble and bronze and gold."

"There is even more gold inside the temple building itself. It lines the ceiling and the walls. But only priests can enter it."

"More steps," Tullia says. "They must be two more man-lengths high."

"Yes, my friend, and that is only for the men," Abelia says. "We women will stay in our courtyard while Simon shows them the rest."

The men ascend the steps to the Courtyard of the Israelites.

"We can only walk around this end because the part with the alter and lavers is only for the priests.

"Look at that temple," Stephen says, staring at the large double doors leading inside the sacred temple building itself. "Steps another two man-lengths high to just get to its portico. No wonder the temple can be seen from such a distance."

"I would like to make a simple sacrifice of thanksgiving for our safe journey here," Ezekiel says. "But, I did not bring anything to sacrifice."

"Follow me," Simon says, smiling. He leads the men back down the steps into the Treasury Courtyard. They look among the crowd and spot Tullia and Abelia, who then join them. They re-enter the larger outside courtyard on the opposite side from where they had come in from the city.

"The outside Courtyard of the Gentiles is half a *mille* long," Simon says as they walk through it.

"What? What is all this?" Stephen asks. "A market in the holy temple complex?"

"That is what it has turned into," Simon explains. "You can buy whatever you want to sacrifice here. Of course, the priests and merchants split the profits."

"Look around for a booth selling unleavened wafers. There's one," Simon says.

Ezekiel makes his purchase and heads for the gate they had just come through. Stephen and Simon go with him.

"We will wait for you here," Tullia says. "We will just look around among the booths. There may be something we'd like to buy."

An hour later, the men return.

"All set to go home?" Simon asks.

They near the west gate from the street they had entered through earlier.

"What are those piles of rocks for?" Stephen asks.

Simon grows silent.

"Go ahead and tell them. They will need to know eventually," Abelia says.

"They are kept handy in case they want to stone someone."

"To death?" Stephen asks. "What for?"

"For adultery or fornication. For blasphemy. For bringing a Gentile Pagan beyond the Court of the Gentiles where we are now."

"Have you ever seen anyone stoned?" Stephen asks.

"No, and I do not ever want to."

They arrive back at the gate leading to the newest part of Jerusalem and where the fortress and *insulae* are.

"Tullia and I are going to stay at the market to pick up food for tonight and tomorrow," Abelia says. "Do not forget tomorrow is the Sabbath."

The rest of the day, while Simon sleeps, Tullia helps Abelia cook down in the tenants' courtyard where the commune ovens and well are. Ezekiel naps. Stephen leaves to explore the city some more."

Late in the day, Stephen arrives back.

"So, did you see anything more interesting than the temple?" Abelia asks.

"Pools. You have pools all over the city. A pool down from Herod's palace. A pool by the three towers. A pool at the south end of the city."

"That is the Pool of Siloam," Simon says, just having risen

from his sleep. "We've also got the Pool of Israel and the Pool of Bethesda. That one is really fancy with columns all around it. We will go see it the day after the Sabbath."

"Where is your synagogue?" Ezekiel asks, having just awakened from his afternoon nap.

"It's north of here over by the Sheep Gate."

The rest of the evening is spent in happy recollections of their city tour, talking about experiences aboard ships, and entertaining Alexander and Rufus.

Morning of the Sabbath. They talk as they break their fast.

"Which Synagogue do you attend?" Ezekiel asks.

"The Synagogue of the Greek-Speaking Freedmen."

"Why? You were born free."

"There are no Berber-Speaking Synagogues here, and we do not feel comfortable with any of the Jewish-Born Synagogues, or the Greek-Speaking Synagogue where Roman citizens attend."

At least you aren't persecuted for being a Jew here," Stephen says. "You do not have to resort to secret meetings and secret words to identify each other, and whispering your songs and watching what you say in public. It must be so wonderful to be able to worship openly and even be respected for it."

"You are not only respected for it; it is all but mandatory," Abelia says. "Here, anyone who skips going to the synagogue or temple on the Sabbath without a legitimate reason has to go into hiding. He is the one who is persecuted around here."

They arrive at the synagogue and walk up the portico with six columns on one side and six on the other, then through the wide double doors.

Stephen and Ezekiel stop and stare.

"It's so big."

The worship hall has doors all along both sides.

"Do your boys attend synagogue school here?" Tullia asks.

"Alexander does," Abelia replies.

"It's so big in here, I cannot distinguish faces way down in the front," Ezekiel says.

"How many do you have in your congregation?"

"A few hundred, I guess," Simon says.

The men and women split up and find their seats. The boys go with their mother.

The rabbi stands wearing his official blue and white, raises his hands heavenward, and pronounces the benediction.

He seats himself in one of the ornate ivory inlaid chairs on the podium. A choir of thirty Levite men rises and sings four psalms of David.

Prayers.

"Now we shall have the scripture readings for the day," a second rabbi announces, standing behind a table made of acacia wood in the shape of the altar of incense in the temple and with horns on each corner made of gold.

Hear my complaint, Oh God.
Hide me from secret evildoers.
They sharpen their tongue like a sword.
Their words are like deadly arrows.
They have only evil purposes
As they make evil plans in secret.

The leading rabbi rises again. "We are blessed today to have a visiting rabbi with us: Solomus of Cyrene."

30 ~ THE IMPOSSIBLE

"**W**ell, that was a surprise," Stephen says as they squeeze through the crowd and go out onto the street.

"I guess ole Solomus has as much right as anyone to come to Jerusalem and spread his prejudices here," Stephen says. "Do you think he found out we were here?"

"You cannot keep many secrets in Cyrene, Son. Even your secret synagogue meetings were known."

"They were?"

"Tomorrow is the beginning of the Passover rituals," Simon says. "Tomorrow, we select our lamb. Then we have four days to fatten him up for our feast.

"I do not really want to buy one from the priests," he adds. "It seems they shouldn't be making a profit when the people already support them."

"I agree, Ezekiel. Our synagogue is close to the sheep gate. There are sheep pens all up and down the road there. We will come back here tomorrow and choose one of them."

"Where will we keep him until we eat him?" Stephen asks.

"The owner of our *insulae* said the tenants can use the back courtyard to tie them up and feed them. The well is right there for water."

The following day, they go to the stockyards. People are already lined up, pushing and shoving at each other. They wait three hours before having their turn. A lamb is selected. Ezekiel helps pay for it.

"I think I'd like to go back to the temple now," Stephen says. "Maybe I can find Achaius while I am there."

"Good idea, Son. I am tired, so I hope you do not mind if I do not go with you."

When they arrive back at the *insulae,* Stephen just keeps walking. He arrives at the temple using the same west entrance ramp off the street near the high priests' palaces. Crowds bump each other, but smile and go on their way. Once in the Gentile Courtyard behind the temple, he walks around the side toward the gate to the inner Treasury Courtyard.

He hears shouting where the merchants are. A sheep races by. And another. Doves fly overhead. Heavy footsteps. More shouting. More sheep. Now clanging. When he rounds the corner to see what is going on, he sees people on their knees scooping money off the tiles.

A man a little older than him and a little younger than Simon stands in the middle of the ruckus with a whip made of rope. His face is red with anger. He is shouting something about "My Father's House." The temple merchants are shouting back at him.

"Excuse me," he hears. "Excuse me." Priests from the inner courtyard run past Stephen. They shout at the man with the whip.

The man with the whip does not stop, despite efforts of the priests.

"Ha, ha. He showed them."

Stephen looks around to see who said this. The voice is soft but loud enough to be heard above the din.

"Ha, ha. I knew he would someday," the sweet voice says again. "Someone should have thrown them out of the courtyard a long time ago."

Stephen looks around again, then looks down.

A young lady looks up at Stephen and giggles.

Stephen is startled by her large black eyes and the fact that she is more petite even than his mother.

He smiles. "Oh, there you are," he shouts over the commotion.

"I have heard him speak. He's smart," she shouts up at him in her sweet voice. "He has the nerve to say what all of us want to say and do not have the nerve. Now he's done what all of us decent people have wanted to do but never did."

"What did you say?" Stephen shouts as the commotion increases.

"My name is Livia. What's yours?" she squeaks.

"Oh, uh, Stephen," he shouts back. "Is the temple always this exciting?"

"It has been since he appeared a year ago."

"Who is he?"

"Jesus. He's a carpenter, but do not let that fool you," she replies, cupping her hand around her mouth to direct her voice more clearly to Stephen.

She looks around and sees a member of the Sanhedrin headed toward the commotion.

"Uh, oh. Guess I'd better go," she squeaks again.

"Wait!" Stephen calls out. "Where do you live?"

"Not far from here," she shouts while walking backward and bumping into people.

"How can I find you?"

"Ask for my father."

"Who's your father?"

"Nicodemus."

"Who?"

She is gone.

He stretches but still cannot see her. He gives up, turns back and watches just as Jesus throws his rope whip on the tile floor, and marches back out of the temple complex. Stephen edges over to a side wall to get out of the traffic, and watches.

When the excitement dies down, Stephen looks for a Levite or priest not rushing somewhere. He spots one.

"Excuse me, sir. But do you know a man named Nicodemus? He apparently lives near here."

"Of course, he does. Nicodemus is a member of our Sanhedrin. Very dignified and respected. Would you like to meet him? He is right over there wearing the white tunic with a scarlet robe and turban."

Stephen watches Nicodemus. Their eyes meet momentarily. Nicodemus does not smile. "Uh, I do not guess so."

"Hey, were you here for the excitement?"

Stephen turns in the direction of the familiar voice. "Justice! Of course, I was here. Where are the others?"

"Oh, Achaius is down at the market buying a supply of parchments so he can sell them back in Cyrene as souvenirs from Jerusalem. Trophimus is buying food for our dinner tonight, and Secundus is taking a nap."

"Where are you staying?"

"At a hostel not too far from here near the Governor Pilate's palace that he took over from the Herod family."

"Hey, if you do not have any plans yet for Passover, Simon and Abelia want you to join us. We picked up our sheep this morning, and it's a fat one."

"That would be grand. Of course, we will help pay for the food."

"By the way, did you see a girl?" Stephen adds.

"I've seen lots of girls."

"This one is really small. She is smaller even than my mother, and has big black eyes, and hair down to…"

"Ah-ha. So, Stephen has finally been smitten. No, I haven't seen any real small women lately, but I am sure you'll figure out something. See you on Passover. And thanks for the invitation."

Just before dark, Stephen returns home and spends the evening talking about the carpenter that scared away a bunch of merchants with a whip of rope, and actually called the temple his father's house.

The next day, Abelia and Tullia shoo the men out of the apartment. "Cleaning day," Abelia announces. "We've got to search everywhere for any leftover leavened bread. Then we've got to move everything around so we can sweep and scrub all the floors and shelves. Those pesky leaven crumbs could be anywhere."

"So, out," Tullia adds. "Go sightseeing or something. I heard David's tomb is on the far side of the city in the old section. Go sightseeing."

The three men obey and do not show up at the apartment until noon.

They untie their sheep in the *insulae* courtyard and lead it through the streets along with everyone else in the city. They head for the temple, pushing and shoving their way as tens of thousands of others go for the same reason.

Levites are out on the streets trying to control the multitudes of pilgrims. Wagons, carts, and chariots are forbidden today. Only foot traffic is allowed.

"We can only sacrifice our sheep between the ninth and eleventh hour of the day, as you know," Simon says. "You've never seen a hundred thousand people squeeze into the temple to get it done that fast. You are about to, though."

The line starts in the outer Gentile Courtyard. When they reach the Treasury Courtyard, priests are on hand standing next to tables lined up on both sides. Two priests man each table. One kills the sheep, the other collects its blood and hurries it to the Men's and Priests' Courtyard, where it is sprinkled on the altar.

To keep people calm during the process, the Levite Choir stands on the steps of the temple building and sing psalms of David.

At last, the lamb brought by Simon, Ezekiel, and Stephen is slaughtered, its blood duly delivered to the altar. The channel around it catching the blood and sending it to a drain below permeates the air above with the smell of death.

They struggle to find a place in the line leaving the Treasury Courtyard. Eventually, they are out of the temple and back down on the street.

Simon carries the bloody lamb in a cowhide sack over his big, broad shoulders. Once at home, they hang the sheep upside down, take its hide off, and let it finish bleeding. A fire is built, and the sheep is put on a skewer to roast until dark.

At sundown, according to Jewish custom in Palestine, the Day of Passover begins. By now, Achaius, Trophimus, Secundus, and Justus have arrived. The apartment is filled with a mixture of excitement and awe, speaking, and silence.

Simon brings the lamb up from the courtyard easily with no help and sets the cooked carcass on a low table in the middle of the room. It is surrounded by bitter herbs and unleavened bread. Each person is given a goblet of warm red wine.

They are seated. Simon has asked Ezekiel to lead them in the ceremonies. They have their first hand washing, then drink the first cup. Ezekiel quotes God's first promise to the enslaved Israelites. "I will bring you out from your slavery to the Egyptians."

They pass around a bowl of bitter parsley mixed in saltwater and dip their unleavened bread in it. They drink their goblet of wine, and it is refilled.

Everyone looks at the youngest. "Okay, Rufus," Abelia urges. "Ask your question."

"Why, why…"

Rufus looks over at his father. Simon smiles.

"Why is tonight different?" the boy says.

Everyone nods their approval.

Ezekiel talks about Abraham, his descendants suffering in slavery for four hundred years in Egypt, and Moses leading them out to freedom. He explains how the unleavened bread, bitter herbs, and lamb represent what their ancestors went through.

They drink their second cup of warm red wine.

They wash their hands again out of respect for the unleavened bread. Ezekiel breaks it, and the bitter parsley is passed around again for dipping with the bread.

"Ah, that mutton smells good," Justus says.

The family enjoys their meal. Now it is time to be serious

again. The third cup of warm red wine is poured, more promises of God are recited, and they drink it.

The fourth cup of warm red wine is poured, and Ezekiel quotes God's final promise, "I will be your God. Never forget I brought you out of your Egyptian slavery, for I am your Lord."

Ezekiel leads the other ten in a hymn taken from one of David's lengthy psalms.

To your name, give glory....
God has rescued my soul from death....
I shall lift up the cup of salvation....
Precious to the Lord is the death of those he loves
.... His lovingkindness is eternal.

"Why do not you all attend the Greek-Speaking Roman Citizens Synagogue with us next Sabbath?" Trophimus suggests before he and his friends leave.

"It's not too far from your Synagogue. It's over between the Sheep Gate and the Antonia Fortress. You all are Roman citizens—well, except for Simon and Abelia. But you can attend as our guests. Please say you will join us."

While the couples confer with each other in whispers, Stephen speaks for them all. "We would be glad to join you. Oh, and shall I be Stephanus again?"

Sabbath arrives. Everyone at Simon's apartment walks east, and pass the fortress named after Marc Antony. A little way past that is the Pool of Bethesda.

Shortly, they arrive at the synagogue attended by Greek-Speaking Roman citizens. Their building is majestic, their furnishings opulent, and their service magnificent.

Afterward, Secundus urges everyone to take a closer look at the Pool of Bethesda. "It has five marble porticos with pillars."

"They say an angel stirs the water every once in a while, and whoever jumps in the pool first gets healed," Trophimus says. "I personally do not believe that. The pool is fed by a spring, and the spring builds up pressure and a surge of water rises sometimes."

"I am in favor of it," Tullia says.

As they walk, they notice some of the elders and rabbis of the synagogue are going there too.

Drawing closer, they see a crowd larger than usual assembled at the pool.

"Where did all these people come from?" Achaius asks.

Stephen works his way through the crowd and sees him. The carpenter from a province in the far north of the country. He is kneeling by a middle-aged man and talking to him. Stephen pushes his way through the crowd and down the fifteen steps to be able to hear better.

"I haven't been able to walk for thirty-eight years. But, every time the angel comes, someone else beats me into the water."

"Then, Abihu, we are going to have to do something about that," Jesus replies. He stands and stares down at the man. He smiles. "Ready?"

The man on the mat looks up at Jesus. They both stare so intently, Stephen is not sure which one to watch the closest.

"Well?" Jesus says with a grin. "Why do not you stand up?"

"Huh?"

Jesus holds out his hand. The man on the cot reaches up and takes it. Then Jesus lets go and backs off. "Come on, Abihu. Stand up."

The crippled man forms a broad grin and looks down at his legs. Muscles develop. Legs fill out. Strength returns.

Stephen wishes he could get just a little closer. *Surely not. Muscles do not grow back that fast. Legs do not fill out that fast.*

"I think I will just do that," Abihu mumbles from his mat. He props his knees up, pushes with his arms, and jumps up.

"Ha, ha!" Abihu shouts.

Stephen gasps. *No. This cannot be. I am imagining it. What's going on?*

"I did it!"

Abihu stares at Jesus. "I did it." He looks around him at the others. "I did it." He looks over at Stephen. "I did it."

Stephen looks back over at Jesus. Jesus has disappeared. He looks over at Abihu and sees him pick up his mat and roll it up.

"Well, everyone," he says to the other disabled ones. "I have enjoyed knowing you. But now I am going to go over to the temple and inform the priests so they'll declare me clean, and I will be able to worship with them again. Won't they be surprised?"

"Hey, you. Stop!"

The rabbi from the Greek-Speaking Roman-Citizen Synagogue stands at the top of the steps. "Stop carrying your mat. You are not allowed to work on the Sabbath."

Abihu squints at the rabbi. "I am not working."

"Oh, but you are."

"I was healed. I am just going to the temple, so the priests will declare me clean, and I can worship there."

"First of all," the rabbi declares, "you were not healed. Second, you are a sinner. How dare you work on the Sabbath."

Abihu looks around and catches the eye of Stephen.

"Go ahead," Stephen urges. "Do not let them stop you. Go to the temple."

The crowd steps aside to let Abihu up the steps of the pool and over to the temple.

Stephen follows along with many others who had followed Jesus that day just to see what will happen next.

Though many who came for the Passover have already left for home, there are still plenty of pilgrims to dodge on the street. Stephen follows as close as he can despite the crowds.

He watches at a distance as the man leaps and dances through the expansive Gentile Courtyard through the Song Gate up the steps to the Treasury Courtyard, more leaping, then through the Nicanor Gate and more steps up to the Courtyard of the Men. He watches as Abihu approaches the priests. They do not smile. There is a lot of pointing, and finally, Abihu turns away, still clinging to his pallet. He does not smile.

Stephen turns and spots Jesus walking toward Abihu. They are lost in the mob of worshippers, so Stephen heads for Simon's apartment.

"Where have you been, Stephen?" Ezekiel asks. "Your mother and I have been worried about you."

Stephen goes to a corner and sits on one of the cushions. He puts his face in his hands.

"What's wrong, Son? What has happened?"

Stephen looks up. His eyes are half glazed. His voice is almost inaudible.

"I have seen with my own eyes."

"Seen what?" Tullia asks, her brows furrowed over worried eyes. "Seen what?"

"He did the impossible. He made a man with atrophied legs fill out, stand up and walk."

"Who? What?"

"I have seen a miracle. I have seen the impossible become possible."

Quiet. Everyone in the room waits.

Simon and Abelia cling to their sons when they want to pounce on Stephen's lap and play.

Stephen presses his lips together and looks around, though he sees nothing. He looks up, takes a deep quick breath, and looks back at everyone.

"I think he is here."

"Who is here?" Ezekiel asks, trying to be patient.

"Him. The one we have looked for many thousands of years. Him. The Deliverer. The Messiah. I think he has come. At last. I think he is here."

31 ~ HEARTS

"**S**on, we're going to have to think about returning to Cyrene. You have a business to run, and Mother and I need to sleep in our own bed and sit around our own courtyard."

"I know, Father. But can we stay just a few more days? I want to go over to the temple to see if the carpenter is still here. I need to talk to him."

"Where does he live? I want to talk to him before he goes home."

"Up north in the province of Galilee."

"Oh. Well, I am really tired, Son. But your reason is valid. Take two more days."

"Three?"

"If it is warranted, three."

Morning. Stephen breaks his fast as quickly as possible while being polite to their hosts. He skips down the three flights to the street.

Is the carpenter the one you have sent, Jehovah God? Is he the one? I wish I could talk to someone else who has seen him perform miracles—if, indeed, he has performed others. And heard what he has to say. Is he political? Is he pious? He seems to have two sides—powerful and peaceful.

Stephen arrives at the long ramp leading up to the temple on Mount Moriah. No bumping and shoving today. No jostling and needing to say excuse me over and over. Most people have left Jerusalem and headed for home. Things are going back to normal.

Now within the walls of the complex that is the size of a small city, he walks through the Court of the Gentiles. He wanders over to where the merchants usually are. *Not as many today. They'll all probably be back once he leaves town.*

He sees a bench and sits a while. Not sure why. Not sure

what he expects to do at the temple today. But hoping the carpenter will return so he can talk to him. He will know of his arrival easily enough. Crowds. Always crowds following him around asking questions, listening, watching. *I hope he doesn't have a big crowd around him.*

He stands and ambles over to the gate up to the Treasury Courtyard. He walks up the eight steps. *Not as many people today. The Levite Choir is singing, though. I guess they sing every day.*

He notices benches under the north and south columned porticos situated between each bronze trumpet-shaped coin collection container. He wanders over to one and sits. *I hope I remember everything I was going to ask him.*

A woman with three children hanging on to her skirt wander over and deposit three coins in one of the containers. Stephen smiles when the coins make a tinkling sound against the bronze on its way down from the neck to the belly of the container. *I wonder what it sounds like when lots of big coins are deposited in them.*

Stephen stands and walks around the almost-empty courtyard. He walks back to the immense Gentile Courtyard that is half a *mille* long and circles the complex. *Sure hope he comes.* He watches the younger Levites sweep up after the onslaught of multitudes and tries to count them all.

He shuffles back up the eight steps to the Treasury Courtyard, kicks a loose piece of floor tile, wanders up the ten steps into the Men's Courtyard, watches the Levites clean up under the altar, and returns to the Treasury Courtyard.

He sits back on his bench. *I hope I do not miss him.*

After a while, another man comes in and sits on a bench next to Stephen. He is wearing a gold tunic and green robe, but that is all Stephen notices. They pay no attention to each other. They sit in silence. *Is he waiting for the carpenter's appearance too?*

"When he was here last year," the stranger growls, "he sat on one of these benches and praised a woman for giving two minuscule mites to the treasury."

Stephen, out of politeness, tries not to listen.

"While she was doing that, we were all over in our fancy chamber, dividing up millions of shekels to build bigger synagogues, expand our territories, decorate the temple more, wear finer clothing."

Stephen glances in the man's direction and sees there is no

one with him.

"Uh, sir," Stephen says in a low voice, unsure he should be saying anything, "are you talking about the carpenter?"

The stranger looks toward Stephen. "I guess I am."

"You have heard him speak? I only saw him perform a miracle."

"Yes, I have spoken to him. But I keep his words to myself. For now, maybe it's better that way."

"Father! There you are."

Stephen looks in the direction of the voice. "Livia?"

"Well, hello there," the sweet voice says, batting the lashes over her big black diamond eyes. "Stephen, is it? I see you have met my father."

Stephen jerks his head back and stares at Livia, then the stranger. "This is your father?"

"Yes, Nicodemus."

"Oh, I am sorry, sir. I presumed too much to speak to a member of the Sanhedrin."

"That is quite all right, son," the man says in his growly voice. "Daughter, I seem to have forgotten something in my *officium.* Wait for me here."

Rabbi Nicodemus climbs the ten steps up to the Men's Courtyard. Stephen assumes he will also be climbing the eleven steps up to the temple proper.

Livia sits on her father's bench and pumps her foot. She shifts and wags her head back and forth. Stephen wonders if her head is keeping the tempo to some song she is singing.

"Have you been..." they say at the same time.

"Pardon me," Stephen says. "I was rude to interrupt." He sneaks another sideways peek at Livia.

"Oh, that is okay. Well, what I was going to say is, 'Have you been able to hear the carpenter speak?'."

"Uh, no, I haven't. Have you?"

She turns her petite frame sideways on the bench. She hugs herself and looks up at the sky. "Oh, yes. I have heard him speak. He is like an angel."

"How do you know what an angel sounds like? Did you ever hear one?"

She puts her hands on her hips. "Well, no. But that is what an angel sounds like anyway, and you cannot prove me wrong."

Stephen smiles. "Well, tell me what this angel man talks about."

"He says we have to love our enemies and even pray for

them. He says we are the light of the world and have to shine with good works all the time and be nice to everyone. He says…"

"Whoa. Wait a moment. He says we have to talk about God in public so our light will shine?"

"Well, there are private things he says we should do too. He says we have to pray in secret and give alms in secret and stuff like that."

"Now, that part I agree with. I am rather a private person, myself."

"Do not tell me you are like my father?"

"How?"

"He is a private person too."

Livia stands and steps over to Stephen's bench. She pushes him over to make room for herself and plops down. She turns and whispers in his ear.

"Do not tell anyone I told you, but my father believes Jesus is the Messiah. He just doesn't say so in public so he can keep his job. He says he needs to stay in the Sanhedrin to counter the extremism and ego of the high priest."

"Which one?" Stephen asks with a slight smile.

"Both of them. Of course."

"Do you think he will be here later today?"

"My father? Probably."

"Not your father. The carpenter. Jesus."

"Oh. No, he's gone. He has left the city and gone back up north."

"Oh."

They sit in silence and look around. Stephen watches an ant explore his foot.

"Well, I agree with your father. In order to do the most good, we must keep our beliefs secret and wait for just the right time to reveal them. Kind of like Queen Esther."

"Kind of like who?"

"You know. She kept her beliefs as a Jew secret until the right time. Then, when she did reveal her beliefs, it saved thousands of Jewish lives. I call it the Esther Quest."

Livia laughs her sweet laugh. Stephen's heart skips a beat when she does.

"So, have you been on Esther's Quest?"

"I did for about a year. We met in secret. Our synagogue was a room in an *insulae*. We had a secret word, so, as we grew, we could find each other—Sesom, which is Moses said backward.

We would write the Ten Commandments on pieces of parchment, then at night, go different places in the city to hide them so they'd be discovered the next day. We taught a lot of pagan Gentiles that way so they would be less prejudiced toward us."

"Did it work?"

"Well, it did for a while. But eventually, we had to disband. A spy managed to infiltrate, and...well, you do not want to hear that boring stuff. So, what do you do when you can do anything you want?"

"Me? Well, I decorate mezuzahs for people's doorposts. And I write scriptures on tiny pieces of papyrus to put inside."

"Oh? My father was a scribe. Still is, I guess. He ran a scribe school in Antioch and a while in Cyrene."

Livia stands and twirls in a circle. "And what do you do?"

"I am a locksmith. I make locks and door pulls and hinges mostly. Sometimes I make a chest with a lock on it. I have my own booth at the market. And..."

"Are you ready?" The voice booms.

Stephen stands, his hands to his side, his eyes straight ahead. "I am sorry, sir. I did not touch your daughter. We started talking about the carpenter, and..."

"Well, we have to be going on home now. Her mother will have our supper ready by the time we arrive."

Nicodemus does not smile. "Come along, Daughter."

Stephen watches as they leave. When they reach the steps of the Song Gate leading down to the Courtyard of the Gentiles, she calls over her shoulder.

"My father wants me to help him with some writing tomorrow."

They disappear down the steps. Stephen watches the empty gateway, wags his head back and forth as he had seen Livia do, looks up at the late-afternoon sky, and smiles.

He walks over to the same stairs, skips down them, and trots toward the outside ramp. Once down on the street, he walks a few paces, jumps in the air, walks a few more paces, and jumps in the air again.

Stephen does not know how long it takes him to arrive at Simon's *insulae* but thinks he has flown. He takes three steps at a time going up to the apartment, opens the door, and grins at everyone.

"Did you see him?" Simon asks.

"Uh, no. But I talked to a couple of people who have spoken to him. What they said about him was good. I need to return tomorrow. I do not think we were through talking."

"You sure do look like a man who has discovered a treasure," Tullia says.

"I have that, Mother. Indeed, I have discovered a treasure."

The following morning, Stephen takes a little longer to wash, puts on a clean tunic, adds a little cucumber mixture under his arms, works a little scented oil into his hair, and cleans his fingernails.

"What's going on with that boy?" Simon asks. "I think there is more going on over there than just the carpenter."

Stephen rushes to the temple and sees that she is already there and sitting on her father's bench.

"Did you come in the dark?" he asks, sitting on his own bench.

"Yes. Why not? No one is going to hurt me. I trust everyone."

"Well, you shouldn't."

She puts her hands on her hips. "Well, I am going to. So, there."

"I forbid it," he declares.

"You what? You're not my father. And you're certainly not my husband. Besides, my husband is going to let me do anything I want. By the way, what's that smell?"

"Oh, nothing," Stephen replies.

"Yes, it is. Yes, it is." She moves over to Stephen's bench and sniffs. "You're as bad as my father."

"What do you mean? I am nothing like your father."

"Oh, but you are more like my father than you think. He loves fancy clothes and spiced oils. I guess you noticed."

"Not really."

"Now, my mother and I. We like plain and simple. We're too busy with, well, life to worry about such menial things."

Silence. She moves back to her bench.

She pumps her feet.

"Stop that. It's making me nervous."

"Oh, you are sooo much like my father," she says, rolling her eyes heavenward.

Silence.

"Hey, did not you say your father was a scribe?" she asks. "Would you like to see my father's *officium*? He has lots of scrolls."

Stephen smiles. "Well, uh...I cannot. Not without your father being present. It wouldn't be proper."

"Do not worry. He's been there since dawn. We came together."

"Oh. Well then. I guess it would be okay."

"Let me go first. We do not want to give those stuffy priests something to gossip about. Walk all the way around the Courtyard of the Gentiles. By then, it should be decent for you to go up. Oh, and he is in the first building left of the temple and upstairs."

Not waiting for a reply, Livia hurries toward the Nicanor Gate and steps up to the Courtyard of the Men.

"You cannot go up there," Stephen calls out.

"Watch me." She laughs that sweet laugh, and his heart skips another beat.

He turns and jumps down the steps to the large Courtyard of the Gentiles and runs. He runs down the south end, turns and runs down the west end, then the north and, and finally back to the east end.

Out of breath, he sits on his bench in the Treasury Courtyard to ease it back to normal. *Mustn't look anxious.*

He stands, runs his hand over his hair, waves his hand under his arms, and straightens his tunic. He walks with sure steps toward the Men's Courtyard. At the top, he turns left and looks for the building Livia had told him about.

He walks around to the entrance, climbs the steps to the second floor, and walks down a long corridor with columns on both sides and marble urns between each column. He notices doors on each side and wonders which one belongs to Rabbi Nicodemus.

He stops in the middle of the corridor and sings one of David's psalms. With great robust.

Why do you stand afar off?
Why do you hide yourself
in times of trouble?

He pauses to listen. No doors are opening.

Why do you stand afar off?
Why do you hide yourself
in times of trouble?

"Down here," Livia calls out. "You are embarrassing my father."

Stephen turns and follows Livia's sweet voice into her

father's *officium.* He touches the alabaster urn. He stares at the multi-design carpet. He lifts his eyes toward the gold-plated wick lamps hanging from the ceiling.

"Father, Stephen said he would like to look at some of your ancient scrolls of the Torah. Did not you, Stephen?"

Stephen clears his throat. "Yes, sir. I surely would like to see them."

Nicodemus pulls one out of a cabinet of cubicles made of acacia wood and inlaid with opals. Livia directs him to another and larger table in her father's *officium.*

Stephen sees a bench at the table and seats himself. With the utmost care, he rolls through it.

"Hey, have you forgotten me?" Livia says. "What is more important? That old scroll or me?"

Stephen looks up at her, smiles, and looks toward her father.

"Rabbi, sir, these are some of the most superb examples of writing I have ever seen. On the market, they would bring almost as much or more as the scrolls of my grandfather, written out by my father."

"Your father's father had writings?" Nicodemus growls, looking up.

"No, my mother's father. He was the tutor of Augustus Caesar—Athenodorus."

Nicodemus sets down the scroll he has been reading and turns toward Stephen.

"You are Athenodorus' grandson? I have heard of him. I have never read his writings, but he was a good stoic with good moral standards. I approved of him."

Stephen does not reply.

"Well, I have a lot of things to do," Nicodemus says. "You will have to excuse me."

"Let us go, Stephen. He's busy again."

The young people go out into the corridor and Livia squeals.

"What's wrong?" Stephen asks.

"He likes you!"

"He does?" Stephen's eyes cross momentarily, then straighten themselves out. Without saying more, he turns to leave.

Stephen is not sure how he arrives back at Simon's apartment.

He knocks on the door, and Simon answers it. "Why are

you knocking? This is your home as long as you are here."

"It is?" Stephen says to the air.

"It is almost time to eat," Ezekiel says. "So, did you see him? The carpenter? What did he have to say? Do you still think he might be the Messiah?"

"Huh?" Stephen responds.

"Come, Son," Tullia says. "After dinner, I think the three of us ought to have a talk. Besides, we are probably going to leave tomorrow."

"You cannot do that," Stephen barks at both parents. He stops, surprised by his rash response. "Oh, I did not mean for it to come out like that."

"We shall talk later," Tullia says.

The meal is made up of bread and raisin sauce dip, cheese, figs, and olives. Stephen takes a few bites of each, then stares at the rest of the food.

A banging at the door.

Simon looks at Abelia in shock. He looks over at Stephen. "What did you do while you were gone?"

"Nothing. I was at the temple all day."

"The temple has its own guards on call," Simon says.

More banging.

Simon takes a deep breath and opens the door. There, standing before him is Nicodemus, rabbi and member of the Judaic Sanhedrin.

32 ~ GOODBYES

"**I**s this the residence of the young man, Stephen of Cyrene?" the voice growls.

"Uh, yes, sir," Ezekiel says, joining Simon at the door. "Whatever he has done, I will repay you double."

"No need. He has done nothing. Which one of you is Stephen's father?"

"I am afraid it is I," Ezekiel responds.

"And his mother?"

Tullia steps forward and takes her husband's arm. Her voice trembles. "I am his mother."

"May I come in?"

"Oh, of course," Simon says, stepping back and motioning for Abelia to find a bench for him to sit on.

Nicodemus places his bulky frame on the bench and stares at Ezekiel and Tullia.

"Oh, uh, Simon, I think we need to grab the boys and take a walk," Abelia says.

Simon ducks out the door, tipping his head as always to avoid hitting the top frame. The door shuts. Nicodemus takes a deep breath, stands, takes a few steps toward the other side of the room, and turns.

"I may as well come out with it. My daughter would like to marry your son."

Tullia sucks in her breath. Ezekiel gasps. Stephen stifles a grin.

"Pardon me. I have not introduced myself. I am Nicodemus..."

"Sir, I have told them about you," Stephen says. "Uh, and all about your work. They admire..."

"As I was saying, my daughter would like to marry your son."

He seats himself back on the bench. "There are some things that need to be worked out. First, she is seventeen years old. Is that satisfactory with you?"

"Uh," Ezekiel responds. "Uh, fine."

"Second, she is a stubborn child with a mind of her own. She is educated like me, but I fear the resemblances to her father end there. She is like her mother—carefree and innocent. She fears no one because she does not understand what there is to fear. Therefore, she requires protection."

Stephen prays as he listens to the miracle before him. *My wife? Livia is going to be my wife? Thank you, Jehovah God.*

Without pausing, Nicodemus goes on. "Third and last, you live too far away. Jerusalem is the hub of the greatest and only true religion in the world. She cannot be exposed to Pagan Gentiles. It is too dangerous." He pauses.

"She cannot be subjected to persecution in any form. She cannot risk her life living there the way you are doing. And my grandchildren will not be raised by a widowed mother. She cannot marry Stephen. That is my decision."

Nicodemus rises, steps to the door, opens it, and leaves. They can hear his heavy footsteps going down all three flights of stairs.

Ezekiel, Tullia and Stephen sit where they are dumbfounded by what nearly happened, and stupefied that it did not happen.

They stare at each other, brows wrinkled, eyes squinted, trying to grasp what had just almost transpired.

Stephen stands. He paces. "Father, I do not know what to say."

"Then I shall say it," Ezekiel responds. "We leave Jerusalem tomorrow."

"Will I have time to return to the temple and see her one last time?"

"No."

They hear voices. The door opens.

"Well?" Simon says with a broad smile, "What did he want? It must have been important for him to come all the way here at night to a Gentile neighborhood."

"Yes," Abelia says, setting Rufus down to play. "Tell us what happened. We want to hear it all."

"Well, it was about Stephen."

"So, was it good or bad?"

"It started out good. A least that is the way Stephen saw it. Then it ended bad. But it was all for the better."

"What was?"

Stephen stops pacing. "His daughter wants to become my wife."

"That is wonderful. So, what was so ba..." Abelia pauses. "He said no."

"Yes, he said no. He thinks it would be too dangerous for her to live in Cyrene with all the Pagan Gentiles."

"Well, Cyrene does have its challenges," Simon says, sitting down with Alexander, who has fallen asleep on his bulky Berber shoulder.

"We're leaving tomorrow," Ezekiel says. "Passover is done with, and we are glad we came."

"And we are most grateful for your hospitality," Tullia adds. "Now, I must gather up our things to be ready at dawn."

Stephen does not sleep that night. Or, at least he thinks he does not.

Dawn comes, and the three head out toward the Flower Gate at the three towers next to Herod's palace now taken over by Roman Governor Pilate.

Stephen carries the wicker chest on his strong back. Tulia carries miscellaneous supplies in her handbasket, and Ezekiel carries the food in his large basket.

On the second day at noon, they arrive at Joppa.

"Dear, did you arrange for return passage in Jerusalem?" Tullia asks.

"No," Ezekiel replies, "Everyone said there are always a lot of ships at nearby seaports, ready to take passengers home after the Passover."

"Stephen, you are younger and have more energy than us," Ezekiel continues. "Take my money pouch and find us passage home."

Stephen takes the money but says nothing. He sets down his mother's wicker chest, and walks along the pier, stopping at each ship. On his third try, he succeeds. He walks back to his parents, who are sitting on a bench, resting and watching him.

"Well, I found us a ship. The *Ortus*. They're leaving when the sun is highest."

He sighs and looks off in the direction of Jerusalem.

"I think this is the quietest we have ever seen our son,"

Tullia says.

"Ha. We'd better take advantage of it," Ezekiel says. "Someday, he will get over it."

"I will never get over it," he says. He sits on the ground next to them, raises his knees, and rests his head on them. The dreaded hours pass. Dreaded because each one takes him farther from his Livia.

They hear bells from the *Ortus*. "I guess that is our signal," Ezekiel says, standing. "Now, Son, when we get on board, be sure to store your mother's chest somewhere safe."

Stephen says nothing. They board the ship and find places out of the way of the crew where Ezekiel and Tullia can stand and watch the ship pull away from shore. Stephen descends below deck with his mother's chest and stays there.

Sails hoisted, anchor weighed, dowsers unwound from pilings. Bells now ring to warn other ships.

Oh, Jehovah God. How can I live without her? Stephen sits alone in his darkness. When other passengers come to the orlop deck, he wishes they would disappear. Disappear like his Livia. Disappear like his world. Like his very life.

Sometimes Tullia goes below and gives him his portion of their food. "Come, Son. You must eat. When we arrive home, you will have a lot of catching up to do so you do not lose your customers."

The evening of the second day, they dock in Pelussium. Next is Alexandria, then Paraetonium.

They are at sea on the Sabbath. Ezekiel finds the other Jews and organizes an hour together to pray a little, chant a little, and recite the Torah and Prophets a little. They meet below in a corner of the orlop deck where everyone takes his own torch. Ezekiel insists Stephen join them. He does, but he does not speak.

"We have been at sea nearly a week," Tullia tells Stephen after the service. "We will be home in two days. Then it's life back to normal. I am glad we went but happy to be home again too."

"You are right, woman," Ezekiel says. "As always. You are right. And you, young man," he says, turning to Stephen, "you need to do something with your demeanor. When we dock in Apollonia, I want a smile on your face for everyone you meet, whether or not you know them."

Stephen's parents return above board and leave him in his darkness a little longer. He sighs. *Okay, I will smile again, but I will never forget her.*

Clanging of bells again. Two more days have passed, and

the ship's sails are being hauled in. He hears heavy feet rushing around above board. Stephen takes a deep breath, picks up his mother's wicker chest, and takes it up to the main deck.

As they walk down the gangplank, the chest carried on Stephen's back, Ezekiel mutters, "Smile, Son. Smile." So, Stephen smiles.

Men with carts line the dock for the debarking passengers' convenience.

"We will take one, sir," Ezekiel says.

Within half an hour, they are back in Cyrene. The cart takes them through the North Gate and market.

"Hey, isn't that Stephen? Welcome back, Stephen. Did you have a good time?"

"Answer them, Stephen," Ezekiel warns. "You're your head up. And smile."

They pass the Jewish-born Freedmen Synagogue on their right and the *hospitium* on their left. They pass the bathhouses and the amphitheater. The cart stops in front of their gate.

They go inside, look around for assurance everything is as they had left it, and set down their baskets. Stephen sits.

"You know what you have to do, Son. Now go do it,"

Stephen looks at his father. "Thank you for your patience. I will be okay now."

He walks back out the gate and toward the market. Out of habit, he walks down to the shop he had shared with Ovidius. He stops and stares. He looks around. The shutters along the front counter are still closed. He tries the back door, but it is locked. He looks around and calls, "Ovidius, are you in there?"

No answer. *Maybe he went on a vacation. Or he's homesick.*

Stephen walks back to the main aisle and works his way down to the last one, the Jewish row.

"Hey, Stephen is back." It is potter Joshua.

"Hey, there, Stephen," Ebron says from his bakery booth.

"So how was Jerusalem?" butcher Eben asks.

"Yeah, how was it?" Midyan the tanner asks.

Stephen stands in front of his booth, stares, and smiles.

"I thought you fellows were all mad at me."

"We were," Joshua says. "But we have better things to do than that, so we're over it."

"Have many customers come while I was gone?"

"Some," Eben says. "But I think a lot of people knew you were gone to Jerusalem."

Stephen walks to the back door to his booth, now converted into a shop to protect his equipment, and goes inside. Out on the street, the men watch as he opens the shutters to his front counter.

"I guess there is enough daylight left that I can fire up my forge and get a little work done."

"Uh, Stephen, there is something you need to know," Joshua says.

"Bad things have been happening to the metal workers," Midyan says.

"Like what?"

"You know Ovidius, who you used to work with?"

"Yeah. I noticed his shop is locked up."

"He caught fire and burned to death."

"He what?" Stephen stops what he is doing and stares at Midyan. "How?"

"He was at the temple to Apollo, making an offering of raisin cakes. Suddenly he burst out in flames. At least that is what High Priest Dialis says happened. All we know is that he burned up."

"Did he get too close to the altar fires?"

"No. He was just offering raisin cakes. There were no altar fires."

"Just this morning," Eben says, "it almost happened again. This time to Nikon, the brass smith. Only this time, he was at the temple to Zeus-Amun Re, offering a basket of corn. No altar fires around. Just him. Luckily, there was holy water nearby, and he doused the front of his tunic. Still, he's injured pretty bad."

"I did not know that," Ebron says to his friend.

"Just happened this morning," Eben says.

"Well, you had better be careful. The pagans are claiming the gods are after you men who formed the metalsmithing guild."

"But we disbanded," Stephen says.

"They claim Apollo is the brother of Vulcan, and Zeus is his father, and they're taking revenge on behalf of Vulcan. We do not believe it, of course."

"But why?"

"Because Vulcan is the god of fire they claim, and only priests of Vulcan can form metalsmith guilds."

"How ridiculous," Stephen says. "I am going to see Nikon right now."

The shutters back in place and the door relocked, Stephen heads out in the direction of Nikon's house.

When he arrives, his wife answers the gate.

"Do not you come in here," she objects when she sees who it is. "You have caused enough trouble."

"Sweetheart," Stephen hears from the other end of the courtyard. "If it's Stephen…let him in."

The gate is opened wider, and Stephen rushes in.

"Oh, Nikon. What happened? Where are you burned? You must be in terrible pain. It's all my fault."

"Yes, I am in pain. No, you are…not at fault. We decided together…to create the metalsmithing guild. But it was…too late. By the time we disbanded, the anger…of the god Vulcan was hot."

Stephen seats himself. "What can I do?"

"You can stay away from…Apollo and Zeus. That is what. Ovidius and I thought…we were doing the right thing."

Nikon takes a deep breath and lets it out, trembling. "We thought…we thought he would be pleased …ughhh…with us and forgive us."

"Those gods are not causing you to break out in flames. They do not exist."

"Stop that, Stephen, …ugh. Just stop. Do you want…ughhh…to make them madder…ughhh…than they already are?"

"I will prove to everyone they do not exist."

"No one can do that. You'll…break out…in flames yourself if you try it. Ughhh. Do not try it." Nikon throws his head back.

"Ahhhh. I am begging you, Steph…"

"Get out. Get out of my house!"

Stephen turns and sees Nikon's wife standing in the doorway.

"Look what you have done. Isn't he in enough pain? Haven't you done enough? Leave!"

Stephen looks back at Nikon and sees he is no longer conscious. He stands and looks at his wife. "I am sor…"

"Get out!"

Rushing out of the room, across the courtyard, and out to the street, Stephen lays his forehead on a wall, heaves, and throws up. He turns to face the street, tears in his eyes. "Jehovah God. Help me prove it. Help me figure out a way."

Realizing it is nearly dark, Stephen returns home.

"Son, you've got to get over it," Ezekiel says when he sees the agony on Stephen's face.

"It's not that, Father. Ovidius suddenly burst out in flames while sacrificing food to the god Apollos, and the same thing happened to Nikon offering food to the god Zeus. The flames just came out of their bodies."

"What's going on?" Tullia asks, stepping over from the kitchen end of the courtyard. "Who got burned to death?"

"Ovidius and Nikon almost did. Nikon says Zeus is the father of Vulcan, and Apollo is his brother, and they are seeking vengeance because only priests of Vulcan can form metalsmithing guilds. I've got to prove those gods do not exist."

"No. You've got to stay out of it," Tullia says. "Look what the high priests of Apollo and Zeus did to you before we left for Jerusalem. Stay out of it."

"But the same thing may happen to me."

"Nonsense. They just got too close to the fire."

"They claim there was no fire on the altar."

Ezekiel leans forward, elbows on his knees. "You know, maybe Stephen is right. You must take the Daniel approach. Declare your beliefs openly. No more hiding. This will be your Daniel Quest.

"It happened when they both were at the temples offering food, right?" Ezekiel continues. "Do you know what my father would tell you to do? He would tell you to go to those temple altars and figure out their secrets."

"Well, if I enter those temples to prove those gods do not exist, surely the only true God will forgive me. I will go tomorrow morning. Tomorrow I shall be a Daniel. He worshipped Jehovah openly, and he was made second to the king."

Stephen stands, squints, then squats in a corner to think alone.

33 ~ THE DANIEL QUEST

"When you are through breaking your fast, I have put some honey cakes in a bowl and some corn in another for offerings to their so-called gods. They are in this basket. Take it with you," Tullia says.

"When you arrive, observe everything, but do not touch anything," she continues. "Take slow steps. Look around as you do. If a priest tells you how to make your offering and he says anything suspicious, do not do it. Remember, do not touch anything."

"Maybe I should go to my shop first and get my leather apron just in case. Nikon said the fire started in his lap."

"That may make them suspicious. You are smarter than them. You know fire. You know how to make it different levels of heat, depending on what you want to do with your iron. You know what kind of fuel makes your iron turn orange, yellow, white. You know that, Stephen. But do not stay long. Go in, avoid talking to anyone, make your offering without touching anything but observe everything. Then leave."

Stephen steps over and picks up the basket.

"Come right back home afterward, so we know you are safe," Ezekiel says. "Then we will talk about what you discovered. I wish my father were here. He could help you understand the fire."

"My dear husband, by now our son knows as much or more about fire. Trust him. I do."

"Well, I want you to have this. It is my father's ring. He said it's forever roundness is a reminder of God's forever protection. Take it."

Stephen takes the ring, leaves, and heads back to the

market where his shop is but does not stop there. He continues on to the Sanctuary of Apollo and its temple.

He enters, looks around for the alter. He sees a large one, a medium one, and a large one. The large one has fire in it. The smaller one smells of incense and has a candle next to it. He looks at the floor for anything that could be tripped over, the ceiling for anything that could be dropped down onto him, the walls for anything that could be pushed out from it. He walks toward the middle-sized altar.

"May I help you?" a priest says.

Oh, no. I forgot about being recognized. Maybe this priest wasn't here that day. Stephen keeps walking as though he had not heard the priest.

"Oh, it's you. May I assume you have come to ask Apollo to intercede for you with his brother. It's about time. Well, just step up to that alter and lay down your sacrifice."

Stephen does not acknowledge the priest. He steps forward a little at a time. Watching for anything suspicious. Listening for anything suspicious.

He reaches the altar and lays his bowl on the edge.

"No, no, no. That is not the way it is done. You must place your sacrifice in the middle of the altar. You must lean over as far as is needed to place it in the middle of the altar. Here, let me show you."

The priest walks toward Stephen, carrying a small golden lamp.

As soon as Stephen spots it, he steps back. The priest draws closer. Stephen leaves his bowl of honey cakes on the edge of the alter and rushes outside.

"Come back! I am not through with you yet. You must make your offering, or Vulcan will take his wrath out on you. Come back!"

Stephen runs out of the sanctuary, picks up the basket with the other offering in it, then slows his pace.

Did I learn anything? Should I just go on home now? Well, while I am at it, I may as well go to the temple to Zeus. How I hate this. How I hate everything they stand for. How I hate their priests.

Stephen stops in the middle of the street. *Love my enemies? Did the carpenter really say I must love my enemies? How can I love the enemies of God? What did he mean to love my enemies?*

Stephen continues on and sees his house ahead on the left. He keeps walking and passes the Greek-Speaking Synagogue, made up primarily of Roman citizens. He passes that on his right, then starts up the hill. Ahead of him is the grand temple to Zeus, even larger than the Pantheon.

To his right is the hippodrome for races dedicated to the glory of Zeus. He walks up to the steps into the grand structure. *Jehovah God, forgive me.* He takes the first step. It is higher than he had expected. He makes his way closer and closer to the top and the magnificent statue of Zeus on his throne as father of gods, father of Vulcan.

He enters and is astonished at the size of the statue. *How can anything carved be that large?* He stops and looks both ways, behind him, and in front of him. Now the walk.

He takes his bowl out of his basket and sets it down at the entryway as he had done at Apollo's temple. He starts forward, once again observing the floor, the ceiling, the walls. A hand span at a time he walks. Watching. Listening. Smelling. Straining his entire being to encounter the lies of Zeus and Apollo and Vulcan.

"Oh, there you are," he hears.

High Priest Diokles strides into the temple from the other direction. "Zeus told me you were coming. He tells me everything."

Once again, Stephen keeps walking without acknowledging the other man's presence. Eyes straight ahead. Analyzing what he sees.

Once again, he sees three altars—one large with fire on it, one small with incense and a candle near it, and one middle-sized. He walks toward that one.

"Good choice," High Priest Diokles says. "You wouldn't want to get close to either fire. Fire is dangerous. You should know that. It is not wise to toy with what and who you do not understand."

Stephen continues in silence until he reaches the altar.

"I see you brought a peacemaking sacrifice. That is wise of you. You must appease the gods. No, no, no. Do not set it there. You must not set it on the edge of the altar. You must set it in the middle. Lean over as far as you have to in order to get it in the middle."

Stephen realizes the high priest is approaching. His hands are cupped over something.

"Come now, get that offering way over in the middle of the altar."

Alarms ring in Stephen's head. He drops the bowl of corn and rushes out of the temple, down the steps, down the hill and home.

He knocks on the gate and Ezekiel opens it for him. "Come in. Sit. Catch your breath. Did they follow you? Are you still in danger?"

Tullia joins them. "Here is a cup of water. Now tell us what you saw and what happened. Anything suspicious."

"I think I know," Stephen whispers between gulps of water.

"Well?"

"I have to explain it when everyone is present."

"Everyone who?"

"All the merchants in the North Market for one."

"You're not going to invite the pagan priests, are you?" Ezekiel warns. "You're already in trouble with them. They are dangerous."

"Believe me, I know how dangerous they are. The high priests of the city practically rule the city. Even the governor dares not go against them. So, I guess I won't invite them."

"So, when are you going to explain everything?" Ezekiel asks. "Can you convince people not to believe in these gods without getting yourself into trouble again?"

"Yes. First, here is your eternal-protection-of-God-ring back. I will go over to the market now and tell everyone. I will make my explanation tomorrow during the time of their mid-day respite."

The following morning, Stephen returns to the market and opens his shop. There is a vacant field on the other side of the Jewish row in the back of the market. A crowd begins to assemble in mid-morning.

They watch as Stephen buys a large bull hide from Midyan, the tanner, that still has the legs on it. He fills it with sand and sets it near a large boulder. He decorates the boulder to resemble an altar. He takes over a bowl of corn for his sacrifice.

When he decides it is the middle of everyone's break, he stands next to the stuffed bull. He notices his parents in the crowd and smiles at them. Ezekiel nods his head, and Tullia winks.

"Now, ladies and gentlemen, I am going to demonstrate to you that our friends were not stricken by Vulcan or Apollo or Zeus or any other god and that fire did not come out from within them. Those gods do not exist. They are products of the imagination of people who want to control you, not like the one true God, Jehovah, who wants to love you."

The Jews in the crowd nod their approval.

"Get on with it, Stephen," the Gentiles say. "We do not want to hear your drivel. Prove these men did not punish themselves with fire leaping from within their evil hearts."

Stephen picks up the bull from behind, but upright. Everyone laughs. He leans over and picks up the bowl of corn with the bull's front hooves and walks the bull over to the altar, where he sets the bowl on the outer edge.

"Now, notice, everyone, he has not set himself on fire from within where his evil heart is."

The crowd laughs. Stephen smiles with them.

"However, it is not allowed to make food offerings of appeasement to the so-called gods from the edge of the altar. The offering must be set way over in the middle of the altar."

Stephen, still standing behind the bull, leans it forward far enough to set it in the middle. He turns toward the crowd.

"Will someone come forward and take control of our worshipper here while I become the priest?"

The crowd grows nervous. People whisper to each other and shake their heads.

"Not me."

"Me neither."

"I am no fool."

"Well, I can prop him up."

Stephen then steps over to a tree stump where he has laid simulated priest clothes. It includes an old blue robe, and a copper bowl turned upside down on his head.

The crowd snickers.

He walks with great solemnity with his hands folded solemnly together over to the bull, pauses, then steps back.

"Huh?"

"Look. The bull is on fire!"

"Get back, everyone."

"The gods are angry."

"Vulcan is angry for making fun of him."

"Run, everyone."

Stephen pushes the burning bull out of the way and climbs up onto the makeshift altar. He raises both hands as he had been taught in oratory lectures.

"Everyone. No god caused the fire. The fire did not arise from within the bull's evil heart."

"Then what just happened?"

I had to go to both temples before I recognized the pattern. Both times the priest showed up, recognized me as a metalsmith, and told me I had to lean way over the alter to put my sacrifice in the middle. Both times the priest then approached me, one holding a small lamp in his hand, the other holding something hidden in his hand, which I assume was a small burning piece of wood.

"In both cases, I could smell the small fire they were carrying. I work with fire. I know what fire smells like. So do all of you."

"But that wouldn't make a man suddenly be on fire from inside," someone calls out.

"Did you notice the decorations on my altar? I made the entire front black. I made the entire top gold."

"Yes, we saw that," another observer says.

"The gold on top was resin made from the sap of cedar trees up in these mountains behind us. I use cedar all the time in my forge. I use cedar chips to start the fire. If I want the fire to burn hotter, I have dried pieces of resin to throw in the fire."

"But what about their legs? Their legs were burned as bad."

"I was unsure about it at first. But I remembered smelling rotten eggs when I neared the altar. When I was in our desert south and west of here, sometimes when I was in a low place where I hoped to find water, instead I found something black that smelled like rotten eggs. I built a fire one night near one of those small black pools. Suddenly, my fire was large enough to light up an entire camp of Roman brigands." He pauses.

"While Simon and I and the boy were recovering from our ordeal, I told a local tribesman—Simon's uncle—about it. He said they kept a supply of the black liquid to build fires with since they had so few trees in the desert. They gave me two vials of it. I used one of those vials on the front of the rock."

Stephen stops speaking. People in the crowd mutter to each other, then walk forward. *Will they grab me up and kill me? Will they make me their hero and forgive me for all the times I've made them mad and did not mean to?*

He jumps down from the boulder and stands over to the side. Men step forward and touch the boulder where the gold resin had been, and the strange, foul-smelling black substance had been.

"Well, we have to admit, it smelled really bad," someone says.

"Well, I use resin sometimes in my fires if I run out of kindling, and it's too late to go get any."

"Well...."

People wander off. No one speaks to Stephen. He stands

and watches them leave. The only audience left now is Ezekiel and Tullia.

"What do you think?" Stephen asks. "Did I convince them?"

"You convinced those who already had doubts. You did not convince the staunch believers. You will never convince them, even if you were God himself standing there and talking to them."

"I want to stay here and do some work. I want to get my customers back."

Stephen goes inside his shop, uses some of the dried resin and a bow drill to start his fire, and pulls out a thin slab of iron he had flattened before leaving for Jerusalem, but not flattened enough.

He works the rest of the afternoon and is satisfied.

On his way out of the market, he stops and buys a small jar of honey for his mother.

"My, you are in a good mood," Tullia says when he arrives.

"And to prove it, dear Mother, here is some honey to make up for what the priests got to eat of your delicious honey cakes."

After the evening meal, Stephen paces.

"Son, you pace when you are upset, and you pace when you're happy," Ezekiel says. "Let me guess. This is a happy pace. Well, sit and be happy. You're making me nervous."

That night, Stephen dreams he is second to the king of Libya with his own throne, and in the smaller petite throne next to his is Livia.

Morning.

"Ah. This is going to be a great day. It is great to be a Daniel, after all. Father, how could I have been so wrong, and you so right?"

"Oh, it happens all the time, Son. You just do not admit it. Well, enjoy your day at the shop and make happy customers."

Stephen grabs a few dates to stuff into a cotton pouch and all but skips through the gate. He walks up the street, swaggering. He wonders why people are staring at him.

Well, it's because I won and they lost. That is all. They'll get over it.

As he draws closer to the north market, more people stare at him. They do not smile. He grins at them to get them to relax and enjoy life as he does.

Two men come running toward him. He stops on the street until he recognizes them. "Oh, it's just you, Joshua and Eben. Come to greet me on victory day?"

They do not smile.

"Come quickly. It's terrible."

"What's terrible?" he says, not smiling now.

He runs after them to the entrance into the market. He follows as they rush down the main aisle to the back row. When he nears his shop, he slows.

"No, it cannot be."

He runs the rest of the way. And stops. And stares in disbelief.

"My shop. It's gone!"

"We're really sorry, Stephen. We do not know who did it. There were no witnesses. But we have our strong suspicions."

"The priests?" he mutters.

"The priests. You defied them."

Stephen sits in the middle of the aisle. Gawkers come to the last row, partly to see the destroyed shop, partly to see the destroyed man.

An hour passes. Two. Three. Stephen remains where he is. Sitting cross-legged in the middle of the aisle.

"Someone needs to go get his father," Joshua says.

"I will go," Eben says.

Sometime later in a realm where time no longer exists, Stephen hears his father's voice. His gentle voice. The kind of voice he used to use when Stephen had been a child and skinned his knee.

"Come, my son." His voice is so low, only those nearby hear him.

Ezekiel leans and takes his son's arm. He pulls on it.

"Come along. It's time to go home. We will figure out something at home. Come along now."

Stephen shrugs off his father's hand.

Ezekiel steps behind him and takes Stephen's other arm.

"Come along now."

Stephen stands, throws up his arms, and shouts at the sky.

"WHY?"

34 ~ THE MIST

Stephen looks over at his father as though seeing him for the first time.

"Come along, now, Son. Your mother is waiting for you at home. She will worry if you do not come home. Come along now."

Ezekiel puts an arm across his son's muscular shoulders and supports him at his elbow with the other hand. He guides his son away from his destruction.

"That is right. One step at a time. No hurry. Just one at a time. Just like I taught you when you were small. One step. Then another."

"We forgave you too soon!" someone shouts behind him. Ezekiel recognizes the voice.

"We shouldn't have forgiven you at all!" another shouts.

"Do not pay attention to them, Son," Ezekiel whispers.

"Next thing we know, all our booths will be burned down!"

"You've been nothing but trouble to the Jews since you moved here!"

"Keep walking, Son," Ezekiel says under his breath. "Do not listen to them. Come on. Take another step. That is right. Now another."

Shadows of a daytime sun filter through to them as scarce clouds bump into each other overhead.

"You're doing fine, Son. That is right. One step. It doesn't have to be a big one. Just lift your foot a bit and scoot it forward. That is it."

Stephen trips on a hidden stone. Ezekiel clings fast.

"Easy now. That is it. Take another step. The stone is gone. God took it away for you."

Stephen leans his head onto his father's shoulder.

"Do not do that. Lift your head up, Son. Be proud. Do not let them think they got to you. Do not show weakness. Lift your head. That is it. Lift it high."

Stephen obeys, though his eyes are now closed. Closed to the world. Closed to his thoughts and dreams and visions. Closed to joy and sadness and all feeling.

"I am so proud of you, Son. We're almost home. Isn't that great? Home where you're always safe and loved. Just a little farther. Another step. You're doing fine. And another step. Just a few more now."

Ezekiel takes his arm from Stephen's shoulder, reaches over and picks up a long branch dropped from someone's haul of firewood. He reaches ahead, taps his gate with it, then throws it back on the street.

"I am here, Son. I will never leave you. We're almost home. Oh, look. There is Mother. She loves you, you know. That is right, another step. Just a little farther. Another step and…"

Tullia extends her arms to embrace her son. Ezekiel shakes his head.

She backs off and opens the gate wider to let the two men in at the same time.

Ezekiel takes Stephen over to a long bench and sits beside him. Tullia sits on the other side and lays her head on her son's shoulder. Once again, Ezekiel shakes his head no.

"Stephen is so strong. He is strong, like his grandfather. Both his grandfathers."

For the first time, Stephen looks into the eyes of his father. Both men fight back their tears. Ezekiel looks away.

"I made some raisin cakes while you were gone," Tullia says, standing. "You love my raisin cakes. They are your favorite. And I put some of that honey in them you gave me yesterday. And…"

Not knowing what else to say, Tullia steps into the kitchen area of their courtyard. She returns, carrying a small plate with a raisin cake and a goblet of milk on it. She hands it to Stephen. He does not reach out for it. She sets it on his lap, but it begins to fall when she takes her hand away.

"Well, I will just set it on the bench next to you. It'll be there when you are ready to eat."

She looks at her husband, tears now in her own eyes. Her brow furrows.

Ezekiel shakes his head. He has no answers, either.

They take turns sitting next to their son until the shadows

come.

"You haven't eaten all day," she says. "Well, that is okay. There's always tomorrow. I have a nice pallet for you on your bed. Let us go to bed now."

Ezekiel stands and helps Stephen up. He takes one hand, Tullia takes the other.

"Come on, Son. Time to take another step. It's not far. Your bedroom is not far. Remember when you let Abelia sleep in your room when she was so worried about Simon and her little boy? It's a special room. She was comforted in it. You will be too."

When Stephen opens his eyes during the night, it is dark and black all around. He cannot tell if he is awake, asleep, or dead. He cannot tell if he can touch or taste or feel anything. He tries to sort things out.

He remembers Esther. Why does he remember Esther? He remembers secret synagogues and sneaking around at night with the Ten Commandments and extra robes and food. It had not worked. Why had it not?

He remembers meetings with metalsmiths in private but not secret. And beatings. And a screaming back. It had not worked. Why?

He remembers Daniel. Why does he remember Daniel? He remembers statues and people bowing down to them. He remembers priests and people bowing down to them. He remembers fire. People on fire. Shops on fire. Stephen remembers who he is.

"WHY?"

His voice echoes around his room and out to the courtyard.

Tullia runs into his room. Ezekiel follows with a lamp and sets it on a small table. Stephen sits up in his bed, his arms reaching for heaven. He looks at his parents.

"Why?" It is a soft why. A whispered why. A why that cannot be answered.

"Esther wasn't right," he whispers. "Daniel wasn't right."

"They were right for their time, Son," Ezekiel says. "Perhaps you will find your own time."

My grandfather, the one who was a slave: He gave up his freedom for yours, did not he?"

"Yes, he did. I could never repay him. He was the finest, most noble man I ever knew."

"Your father is right," Tullia adds. "Your grandfather kept his dignity the whole time he was a slave."

"But he was wrong, Father," Stephen says, still whispering. "He spoke out to the Roman invaders, and it cost him his life. Speaking out does not work. Keeping things secret does not work."

"Son, it is still dark out. Go back to sleep. We will talk more in the morning," Tullia says.

Stephen scoots back down in his bed, and Tullia lifts the covers over him as she had done countless times when he was small. She kisses him on both cheeks and his forehead as she had always done in those days of his innocence.

They leave.

Stephen falls asleep and dreams, but it is a dark dream. He fights it until he awakens. It is morning.

He walks out into the courtyard in his nightclothes. He shuffles to his bench and sits. He stares. He does not respond when Ezekiel or Tullia speak to him.

He hears them whisper but does not know what about. It does not matter what about. Nothing matters. Not anymore. Nothing left but dreams and visions and goals all turned to ash. All melted into oblivion.

Sometimes he mutters. "Nothing works. Nothing works. Nothing works."

Then silence again. Silence for a very long time.

Through the fog, he hears his father say the word *mourning*. He hears his mother say *patience* and *food* and *new beginning*. Through the fog, he hears.

What do they mean? What do those words mean?

Drifting. Roaming in and out of oblivion and nothingness in a world of no meaning.

Time runs and hides. Hours. Days. A week? A month?

He thinks he hears a knock at their gate.

"Hello, Joshua," he hears his mother say off in some distant world.

"Come in. Come in," Ezekiel says.

"How is he?" Joshua asks

"See for yourself."

Joshua steps farther into the courtyard and sees Stephen sitting in his bedclothes. Hair in his eyes. Unshaven. Arms limp at his side. Eyes closed.

"May I try?"

"Please do," Tullia says. "We just do not know what else to do."

Joshua steps over and sits cross-legged on the rough tile in front of Stephen.

"Some of us went together and rebuilt your shop. It's not as good as it was before. Well, actually, it isn't a shop. It's just a booth. But it's a start. And we salvaged a lot of things. It's not as though you work with wood or pottery. Iron survives. Your supply of iron nuggets was still there. Well, the wooden bin you had them in is gone, and a lot of the nuggets were fused together. But that is good. Isn't it? And your tools. They were all made of iron, so they're okay. I am afraid the locks you were crafting have melted. But you can make new ones."

Ezekiel and Tullia stand behind Joshua. He turns and looks at them. They each give him a weak smile and a nod. He turns back to Stephen.

"So, come on back. No one is mad. The priests did not burn down any other booths. And the Jews do not completely accuse you of the growing persecution here."

Stephen squints his eyes at the word "persecution."

"No, I did not mean it that way. Well, anyway, everyone likes you. They think you're brave. And you have always stood up for what is right. No one has ever known anyone like you. We admire you."

"It has only brought disgrace," Stephen finally answers in a whisper. "Disgrace and failure."

"No, you're wrong."

"I wish I could die."

"No, you do not mean that, Son," Ezekiel says.

Silence.

"And all the customers who were waiting for their lock and hinge orders. They came back and paid you ahead of time. Here is your money, Stephen."

Joshua hands him a money pouch. Stephen opens up his hand but does not reach for it. Joshua puts the money pouch in his palm and folds Stephen's fingers around it.

"You can use this money to buy anything you need to replace, though I doubt you need to replace much."

Joshua stands. "Come on, Stephen. Everyone down at the market is waiting for you. Come on. Get dressed. Splash some water on your face. Comb your hair. And let us pretend you are growing that beard for the Lord."

He takes hold of Stephen's free hand and tugs on it.

"Man, you are heavier than I thought. All those muscles. Well, get up. You've got customers waiting and orders to fill. You can do it. Or you aren't the man we all thought you were."

Joshua turns and looks back at Ezekiel and Tullia. Their smiles are broader. Ezekiel nods.

Joshua turns back to Stephen and sits next to him on the wide bench. He puts one arm across his shoulder. With his other hand, he pulls up on Stephen. He gets Stephen halfway up and starts laughing.

Ezekiel and Tullia laugh too.

Stephen lets out a small laugh.

"Well, you're going to have to help me, Stephen, or we are going to both land on the ground. Then we will both be in a mess. C'mon, Stephen. Yeah. That is right. Up, up, up."

Once Stephen is completely standing, Joshua turns to face him.

"Whew. Remind me to never get in a fight with you. Those muscles. Where did you get those muscles? Oh, yeah. I seem to remember an anvil and big heavy hammer that I couldn't lift with two hands. You lifted it with one.

"Oh, here's your mother with a clean tunic. Whew! You smell like a horse! When you take that thing off, she's going to have to bu...to throw it away. We could use it as a camel blanket, but I do not think the camel would take it."

Joshua steps aside far enough that he and Ezekiel can pull his night tunic off. Joshua laughs. Ezekiel laughs. Stephen laughs in his throat, though his eyes doubt.

"Whew, Tullia. Why do not you just throw the whole pail of water on him? Or dip him in that well over there?"

Ezekiel reaches into a pail of water Tullia has brought and sponges Stephen down. Stephen lets him.

"Now for your clean tunic," Joshua says. "Not your best one, though. You've got some dirty work to do the rest of the day."

He puts the tunic on Stephen as one would a baby. His arms remain limp.

"Okay, big guy. Sit a moment so your mother can put your sandals on your dirty, smelly feet." He moves out of the way so she can do her job.

"I sure wish my mother were willing to put my sandals on my feet every day. She throws them at me and tells me, 'Do it yourself.'"

Stephen sits, looking straight ahead.

"All right. Stand back up. Your mother has a basket of food to take in case you get hungry. Take your basket."

Stephen obeys.

Joshua signals Ezekiel, who steps to the gate and opens it.

"Have a good day at work, Son," Ezekiel and Tullia say in unison and wearing artificial grins.

Stephen lets Joshua take him out into the street. When the gate closes, he thinks he hears his mother cry.

They start for the market with slow steps.

"All right, Stephen. We've got a little planning to do on our way there. What is the first thing you're going to do?"

"Unlock it," Stephen mutters, his eyes still glazed.

"Ha, ha! I forgot about that part. Then what?"

"Sort through my tools and put them where I can find them."

"Good. Good. Then what? Oh, here. I forgot. This clay tile has all your old orders on it." He takes the rope off his wrist and puts it on Stephen's wrist.

Stephen does not look at it.

"You'd better read it, so you'll know what to start on when you get there."

"Do not need to," Stephen says, still looking straight ahead with a stoic expression. "I know what they are."

"Ha! I should have known. Well, here is a tile with all your new orders on it." He hands it to Stephen.

"Well, are you going to read it?"

"Not until I get there."

"What did your mother make for your mid-day respite?"

"I have no idea," Stephen replies.

"You know she spoils you."

Stephen grins. "I know."

"Well, we're almost to the market. So, you did not tell me everything you're going to do when we get to your booth."

"Kick you out."

"Huh? Ha, ha, ha. You'd better be nice to me. I have some pottery bins you can put your pieces of wire and other supplies in. I won't sell them to you if you're not nice to me."

"Then I will buy them from someone else," Stephen says, still looking straight ahead, but still grinning.

Joshua reaches over and ruffles Stephen's hair.

"Stop that," Stephen says. "My mother just combed it."

Then they hear it.

"Hurrah!"

"There are your friends, Stephen. See, at the end of the aisle? Didn't I tell you they still like you? You're a little strange sometimes. But they still like you."

"Well, I think they're strange. And I think you are the strangest of all." He continues to look straight ahead with no expression.

As Stephen and Joshua draw closer, the merchants from the last aisle—the aisle of the Jews—rush up to meet him.

Pats on the back. Cuffs in the arm. Shadowboxing. Roughhousing.

For the first time, Stephen stops looking straight ahead. He turns and looks in the faces of his friends. He smiles. He manages a few more throaty laughs.

A few at a time, the others go back to work. All but Joshua. Stephen looks at him. "I do not...."

"No. You do not have to thank me. It's what friends do. Some day you can drag me out of bed for a little payback. Are you going to be all right now?"

"I think so."

Joshua walks away. Stephen walks into his unlocked booth. He looks around at what his friends had done for him. He sees his tools piled in a corner. He picks them up and sets them on a work table they made for him.

He notices his walls go out a little farther with only part of it under a roof. When he steps over to the unroofed part, he sees a pile of bricks.

"For my forge," he whispers. "They did not know how to build a forge." He sighs. "I do not deserve this. He stands and looks up. "Jehovah God, I do not deserve this."

He arranges his tools the way he wants them and hears a voice at his front counter. He peeks around and sees a stranger.

He steps up to his counter. "Yes? May I help you?"

"I just bought a house in Cyrene and need some locks made. I need a heavy one for my front gate. Oh, and another heavy one for my stable."

Stephen hears a muffled laugh. He looks beyond the new customer. Joshua is out on the street. He is turning his thumb up.

Stephen smiles, nods, and returns to his customer. He clears his throat.

"There are a few other customers ahead of you, but I think I can have them to you by next week. Would that be satisfactory?"

35 ~ DREAMING

*T*he summer heat has arrived. As always, everyone now reverses night and day. Now being outdoors is limited to the night hours, a little in the morning, and a little at sunset. In the day heat, people hide under the covers of thick goat hair thrown over their booths or just stay home where the walls are thick and fight off the relentless rays of sun. Many merchants only open their shops during the night and sleep during the day. Customers do not take to the streets and shop in the heat.

During the cooler months, Stephen had built up his supply of flattened iron for locks and hinges, so he does not have to fire up the forge very often in the summer.

It is mid-morning, and Stephen has not had a customer since dawn. He closes up his shop and heads up from the back aisle in the Jewish row and out of the market.

"Hey, you."

Stephen turns to see who is calling him. The voice is not familiar.

"Are you Stephen, the locksmith? I was told you were skinny but had big muscles." The man has a dark tan and leathery skin.

Hmmm. Must be a sailor. "Why are you looking for him?" Stephen asks. "He's a private man."

"I have a message for him."

"I can take it to him."

"No. My captain told me he was paid a lot of money to deliver the message, and it has to be handed only to Stephen himself. I will receive a bonus if I can find him."

"Who would pay a lot of money to get a message to Stephen? He's not a government official or anything important."

"I have no idea."

"Where is the message from?"

"Jerusalem."

Stephen sucks in a quick breath. "Is it good news or bad news?"

"Sir, just tell me where Stephen is."

"Well, I guess I am Stephen. I had to check you out first."

"Then take the message. And etch your signature on this tile so I will get my bonus."

The message is on a parchment scroll with a red waxed seal. Stephen takes another deep breath. His heart races. He looks up and around the nearly-empty street as though wanting someone to tell him whether or not he should open and read it.

Is she dead? Or is it about Simon? No, he wouldn't have the money to have a message delivered so far away. Did Father's scribes stay in Jerusalem? I haven't seen them since Passover. But why would they be writing me?

Did Jesus come back and destroy the whole temple? Did he heal an entire city? No. It's about her. But what about her? Is she sick? Is she dying? Does she need me?

"Ha. You are going to melt if you do not get out of this heat."

Stephen looks over and sees Xenon, a member of the Greek-Speaking Freedmen Synagogue.

"Oh. Yes. Of course. You're right," Stephen replies, looking back down at the small scroll. "I guess I will take it home to read."

"Hey, are you interested in doing the scripture reading next Sabbath?" Xenon asks. "Usirus, Agathon, and Balios have all taken their turns. Helios has been sick lately."

"I would like that," Stephen replies with a smile. "Thank you for asking. Now I guess I'd better get home and read my message before we both melt."

"Uh, tomorrow is the Sabbath."

"I will be there."

Stephen turns and passes the *hospitium* on his left and the Jewish-Born Freedmen Synagogue on his right. He passes the theater where he had temporarily won the laurel crown for javelin throwing and arrives home.

He knocks on the gate, and Tullia takes the bar down from the inside. He walks in, staring at the scroll.

"Well, hello to you too," Tullia says.

"Oh, I have this message. It's from Jerusalem. I am afraid to open it. And I am afraid not to open it. What if it's bad news? What if something terrible has happened back there?"

"Son, you know the obvious answer to that. I am going back inside where it's cooler."

Stephen sits on his usual wide bench and tries not to pay attention to the heat it has absorbed nearly burning through his tunic.

He stares at the scroll. He turns it over and over in his hands. Tears form in his eyes. What if she's... He stands and walks to the kitchen area of the courtyard that has been abandoned for the summer in favor of food not requiring an oven.

He walks over to the well and tries to look down at his reflection. It is the dry season. He cannot see the water. He thinks about throwing the scroll down the well. *Then I will never know what the bad news is and will drive myself crazy.*

He walks out into the mid-day deserted street and looks to his left up the hill at the temple to Zeus-Amun Re. He comes back in and reseats himself.

"Oh, Jehovah God. I cannot take any more bad news. What am I going to do?"

"You're going to open the thing," Ezekiel growls, "so you'll quit making noise out here. I am trying to sleep. What have I told you before? Be a man, Son. Be a man."

Stephen takes a deep breath, breaks the seal, sits, unrolls part of the message, but does not look at it. "Here, Father. You read it."

Ezekiel sighs, rolls his eyes heavenward, takes the scroll, and seats himself on his own usual bench, which Tullia has covered with a cotton cushion.

He reads the first few lines and throws his head back. "Ha, ha, ha, ha." He stands and steps over to Stephen. He throws his head back again. "Hee, hee, hee." The old man grabs his side and laughs harder.

"What's so funny, Father?"

Ezekiel hands it back to Stephen. "Read it yourself. But read it aloud. I am going to enjoy this. No, wait. Tullia, come out here! This is going to be fun."

"In this heat?"

"In this heat." Ezekiel waits for his wife to sit next to him. "Now, Son, read it aloud so we can enjoy it with you."

From Nicodemus, rabbi, and member of the Sanhedrin of all Israel, to Stephen, son of Ezekiel former slave, and grandson of Athenodorus former philosopher and mayor of Tarsus. Greetings from

Jerusalem. I trust this finds you well and prospering.

I have been in negotiations with Simon, the Berber of Cyrene, about my daughter.

Stephen looks up. "He's going to let Simon marry her? No! What happened to Abelia?"

"Ha, ha. Keep reading, Son."

If you meet my terms, you may marry Livia.

Stephen jumps up and raises the scroll over his head. "He says I can marry her. I can marry Livia!" He jumps around the courtyard, then over to his parents to give them a sweaty kiss.

"Okay, read the rest of it aloud," Ezekiel says. "I want to know what Simon got you into to qualify for marrying this important man's daughter."

Stephen reads on.

I have thoroughly investigated the situation in the province of Cyrenica in northeast Libya. My investigation has revealed growing persecution against Jews with the Roman governor's blessings.

As I explained to you and your parents while you were here, she is very naïve. She believes and trusts everyone. She has no sense of fear. You must give up everything that is familiar to you and live according to my instructions. You must protect her with your very life.

Stephen looks up, pauses, and says, "I can do that. I will give my life for her."

"Keep reading," Tullia urges. "What does he want you to give up?"

"Ha! He's got the rest of them numbered," Stephen says. "Let me see."

Number One. You will stop all associations with the Jewish-born and Greek-Speaking Jews. That means you give up your locksmith business among them.

"How am I supposed to support her?"

"Keep reading," his grinning parents say in unison.

Number Two. You will stop worshipping with any Jewish-born or Greek-Speaking Synagogue.

"Huh?

Number Three: You must live in disguise. Secrecy is what will protect her. You will, therefore, live as a Berber. You will dress like a Berber, eat like a Berber, speak like a Berber. You will live among the Berbers.

"I only know a little of their language," Stephen responds.

Number Four: You will not give up worshipping Jehovah God, the only true God. You will worship with the Berber Synagogue.
Number Five: You will pray five times a day, you will read portions of the Torah every morning before breaking your fast, and you will read one of the prophets every evening before retiring. This will be done aloud for the benefit of your wife and children.

Stephen holds one finger up and paces.

Number Six: Should you decide to leave there and move to Jerusalem, all stipulations in number one through five are rescinded.

"If I give up my locksmith shop and live in disguise, how am I supposed to support her?

Finale: Should you accept these stipulations before witnesses which shall be your parents and any Jewish Berbers you are intimate with, you will be officially betrothed to my daughter from whom you will never divorce.
What follows is from Simon, the Berber.

"Ha! He started over. He wrote his letter in Aramaic, then wrote it in Greek." Stephen skips the Greek and moves down to Nicodemus' signature.
"What a flourished hand he has. But, I wonder what Simon has to do with it?"
"I think I know," Tullia says in a sing-song voice, tipping her head and grinning at Stephen.
"Do you really think so?" Ezekiel asks his wife.
"Think what?" Stephen replies.
"Keep reading," his parents say in unison with broadened grins. Stephen sits again.

From Simon, the Berber, former outlaw, fisherman, and vine keeper, to Stephen, who helped me save my son's life. Greetings from

Jerusalem.

You may have my vineyard in the foothills of the mountains behind Cyrene. You may have my house with the winepress in it.

"Huh? He's giving me his house and vineyard? I cannot go along with that."

"Just keep reading."

If you ever move out of it, it all reverts back to me. Go to my Uncle Twafa and Aunt Tazerwat to learn more of our language. While you're there, ask Aunt Tazerwat to make you and Livia some Berber clothes. You may remember they rescued and nursed us until we got well enough to travel. Look in my stable. The cart they loaned me is still there. You can take it back to them.

When you are able to, write me a letter in the Berber language, I will tell Rabbi Nicodemus you are ready to marry his daughter. Good luck with Livia. I heard she is a handful.

The scroll ends with Simon's condensed signature. Stephen stands and grins at the heavens above.

"Let me see that," Ezekiel says, reaching for it. As he reads through it, he shakes his head and grins. "I thought we were too protective of you. That is a drop in the Great Sea compared to his over-protection of his daughter."

"She's only seventeen. Well, I guess she's eighteen now. I am twenty-four and fully capable of taking care of her."

Ezekiel looks over at his son. "Yes, I think you are. You have experienced more of life than most young men your age and survived them all. You are a survivor, a conqueror, and will live a long life."

Stephen sits back across from his father. "Wow. You have never said anything like that before."

"Well, I thought it."

"I think we should celebrate, but it is too hot for me to bake you any raisin cakes," Tullia says.

"Tomorrow is the Sabbath. I guess I should go to my synagogue one last time. They have asked me to read the scripture tomorrow. Just when things are going better over there, I have to... Well, it's not important that I stay there."

The Sabbath arrives. Ezekiel and Tullia go over to the Jewish-Born Freedmen Synagogue. Stephen goes over to the

Greek-Speaking Freedmen Synagogue.

"Today, we are pleased to have Stephanus read our scripture," Rabbi Solomus announces.

Stephen rises and walks up to the podium. He stands behind the ornate table, turns, and pulls out a scroll with the scripture he wants to read.

"I trust you will pardon my diverting from the norm. Instead of reading just one of David's psalms, I would like to read the first part of his second psalm and the first part of his fifth psalm."

Xenon rises in the audience. "This is highly irregular."

"We only read one psalm at a time," Agathon says from the audience.

"We did not ask you to divert from the norm," Halios says.

"Well, just this once because you are new," Balios says.

"I think we should find out just what Stephanus is planning to do with those psalms," Rabbi Solomus says. "Go ahead, young man."

Stephen opens the scroll to the psalms:

God decreed,
I have crowned My King
Upon holy Mount Zion.
The King declared the decree
to kings of the earth:
God said to Me
"You are My Son.
Today I have begotten you.

David replied,
Heed my cry, for you are
My King and my God.

The congregation stirs. The rabbi fidgets. Stephen rolls the scroll back up.

"My brothers, I heard a rabbi in Alexandria speak of this, and I believe he was right. My brothers, the Messiah, the holy King we have been waiting to come rule us in purity and peace will be God himself in some form."

Whispering throughout the ornate room. Whispering and shuffling of feet and stirring. Rabbi Solomus rises.

"That is fine, Stephanus. You may be seated now."

After the service, as Stephen walks out, he hears Xenon

whisper to Balios. "Remind me to never ask him to read again."

Stephen smiles to himself as he heads toward home.

"You will not have that chance, my friend," he mutters under his breath with a grin.

When he arrives home, he sees three Berber couples in the courtyard sitting on cushions under the shade of the thick canopy of goat hair. He looks at them, then over to his mother.

"Stephen," Ezekiel says, "These are Simon's and Abelia's friends who joined him in celebrating Alexander's second birthday the night he was kidnapped. They came here a few moments ago after their synagogue service instead of going home."

"Oh, yes, I believe I remember everyone now," Stephen says." But I do not seem to remember your names."

One of the men stands. "I am Cheber, and this is my wife, Delylah."

"Oh, yes. I got you out of jail, didn't It?" Stephen says.

A second man stands. "I am Talam, and this is my wife, Zilpah."

Stephen looks over at the third couple. The man stands. "I am Nebo, and this is my wife, Nissal."

"We received a message from Simon yesterday," Cheber says. "He said we were to befriend you and help Berberize you, beginning with being witnesses, then helping you celebrate your betrothal."

"Berberize? You're going to Berberize me?" Stephen laughs. "Okay, then Berberize me," he says, seating himself on his favorite floor cushion.

"Simon sent us a copy of the message he and the father of the bride drew up," Talam says. "You are going to have quite a father-in-law. Well, do you agree to the stipulations?"

"I do," Stephen says. "I do, I do, I do."

"Okay. Then sign below Simon's signature. Your parents and we will sign below yours," Nebo says.

Stephen signs, then stands and walks around the courtyard his hands raised heavenward. "Livia is mine. Livia is mine. Forever mine. Livia is mine."

"Come sit," Tullia says. "The women all brought food with them they prepared yesterday. Enough for a feast, I must say. A betrothal feast.

Everyone indulges and occasionally congratulates Stephen, or asks him what his plans are.

At sunset, the three couples leave.

"Now that it is no longer the Sabbath," Stephen tells his

parents, "I want to go over to Simon's—er, uh, my house and see it."

"Of course, you do," Ezekiel says. "Good thinking. Do not come back here tomorrow until the sun is at its hottest and most people have gone inside. Bring the cart he told you about, and take it over to the market. No one will be there in the heat of the day. Put your tools and equipment in the cart and bring it home."

"What will I use for a horse to pull it?"

"I have a neighbor who has been wanting to sell me his donkey. It's an old donkey, so maybe he won't want much. Wait while I grab some money and go next door."

"I will pay you back when I sell my shop," he tells his father.

"Seems to me that shop was mine to start with."

"Well, I will pay you back somehow."

Stephen rides his father's newly-acquired donkey to Simon's house. The following day at the hottest part of the day, Stephen rides over to his shop, empties it, and delivers his supplies and equipment over to his new house.

He takes a few days to settle in, then says goodbye to Ezekiel, Tullia, and the three couples who have checked on him each day. He heads south over the Gebel el-Akhdar Mountains and down into the desert with the cart and donkey.

Over the next three months, Stephen stays with Simon's Uncle Gwafa and Aunt Tazerwat south of the mountains in the Nassamonian tribal lands.

Autumn is here. The heat has eased up enough, the markets can stay open during the day. It is nearly time for the Day of Atonement, though Ezekiel and Tullia have decided not to go to Jerusalem for the autumn festivals.

"One long trip to Jerusalem a year is enough," he says.

There is a knock at the gate. Ezekiel opens it. A man stands there with a pigtail on each side of his head, a long multi-colored embroidered tunic, and a cape of matching colors but different pattern.

"We're not interested in whatever you're selling," he tells the stranger. "Perhaps your own people will give you some of their business."

Ezekiel eases the gate closed. A foot is stuck in the way.

"I am sorry, sir, but..."

"Would you be interested in a lock," he interrupts with a Berber accent.

Ezekiel stares. Tullia walks toward the gate. "I thought I

heard Stephen's voice. I must have been mistaken. What is this man selling?"

Ezekiel does not reply. He stares at the Berber at his gate. Tullia joins him.

"What?" she asks her husband.

"Look at his eyes."

"Stephen? Is that you in there?" she says, folding her hands together as though in prayer.

"Greetings, Mother. Greetings, Father."

The gate is swung wide. Stephen steps in.

"Oh, my. You fooled both of us."

"Do not close the gate yet. I need to know where to put my camel."

"Your what?"

"That is all anyone travels on down there for long trips. My donkey almost did not make it the whole way in that desert."

Two weeks later, Stephen has moved completely into Simon's house and cleared the land of weeds around Simon's grapevines.

Today, he sits at a table with a new but small scroll and writes a letter, first in Berber, then Greek, then Aramaic, and finally in Hebrew. *That should impress him.*

Stephen, a proud Jew, former locksmith of Antioch, runaway slave from Crete, and now a Berber vine keeper. Greetings, from Cyrene in the land of Libya. Rabbi Nicodemus, I have fulfilled all the stipulations you have made. Simon will confirm that the first part of this message is written in proper Berber language.

All things are ready. Kindly send me my bride.

He hears a knock at his gate, answers it, and smiles at his parents.

"Well, hello there. You're just in time. Your son has just written his letter to the rabbi," Stephen says. "Before you know it, his bride will be here."

"Oh, indeed?" Tullia says with a broad grin.

"Let us go for a little ride to celebrate," Ezekiel says.

"Ride on what?"

"Oh, someone loaned us a chariot and horse. Come. Let us go for a ride."

Stephen puts on his multicolored cape to protect him against the autumn air and joins his parents in the chariot.

As they ride through the city of Cyrene, he realizes they are headed toward the North Gate Market.

"I do not think we should go there. I am in disguise, but I do not want to test it here."

"Okay," Tullia says. "It's such a nice day, why do not we ride down to the seashore? Maybe we will find some seashells."

"Oh, Mother. I do not want any seashells."

"Well, I do. And since we won't be able to do things like this with you much longer, you will indulge us and do what we want."

"Yes, Mother."

He hangs on to one side of the chariot behind his father while his mother sits on a bench on the other side.

In less than an hour, they are at the seashore of Apollonia.

"This is close enough to the water. There are hitching posts here," Ezekiel says.

They climb out of the chariot, and Stephen walks behind his parents as they oooh over seashells.

"Son, if you're bored, why do not to go over to the bench by that fountain and wait for us?"

Grateful for a way out, Stephen walks up from the beach.

He stops short of the fountain.

He stares.

His knees grow weak.

He blinks.

He squints his eyes.

He looks back at his parents, then back at what is before him. A dream? A vision?

"Well, aren't you going to welcome your bride to her new home?" she says.

36 ~ SECRETS

Stephen's eyes grow as big as a full moon. He sucks in his breath, his insides turn upside down, and his heart leaps. He cannot run fast enough. What if she disappears?

The smile on Livia's face grows broader, her dimples larger. Her eyes sparkle as though the very stars are in them. They run toward each other, holding out their arms.

Stephen forces himself to stop a pace from her. "I want to take you in my arms, my love," he whispers with a voice that is both husky and scratchy and not completely in his control.

"Then, why do not you?" Livia responds, her words like honey.

"Oh, my darling, my bride. How I want to." He takes a deep breath and presses his lips together. "But if I do, the good citizens of this fair land would probably throw me in jail for immoral public behavior."

She laughs. That laughter that had stolen his heart in Jerusalem. "Well, we need to do something about that, do not we?"

"I see you found her," Tullia says, walking up behind Stephen.

"Welcome to our humble family," Ezekiel says.

"I hope it's not too humble," she replies. "Oh, I was just teasing. And I humbly accept your welcome."

Livia looks back at Stephen. "It's a good thing your parents and those four men who guarded me on the ship warned me what you were going to look like.

"Well, here's a long colorful robe for you," Tullia says, so you will look as odd as our son does. Put it on quickly. There are several outfits for you at your house."

"My house! I have a house! We have a house!" Livia says, putting on the strangest multi-colored robe she has ever seen.

"Are you sure people wear clothes like this around here?"

"Positive, my love. Just look at me. Here I am out in public, and no one suspects it is me."

"I still do not understand why we have to wear disguises," she replies.

"There is persecution of Jews in this city, and it is growing worse. Your father insisted you not be identified with them for your own protection," Ezekiel says. "We must keep you alive long enough to give us grandchildren, and for you yourselves to have grandchildren when you are old."

"Okay, how do I look?" she asks in Berber.

"Very Berberish," Stephen replies. "And where did you learn to speak Berber?"

"Who do you think? Simon."

"Our chariot is right over there," Ezekiel says, pointing. "Let us get you over to your house."

"But, what about finalizing our marriage?"

"We have taken care of everything," Tullia says with a large grin and a wink. "Do not you worry."

"You own a chariot?" Livia asks when she steps onto it.

"Only for special occasions," Ezekiel replies. "Today, it is your wedding chariot."

"And you thought our little ride down to the seashore was going to be boring," Tullia says with a little tug to the pigtail on the side of her son's head. "Never under-estimate your parents."

As the chariot takes them up the steep beach, through the city of Apollonia, and up the steeper hill leading into Cyrene, Livia looks behind them at the panorama of open water and ships and seagulls. "I've never been near the sea before. Never even saw it until I left on this trip."

They enter through the North Gate of Cyrene.

"Shhh now," Stephen says. "Sit on this bench by me and try not to be noticed.

"Why?"

"Because we're going through the market where I used to have my locksmith business."

"They wouldn't recognize my voice," Livia objects.

"They would mine," Stephen counters, "and they would recognize yours as a new voice they will be curious about."

Ezekiel leads the horse through the market as fast as he can without endangering pedestrians. He directs the horse to turn right past the sanctuary and temple to Apollo. Behind that, they enter the Berber section of the city.

"That is the Berber Synagogue we will be attending over there on the left," Stephen explains. "It is made of mud-brick like most other buildings."

"It sure looks odd. I never saw a synagogue look like that with that cone-shaped roof," she says. "Is it okay to talk now?"

"Yes, it's okay. Oh, our house is right ahead."

Ezekiel pulls on the reins of the horse and the chariot stops. He turns. "Well, are you ready to see your new house?" he asks Livia.

She does not leave the chariot. Stephen notices tears in her eyes.

"What's wrong, my love? Whatever it is, I will fix it."

"Oh, Son, you have a lot to learn about women," Tullia says. "Those are tears of joy."

Stephen reaches his hand out to his bride, and she takes it. They take slow steps as Livia drinks in what is now hers.

They pass through the gate. Stephen stops. "Who? What?"

"We came to help you celebrate your wedding," Justus says. "We slipped up here to the house while the two of you were gawking at each other down at the beach. Achaius, Secundus, and Trophimus, too," he adds.

"Thank you," Stephen says, reaching out his hands to the four scribes. "Thank you for bringing her safely to me."

"Well, sometimes it was more like we were the ones who needed guarding," Trophimus says. "She was all over that ship."

"Ha. We had to divide and set up stations for each of us so we could keep her located," Secundus says.

Stephen looks around at the others in the courtyard.

"Come, my darling, my bride. Meet our Berber friends. They were friends of Simon and Abelia," Stephen says. "This is Cheber and his wife Delylah, these are Kehath and Liba, over here are Nebo and Nissa, and seated over there are Telem and Zilpah."

"Oh. People really do dress in these strange clothes," Livia says.

"They're not strange to us," Delyhah says.

"You'll get used to them," Nissa says.

"After a while, you'll prefer them," Zilpah says.

"Gentlemen, be seated," Achaius says. "This large table should be enough for us men. We will let the women sit at their own table so they can tell the bride how to make Berber food."

"Livia," Tullia says, taking the young lady's arm. "Come with us, women. They have prepared a beautiful wedding dress for you."

Moments pass. Half an hour.

Stephen paces. "What are they doing in there?"

"You will see. Women always take as much time as they can to present themselves to their men," Cheber says.

"Sometimes too long," Kehath declares in mock anger and a twinkle in his eyes.

The banter continues until they are interrupted.

The women walk back out to the courtyard. They are in a line. They pause, then part. Behind them is Livia in her wedding dress.

She wears a long tunic with splashes of yellow, gold, orange, and the tan of sand dunes scattered everywhere on it. Her long robe is stripes of red and gold sometimes, and large balls of green over red and blue sometimes. The sleeves are long and full, and when she holds her arms out, they resemble wings.

On her head is a cone-shaped crown of blue, many-folded, with brass and silver bells hanging from each fold.

She wears three necklaces. The first reaches almost to her waist and is of silver with coins dangling in rows a hand-span long each. The second is wood beads about the size of small eggs. The one closest to her neck is small gold beads attached to each other by thin cords of woven gold and in five strands. On her tiny feet are sandals of leather straps dyed purple, with a bronze coin attached where each strap crosses the other.

Livia smiles as though half-embarrassed by the strangeness of her attire, but proud that she can be counted worthy of such an ornamental wedding dress with crown.

Stephen, who had been seated with the other men while waiting for her, stands and stares. As he absorbs her beauty, he says nothing. He breaks his silence with a whisper.

"This is my bride? This is my Livia? You are beautiful beyond words, my love."

"Go ahead and take her hand," Nebo calls out, laughing. "It's allowed now."

Stephen reaches for Livia's hand and steps beside her.

"Atta boy, Stephen," Kehath bellows.

Tellem walks out with a smaller table. One just large enough for two.

"This is for you and your bride. We weren't really going to make you sit apart from each other. Not on your wedding day, at least. Isn't that right?"

The other men let out hoots and hollers.

"Ladies, we need to go to the kitchen area and start bringing out the food," Tullia says.

The day is spent in celebration. One couple plays the flute and lyre and performs happy tunes to keep things lively. Another tells an old Berber folk story.

When the evening shadows appear, everyone rises.

"Have a happy life together," each one says as they leave.

A month goes by. Stephen has bought a second camel for them to ride to and from the market and further identify them with the native Berbers.

Livia has learned to cook in the Berber style, but still cooks dishes her mother had taught her.

"I think I want to enter the medical school at the university," she says one evening as they break their fast.

"You cannot."

"Why?"

"It would draw attention to you."

"I could go disguised as a man."

"As tiny as you are? They'd never believe you."

"Well, I do not know why they wouldn't accept me. My mother went to a university. It was before she met my father, but still."

"I never met your mother. What is her name, and what is she like?"

"Her name is Naomah, and she is so much fun. I really miss her."

"Fun, how?"

"Well, she taught me how to paint. Remember I told you I paint mezuzahs for people's doorposts, and even write out miniature scripture scrolls to go inside."

"It's too bad you cannot do that for the Jews here. But it would…"

"I know. I cannot write Berber. I hate keeping it a secret that I am a Jewess. I wish we could live in Jerusalem, where everyone is proud to be a Jew."

"Well, perhaps someday. But I make my living with Simon's vineyard now. Cannot take it with us."

Livia jumps up. "I know what I will do."

"Huh? Oh, you've got that mischievous grin on your lips," he says.

"I can go to the gymnasium academy disguised as a boy."

"My dear, darling wife. They spend half their day in

lectures, and the other half at their amphitheater playing games in the nude."

"They do?" She squeezes her eyes halfway shut, tips her head down, but looks up at Stephen. "They do? Is that what Achaius, Justus, Secundus, and Trophimus do?"

"They're instructors at the academy. I doubt they spend much time at the amphitheater. Besides, I never knew any of them to take much interest in sports other than watching them."

"Then what am I going to do? I have to do something."

"Tomorrow is the Sabbath. Why do not we have Cheber, Kehath, Nebo, and Telam over with their wives after synagogue, and the women can explain to you how to make your own cloth."

"You mean weave it? I do not want to weave it. I know. I will paint the cloth."

"People do not do that."

"Well, I can, and that is what I am going to do from now on. I am going to paint cloth."

Two days later, when Stephen comes in from the vineyard, he is greeted with a happy wife.

"Well, what did you do with your day today?" he asks, headed for his favorite bench.

"I went to the market and bought my paints."

"You do not speak Berber that well," he replies.

"Oh, I did not go as a Berber. I put on one of the tunics I brought with me and wore that."

Stephen jumps up. "You did what?"

"Do not worry. No one recognized me. And besides, I do not actually look Jewish."

"Women do not ever look Jewish. What were you thinking? Do you realize how dangerous it was for you? And maybe also for me?"

"Oh, pshaw. Everyone was really nice. They were anxious to wait on me. They were all smiles. Everyone was nice."

"Of course, they were nice. You're pretty, you were alone, and, and, I will bet they asked your name and where you were from."

"Of course, they did. I just told them they had to guess my name and where I was from, but that my father was important enough to give them a lot of trouble if they charged me too much."

"You told them about your father?"

"Not exactly. They do not know where he is."

Stephen draws petite Livia close to him and surrounds her

with his strong arms. "Oh, my darling. Do not scare me. The world is not as innocent as you think. I do not know what I would do if I ever lost you."

"Oh, pshaw. You're not going to lose me. We are going to have a long and happy life together."

"By the way, I am with child."

Stephen pulls back an arm's length from her and grins. "You're, you're…"

"Yes. You are going to be a father."

He embraces Livia until she screams for freedom. He steps back and paces. "Now, let me see. We can quit using that room over there as a storeroom so the baby can have his own bedroom. And, is there anything dangerous around here he could fall in to?"

"Stop. He's not going to be born until early next spring. You have plenty of time to change things around."

"Just think. Me, a father. Father Stephen." He struts and grins. He holds up a finger. "'Father, may I walk over there?'" He holds up his other index finger. "'Father, will you lift that for me?'" He holds a fist up in the air. "'Father, will you pick me up?' A father. A father!"

"That is why I have been so sick in the morning and couldn't eat," Livia explains. "And why I had a hard time fixing mutton for you to eat in the morning. Fried mutton smells awful to me. From now on, you're going to have to eat dried mutton. And that is that."

"Oh, I forgive you, my darling, the mother of my baby boy."

"Oh, you're not going to pull me into that argument, sir," she says from the kitchen area where she picks up a plate of cheese, dates, and bread.

"What? No sauce? Oh, I forgot. You are forgiven."

"And stop saying that," she says.

"Yes, Mother," he says.

The winter continues.

"Did you see the snow up in the mountains behind the city?" Livia asks Stephen one morning.

He jumps out of bed, runs out to the courtyard, and looks south toward the mountains.

"Libya, the hottest place on earth has snow?" he says. "Well, well."

They hear a knock on the gate. It is Tullia. She is alone.

"I am worried about your father," she says. "A few days ago, he and several of the other men went up into the mountains to look for wild goats or sheep or deer or whatever else is up there they could bring back."

"Yes," Stephen says. "He came by here and picked up a camel-hair cape Simon left behind. He'll be okay."

The following day, Tullia returns. "The men are not back yet."

"If they're still gone after a week, I will join some other fellows, and we will go up and look for them."

As Tullia returns to the street, she and Stephen hear whooping coming from the direction of the South Gate.

"They're back!" they hear a woman call out while running in the direction of the gate.

Tullia and Stephen head in that direction in time to see a group of men walk through, tattered, some limping, but in good spirits.

Stephen spots his father and motions for him. He and Tullia embrace Ezekiel and take him back to Stephen's home.

"How did you survive the sudden cold and snow? Was it very deep?" Tullia asks.

"You could say it was deep. We just cut some branches and made ourselves a two-sided shelter and built a fire."

"What about food?"

"We hadn't had much luck finding any. But Jehovah was with us. Right near where we stopped to wait out the storm, someone spotted a wild goat that apparently had dropped dead a couple days before the snow. It was in good shape because of the cold, so we skinned it and roasted it. It was just enough for each of us to have some for a meal. It gave us the strength we needed so that, when the snow stopped, we were able to wade out. And here we are!"

Tullia shakes her forefinger at her husband.

"Do not ever do that to me again, Ezekiel. Do you understand?"

Ezekiel embraces his wife, grins, and promises to never do it again.

37 ~ THE SACRIFICE

Spring arrives. One afternoon when Stephen arrives home, he sees his father out in front of the gate, blocking the way.

"What are you doing here? Is everything all right?"

"Well, if you can call being kicked out of my very own son's house all right."

"Why? What did you do?"

"It's not what I did, Son. It's about what you are going to do." His grin is broad.

"Me? I am not going to do anything. I've been working all day and have come home to do nothing."

Ezekiel sits in silence a few moments, hears a scream, and grins, "You are about to."

"To what?"

"Be a father. She has been in labor all day. I think your son or daughter will be saying hello any moment now. You can come out now, men!" he calls out.

The Berber neighbor men all peek around from the side of Stephen's house and step out, grinning.

"Sit," Cheber says. "We men have some valuable advice to give you."

"Now, Stephen, what you do when your baby cries in the middle of the night is give out a real loud snore. Then your wife will pick up the baby and leave you to sleep." Ezekiel leans back and grins.

Moments later, the gate opens.

"You can come in," Tullia says. "No, not you other men. Just Stephen."

His eyes glaze over, and a grin grows large on his face. He walks straight to the bedroom and sees Livia lying on their bed with a bundle in her arms. He joins her. He looks at his baby for the very first time.

"You have a son, my husband," she whispers.

Stephen embraces his wife and son. His lips tremble. He smiles. He looks off in the distance somewhere.

"We shall name him Abraham," he says.

"He was very special to you," Livia responds. "Yes, he shall be Abraham."

They become used to a third member of the family. Today, the parents are sitting under the goat-hair canopy across their courtyard for relief from the noon-day sun.

"Stephen, little Abraham is nearly a month old. We need to take him to the temple and dedicate him to the Lord."

"And see your mother and father while we're there," her husband adds.

"Of course. My father has grown to like you, she says, handing Abraham to Stephen."

"Well, that is progress. Did he come right out and say it in one of his letters?"

"Not exactly, but I know he does. My father may look grumpy, but he has a heart as soft as a cotton boll," she says while spreading out another strip of cotton cloth to paint.

"How can you paint even in the summer?"

"I like to paint. That is how."

"Has your father said anything more about the carpenter?"

"He does in every letter. Jesus is down in the province of Judea sometimes, up in the province of Galilee sometimes, over in Lebanon, up in Syria—just everywhere."

"Is it doing any good? Is the country any better off than it was?"

"He says Jesus heals people everywhere he goes. It's instant too. He makes arms and legs of the maimed grow back. He makes blind people able see again. He cures leprosy. All in an instant."

"Well, then, Israel must be growing very healthy."

"He's speaking too. More than ever. Crowds are following him all the time. He clogs up the highways. Hundreds and sometimes thousands follow him around, wondering what he is going to do next or say next."

"Say what kinds of things?"

"Things like repenting of our bad habits—our sins. Things like loving our enemy. Things like not hiding our light under a bowl."

"So far, so good."

"But Father admits he has a lot of trouble with the last one. He thinks a movement will grow better if it stays secret until it is strong enough to be accepted by everyone."

"Did you say he went to see Jesus one time and talked to him alone?"'"

"Yes. He slipped over there at night."

"Is the other reason that he doesn't want to lose his job with the Sanhedrin? Or worse?"

"He shouldn't be so secretive," Livia says. "I know what he says. But I think he is wrong. Especially about the Sanhedrin."

She stirs some blue in with her jar of yellow.

"I grew up around those men," she continues. "They bounced me on their knee. They have hearts of gold. Just like my father. I do not know why he won't listen to me. Besides, we wouldn't have to dress like Berbers if he wasn't so afraid."

"Livia, he is a strong and wise man. He is just taking his time."

"For what? Jesus is a good man. What is there to decide?"

"I have heard talk by some of the merchant marine captains who come to inspect my wine. They say Jesus is not popular."

Livia puts her hands on her hips. "Who said? The people love him."

"Maybe the people do, but the leaders…"

"We're back to that. Well pshaw. I do not care what you or he say. The Sanhedrin is harmless. And I've made up my mind."

"Well, I think you're right about one thing. We need to go to Jerusalem. Your parents need to see their grandson, and we need to dedicate our boy to the Lord at a temple ceremony."

Livia jumps up and hugs Stephen's neck. "So, when are we going?"

"In two days," Stephen says.

"You cannot get ship passage that fast."

"Oh, we got that last week."

"Last week? Who?"

"All of us. My parents, Achaius and the other three, and you and me. There will be nine of us."

"Oh, my. I need to put this cloth away and start looking through our clothes and food supply," she says, kneeling on the rough pavement of the courtyard. "And I've got a couple baskets to mend so we can put our food in them as we travel. And, oh, another basket for Abraham. So much to do."

She punches Stephen on the arm.

"What's that for?"

"For not telling me last week."

As she steps away from him, she squeaks, "Yippee. I get to wear decent clothes again and talk my own language in public."

Two days later, the nine are aboard a corn ship headed for Egypt, Palestine, and eventually on north to Lebanon, Syria, and Anatolia.

"Hey, Stephen," Usirus asks on the second day of their voyage. "Where did you disappear to? We have been missing you at the Greek-Speaking Freedmen Synagogue. Everyone has been asking about you."

"Oh, you're going to Jerusalem too?" Stephen asks. "Well, I picked up a new venture. So how are Balios and Rabbi Solomus?"

"Fine. Fine as ever."

The wind is good to them. They arrive in Joppa in four days instead of five. The men pool their money and buy a wagon with two mules so all nine can ride in moderate comfort and arrive in Jerusalem within a day.

As always, just before the sacred Day of Passover, the road is crowded with pilgrims. Some walk. Some ride on animals. A few have wagons.

Baby Abraham grows more restless and fussy. Stephen and Livia take turns holding him and trying to convince him to stop crying.

"I am sorry, everyone," Stephen says. "We're going to have to rent a room in Emmaus. You all go on ahead. We will meet you tomorrow at Simon's apartment."

"No, you're not going to stay there alone," Achaius says. "Too many strangers. Too dangerous."

"I am rather tired myself," Ezekiel says. "I am sure Tullia is too."

The group stops for the night. There is no room at the inn. Ezekiel surprises them with a goat-hair tent. "You wondered why I hauled those poles on board the ship and in the wagon?" Ezekiel snickers. "This is why."

That night, baby Abraham sleeps, and so does everyone else. Morning comes. They join the crowds on the highway for the last little bit of their long journey.

An hour later, they see ahead of them the three towers of Jerusalem.

"Oh, this is going to be so exciting," Livia says. "Plus, I did not tell my father we were coming—did not have time. My parents are going to be so surprised."

As they draw closer to the towers and the city, they hear shouting.

"Are we close enough to hear audiences in ole Herod's theater and its Roman abominations?" Ezekiel asks. "We surely cannot hear this far away."

"So, what's going on?" Stephen asks.

"Be careful," Achaius warns. "It sounds to me like a mob shouting, not an audience cheering."

They enter through the Flower Gate, what some call the Joppa Gate. They see people running. Running from the palace Governor Pilate has taken over from the Herods.

Running and shouting.

"Hurry," they hear. "We're going to miss it."

The Cyrenians stop to let the crowd go by, but it is slow to thin out.

"What do we do?" Tullia asks.

"It's something bad," Trophimus says.

"People shaking their fists, others crying."

"Well, there is no place for us to go," Trophimus says in a loud voice. "We cannot go back to Emmaus."

"Looks like we're going to have to go where the crowd goes," Secundus shouts.

"At least they're going in the direction of Simon's *insulae*," Ezekiel calls out over the sin.

"Kill him!"

"Kill him!"

The more progress they make up the street, the faster people run, the meaner they get. Pushing. Shoving. Threatening. Defying.

"Kill him!"

"Kill him!"

"Crucify him!"

Stephen puts his arm across Livia's shoulder as she hugs baby Abraham close to her breast.

Achaius calls to a beggar sitting along the edge of the street. "Who? Who are they wanting to crucify?"

"The carpenter. Jesus!" he shouts. "The people made him king, so the Sanhedrin is killing him. He never hurt anyone."

Stephen holds Livia closer, moving her to the edge of the street so he can be a buffer between her and the mob.

The closer they draw to Antonia Fortress near Simon's house, the madder the mob becomes.

"Kill him!"

"Crucify him!"

"Crucify him!"

Fists in the air. Shouting. Bellowing. Pushing. Shoving. Calling out for blood.

"Crucify him!"

"Crucify him!"

"Crucify him!"

Stephen and the others become one with the mob as it moves together like the body of a monster.

"That is Simon's *insulae* over there," Justus shouts. "But, we cannot break out of this mob to get to it."

"The sheep gate is up ahead," Tullia shouts.

"That is where the shepherds come in to supply the temple with their sacrifices," Stephen shouts, though he is unsure anyone can hear him.

The mob slows. Why? What has stopped the mob?

Romans legionnaires now line the street, making the mob split off to the sides.

Then quiet. An eerie quiet. Dead. Dead silence.

They hear scraping.

As the crowd parts to either side of the street, the spectacle lies bare in front of them.

Three condemned men carrying their own instruments of torture, their crosses.

"Who is the one that keeps falling?" Stephen asks Livia.

She stares. "I think... No, it cannot be."

"Couldn't be who?"

"They finally got him. Took them long enough."

Stephen turns around to the person talking.

"Who is he? The one that is going to be dead before he gets there?"

"Jesus."

"Which Jesus?"

"From Galilee. From Nazareth."

"The carpenter?"

Stephen does not wait for an answer. He looks over at the three condemned men. "Livia, I think the one they've already beaten is, well, I think it's Jesus."

Livia gasps. "No!" she screams. "No!"

Before Stephen can stop her, Livia is running down the middle of the street, clinging to baby Abraham and screaming,

"No! No!" As she does, Jesus falls on the street again. Bloodied and nearly unrecognizable.

She reaches Jesus and kneels. "No," she whispers to him. "Please, no."

"Grab her," a legionnaire bellows.

Jesus reaches up to her. "Do not cry for me." He looks over at other women crying nearby.

"Cry for yourselves…ughh…and your children. One, one day…ughh…you will…ughh…weep at what will happen, happen…ughh…to your children then."

"Get that woman out of the way," a legionnaire barks.

The Roman shoves at Livia just as Stephen catches up with her. Stephen grabs her as she stumbles into the crowd and holds her close. She buries her face in his chest and sobs uncontrolled.

Stephen sees Jesus fall again. *How can he still be alive? They've beaten the skin completely off his back. His eyes are swelled shut. His lips are broken open. Those thorns on his head are digging into him. His beard. All blood now.*

"Sir, this one isn't going to make it out the gate and up the hill," he hears one of the legionnaires tell the centurion. "He'll be dead before we can carry out the sentence," he bellows.

"Then get help," he barks.

The legionnaire looks around. He sees a big red-headed man with a pigtail on each side of his head. The man is in the back, looking over everyone's head.

"Hey, you. Yes, you! Here! Now!"

Stephen sucks in his breath when he sees his old friend. "No, not Simon," he whispers.

The crowd parts and big Simon works his way through it. He stands at attention before the legionnaire staring into nothingness over his head. His fists are clenched.

"Pick it up!"

"Sir?"

"I said, pick it up!"

For the first time, Simon allows himself to look down.

"Master," he whispers.

Jesus looks up at him. "Thank you," he whispers.

Simon now reaches down his strong arms and lifts the beam. It is heavy and roughly hewn. His muscles strain.

"Get up there," the legionnaire orders Jesus. "You have no excuses now."

And so, the crowd moves slowly out of holy Jerusalem with its mission of death.

Stephen and Livia stay as close to Simon and the carpenter as they can. Their tears and sobs mingle with merciless shouts and rush to the ears of the victim.

The Lamb of God shuffles out through the sheep gate.

Jesus staggers on the road leading out of the holy city. His steps are short. He trips and stumbles forward.

He once more falls to the ground. He is on his knees. He puts his hands down in front of him like an animal. He crawls. Like an animal. Up the hill. The hill of his condemnation.

Stephen sees Simon stop and let the beam down a moment to rest. He watches Jesus' every movement.

Where is he getting the strength?

"Oh, Jesus..." Stephen whispers, "you'll never make it."

Jesus stops. The hill is too steep.

Just a little rest. Just to lie here and die.

"Get up!"

Struggling, Jesus manages to stand once more. He gasps for breath and takes a few more steps.

Once again, he is on the ground. Someone from the crowd steps forward to help.

"No! Leave him alone!" shouts a legionnaire.

"Oh, Jesus," a woman in the crowd utters softly. "No man deserves to be treated like this."

"You just loved them," another says.

"That is his mother," someone in the crowd says.

Tears flow freely. She kneels and puts her hands on his bloody face.

"Get her away," the centurion shouts.

Stephen watches as Jesus, with every weakened muscle, with every pain-embroiled nerve, with every ounce of tenacity, pulls himself back to his feet to take a few more steps.

One step...now another...and another...and another. But again, he stops.

Once more Simon stops behind Jesus

"If I could just help you more," Stephen hears Simon say. "Why did you let them do this to you?"

"Get going there," the centurion demands.

"I cannot stand this," Livia says, clinging to her baby. "This isn't happening. This cannot be happening. I am going to Simon's and Abelia's apartment."

Stephen embraces his wife and baby. "Good idea. They live just a few blocks away. I do not know how long I will be. It's like that day when I was seventeen and, well, go on."

He helps her escape the mob, then turns back to what he does not want to see.

"Sir, he'll never make it," a legionnaire tells his superior.

"Well, he's got to live long enough to be crucified. If we do not carry out the sentence, we will be executed ourselves. All right, you and you, pick him up and carry him!"

Two legionnaires march forward. They yank Jesus up and throw each of his bloody arms over their shoulders. They proceed up the hill with Jesus between them. His feet drag and hold them back. They stop. Still holding his arms over their shoulders, they clasp hands to form a makeshift seat.

Simon follows close, his eyes misty with unmanly tears.

Stephen struggles in the crowd to stay close to his friend.

The death march continues up the hill. Simon has the large beam across his big shoulder, "Forgive me, Master," Stephen hears him groan over and over. "Forgive me."

38 ~ GUILT

Having reached the crest of Golgotha Hill, Simon lets loose of his Master's cross, and it falls to the ground. One end strikes a rock.

"You fool! You want to crack the thing?" a legionnaire barks. "We'd have to wait around another hour while they prepared another one. Here you. Jesus. Get down on that beam where you belong."

Simon moves out of the way. A hand is on his shoulder. He turns.

"Stephen? Stephen, this is terrible. This kind of execution is for hardened criminals."

When the three condemned men—Jesus and two thieves— cry out in agony as the spikes are driven through their flesh, Stephen thinks back nearly ten years earlier when they had nailed his best friend to a cross. He had run away that time. He will not this time.

Once the spikes are in place, Jesus is forced to stand and back up to the upright beam permanently in the ground, the blood of other victims of justice dried and black on them.

Once more, the cries of agony as the soldiers lift Jesus up and wedges the crossbeam his body is nailed to into the upright beam.

Then the sign designating the crime.

"What crime can they possibly accuse Jesus of?" Stephen whispers.

After the hammering is over and the soldiers move away, they read the sign. "Good for him," Simon says.

"What?" Stephen asks.

Governor Pilate. Good for him. He called him the King of

the Jews."

"Why?" Stephen asks.

"Because that is what he is. He has become everyone's king."

They find a place to sit. They lean against a boulder and watch the spectacle.

"This is the end of the greatest man who has ever lived. I do not want to miss a moment of his last day," Simon says.

They are quiet.

"Why did it have to be me?" Simon asks. "Why did I have to come in from the vineyard when I did? Why couldn't I have done something different this morning?"

"What about Abelia?" Stephen asks. "What does she think of the carpenter, Jesus?"

"She thinks he is the promised Messiah."

Stephen takes his eyes off the cross and onto Simon. "She does? Do you?"

Simon looks at Stephen, then back at the cross. "Yes. Yes, I do. But now this. It makes no sense. He was able to perform miracles. He could have willed all his enemies dead."

Some in the mob grow tired of the boredom and heads back down the hill and to their jobs.

After a while, more people arrive.

"They must be spreading the word in the city," Stephen says.

Soldiers now laugh, sitting in a circle. "How much do you think this tunic is worth? And those sandals? Anyone need sandals?"

"He's not even dead yet," Stephen says, "and they're gambling his clothes away."

Someone steps out from the crowd and bows before Jesus' cross, his head touching the ground. People become quiet, wondering what he is doing so openly. When he raises his head back up, he lets out a bellow. "Ha, ha, ha. What a king. What a fake." He stands and shakes his fist. "Thanks be to God, we won't have to put up with you any longer."

Many in the mob hoot their approval.

"How long did Jesus teach and perform miracles?" Stephen asks.

"Three years," Simon replies. He shakes his head. "He had so much to give us. And he never asked for anything in return."

They watch as Jesus struggles to take each breath. They hear him cringe as he scrapes his raw back up the beam so he can be in the right position to breathe. They see blood gush out of his wrists and know he cannot stay in that position.

"He turned Israel upside down in three years?" Stephen asks.

"Yes, and we needed him. We needed him to take over our country and be our king."

"Why would he himself be cut off so young in life? He had so much to offer," Stephen replies, still not taking his eyes off Jesus. "Death only brings the end to everything."

"Huh?" Simon interrupts. "Did he say something?"

"Father! Give…them…a full par…don."

Stephen shakes his head. "The first time I saw him, he was calling the temple his Father's house."

"He has said the same thing many times since then." Simon pauses. "Oh, Stephen, what have I done? Have I helped them kill…helped them kill…how can it be?"

"A couple years ago, I noticed David's psalms mentioned God being our king on earth. Are we thinking the same thing, Simon?"

An hour passes.

"Hey, if you're so special, Jesus of Nazareth, jump down off the cross," a Levite shouts. "Go ahead. Do it. Right now. Jump off. If you do that, we might consider believing you are who you claim to be."

One of the priests walks up to the cross and spits at Jesus. He turns to the gathered mob. "Ha, ha, ha. He's a nobody."

"Hey, you! Blasphemer. You're getting what you deserve. How I hate you."

"Saul, just be quiet," Simon whispers.

The young scoffer merges back into the mob.

Simon walks forward. He looks into Jesus' eyes. "I am so sorry, Master. I wish I could have freed you. I did not know how. Can you forgive me too? Can you? I wouldn't blame you if you did not."

Simon gasps when he sees what Jesus does next. He smiles at Simon. "Oh, Master. I do not deserve your forgiveness. I couldn't even save you."

Stephen hears whispering in the mob and among the soldiers.

"Isn't that big guy the one who carried Jesus' cross?"

"Is he from around here?"

"I do not like his looks. That red hair and those pigtails

beside his face."

"What is his name?"

"I wonder where he lives."

Stephen stands and walks over to Simon, who is silent now. "Come on now, friend. They are growing suspicious of you. We cannot afford to lose you today too. Come on."

Stephen takes Simon by the arm and urges him to break away from the cross.

They sit on a different part of the hill.

They sit in silence.

Another hour goes by.

"Who is that woman?" Stephen asks.

They watch as a woman reaches up and touches Jesus. She speaks to him between sobs. She clings to his legs.

The young man with her puts an arm around her shoulders, and she lays her head on his.

Jesus says something to both her and the young man. The young man nods, then guides her back toward a crowd of weeping men and women.

"Those are his apostles, his ambassadors," Simon says. "At least I think that is who they are."

Now and then, Stephen hears Simon whisper, "I am sorry. I am so sorry. I did not want to."

They sit, mostly with their chin on their raised knees. They listen as people down on the highway leading into the holy city shout up at the condemned men.

"Whatever you did, you must have deserved it!"

Stephen notices a new stillness.

"Simon," he whispers. "Do you feel it?"

"Yes, I feel it. There is no breeze. Not even the birds are here anymore."

"What?"

They look up and see the clouds bumping into each other. One floats in front of the sun and stays. The shadow deepens.

Darker. Ever darker. No more shadows. Night. The shadows have given way to night. Where has the night come from? Will it never leave? Bitter, bitter blackness.

Stephen stands. Simon stands. People look up into the sky.

"What's going on?" someone shouts.

The soldiers come to attention. They extend their spears and swords ready to strike an unknown, unseen enemy.

The breeze returns. Wind whips around people's heads. Leaves and debris and dust fly through the air.

Deeper the darkness and deeper.

The centurion shouts to the sky.

"Who are you? Zeus? Apollo? Vulcan? Who are you? Come out. Show yourself."

Silence again. Dead silence. Stillness No more wind or breeze, as though the earth has stopped breathing.

Still, the soldiers stand at attention.

Simon clenches his fists.

Stephen stands and holds his arms heavenward. "He has come to punish us," he says. "God has come to punish us!"

Simon slips over closer to Jesus' cross so he can see. He comes back to Stephen.

"He's still there. I was hoping he had come down. How dare I hope? The world will come to an end now. We have rejected him. We have rejected God's king.

They, as do the rest of the crowd, stand in place, watching the cross.

"What is happening?"

"What have we done?"

Simon sits back on the ground and puts his head on his raised knees, hugging his legs. "We cannot fight it. We have done a terrible thing. And I am part of it."

Stephen sits too. "How long will it be dark, I wonder."

"Till God is through punishing us," Simon says. "Forever, maybe."

"We may never see the sun again."

Another hour. The mob has thinned. Not many left on the hill. Most of the hecklers have gotten bored and gone home or back to their jobs. The women stay. The men behind them stay.

Stephen looks around and stands. "Over here, he calls out."

"I guess we got separated from each other," Trophimus says. "When we saw what was happening, we went over to the temple to see if any of the priests had enough influence over Governor Pilate that they could put a stop to it.

"Instead, they arrested us," Secundus says, carrying a torch.

Locked us in a room just inside what we have heard called the Women's Courtyard," Trophimus says.

"When it got dark, they let us out and said they would kill us if we ever returned," Justus says.

"His cross is over there in case you want to say goodbye to

him," Stephen whispers.

"Is he talking?" Aurelius asks.

"Hasn't talked since it got dark."

The four step to the cross, speak a few words to Jesus, then return to Stephen and Simon.

"Is he still alive?" Trophimus asks.

"We think so, but barely," Stephen says.

"You're really quiet, Simon," Aurelius says, sitting next to him.

"We will explain later," Stephen says. "Just sit with us."

"What did he do so wrong?" Secundus asks.

"Nothing. He was too good for us," Simon says. "He was too good for the world. Now we are being punished."

Another hour. Darkness when the sun should be brightest. Cold when the earth should be warmest. Tears where there once had been joy.

Stephen wonders who has stayed in the darkness. He thinks he sees two men dressed in fine clothes. Like the clothes members of the Sanhedrin would wear. He thinks one of them looks familiar. And wonders.

And another hour. Not many left on the hill anymore. Just sitting. Sitting and waiting for the world to end.

"What was that?" Stephen stands. "He said something."

They watch as a soldier touches a sponge to Jesus' lips. Stephen and Simon move closer.

"It...is...finished," Jesus whispers.

The wind picks up again. Jesus lifts his head up and calls out. "My spirit...it's yours." A loud piercing scream. Jesus drops his head.

"Is he dead?"

The foundations of the earthquake and rumble. The ground trembles. Boulders shake loose and roll; they care not where.

The women scream. The men move their legs far apart to steady themselves. The soldiers stand once again in defensive position.

The centurion looks around. His jaw is taut, his face red, his eyes wide. He stares at the torn figure, pulls out his sword, stumbles over to the cross, hangs on to its shaking base with his other hand. He turns and calls out to the universe, "We have crucified the Son of God!"

"Come on, Simon," Stephen says. "It's all over. We've got to leave."

The six men make their way down the hill, back through the sheep gate, veer to their right, and soon are at the *insulae.*

When they arrive at the third floor, the door opens.

Abelia sees her husband with his blood-smeared tunic and falls into his arms on the landing. Neither speaks. With bloody hands, he embraces his wife.

The others walk around them and enter the apartment. Ezekiel rises off his cushion.

"Is it all over? So soon?" he asks Stephen.

Stephen nods.

"Oh, I see the other men are with you," Ezekiel continues without smiling. "That is good."

When everyone is inside, Tullia closes the door and re-seats herself between her husband and daughter-in-law. Simon hugs Alexander and Rufus, who are now eight and six. When he sits, they hug his neck.

"Daddy, do not cry," Alexander says, then lays his head on his father's shoulder.

Rufus returns to his mother.

Each finds a cushion to sit on. Silence returns.

What can be said? Stephen thinks. *What can be done? It is too late. It is all over. Our hope—the king of our hearts—is gone forever. He was not the Messiah, after all.*

When night comes, Ezekiel shifts onto his knees then stands in front of his cushion.

I guess the Passover has arrived. We have no lamb.

There is a knock on the door. Everyone tenses, their eyes dart from one to the other.

"They must be after us," Simon says. He rises and answers the door.

"Father!"

Livia stands and rushes to Nicodemus. "What are you doing here? You have blood and dirt all over you."

"We buried him. Joseph and I. A few women said some words over him," the rabbi rumbles. "At least he had some kind of funeral."

He looks at his daughter. "I am ashamed."

"Why, Father?"

"I spoke to him in person. I saw him perform amazing miracles. I heard him speak. I knew who he was. We all knew. The whole Sanhedrin knew. That is why we were all afraid."

"Come sit here," Stephen says, pulling out one of the few benches in the apartment.

Nicodemus obliges, and holds his dirty hands up to his face."

"Afraid of what?" Livia asks.

He takes his hands down. His eyes are red and puffed.

"Afraid Jesus was going to replace us leaders and take the priesthood away. I wasn't. I knew he already had. I thought I could do more for Jesus by working in the background, going to see him in secret, and keeping my mouth shut about him in public. I called myself a secret believer. Well, I wasn't a secret believer. I was a secret coward."

Stephen realizes everyone in the room is staring at his father-in-law at the height of his embarrassment.

"Father," he says to Ezekiel on the other side of the room. "Why do not we have the Passover tomorrow. It will be Passover until tomorrow night."

Nicodemus stands. "You are right, young man," he says to Stephen. He takes a deep breath. "I would like to invite all of you to my home tomorrow for the Passover. My wife has made all the arrangements. We will struggle through it together."

Nicodemus steps to the door and leaves without saying anything more. They can hear his heavy footsteps going down the three flights.

Stephen sees others have risen and realizes they are retiring for the night. Nothing more to say. There is nothing more to do. Other than to sleep and dream that this day never happened.

The next morning, they go through the newer part of the city and past the temple. Livia leads them to her girlhood home. When they arrive, a servant washes their feet in a room of marble floor tiles and white granite columns. She then leads them to a courtyard with a large reflecting pool in the middle and small trees planted around the edge. Nicodemus stands, and a woman walks next to him.

He is wearing a plain brown tunic with a brown toga. He wears nothing on his head and no jewelry.

"Everyone, thank you for coming," he says in a soft voice. "This is my wife, Naomah."

Livia's mother is wearing an unbleached wool tunic. Her gray hair falls down around her shoulders.

"We are gratified you came and brought our daughter. I fear she is a handful, just like I was at her age," she says.

Stephen is grateful for some deflection from their sorrow.
"Oh, Mother."

Another man joins them.

"This is my close friend, Joseph," Nicodemus says. "He lives in Arimathea when he is not helping to rule the country with the rest of us Sanhedrin hypocrites."

Joseph steps forward. His clothes are tattered as though he had torn them climbing a mountain or descending into a cave. Blood cakes on them as well as his face and hair. His eyes are puffy, and he smells similar to what Nicodemus had smelled the night before.

They recline on fine Romanesque couches surrounding a large low table. On it are bitter herbs.

"Where is the lamb, Father?" Livia asks.

Nicodemus takes a deep breath. "We sacrificed him yesterday. And the earth has swallowed him. Now, all that is left is the guilt. The bitter guilt."

39 ~ CONFUSION

*T*he Passover is not the joyous occasion it had been the years before. It is not what Stephen or any of the others had expected when they had happily left Cyrene eight days earlier. How can the Passover ever be the same again?

They manage to make it through the stories of ancestors being freed from slavery. They manage to get through eating the bitter herbs and drinking the blood-red cups of suffering. They manage the psalms of David about God now being their king, but not very well.

Is he really? Is God the king everyone had always thought? Does God care?

The feast of sorrow ends, and the guests walk toward the gate to leave. Stephen hangs back. "Go on back to the *insulae* without me. I will be along later."

"I need to talk to my father-in-law. Please, everyone. I will join you later."

Joseph leaves as the others do. Naomah retires to another room.

Nicodemus leads Stephen to the private courtyard. He leans forward.

"First, before you say anything," Nicodemus begins, "I want to thank you for the fine way you have taken care of my daughter."

"I was most happy to..."

"Do not interrupt me, Son. I have needed to say this to you. I know she can be difficult sometimes. But she is happy. So, you must have figured her out—something I was never able to do."

"We love each other, and..."

"You're interrupting again."

"Sorry, sir."

"I never had a son. So, I would be proud if you considered

me a second father. You are far more than I expected in a young man for her. You have showed wisdom in your decisions, though I do not know all."

"Sir. Please. I thank you for your kind words, but I am so mixed up. I used to say that to my father—my first father—a lot. Now I am saying it to you. "After my friend, Abraham, was crucified…"

"Abraham. Is that who you named my grandson after?"

"Yes, and he was crucified in Antioch for standing against the patron goddess of the city and trying to declare Jehovah as the only true God. After that, I decided the only effective way I could stand up for God was to do it secretly.

"When it became too dangerous for us to live in Antioch, we moved to Cyrene," Stephen continues. "I decided I had to be a secret Jew. I had everyone call me Stephanus, I no longer wore a beard—something I kind of liked, so never went back to—and I set up my shop in the Gentile section of the market.

"Eventually, I started a secret synagogue open to all languages and nationalities and levels of freedom. We met in a secret location, had a secret word, whispered our songs, and did secret good works, sneaking around the city at night.

"We thought we could convince the Pagan Gentiles that Judaism was good and right and Jehovah the only true God. Instead, when we were discovered—betrayed by one of our so-called converts—I became a disgrace in the whole city."

Stephen takes his time giving details as Nicodemus waits patiently, sensing Stephen needs desperately to talk. The night continues on as the young man empties his heart.

"Later, I started a guild for the metalsmiths because people were underpaying us. The priests beat me and threatened me with worse. Later I proved their god wasn't real, and they burned me out."

The night continues. Stephen puts his elbows on his knees and his head in his hands. Nicodemus does not say anything.

He raises his eyes. "Sir, I do not know what to do. And now, I am more mixed up than ever. I never was around Jesus much. But I did see him declare the temple his Father's house, and saw him perform miracles, and heard him tell people to love their enemies. A lot of good it did him. They killed him. Our carpenter is dead."

Stephen speaks of all the scriptures that had convinced him who Jesus was, then all the confusions that followed. The night wears on.

"Why? Why is the world so upside down?" he asks his father-in-law. "Why doesn't God come down to us to be our king like he has promised us for thousands of years?"

Nicodemus stands and rushes to the other side of the courtyard. He faces the outer wall away from Stephen. He looks up at the sky, pulls out a kerchief, blows his nose, and returns to Stephen.

Stephen notices his red eyes and is embarrassed.

"Son, you have asked the wrong person. I do not have any answers for you. I am as confused as you. Well, almost. I have, however, come to one conclusion.

"I will never hide what I believe again. They can dismiss me from my job on the Sanhedrin. They can take my house from me. They can force me out of Israel. But I can no longer hide what I believe Jesus to be."

Nicodemus speaks at length of the things he had seen Jesus do and heard him say.

The night continues.

"I need to know, sir. What or who did you decide Jesus was?"

"Somehow, in a way I do not understand," Nicodemus replies, "I believe he was the Messiah promised by God those thousands of years ago. I do not understand how it could be since they killed him."

"Sir, what are we going to do?"

The two men kneel—one young, one old. They pray. Sometimes together. Sometimes silently. They do not know for how long. Their hearts unite as they empty their hearts to God.

"Nicodemus. Someone is at our gate."

Nicodemus hears Naomah's voice. When he looks over at her, he realizes it is daylight on the first day of the week. He rises. "I shall answer the gate. Stephen, stay by my wife. Protect her as you have protected our daughter."

Nicodemus walks to the gate, takes a deep breath, unlocks the night lock, and opens it.

"If you are through with my son—our son—let us go over to the temple and see if anything has changed." It is Ezekiel. Simon is with him.

"I would think they would be happier today," Nicodemus groans.

Stephen walks up and stands next to his father. He looks at his father-in-law.

"We were just thinking and praying about that, Father. We are going to be bold and march right into the temple—not that they will notice us."

"They will notice me," Nicodemus says. "That is fine. Let us go over to the temple and do some marching."

When the four men arrive, they are shocked. The priests coming out are angrier than ever.

Nicodemus steps over to one of the Levite guards.

"What is wrong?"

"I am not supposed to tell anyone, but since it is you, sir. I can tell you: He's alive again."

Nicodemus jerks his head back. "What did you say?"

"Our guards saw it happen. That cave he was buried in with the stone rolled up to the entrance—it was sealed with concrete all the way around, then chained. Jesus himself—or angels maybe—pushed it over like it was a feather, and Jesus walked out, just as alive as you and me."

The guard straightens and looks ahead. Nicodemus turns to see which priest is approaching. When the priest sees Nicodemus, he turns to walk the other way.

"What happened?" Nicodemus calls after the priest. He receives no answer.

"We made an agreement with God last night," he says, turning back to Stephen. Let us keep our promise." He looks at Ezekiel and Simon. And you are part of the agreement. Let us go."

Nicodemus leads the way through the Courtyard of the Gentiles. They climb the eight steps up to the Treasury Courtyard. As they walk through it, they see the Levites rushing to gather up coins from the eleven receptacles.

They climb the steps up to the elevated Courtyard of the Israelite Men. Nicodemus turns to Stephen, Ezekiel, and Simon. "Wait here."

He walks to the end of the courtyard closest to the holy temple itself and climbs the final steps to the grand columned temple portico.

Though not a priest himself, he is allowed to look inside the holy place, ceiling to floor covered with gold. He gasps. He looks around for someone to ask about what he sees.

"Do not. No one is allowed to see in there. Someone close these doors."

Nicodemus turns toward the priest.

"What happened?"

"Nothing. Go home, Nicodemus. Go home."

"But I saw..."

"You saw nothing. Go home."

Nicodemus turns and walks back down the grand stairs and motions for Stephen, Ezekiel, and Simon to follow him.

They walk across the temple complex, not able to tell if Nicodemus is happy or angry. As always, Simon remains silent and shows no emotion. They leave out the west gate and descend to the street below.

"Well? What happened?"

"The grand curtain that hides the Most Holy Place in back of the temple has been torn. Everyone can see inside it. It is not allowed even for Levites and priests to see inside it."

"Is that good or bad?" Stephen asks, confused.

"I think it is good. There is somewhere else we need to go."

"I need to go back to the *insulae*. I've walked too far," Ezekiel says.

"No problem. Where we are going is near the *insulae*. Just outside the Sheep Gate. If we find what I think we will find, I shall start calling it the Lamb Gate, or the Lamb of God Gate.

Nicodemus controls himself and walks slower for the sake of the older Ezekiel. Simon, still brooding, is glad for the slower pace too.

When they pass the Fortress of Antonia, without saying anything to the others, each begins looking closer at the cobblestones between it and the gate. They look for signs of blood. Their Master's blood.

When they draw close to the Sheep Gate, Simon stops.

"No. I will not go through that gate with you. I will never pass through that gate again. Never. I shamed him. I helped them kill him. I am as guilty as they are. Ezekiel, if you want to go back to the *insulae*, I will go with you."

Stephen and Nicodemus continue to the Sheep Gate and walk through it. They are careful to stay on the road and not veer to the left where the dreaded hill is. When they pass the hill, they resist looking up toward the crosses at the top.

"Okay, this is where it is. Come on, Stephen. Let us go see a miracle."

Stephen follows Nicodemus down the path into a garden.

"Where what is?"

"You'll see," Nicodemus says.

Moments later, they come to a clearing in the garden. "This

is where Joseph's tomb is. We buried Jesus here," Nicodemus explains.

They walk side by side through the clearing until they come in full view of the burial cave, the death cave.

"What's the stone doing over there?" Stephen asks. It's not even on its track.

His father-in-law is not with him. He turns to see where he went.

Nicodemus stands before the cave, feet wide apart, laughing at the heavens.

"What's so funny?" Stephen asks.

"He did it! He is alive again! He's back, Stephen! We've got him back!"

Nicodemus grabs Stephen's hands and makes him jump and jig with him. "Celebrate with me, Stephen. He's back! He outwitted us all."

He stops. "Why are we lingering here? You have to go back to the *insulae* and tell Simon. And the others. I have an old friend—Joseph—I need to go see. "Ha, ha, Stephen. He's back."

A little at a time, word spreads throughout the city. "They couldn't keep him dead. Jesus came back to life. We have him back. But where is he?"

After hearing the good news, Simon convinces everyone to stay with him at least until Pentecost fifty days hence. "When Jesus reappears, you want to be here for it," Simon urges.

A week later, Achaius announces he and his friends have decided to stay in Jerusalem and set up a scribe school. They find an apartment in one of the *insulae* in the Greek-Speaking newer part of the city near the Fortress of Antonia.

They do not forget their friends, however. One day, there is a knock on Simon's door. He answers it.

The four stand at the landing of the stairs with two other men.

"May we come in? I want you to meet our friends, Philip and Andrew. They were, they are apostles—ambassadors—of Jesus."

Stephen pulls out extra cushions for the six visitors to sit on.

"You know what it has been like for you—Stephen and Ezekiel—to be Jews in Cyrene. It is like that for Gentile Greek-Speaking Jews here in Jerusalem," Trophimus explains.

"Not long before they killed—well they tried to kill—Jesus—

he was speaking in the Gentile Courtyard of the temple. He kept speaking about all nations repenting and entering the Kingdom of God," Secundus explains.

"We tried to get Jesus' attention, but the local Jews kept pushing us back. We found Philip, and he found Andrew, and together they helped us gain an audience with Jesus," Justus explains.

"It was wonderful. He accepted us completely. So, Philip and Andrew are special friends. We wanted you to meet them," Achaius says.

The rest of the day is spent listening to Philip and Andrew tell their stories of what it was like to live with Jesus.

"You should have been there the time it was pouring down rain in a fierce gale, and our boat was sinking in the storm," Philip explains.

"He just stood up and, in a calm voice, talked right to the storm. 'That is enough. Be quiet now. Be still.' So, the storm obeyed!" Andrew says. "Stopped in the blink of an eye."

"Stay in Jerusalem," Philip says. "Do not go back to Cyrene. We understand they are hostile to Jews there. Stay in Jerusalem."

Stephen looks at his father.

"You could go to work with me in the vineyard," Simon says.

Stephen looks over at Livia. "Well, little Abraham may enjoy playing with his cousins," she says, winking at Abelia.

The decision is made. Stephen goes to work with Simon, and the whole family stays with Simon until they have enough money to rent a place of their own.

Another week goes by. Two weeks. A month. It is now early summer.

"Tomorrow is Pentecost," Simon explains to Stephen and the others. You will enjoy it."

"Is that why there are so many people in the city?" Tullia asks.

"Why do we enjoy it, Father?" Alexander asks.

Simon picks up his eight-year-old son. "Because, God through Moses freed our ancestors from being slaves during what we call Passover, and seven weeks later when they were out of Egypt, and away from danger, God gave our ancestors our law, our Torah, on Mount Sinai. Then the nation of Israel officially began."

"It is a happy time," Abelia adds. "The farmers come into Jerusalem with the first of their winter crops loaded on ox carts, and the oxen decorated with flowers. They go to the temple and offer their first fruits to God."

The next morning, the whole family is up early. They break their fast and hurry toward the temple. As they draw close, they notice a fierce wind above the city.

"Oh, no! Not a storm today," Livia says. "It'll ruin everything."

"Look!" Stephen says. Everyone stares in the direction he is pointing. "The wind went inside that big hostel."

They rush in that direction. Everyone else in the city who has heard or seen the wind rush to the same place. The hostel is so large, it takes up an entire city block. People stand around it, wondering when the building will explode or collapse. It does neither. Instead, twelve men walk out onto the roof.

As with all national holidays, Jews from all over the world are here. All dressed in different ways, many speaking different languages and needing interpreters, all either born Jew or proselyted to Judaism.

"Hey! There is Philip!" Simon tells Stephen, pointing. "There's Andrew!"

The apostles divide up. Three stand on each side of the large hostel roof. They all begin to speak.

"Ha! He's speaking Berber," Simon declares.

"He's speaking Egyptian," they hear someone say.

"He's speaking Persian," still another says.

"Quiet. Quiet, everyone. What are they saying?"

In the hush of the bright early-summer morning, they listen.

"Jesus—the man every one of you nailed to the cross—has come back to life. He has overcome death for mankind."

The apostle pauses. People look at each other. "I did not nail him to the cross. Did you?"

"David prophesied it would happen. God declared he would not abandon his soul in hades or his body to decay. We have all seen him alive again. We have walked with him, talked with him, eaten with him."

"They have?"

"And now this very Jesus reigns in heaven on the throne of God—the one you crucified."

"We did not mean for it to happen," someone calls up.

"We loved him," someone else shouts up to the roof.

"We wanted him to be our king. Remember?" someone else

bellows.

"What are we going to do? We cannot face God."

They hear the answer plain and clear.

"First, be sorry for your sins and decide to do better. Second, be immersed in water and the Spirit. Then you will receive the gift of the Holy Spirit."

"Can we? Is that all we have to do? We're sorry we crucified Jesus. We're sorry."

"Baptize me," someone cries out.

"Baptize me," another shouts.

"Baptize me," Stephen declares.

"Baptize me, and me, and me."

From up on the roof, they hear their instructions. The twelve apostles divide up, with two going to the Pool of Bethesda, two to the Pool of Amygdalon, two to the Serpent Pool, two of the Lower Pool, two to the Pool of Siloam, and two to the Gihon Spring.

For the next ten hours, Stephen and his family sit near the pool where they were baptized and watch as each apostle baptizes twenty-five people each hour.

"God must be giving them the strength to keep going," Tullia says.

By midnight, Philip and Andrew have baptized two hundred and fifty people each.

"That is three thousand people baptized today," Ezekiel says.

On their way back to Simon's apartment, Livia smiles and says, "Guess what today is? It's the day Stephen was born."

"Well, happy birthday," the others say.

"And something else," Stephen adds. "Today is also the day I was born again, just like Jesus told Nicodemus that night in secret."

At the apartment, they stay up all night talking. They recall over and over what had happened that day, and ten days before and fifty days before. Their emotions alternate between inexpressible joy and overwhelming awe.

"Apollos was right that day in Alexandria," Stephen says. "God returned to earth and walked among us. We did not understand, but he forgave us of that."

He stands. And paces. The others watch him, though their thoughts transcend the apartment.

"Jesus became the Lamb of God." He stops and looks at Livia. "He died on Passover Eve, the night we were supposed to eat the lamb we had killed."

"He paid our penalty for our sins on the cross. Somehow he did," Ezekiel says, trying to comprehend his own words.

"So much to understand," Simon says. "So much to grasp."

"Father," Stephen says at dawn. "We have to go back. We have to return to Cyrene. We cannot keep this a secret."

40 ~ THE PLAGUE

*T*he ship is full of passengers who had gone to Jerusalem for Pentecost and are on their way home.

Ezekiel and Tullia are more quiet than usual. Stephen and Livia are more quiet than usual other than doing and saying whatever is necessary to keep Abraham safe now that he is learning to walk.

"Father," Stephen says. "I am mixed up. What makes a man die for someone else? Take Jesus, for example. He had his entire life ahead of him. Why did he do it?"

"He was the Son of God," Ezekiel responds. "You're asking me to understand the Son of God."

They are quiet for a while.

"You know that prophecy Isaiah wrote?" Ezekiel finally says. "About the Messiah's death? People thought he was being punished for his sins. But really, he was being punished for ours. He was taking our punishment for us."

Stephen wrinkles his brow, squints, and smiles. "Well, Peter said if we call on his name and repent and are baptized, our sins are forgiven, and we receive the gift of God's Spirit. Not only us but all mankind."

"So, there you have the answer to your question. He accomplished more by dying than living."

"But how many people are in such a situation?"

He watches a seagull fly overhead with a small fish in its beak. *That fish died so the seagull could live.*

"Hey, you two," Livia says with Abraham clinging to the bottom of her tunic. "Do not you hear the captain up on the bridge?"

The two men turn in the direction of the voice they had not noticed.

"There are pirates in these waters between Crete and Egypt. They steal cargo and people for trade. If you would like to get off the ship now, we are nearing Alexandria. We will refund the rest of your fare if you had planned to go farther. We will stay in Alexandria just long enough for that and to bring more food and water on board for the crew. Then we will sail again."

Tullia walks over to the men and takes Ezekiel's hand. "What do you think?"

"Wife, we have handled pirates in the past. I think we can handle these as well." His laugh is nervous.

"You've handled pirates?" Livia asks, looking up at Stephen.

"Oh, I never told you how we ended up in Cyrene instead of Rome?"

"You lived in Rome too?" she asks, her eyes wide and her head tipped to one side.

Stephen laughs. "No, we never made it to Rome. We ended up on Crete, and the quickest way to escape was to Cyrene."

"You escaped? And from pirates?"

"Son, there seem to be a lot of things you have not told your wife yet," Ezekiel says.

"Tonight, I promise to tell you about our pirates," Stephen says, picking up Abraham and putting his other arm around his wife.

Another day at sea. The women are sitting near the bridge, letting Abraham play between them. The men are standing at the rail again.

"Jesus overcame death for mankind. He accomplished a lot with his death," Stephen says. "But what if a Christian is threatened with death? What if that happens someday? What would it accomplish?"

Ezekiel looks at his son, then paces a while. He returns to Stephen, wringing his hands.

"Why are you thinking about those things? As a Christian, you will be safe. Cyrenians only hate Jews, and we are no longer Jews."

"But we believe in the same one true God."

Ezekiel pats his son on the back. "Son, God is not going to let you or any other Christian die. You're going to live to be an old man with grandchildren, just like I did. So, quit worrying. Now, when we get back, you're going to have a lot of work to catch up on. The weeds in your vineyard are going to be up to your knees."

"Maybe I will go back to locksmithing, Father. Since I am no longer a Jew, maybe they'll let me take over Ovidius' shop. It was still empty when we left."

"And the vineyard?"

"I left some new wine in vats in the courtyard when we left. I might be able to sell that for enough to hire someone to take care of the vineyard."

"Ha. My son is twenty-five years old and already a cruel taskmaster," Ezekiel says. "Ha!"

Thereupon, Ezekiel resumes pacing and wringing his hands.

"What is going on with your father?" Tullia asks, joining Stephen at the rail. "What did you say to him?"

"Nothing that would cause him to pace so much. I am the pacer in the family. Not Father. He's acting strange."

"He isn't eating anymore, either. Maybe it's just all the excitement of the past week."

The trip takes six days, not counting the two days on the road walking between Jerusalem and Joppa.

At last, they disembark in Apollonia. Ezekiel hangs on to Tullia hard as they walk down the gangplank.

"You know, I think we need to get a cart or a wagon to go the rest of the way home," Stephen says. "Do we have any money left?"

"I have a little my father slipped me so I could buy some fabric to make normal tunics with," Livia says. "He's decided I do not need to dress like the natives anymore. He's decided he was wrong and I was right!"

Grinning, she pulls out a silk pouch from behind a wide belt and hands it to her husband. Stephen hires one of the wagon drivers lined up along the docks. They load up the wicker chests and baskets and larger leather pouches, then climb on board.

"Here, Father," Stephen says as he sees Ezekiel lose his balance. "Let me help you."

"Whew. My legs wobbled there for a moment," Ezekiel says.

The wagon makes its way up the steep incline to the city of Cyrene high and overlooking the sea. They ride through the North Gate.

"Drop my parents off first," Stephen tells the wagon driver. "Then come back."

Stephen and Tullia walk on each side of Ezekiel to their gate.

"I do not need you to hang on to me," Ezekiel tells them. "I am perfectly all right. I am just going to have to get used to the hellish summer heat here again."

Stephen unloads his parents' luggage and returns to the wagon. Being on a city street, the wagon moves at a slow pace.

"Look. That old man over there is staggering," he tells Livia. "Just like my father. Is that what growing old is like?"

They arrive home, unload, and go inside.

"Ah. It's nice to be home again."

"Jerusalem was almost our home. It was for a little while," Livia says, setting Abraham down to explore the home he does not remember. "I am going to the market now and get us some food for the noon respite and tonight."

"Will people be there in the heat of the day?"

"We haven't reached the heat of the day yet, dear. It's still morning. The food vendors will be out." She turns to Abraham, still exploring. "Now Abraham, be good while I am gone, and do not hang on to your father's leg. He has work to do."

"Leg, *Abba*. Leg."

Stephen pulls out his boxes of lock-making supplies to inventory them. He etches his tally on a clay tablet, then makes a list of what he needs.

Livia returns. "Ha, ha. Nobody knew who I was! They were used to a Berber girl. When I told them I was your wife and that we had been married two years, they asked where you had been since you disappeared shortly before our wedding.

"What did you tell them?"

"I just said you'd gone down into the desert until we were married. You took over Simon's vineyard over toward the mountain, then we went to Jerusalem, and now we are back."

"They were satisfied?"

"I guess. By the way, in the market, I saw another man staggering like your father. That is the third man. I hope it's just the heat."

The following day, Stephen takes as many of his clock-making supplies as he can carry on his back and in a shoulder pouch, and walks toward the market. On his way, he stops at the government basilica and obtains a permit to resume selling locks in the city.

He arrives, walks down the aisle where he had formerly worked with Ovidius, unlocks it, enters, and sets down his supplies.

He locks up again and walks around the market.

"Hello, there, Stephen. When did you get back?"

"Well, if it isn't the mysterious Stephen. Where have you been all this time?"

"Hey, Stephen. Where did you disappear to?"

"Down in the desert part of the time, working in the country part of the time, and in Jerusalem part of the time," he answers them all.

When he arrives at the last aisle, the aisle of the Jews, he is welcomed with smiles by some and suspicion by others.

"Oh, Stephen, we are having a special time of prayer tonight," his old potter friend, Joshua, says.

"Did you have a dry winter here? I shall indeed join you and help you pray for rain."

"No, Stephen. It's something else. It's for the men. One in our congregation who had the nervous sickness died last night."

Stephen takes in a sharp breath. He squints and tips his head. "What did you say?"

"Abi. He got the sickness and died last night."

"Oh, no. Did you say others are getting it?"

"A few. It hasn't hit the whole city yet, but everyone is scared."

"I am taking my father to the *hospitium* right now. And, yes, I will join you tonight to pray."

Stephen rushes out of the market, turns left, walks between the *hospitium* and Jewish-Born Freedmen Synagogue, then takes off running. He passes the theater
and bathhouses and arrives at his parents' house.

"Mother, let me in. Hurry!"

Tullia slides the bar off the gate and opens it.

"How is Father? Is he any worse?"

He notices his father in the center of their courtyard pacing and sometimes stumbling. He rushes up to him and puts his arm over Ezekiel's shoulders.

"Father, there is a sickness going around. I think you have it. You need to go to the *hospitium*."

Ezekiel looks at his son. His lips tremble, and tears come to his eyes. "My head hurts."

"I will borrow the cart of the man next door," Tullia says when she hears the news.

"No, I will," Stephen says. "Sit with Father until I return."

In a little while, Stephen walks through the gate. "The cart is hitched to a donkey."

They make their way back up the street and arrive at the

hospitium. They take Ezekiel in and are met by an aide.

"I see he has the sickness. We are keeping all the men together in this ward. Follow me."

They settle Ezekiel on a cot, and the aide gives him a cup of tea. "This is *tiluit* for his pain, *taghiat* for his dizziness and spasms, and *uzuer* to help him sleep," he tells Tullia.

A man on the other side of the ward screams. The aide pretends he does not hear.

Stephen walks back out to the open courtyard and sees someone familiar coming toward him. "Gaius, is that you?" he asks.

The *medicus* pauses and stares a moment at Stephen, then laughs. Oh, yes. I think I remember you. You got an arrow in your lower leg for wandering into desert mountains you knew nothing about and had a silly blue headcover on that looked more like a child's tunic. Ha, ha. You've done some maturing."

Stephen grins. "Got married and have a little boy of my own. He's close to the age of the little boy I was looking for out in those desert mountains I knew nothing about. So, where is Theophilus?"

"Oh, he rejoined his legion and got promoted to tribune. I decided to stay here with ole Blasius, although I hear he is packing up to go to Rome and have a triumphal arch named after him. So, what brings you here?"

"My father, I am afraid."

"The nervous sickness?"

"Yes, I guess that is what you could call it. We just got back from Jerusalem, and he started having symptoms on the ship."

"I've been trying to figure it out. Hippocrates described the same symptoms, but they were for sheep and goats. How old is your father?"

"He is seventy-six. I know. I know. Everyone thinks my mother is his daughter. She is 30 years younger than him. But they have been madly in love with each other since the beginning. Anyway, he's seventy-six years old."

"And you say he just arrived in the city? Let us sit over here and talk."

"How long has it been going on?" Stephen asks.

"About a month now. At first, I thought the men were catching it from each other. But your father hasn't been here. How did he get it? Did anyone else have it on board the ship or in Jerusalem?"

"Not that I saw. What about my mother? Is she safe in there with him?"

"That is another strange thing about the sickness. Only men get it. Not women."

"Doctor! Doctor!"

A woman comes running out of the ward where the plague victims are kept. Tears stream down her face, hair is in her eyes, she is trembling and clenching her fists.

"My husband. My husband."

Medicus Gaius runs into the ward and examines her husband.

Soon the wife catches up with him. Stephen is at her side.

The *medicus* looks up. "I am afraid your husband is gone. I am very sorry. I tried to save him. But the gods apparently had other plans."

The woman falls on her husband's remains, clinging to him and sobbing. "No, no, no."

Gaius stands and looks at Stephen. "That is the fourth one," he sighs.

One of the other men in the room screams. "He's getting me. He's getting me! Get him away from me! No. No! Help me!"

As the *medicus* leaves, Tullia comes over to the new widow. "Aello, I am so sorry," she says.

Stephen follows the *medicus* out. "My father paces and teeters sometimes, and now he's getting a headache. What else will happen if he gets weaker?"

"Exactly that. He will get weaker. He will have pain in his arms and legs as well as his head, and it will grow worse. Toward the end, he will have terror dreams as though he is becoming mad."

"Who else has succumbed to this plague?" Stephen asks.

Gaius pauses. Let me see now. Thales and Carpus were the first. Then there was Spiro and now Agathon.

Stephen returns to his parents. He sits a while next to Ezekiel's cot.

He notices the shadows grow long in the courtyard. "I need to get home to my family," he says, kissing his mother on the forehead. "Livia or I will come back tomorrow."

He leans over and kisses his father on both cheeks, stares at him a moment, and leaves.

"What is happening?" Livia asks when Stephen arrives home.

"It's a plague. Four men have died so far."

"No women?"

"It doesn't seem to affect women."

"Maybe we should not have come back."

"It isn't catching. The men do not give it to each other. No one knows what is causing it. There are more offerings at the temples to the gods, and our Greek-Speaking Freedmen Synagogue is meeting tonight to pray for the city."

"You haven't told them?"

"What? Oh, about being a Christian now? I will soon. But no one's mind is on anything right now except the plague."

"*S'Abba*. I want *S'Abba*," Abraham says, grabbing his father's leg.

Stephen stoops and lifts his son into his arms. "Your grandfather is very sick. If he is still…Well, if it's okay, tomorrow I will take you to see your *S'Abba*."

After breaking the day's fast, Stephen walks over to the synagogue. He greets friends he has not seen in over two years. They ask where he has been, and he tells them his usual brief desert-country-Jerusalem account.

They pray together. Stephen is glad to be back among his old friends again. *God, help this plague leave quickly so they will be receptive to Jesus*, he prays in his heart and mind.

On his way home, passing by a house, he hears screaming. "No! Get away from me! Help! No!" coming from the hidden courtyard of a neighbor.

The next morning, Stephen takes Livia and Abraham to the *hospitium*. Livia takes a change of clothes for Tullia and some food.

The closer he draws to it, the harder and faster Stephen's heart beats. *Please, Jehovah. Let him still be alive.*

They walk in and see Ezekiel sitting up and smiling.

"The *medicus* gave him some opium," Tullia says, rising to kiss her family.

"He said it would make me sleepy, but it hasn't hit yet," Ezekiel tells his family.

Abraham toddles over to his grandfather and lunges at his chest. "*S'Abba. S'Abba*," he says. Ezekiel pulls him up onto his lap.

"Have you been a good boy, Abraham?"

"Yup!"

"You are to say 'Yes, sir'," Livia corrects.

"And *S'Abba*, you are going to be a grandfather again," she adds.

Stephen jerks his head around and stares at his wife. "He is? We are?"

"Next winter. And I insist on giving Abraham a baby sister."

Stephen smiles and holds Livia's hand. They sit in silence a while.

"So, have you met the others in the ward, Father?"

"Well, I am kind of weak to be walking around, and the other fellows are too. But, Xan is here, and Nikator and Hypos. In this heat, everyone is wishing for that snow we had last year. And that goat we shared. Or was it two years ago? I am growing very tired."

Stephen helps Ezekiel slide down in his cot. He falls asleep. The family watches him. Trying to absorb him. Trying to etch everything about him in their memories.

Stephen looks at his mother. "Do you think he will get the terrors?" he whispers, not wanting the answer.

"The medicus said the opium will keep it under control for a while," Tullia replies.

Ezekiel opens his eyes. "Sweetheart," His voice is hard to hear except by those nearest him.

"Yes, my darling," Tullia says.

"I never deserved you. I still do not know what you saw in me. But I have been the most blessed man in the world."

"I am the one who has been most blessed. A woman could never ask for more love than you have given me."

Stephen watches his parents, a little embarrassed, listening in on their intimate moments, but also proud.

"We had a good life together, did we not?" Ezekiel whispers.

"Oh, indeed, we did, my love. Indeed, we did."

"Maybe someone will write a book about us someday," he says, though unable to smile.

Tullia smiles for him. "You know, I suspect you are right, my love."

Ezekiel closes his eyes. His family watches his every breath. Which one will be the last?

He opens his eyes again and looks at Tullia. "Give my blank scrolls to my scribes. And, when you're done with the ones I wrote on, give them to Abraham."

"Thank you, Father," Stephen says. "Abraham will treasure them." He pauses. "And, sir, I just want you to know that you have been the best..."

Stephen's jaw quivers, tears come to his eyes, and he presses his lips hard together.

His father looks over at Stephen and pats his hand with his gnarled, arthritic hand. "I know, Son. And you have been the best too."

"Who can I talk to now whenever I get mixed up about things?"

Ezekiel closes his eyes, then opens them again. "Son," he whispers. "Take the ring off my finger... The one your grandfather...made for me when I was...a boy." Ezekiel stops and takes a labored breath. "He said...it is an eternal circle and...will remind you of God's...eternal protection. Take...it."

He closes his eyes again.

When he screams in his sleep, Tullia moves closer and puts her cool cheek next to his.

They watch him the rest of the day. Just before sunset, Ezekiel, born into slavery, freed in body by Athenodorus and freed in soul by Jesus, dies.

41 ~ WIDOWS

For a long time, they stare at what is left behind of the man they had loved for so long. Sometimes Tullia brushes his hair back and kisses him. Sometimes she holds his face in her hands. Sometimes she pats him gently on his cheek. Sometimes she lays her head down on his pillow next to him and closes her eyes to remember.

"He used to be a big man. Now look at him," Stephen says.

Tullia looks up at her son. Her eyes are strained.

"We must take him home now," she whispers. "He would want his last few hours to be at home."

Stephen and his mother slowly pull the covers down to Ezekiel's feet. Stephen lifts his father's now-frail body into his strong arms. Tullia leads. Livia and Abraham follow. They walk out of the *hospitium*, Stephen still carrying his father, turn left, walk past the theater, and arrive at Ezekiel's house.

When they enter, Stephen sees where his mother had brought their bed out into the courtyard under the goat hair canopy.

"I need to be alone with him now, Son," Tullia whispers.

The following morning Stephen returns with Rabbi Levi of the Jewish-Born Freedmen Synagogue and a cart. "It is being pulled by the colt of a donkey, as you requested, ma'am."

"Thank you, Rabbi," she whispers.

"The congregation has been notified," Rabbi Levi tells Tullia with his gentle voice. "They are waiting at the synagogue."

She nods her consent.

Stephen sees she has dressed her husband in his finest tunic and robe and placed in his hand a scroll.

"It is of the prophet, Zechariah," she tells Stephen. "He prophesied so much about the Messiah's death. He loved it."

She takes the scroll, Stephen picks up his father, and they move out to the waiting cart. Ezekiel is placed on the cart that has been draped with white and blue linen. The colt of a donkey is hitched to it. They walk in slow motion to the synagogue.

The funeral is solemn. Ezekiel is honored for his good and righteous life. They read from the Torah and the Prophets and chant between readings.

Stephen rises. "Brothers, my father was the most honorable man I have ever known. I have been privileged to be his son. He leaves me a legacy I never dreamed possible, a legacy you do not know about. Today I declare that legacy to you.

"In his hand is the scroll he penned himself of Zechariah's prophecies. Brothers, I am here on behalf of my father to tell you what he was intending to tell you himself.

Behold.
I will remove the sins of the land
In one day.

"Brothers, it happened. My father and I witnessed it in Jerusalem."

He pauses as members of the congregation glance at each other, then look back at him. "Just as Zechariah prophesied."

"He came to us just as he promised, with his salvation," Stephen resumes. "He came to us humble and riding on the colt of a donkey. He was betrayed for thirty pieces of silver. He was pierced, and we mourned for him as the only Son. A fountain of blood flowed from the wounds between his arms on the cross for our sins. All just as Zechariah predicted.

"The predicted earthquake came. There was no light in the middle of the day. And on that day, brothers, living waters of salvation flowed out of Jerusalem."

He pauses once again. He waits for the people to grasp what he is saying. His voice grows louder.

"The silver and gold crown Zechariah spoke of has been placed on the head of the Messiah, Jesus the Christ of Nazareth. He is now on his throne as our High Priest and King in heaven."

Stephen whispers his final words. "And we worship him."

He takes a deep breath, pauses, and adds, "The last advice my father gave me was a few days ago when I was talking to him about dying. He said, 'Son, God is not going to let you or any other Christian die.' He was right. Today, my father is more alive than ever because he is with Jesus."

Stephen seats himself between his wife and mother in the front row.

All is quiet. No chanting. No reciting. No praying. Only quiet.

At last, Rabbi Levi stands. "His grave has been dug at the cemetery out the South Gate. The women have prepared food for us when we return. But I believe we have important things to talk about before eating."

It is midnight before Stephen and Livia walk Tullia to her house.

"Mother, would you like us to spend the first night with you? Or even the first week?"

"Son, I will be okay alone. But, before you go," she takes his face into her up-reached hands, "what you said and did. It was exactly what your father would have said and done."

Stephen places his hands on her wrists and looks down at his mother. "But what happened. They all believed, and all became Christians. Not just part of them. All of them, Mother. The whole congregation."

The following day, Stephen returns to his mother's house. When Tullia opens the gate, he sees the women of the Jewish-Born Freedmen Synagogue seated in a circle.

"We are searching through all the old prophets to see what else Jesus fulfilled in his life and death. Would you like to join us?"

Stephen stutters. "Well, no. I am on my way to the market. I am going to set up my shop again."

"We are going to meet the day before the Sabbath from now on. Tell Livia about it."

Stephen walks on past the theater and bathhouses and arrives at the *hospitium.*

"Have any more..."

"Yes," Medicus Gaius answers. "Two more came in from the city, and one more died last night. That is six so far."

"If you have a moment, please come sit with me. I have heard something I need to check with you."

They go to a side room, and Gaius hands him a clay tablet with ten names on it. "These are the men that have passed through my ward so far or are still in it, waiting to die. Do you recognize any of these names?"

"Yes, they were all in my father's hunting party."

Did they run into any diseased animals that might have

been foaming at the mouth or snapped at them?" Gaius asks.

"No. Their trip was pretty uneventful, except that there was a bad snowstorm up there. They found a dead goat in the snow that seemed pretty well preserved, so they cooked and ate him."

"Hippocrates referred to goats getting a madness disease where they paced and got dizzy and lost strength in their legs."

"What are you saying?" Stephen asks.

Gaius leans back against the wall behind him. He takes a deep breath. "That is it. That is what is killing them. If that goat had the disease, they caught it from the goat. It is a slow-acting disease often taking a year before it shows up."

"Does it have a name?" Stephen asks.

"They just call it the Madness Disease. Or, in our case, the Madness Plague." He shakes his head. "I am sorry, Stephen. I am truly sorry."

Stephen clasps Gaius' hand and forearm. "You have done your best," he says. "God bless you."

"Which one?"

Stephen resumes his walk. He arrives at the market and turns down the second aisle. He arrives at the end where the shop is he had shared with Ovidius.

Within an hour, he has the front shutter open, the front door unlocked, and his forge going.

"Hey, what are you doing here, Stephanus or Stephen, or whatever you are?"

"Diogenes, my friend," Stephen says, walking toward the tapestry merchant next to his shop.

"I am not your friend, and you are not welcome here. Jews belong in the back row. You know that."

"But, Diogenes, my friend, I am no longer a Jew."

"You cannot un-Jew yourself. Once a Jew, always a Jew."

"I am a Christian now. I believe Jesus of Nazareth came to earth to rescue us from the clutches of Satan so we can come back to life after we die."

"First, I never heard of Jesus, second, I have no idea where Nazareth is; third, I do not believe people come back to life after they die. So, leave. You are still a Jew."

Stephen's muscles stiffen and bulge. *Love your enemy. Love your enemy. Love your enemy.*

"I am not here to fight. Hey, I can make a special lock for you so no thief in the world will be able to get into your..."

"I do not want your locks. I do not want you. Everywhere

you go, there is trouble. If you do not leave, I will notify Governor Blasius that you were one of TacFarinas' outlaws. Yeah, I know all about you going into his hideout. Everyone knows."

"But, my friend…"

"Stop calling me your friend. I am not your friend and never will be."

Diogenes ducks into his booth and comes out with a weaver's beam. He marches toward Stephen with it. "Dead or alive. I do not care which way you leave here."

"I am sorry you feel that way, friend."

"Stop calling me that. Now you have until I count to one hundred to get everything out of that shop. I do not care where you put it or throw it. One-two-three-four…"

Stephen rushes inside his shop and carries as much to the main aisle as he can by Diogenes' count to one hundred.

Rather than return home, Stephen picks up his most valuable tools and heads for the back row of the market.

All the booths have been taken near the main aisle, including the one he used to have. He walks down toward the far end of the Jewish row where the Greek-Speaking proselyted Jews are.

"Well, well. Look who's back," Usirus says. Where have you been for the past two years?"

"Down in the desert, out in the country, then over to Jerusalem," he replies.

"Setting up shop again, I see."

"Yes. Is there a booth down here that is available?"

"The one at the far end is. The very last one."

Stephen does not smile.

"Too bad. No one ever goes down there. But, at least you'll have a place to work. By the way, are you coming back to our synagogue? We need you. Several of our men have died of that strange disease, that nervous plague some are calling it. Hey, I heard about your father. I am sorry. He was a good man. Well, can I help you with anything?"

"Yes, friend," Stephen replies. "The rest of my supplies and equipment are at the front aisle. If, that is, they are still there."

"So, they gave you a hard time, did they? Shouldn't have tried it," Usirus says, walking Stephen up to the front aisle. "Why did you, anyway?"

"I will tell you next Sabbath, maybe."

The day before the Sabbath, Stephen is at his mother's home on his daily checking in on her.

"Would you like to start going with us to the Greek-Speaking Freedmen Synagogue?" Stephen asks her.

"I think I would. But I thought you were going to stop worshipping as the Jews do and just worship on the first day of the week in Jesus' honor," Tullia says.

"I think I will do both. I want to try something with them."

The next morning for the first time in two years, Stephen's family enters his old home synagogue. They stop and stare.

The women's side is full. The men's side sparse. Livia and Tullia find a seat. Tullia takes the hand of the woman next to her—the most recent widow.

"Welcome, Stephen," Usirus says. "Rabbi Solomus was just telling me how much he missed you, weren't you rabbi?" he says, turning to the older man.

"Uh, yes. Let us now begin."

The rabbi walks to the podium, raises his hands in his usual manner, and pronounces the benediction.

With his amen, everyone drops and puts their heads to the floor, says a silent prayer, and rises.

The rabbi clears his throat. We have lost three more since last week—Linos, Nikator, and Hypos. He looks over at the widows. "Your brothers are all deeply sorrowed for you."

The chanticleer stands and leads the congregation in a psalm. The sound is different. Hardly any more booming voices. Now mostly the soft sound of widows in mourning.

"Stephen," Usirus says from the front, "would you like to come forward to give us our reading?"

Stephen stands and steps up to the podium. He selects one of the prophets—Isaiah.

> Jehovah God's Spirit is on me.
> He anointed him priest and king
> To comfort the afflicted,
> Heal the brokenhearted,
> Liberate captive sinners,
> Free those imprisoned by sin,
> And announce this is the year of the Lord.

Rabbi Solomus rises to speak, but too late.

"Brothers and sisters, this has happened," Stephen announces. "This prophecy has been fulfilled. God's anointed, the one he made priest and king has come at last. He comforted people, he healed people, he forgave people. Jesus of Nazareth freed mankind imprisoned by sins." He pauses.

"This year, my brothers and sisters, is the year it was all fulfilled. This year was the year of the Lord predicted since the time of Adam and Eve and renewed to Abraham and Moses."

Stephen pauses as the audience looks at each other in surprise, then looks back at him in anticipation.

Rabbi Solomus stands, scoots over to Stephen, and nudges him until he is at the edge of the table and Stephen gives up.

"Thank you for the reading. Now, my sermon for today is about peace. Jehovah is the God of peace. Peace and truth..."

The service is over. When Stephen walks to the outside door, Xenon meets him. "You shouldn't have tried to take his place like that. He is a proud man."

"I wasn't trying to do anything but comment on the prophecy."

"It was more than a comment, brother. Do not ever do it again."

"Go on without me, Son," Tullia says. "The other widows and I need some time together."

"Good for you," Livia says, walking home with her husband. "Speak out. It doesn't matter if they do not want to hear it. They do not know what they want. They do not know what they need. They need you here, Stephen. I am so proud of you."

Stephen takes his wife's hand and lets Abraham repeat his mother. "I proud of *Abba* too. I proud too."

The following morning Stephen realizes he had not determined with his mother where they were going to hold their Christian worship.

"I assume we are going to worship with the Jewish-Born Freedmen Synagogue since they all became Christians," Livia says.

"Yes, but they call it the Jewish-Born Freedmen Church of Christ now."

The three walk to his mother's house and knock on the gate.

"Yes, we are all ready to go," Tullia says when she opens the gate.

"We? We who?"

"The widows, of course. I spent Sabbath afternoon with them, telling them about our hope to live again through Jesus. They want to try worshipping with Christians today."

They arrive at what used to be a synagogue building, but

which is now the first church building in Cyrene. Everyone is excited to be Christians. Tullia walks in first, greets her old friends, and the widows follow her in. Extra benches are brought in for the visitors on the women's side.

Brother Levi—as they call him now—rises and proclaims Jesus as the Messiah that had been prophesied all those hundreds and thousands of years.

They sing the same psalms of David, they read the same scriptures—though with new eyes. They pray the same prayers except, instead of asking for the Messiah to come, they thank God that he has come at last.

The only big difference in their worship is that the leader brings out unleavened bread, which everyone takes a bite of to remember Jesus' body broken on the cross. A time of silent prayer and meditation follows. Then everyone takes a sip of warm red wine to remember Jesus' blood given away on the cross. More prayer and meditation.

Then the chants and prayers. The service is over. Stephen is pleased. Tullia and Livia are overjoyed.

As they leave the building, they realize something is not right. No one speaks to the visiting women. Stephen stays behind.

"Were they not welcome?" he asks Brother Levi.

"They are welcome by Jesus, of course. But they are not used to our ways. They used to worship idols, and although they converted to Judaism and may want to be Christians now, they do not have the foundation the rest of us have. They need to be given special attention in the ways only they understand."

Stephen stares. "Brother Levi, I can hardly trust my ears. You surely did not claim Jewish-Born Christians are superior to Greek-Born Christians."

"They do not have as deep an understanding of the scriptures as we do," Levi replies. "It is not their fault. It's just the way things are."

Stephen walks home alone, glad the women had gone on ahead. Though it haunts his mind, he does not speak of it the rest of the week.

He settles in making locks at the end of the last row, where the Jews of Cyrene are forced to sell their wares and services. The week goes by.

The Sabbath returns. Once again, he and Livia stop to pick up Tullia, and they walk to the Greek-Speaking Freedmen Synagogue. Once again, Rabbi Solomus stands, raises holy hands to the heavens, and pronounces the benediction. Then the bowing and praying.

Rabbi Solomus sighs and groans. "Alas. The last two have succumbed—Nestor and Fotios. Our eleven men will be sorely missed. Amen."

The chanticleer leads two psalms of David. The reading is done this time by Helios.

"Stephen, will you please lead us in our closing benediction?" Balios asks.

"Great Jehovah. We bless you for granting us our greatest wish. We praise you. We adore you. We worship you. At last, you have sent your very own Son to be our Savior. At last, it is all fulfilled. At last..."

"And amen!" The voice bellows from the podium. The few men who are left of the congregation file out.

"Stephen, if you cannot keep this vile sect out of our synagogue, we will have to keep the synagogue out of you," Rabbi Solomus says. "You are no longer welcome here."

42 ~ REJECTION

"The widows come every morning now before it grows too hot," Tullia tells Stephen and Livia on one of their daily visits late in the week.

"They bring little things their husbands had made that are dear to them now. They speak of embracing a tunic or coat their husbands had worn, just to remind them of their manly smell. We pray together, then I teach them from Ezekiel's scrolls. From the prophecies."

"They can all read?" Stephen asks.

"Most of them. They have more education than the Jewish women overall. The few who cannot read I am tutoring in private."

"How many want to become Christians?" Livia asks.

"All of them. But they are worried they will not be accepted by the church."

"People who were born Jewish think Gentiles do not understand them," Stephen says. "I am sure they will come to accept the women in time."

"How much time?"

Three days later, while Stephen is at his shop, he hears Greek Diogenes from the second row down near the entrance to the Jewish section of the market.

"You're not letting that Stephen down here, are you? Did you know he claims he is no longer a Jew? He's a traitor and blasphemer to your own religion. What are you going to do about it?"

"Calm down, Diogenes," Joshua says. "You do not understand our ways. You only imagined he said that."

Diogenes swings around and points at his accuser. "Ha! You do not believe me? Go ask him yourself."

"All right. We will," Midyan says. "C'mon, men. We will settle this then kick that pagan Diogenes out of our aisle."

Ebron and Eben follow him. They stop in front of the locksmith's shop.

"Okay, Stephen," Ebon says. "Tell this pagan he is a liar."

"Diogenes, my friend!" Stephen says, siding up next to the tapestry merchant. "I have been wondering when to break the news to them. You have helped me decide."

Hearing the goings-on, other nearby shop keepers gather close.

"Diogenes is correct," Stephen says. "I am no longer a Jew. I am a Christian, and it is the most amazing life in the world."

"Huh?"

"What did he say?"

"Oh, I believe in all the prophets more than ever. And I believe God gave Moses those six-hundred commandments. But the commandments once written on stone are now written in our hearts."

Satisfied with the results of his tirade, Diogenes sneaks away without being noticed.

"That is right, brothers," Stephen continues. "The Messiah we have all been looking for has come. The Christ has come."

"Get him out of here!"

"Throw him out!"

"Do not let him take anything with him."

"Stone him."

By now, Stephen is out in the middle of the aisle and working his way toward the center. His eyes flash from man to man, he is still smiling.

"Brothers! Do not you want to hear about our prophecies finally being fulfilled? Do not you want to know who our Messiah was and is?"

"The rabbi of our Merchants Synagogue did not know anything about it. You're a liar, Stephen."

"False prophets have gotten hold of him."

"He's been cursed."

"He's got a demon."

"Stone him for blasphemy."

The other merchants grab Stephen and push him in front of them. Someone puts a rope around his neck.

They head up the main aisle of the market. Other merchants join in the growing mob as they work their way up to the front.

"He's got the evil eye."

"Zeus denounces him."

"Throw him in the fire. Sacrifice him."

"Neptune wants him. Throw him in the sea."

They reach the exit of the market.

"Halt!"

Centurion Cronos stands full height in front of a *contubernium* of Roman legionnaires.

When the mob stops, the centurion recognizes Stephen as the one he had ordered locks from for the fortresses around Libya.

"Take that noose off him," he orders.

"But he has blasphemed," Sethos calls out.

"Cease all talk."

"Do not you want to know what he did?" Midyan bellows.

The centurion raises his right hand and steps to the side.

His *contubernium* divides up. Three stand at attention to Stephen's right, three to his left, one in back and one in front.

Centurion Cronos marches toward the citadel on the hill south of the market, Stephen now in custody.

Once inside the citadel, Cronos dismisses his legionnaires and faces Stephen.

"I thought you were a peaceful man, young sir. Well, a hard bargainer, but you looked harmless. What did you do to make them all so mad and disrupt half the city?"

Before Stephen can reply, Cronos motions to one of the gatekeepers. "Give this man your cape."

The legionnaire takes off his official cape and throws it on Stephen's shoulders.

"This should help hide your identity. Now, go home. And stay out of trouble."

"Uh, sir, could you get a message to my wife?"

Cronos motions to an aide standing by.

"I live behind the Berber synagogue. My gate has a large lock on it, but it will be locked on the inside. Tell my wife to meet me at my mother's house."

Stephen turns back to the centurion. "Is that satisfactory?"

The centurion makes an about-face and marches away. When the legionnaire opens the gate, the aide leaves and turns left. Stephen follows, disguised in his military cape, and goes straight ahead.

Jesus, what must I do? I am so mixed up. Amidst his confusion, he smiles to himself. *I used to say that to my father all the time, didn't I? Well, I am mixed up. What would my father have done?*

A stray dog trots in front of Stephen as though oblivious of his presence.

By now, Stephen has reached the smallest amphitheater in the city—the one used for slave auctions. There is a bench in front of it. He looks around to see if anyone is following him, is satisfied, then sits. The dog stops and sizes up the stray human.

Stephen clicks his tongue, and the dog wanders over. He scratches the dog behind its ears, and the dog becomes contented. He looks up at the sky. He brings his eyes down to the slave-trading arena.

Grandfather was a slave because he dared talk too much. My father was freed from being a slave because he dared marry the daughter of a great man. What have I dared?

The dog lies down at Stephen's feet. He looks over to the block where slaves are put on display.

Who am I a slave to, God? Is it you? I want to be your slave.

"What are you over here, mumbling about?"

Stephen jerks his head up. "Livia? What are you doing here?"

"Well, since you had trouble in the market, I decided I needed to hurry to Tullia's house by cutting through the middle of town."

"How did you know it was me just now? Oh. I guess the cape fell off."

"I guess it did."

"Doggie, Abba. Doggie."

"Yes, doggie," Stephen says, grabbing up his son from Livia."

"You know you shouldn't be carrying him in your condition. You're going to be delivering soon."

"Not for a month or two."

They leave the slave market, walk past the Greek-Speaking Synagogue for Roman citizens, and arrive at Tullia's house. Stephen reaches out to knock on the gate and feels something on his leg.

"Lookie," Abraham giggles. "Doggie followed us."

Tullia opens the gate.

"Mother, I need to talk to you."

She swings wide the gate, and he sees the other eleven widows in the courtyard.

"And we need to talk to you," she says. "Have a seat and

give me that precious grandson of mine."

Stephen and Livia join the widows in their circle. He looks around, then over at his son. "Well, Abraham, it seems we are the only two men here."

"No, we have a few little boys running around here," Tullia says. "And girls."

"Aello, you begin the discussion. Tell Stephen what you have been telling us."

"I want to be a Christian, but the Jewish Christians do not approve of us."

"Chloe, you're next."

"Did you say Christians who meet together are called the church? Then why cannot we start a congregation of the church?"

"Dione?"

"I am from Greece. Why do not we just all go to Greece? The Grecians are better at accepting outsiders."

"But your family couldn't support us all," Ekho says."

"I am good at embroidery. I could sell a little for our food," Enyo says.

"Everyone could move in with me," Athene says. "My husband built us a large house, and it is too much for me."

Stephen jumps up. "Woah. You ladies are as mixed up as me."

He paces. The women watch.

"Lookie. Doggie."

Stephen looks down and sees that the dog is following at his heels, turning when Stephen turns.

"Ha! He thinks I am his master and want him to go wherever I go. I need to kick him out and make him go home to his real master."

"Stephen, darling. Maybe you just solved the dilemma. Maybe the dog no longer has a home. You have been expelled from both the front and back of the market..."

"How did you know about that?"

"Dear, the legionnaire who came with your message... So, as I was saying, the only thing everyone here has in common is our Master."

Stephen stares at his wife a moment. He stands in place and turns to see each of the widows. The last widow is his mother. He paces again.

He sits back on his bench. He looks over at Keta. Would you be willing to go where our master was? Gia, would you?

Hagne?

"It would not be easy," Keta says.

"We'd be leaving a lot behind. Some of us were born here," Gia says.

"What good is any of that if we are not wanted here and will be miserable here?" Chloe asks.

"Maybe it's not so much what we're leaving behind, but the acceptance and love we will feel somewhere else."

"You mean Jerusalem, do not you?" Athene says.

Quiet again.

"We buried our husbands here," Dione says.

Silence.

"Jerusalem is where the Master died for us."

"Oh, everyone, it will be so wonderful," Livia says. "Jerusalem is so beautiful. It is not as large as Cyrene. But everyone will love us. Isn't being loved worth everything?"

"Well, okay. I will go to Jerusalem," Aello says, standing in front of her bench.

"Me too," Ekho says on the other side of the circle. She stands.

"I suppose I could rent my house, just in case I want to come back." Enyo stands.

"Can I go too, *S'Abta*?"

Tullia smiles. "Indeed, you can go, Abraham."

"May I make a suggestion?" Athene says. "A friend of my late husband has been wanting to buy our house. I will sell it to him. That should give us all enough money to buy passage to Jerusalem."

"Then what?" Ekho says. "My husband and I were poor. We were renting a room at the *insulae*. I have no money to contribute."

"You will contribute in other ways," Athene says.

Four weeks go by. Possessions are sold. Ship fare purchased. Good-byes said to friends and relatives. Last visits to the cemetery.

Stephen closes up all of Simon's house but the front gate. "He may want to come back someday."

The last night is spent in Stephen's house. On the last morning, the women gather up baskets with clothes and food in them. Mothers give instructions to children to stay close and never let go.

They walk past the sanctuary and temple to Apollo. They walk through the market and finally through the North Gate.

No one speaks. They walk down the steep road to the docks

at Apollonia. The smell of seawater grows stronger. Seagulls chatter louder.

Still, no one speaks except an instruction now and then to a hungry or curious child.

Stephen leads the women on board. He shows them where they can store their belongings in a bin he has rented for them.

Bells ring. Anchor weighed. Sails hoisted.

Stephen stands along the rail, watching Cyrene fade in the distance. The city where he had finished growing up. The city where he had attended university and sold fine locks and won a temporary crown at the amphitheater. The city where he had been saved by Simon, then helped Simon save his child. The city of synagogues for every nationality, and pagan temples for every taste.

The city where he had married and had a child. Where his father had left him. And where he had been rejected.

"Maybe things will be better in Jerusalem," he tells Livia.

"Darling," Livia says, just as the ship breaks free of the shore, "I think it's coming."

"What's coming?"

"The baby."

43 ~ GHOST FROM THE PAST

"Well, young man," the ship captain says as Stephen walks down the gangplank onto shore at Joppa. "You certainly are brave. Will you be leading the same bunch of women and children back any time soon?"

"Not that I know of. We're moving permanently to Jerusalem." Livia answers for him while holding her new baby girl close.

"Well, good luck, sir," the captain says, still looking at Stephen.

"Did I hear you are going to Jerusalem?"

Stephen turns to find the owner of the voice.

"My name is Philip,"

Stephen decides the stranger is about his same age. He has a long nose, long neck, and small beady eyes.

"I just came down from Caesarea. I am meeting my friend, Peter, who has been in Joppa a while. Oh, here he is now."

Philip holds out his hand toward his friend. Peter has a big chest and short arms. He has a round head and big mouth.

"Peter, my friend, you did not have to come down here. The climb up to the city is steep."

"Oh, I've been fishing while waiting for your ship to come in," Peter replies. "Who are your friends?"

"I just met them. They are going to Jerusalem also." He turns back to Stephen. "What did you say your name was?"

"I am Stephen, late of Cyrene. This is my wife, Livia; our oldest son, Abraham; and newborn daughter, Naomah."

"Ha. You will have to meet my wife, Patrice, when we get back to Jerusalem. She does love babies," Peter says. "Oh, uh..." he looks over at Philip. "I think I just invited ourselves to travel with them."

"You beat me to it," Philip says. "So, is it agreeable that we travel to Jerusalem together?" he asks Stephen.

Stephen grins, looks at his wife, looks at a group of eleven more women, and a crowd of children of all ages and sizes.

"Other than my two-year-old Abraham, I have not had a man to converse with since we left Cyrene."

Philip and Peter stare at the women and children.

"Oh. I see. Are you in charge of them all? Are they relatives?" Philip asks

"Well, I kind of inherited them. Oh, here comes my mother now. Mother, these are Philip and Peter. They are on their way to Jerusalem also and wondered if they could travel with us."

"Of course, my son said yes. He hasn't had a man to talk to..."

"Yes, I told them. Well, anyway, this is Tullia, my mother. As I said, I kind of inherited these women. All their husbands, including my father, died suddenly in a plague of nervous sickness. They want to become Christians, but...well, there were problems. So, everyone decided to come to Jerusalem, where the Master died."

Livia walks up to Stephen, leading a donkey.

"Where did you get that?" he asks her.

"While you were talking, I was growing tired. So, I rented it to get our daughter and me to Jerusalem. The rest of you can walk." Her coy smile convinces Stephen to agree with the new arrangement.

"Well, shall we go?" Peter says.

Stephen stares a moment at Philip. "I thought I already met you, but you do not look familiar."

"Oh, we have two Philips: This one and the apostle. The apostle Philip is usually with his friend, Andrew."

"Oh, yes. That is who I saw him with."

Once up the steep incline to Joppa, through the city, and out on the highway heading east, Stephen introduces the two men to the widows.

"This is Peter. He was one of Jesus' apostles and traveled with him as he preached and healed."

The women, though tired, brighten up.

"My mother and wife and I taught you onboard the ship about the prophecies Jesus fulfilled," Stephen continues. "Now is your chance to ask Peter all about what Jesus said and did."

When the women flock around Peter, Stephen grins and

says, "Looks like I've been deserted. Ha, ha."

It takes three days to walk the last twenty-five *milles* to the grand capital city of Israel, Jerusalem. The children are fussy. The women are tired. Stephen prays a lot.

Their last night is spent in Emmaus. They get settled in at a large hostel. Peter calls out to them from the inner courtyard. "Here is water, everyone. What hinders you ladies from being baptized?"

The innkeeper gives his consent, and the women are all baptized in the reflecting pool.

On the last morning, the women gather at the city gate and head out singing happy psalms. The children do not understand but are glad their mothers are happy.

Peter answers question after question about the Savior they never met but now believe is the Son of God.

Philip and Peter sometimes try to fill in watching some of the children to give their mothers a break.

"There they are!" Stephen says to Abraham, clinging to his father's back. "Do you see them? Count them."

"One. Two. Three," they say together.

"Yes, the three towers. They are there to welcome us into the city, and to guard us at night when the gates are closed.

"I sent word to my father and mother as soon as we decided to do this," Livia says. "I hope he got word."

She shifts on the donkey. "My mother will be so pleased with little Naomah. Do you think when Abraham and Naomah grow up and marry, they will name their daughters after me and their sons after you?"

"One of each perhaps," Stephen says. "Now, which way is their house? As I recall, it is a big one."

They enter Jerusalem through the Flower Gate, also called the Joppa Gate.

"Uh, may I make a suggestion?" Peter asks Stephen.

"We apostles purchased an old two-story hostel as our apartments and headquarters."

"Is that where you preached from that day?" Stephen asks.

"Yes, my friend, that is where we preached from. Three thousand were baptized that day. The six public pools of Jerusalem were busy until midnight. Anyway, we have a large room on the third floor. The women are welcome to spend the night there. Then we can work out something better for them tomorrow when they aren't so tired."

Stephen stops the busy talking and thinking and doing and

planning he had been submerged in the entire three days on the highway. He looks in Peter's eyes. He realizes just how tired he is.

"Thank you, Peter," he says with a sigh.

"By the way, Stephen and Livia," Philip says. "I have a home in the north part of the city over by the fortress. You will have to come for dinner one evening. We have four daughters who will be happy to spoil your little ones."

The widows follow Peter going straight east in the direction of the temple, Philip turns left to go to the Greek part of the city, and Stephen's family of five turns right to go into the wealthier upper part of the city southwest of the temple.

"My parents' house is one of the older ones built when our people were released from Babylon and allowed to rebuild Jerusalem."

"This house is very old but sturdy. We have a beautiful view from our rooftop. Behind us is the Tyropoeon Valley, which rises to Mount Zion, the original Jerusalem."

"Is that what they call the City of David?"

"Yes. It was small by our standards—the entire temple complex is as large as the original Jerusalem. Anyway, we can see where David's palace used to be, although it is in ruins now."

"What about Solomon's palace?"

"What was left of it after Nebuchadnezzar burned it was filled in by Herod so he could expand the temple complex. Anyway, here we are."

The double gate into the estate is covered in bronze with the Hebrew letter N on each gate.

"Ha! Nicodemus and Naomah. Clever," Stephen says. "I guess I did not notice when we were here before."

Livia slides off her donkey and pats her black hair down.

"You look beautiful," Stephen says.

The door opens. "Yes?"

"Oh, you must be new. I am Livia. I grew up here."

"Whose precious voice do I hear?" Naomah calls out from the courtyard.

The servant steps aside and the women embrace.

"Oh, but I cannot hug you too hard," Naomah says, stepping back. "You have brought us another grandchild."

"Not just any grandchild, Mother. She is Naomah, named after you."

Stephen clears his throat.

"Do not mind the women, my boy," Nicodemus says, joining

them in the courtyard. "Just look how my grandson has grown. Naomah, look!"

The two men turn just in time to see Naomah with the baby swinging in a circle.

"You're too old for that, Naomah. You're going to fall."

"Oh, pshaw."

"I think we're going to have to work out a schedule between the grandmothers," Tullia says.

"So, my boy," Nicodemus says, putting his arm over Stephen's shoulders. "What brings you to Jerusalem? Come over here where it is quieter and tell me. Livia wrote me you may be coming, but did not say why. What has happened?"

The courtyard is surrounded by coral columns of granite. The tile under their feet alternates between coral, white, and green. They step over to the other end and sit on coral granite benches.

Stephen looks at Nicodemus, over at a large urn with a small cedar tree planted in it, up at the sky, and down at his feet.

"That bad, huh? Tell me."

"I tried to set up my business in the Gentile section of the market, telling them I was now a Christian and no longer a Jew. They forced me out. I went down to the Jewish aisle in the back. The Gentiles followed me down and told them I was no longer a Jew. So, the Jews belonging to the new Merchant Synagogue forced me out."

"What about the other synagogues?" Nicodemus asks, taking two goblets of pomegranate juice from a maid, and handing one to Stephen. Stephen takes a polite sip and sets it down.

"My father died. We had the funeral at the Jewish-Born Freedmen Synagogue. When I told them of my father's joy upon learning the Messiah had come, and he was now a Christian, the entire synagogue became Christians."

"May the name of Jesus the Christ be praised. But you're not smiling," Nicodemus says, taking another sip from his goblet.

"Then, I decided to teach the Greek-Speaking Freedmen about Jesus being the promised Savior. Rabbi Solomus told me to never come back.

"However, this was the synagogue hard hit by the plague my father died of. There were many Greek widows, and they decided they wanted to become Christians.

"So, I took them to worship with the Jewish-Born Christians, and they were rude to them," Stephen stands and paces. He turns back to his father-in-law. "Basically, they said the

Greek-Speaking women did not have enough understanding and were not welcome."

"Oh, that is bad," Nicodemus says.

"Why does it get so complicated, sir? All I wanted to do is tell people how to go to heaven and escape hell. Should I have returned to teaching people in secret?"

"Satan, my boy. He doesn't want to lose his following. So, he makes people think like he does. Plain and simple ego. They do not want to lose their followers or friends. Ego, my boy. I should know."

Nicodemus sets down his goblet. "I did not want to lose my position in the temple and my students and my friends. I sneaked to talk to Jesus at night like a coward."

"Hey, you men," Livia says, walking to their end of the coral courtyard. "Mother and I have put together a meal of cheese, fresh grapes, yogurt dip, and baklava. You'd better come before Abraham eats up your share too."

She hands baby Naomah to her father and clasps Stephen's hand.

The following day, Stephen asks if he can go to the temple with his father-in-law for a while.

"Sorry, Son. That is a thing of the past. I have lost my job. I am no longer on the Sanhedrin and no longer a teacher. My house is for sale. I am beginning to tutor, but will have to move to a smaller house."

Livia stares at her father. "Not the house I grew up in. I love this house."

"Your mother does too. But, you had a lot of good years in it. Be satisfied with that."

"Well, I am just marching over to the temple and telling High Priest Caiaphas he has made a big mistake," she says, putting her hands on her hips. "A very big mistake."

"Sweetheart, I know you believe everyone is good, and you are right to some degree," Stephen says. "But some people have that good part of them hidden away. Jesus said we are to be wise as serpents and harmless of doves. Isn't that right, sir?"

"That is what he said," Naomah responds in her husband's place. "Did not you say the widows you brought to Jerusalem slept on the third floor of the apostles' hostel last night? We need to go over there and see what we can do to help. Oh, and I cannot wait to practice speaking Greek with them."

Within an hour, the six have arrived at the hostel.

"Come in. Come in. We have been expecting you."

"Oh, Andrew," Stephen says. "It is so good to see you again. Is Philip around anywhere?"

"If you mean young Philip, I believe he is up on our top floor, helping Peter figure out what to do with all those widows and their children. I will take you to them. They'll be glad for the help."

Before they arrive at the top of the steps, they hear the ruckus. When they open the door, they see children laughing and chasing each other, babies hungry and crying, mothers both laughing and crying.

"Oh, thank our Lord Jesus Christ, you have come," Philip calls out.

Naomah grabs up a child sitting in a corner and wet. Stephen chases down two boys running after each other and grabs one into each arm. Tullia rescues a baby crying near an exhausted mother. Nicodemus sweeps two fighting boys off their feet and into his arms. Livia hands her baby to Peter, takes the baby of a crying mother into her own arms, and sits with the mother on the floor.

Naomah, still hanging on to the wet child, begins to sing. It is a children's song. She marches around the edge of the room, Tullia picks up the signal and marches behind her, then the children do.

"Whew," Peter says. "Now, we've got to figure something out for these new widows. Do they have any money, Stephen?"

"Yes, some had houses to sell, and horses and furniture and equipment, along with their husbands' businesses. They pooled their money so they can live equally and near each other."

"A new *insulae* has just been built between the Sheep Gate and the fortress," Andrew says, having followed their guests to the top floor.

"Perfect. That is near Simon, my friend from Cyrene. He doesn't even know I am here yet. We will take the widows over, then Livia and my parents-in-law and my mother can go see Simon."

Andrew and Philip line everyone up and head north to the newer and Greek-Speaking part of the city. The women pay a year's worth of rent.

"You all go on," Andrew says. "Philip and I will take the women to the market so they can pick up sleeping mats, kitchen supplies, and food, and help them carry it back."

Half an hour later, Stephen is at the *insulae* and knocking on Simon's door.

"Well, look who's here!" Abelia says.

She opens the door wide so Stephen's seven can enter. "Come see, Simon," she calls into another room. "Look who's back."

"Unkee Stephen," Alexander screeches.

The next two hours are spent listening to Stephen's story and coming up with ideas for work for him and a place to live.

"Achaius has begun a scribe school here," Simon says.

"Until I can get my locksmith business started, perhaps they would let me help teach," Stephen says.

"And I could add tutoring to their school," Nicodemus says.

"Tomorrow is the Sabbath. Even though we are Christians now, we still attend so we can keep teaching them," Simon says. "Go with us tomorrow. It's the Greek-Speaking Freedmen Synagogue."

"I wonder if our new friend, Philip—not the apostle—attends there."

"No Philip in our congregation. Perhaps he attends the Greek-Speaking Synagogue for Roman Citizens."

"Then we shall go to them both."

Nicodemus and Naomah return home, but Stephen's family stays with Simon. The next morning, they break their fast and walk over to the Greek-Speaking Freedmen Synagogue.

Stephen feels comfortable with their routine. This synagogue is even large enough for a professional chanticleer to lead congregational psalm chanting.

The rabbi rises. "And now, I would like to introduce to you a guest rabbi from Bethany and the newest and youngest member of Israel's Sanhedrin: Saul of Tarsus."

Stephen thinks back. *I played with a boy named Saul when I was a little boy. Is that him?*

"Those Christians!" Saul screams, rising from the speaker's chair. "Those vile, despicable, blasphemous Christians. They must be stopped!"

44 ~ FRIENDS AND ENEMIES

"I had no idea he was going to be there, Stephen and Livia," Simon says on their way back to the *insulae*. "That was not a very good welcome-back for you."

"I remember him," Stephen says. "We used to play together. We attended the same synagogue in Tarsus when we were children."

"You did?" Simon asks, stopping in the middle of the street.

"Ohhh, yes," Tullia says, rolling her eyes heavenward. "And I remember that father of his, Lucius. He was one man you never wanted as an enemy. Strict? Oh, yes. He kept those three boys of his in line. Beat them so hard sometimes, even the other men tried to get him to ease up. Of course, he would turn on them next."

They resume walking. "Saul's two older brothers—I did not know them very well," Stephen says. "What were their names, Mother? I forget."

"Andronicus and Junias. They were six or seven years older than you. But there was a girl, too—Bethania. She was born the year before you.

"What about their mother?" Abelia asks.

"She died when Bethania was small, but that was before I met your father, and he converted me to Judaism, so I never knew her. I always heard good things about her."

Tullia shakes her head as they walk. "So, it sounds like Saul has turned into his father," she says. "May God provide extra protection to anyone he decides is his enemy."

The following day, they will worship as Christians. They head toward the temple.

"We meet at Solomon's Portico," Simon explains as they walk.

"I thought the original temple was destroyed by the

Babylonians. How could Solomon's Portico still be standing?" Tullia asks.

"All anyone knows is that the wall across the top of Mount Moriah at the drop-off was never touched.

"It goes the whole length of the temple complex. Just how long is it?" Stephen asks. "I forgot."

"Half a Roman *mille* long," Simon answers. "It has a roof over it to keep worshippers out of the rain, is wide enough it could hold ten thousand people if they were all standing up. We always sit, so it doesn't hold that many, but it could."

"How many Christians meet there?" Livia asks.

"Three thousand were baptized last June while you were here," Simon says, "but a lot of them returned to their own countries after Pentecost was over. Another five thousand were baptized during the winter. Many of them left too."

"It wouldn't surprise me if there were five to ten thousand Christians in Jerusalem by now," Abelia says. "Jews everywhere are coming to realize Jesus fulfilled all the prophecies of the Messiah, God walking on earth again, and becoming the king of our soul."

"Do not the priests mind that the Christians worship on temple grounds?" Stephen asks.

"So far, they haven't made us move. But we are making them nervous."

They arrive at the High Priest's palace and turn left onto the long ramp going up to Mount Moriah and the temple. The Courtyard of the Gentiles is busy, most of the people heading to the east side of the massive temple complex.

"One of Jesus' apostles always stands by one of the columns to greet people," Simon explains.

"Welcome. And who do we have here?"

"James, this is my dear friend from Cyrene, Stephen, and his family. They have decided to move to Jerusalem. They became Christians last June on that first day."

"Welcome. Welcome. Come in. I hope you brought a mat to sit on. At least we're out of the sun."

When it is time to begin, the twelve apostles stand side by side in front, then seat themselves on benches along the side.

Philip, the apostle, stands, greets everyone, and pronounces the benediction. The stone wall and cedar ceiling over the roofed portico carries Philip's voice so everyone can hear.

Another apostle Stephen does not recognize stands and

leads three psalms of David. The sweet strains of their voices flows through the portico and out into the massive Courtyard of the Gentiles.

There follows a long period of silent prayer, which is ended by another apostle Stephen does not recognize.

"Now, we come to the main purpose of us meeting on the first day of the weak." It is the voice of James.

He looks at the congregation and smiles at the mothers struggling to keep children quiet.

"I remember the time we were sitting down by Galilee Lake, and women began bringing their children for Jesus to bless. I was so angry at them. Jesus needed to rest. He had gone down to the beach to be alone. But here came all the mothers.

"I am ashamed to say I was one of them who tried to shoo the children away. Jesus stood up and was angry. I knew I was right until he spoke. He said, 'Let the little children come to me. They are good reminders to us of the innocence and tenderness we all should have.' I was embarrassed as were the other eleven."

Stephen looks over at Simon. "Other eleven?" he whispers."

"Yes, James is the twelfth."

"He's one of the apostles?"

"Shhh. Listen."

"Although I had known Jesus all my life—his mother, Mary, was my mother's sister—I never quite figured him out. One time after he started preaching, one village turned on him, and we had to leave. I told Jesus to just call fire down from heaven onto the village. He told me to leave them alone."

His voice carries strong through the portico. James pauses, then holds up one finger.

"But, as you all have seen for yourself, he was never afraid to face down hypocrites. He said they needed to be confronted for denying the scriptures. He was mean to the mean and gentle to the gentle."

Tears come to James' eyes.

"Then, he died. I thought my world had come to an end. I was mad at everyone in the world. But Jesus was in love with everyone in the world. He took the blame and punishment for all our sins as the perfect Lamb of God, then came back to life. I would give my life for him if I could.

He would? Stephen ponders. *What could he accomplish by dying? Wouldn't he leave behind work undone?*

"This bread represents his body..."

Men are posted between the outer columns. Stephen

estimates there are fifty to one hundred of them. Each has a large basket full of unleavened bread. The basket is passed down each row. Each Christian breaks off a bite and passes it on.

It is a quiet time. A time when each person thinks back to Jesus hanging from that terrible cross outside their city.

Stephen's thoughts go back to that day. *Oh, Jesus, I will never forget. I hated the way they treated you. I hated that you had to die. Help me understand a little better why you had to do it—the dying.*

After everyone has been served, Peter stands before the thousands of Christians.

"The night Jesus was betrayed by one of our own, I, too, betrayed him. I denied ever having known him. But he loved me anyway. No matter how horrendous your sin, it could not be any worse than mine. Then he sacrificed his blood—much more holy than the lambs that are sacrificed over there in the temple—so I could be forgiven. So you could be forgiven.

The men return to their posts. This time they have urns into which they pour red wine. The urns are passed down each row. Each person takes a sip.

Stephen, as well as everyone else, meditates in the quiet.

I have been mixed up about a lot of things, Jesus. But one thing I know: You died in my place to satisfy Satan so I can live with you someday. How could you love me that much?

The Lord's Supper is over.

Another apostle stands.

"Brothers, we must take care of our own. We have sick among us who have no money left for elixirs from the apothecary. We have children with no shoes. We have brothers who were injured at work and need help feeding their families until their recovery. We have widows who do what they can, but if they were left with several children, it is never enough."

The men standing by the columns take the baskets that had formerly had bread in them and pass them around for people to drop their coins in.

The final benediction is pronounced. People are slow to leave each other. They have been there since an hour past dawn until the sun is high in the sky. It has not been enough.

Stephen sees James on their way out. "Aren't you afraid to be meeting right on the same grounds as the temple itself?

"We must be bold, Stephen."

"They killed Jesus. What if they kill again?"

The week goes by fast. Stephen has found a locksmith who needs a partner, and his mother has found a small house for them to rent using part of the money I got from selling our house.

The day before the Sabbath, Philip—not the apostles—invites Stephen's family to his home for a meal.

"Come in. Come in," Philip says at his gate.

Tullia walks in first, then Livia with baby Naomah, and finally, Stephen with Abraham hanging on to his hand.

"May I introduce to you my lovely wife, Hestia?" Philip says. "And these are my daughters..."

Before introductions are complete, his daughters whisk Stephen's little ones to their favorite corner of the courtyard.

"Ha! Didn't I tell you my four daughters would have fun spoiling your two?"

Philip leads Stephen to his favorite bench. "My wife just put new cushions on them. Green. Do you like them?"

"Philip, what are things like here in Jerusalem? I mean for the Christians?" Stephen asks.

"Well, as more Jews come to understand Jesus fulfilled all the prophesies of the Savior to come, they become Christians too."

"Yes, I know that, but..."

"But, what about the opposition? It mostly comes from the leaders. And they do not have to be leaders of the temple or entire synagogues. Some are leaders of committees in their synagogues. Or the treasurer or official reader or chanticleer of their synagogue. They like feeling important and do not abide their admirers being taken from them."

"How do they keep their followers?"

"Bribes of money or position, more customers for their business, fine furniture, a vacation to Egypt. Or lies. They take one of our truths and exaggerate it or add to it. They're still telling that we are going to tear down the temple and rebuild it in three days. That is what they accused Jesus of. Now they're accusing us of it."

"How dangerous is it? I mean, should I settle my family here?"

"So far, it isn't dangerous. Not physically dangerous. The Sanhedrin seems to have been satisfied with killing Jesus. But, as they lose more priests to Christianity, I do not know."

"We are ready to eat," Hestia says.

The evening is a happy one.

"I am glad we moved here," Livia says, walking back to their little house that Tullia had rented for them.

"I am going with Philip to the Greek-Speaking Synagogue for Roman Citizens tomorrow. You do not have to go.

"We would love to," Tullia says. "It will be good training for Abraham to learn to sit still.

Morning comes. They walk over to Philip's house, then the two families walk the rest of the way to the synagogue.

"This one is closer to the Pool of Bethesda," Hestia tells the women. Isn't it beautiful down there? Have you seen it? I will take you there if you haven't."

They arrive at the synagogue. The women head to their side and the men to theirs. As Stephen settles in near the back, he notices movement on the podium.

"That is Rabbi Karpos," Philip says. "I do not know that other man, though he does look a little familiar."

"I shouldn't have come," Stephen whispers.

"Why? Who is he?"

"We called him Paul while we were up in Tarsus in Anatolia. His Hebrew name is Saul."

"Saul? I think that is the name of the newest addition to the Sanhedrin. I had heard they had replaced Nicodemus. So, what about him?"

Stephen does not have a chance to respond.

"Brothers, let us all stand for the benediction."

The worship continues as all Jewish worship does.

"And now for our speaker, Saul, Rabbi of the synagogue in Bethany and newest and youngest member of the Sanhedrin."

Saul stands. Stephen notices this time that he has grown into a big and muscular man, though of average height. Saul stares at the audience a moment, then sneers.

"We will get them. We will get all those Christians for blasphemy. We will stone them, crucify them, kill them with our swords. They cannot be allowed to blaspheme the very name of the one God of the universe. God has no son, nor will he ever. God does not get married. The words are sour in my mouth. There is one God, not two.

"When the Messiah comes, he will be our high priest and king. The Fortress Antonia adjoining the temple will be turned into his palace. There will be no more need for fortresses or anything else because he will be the Prince of Peace. Things are only going to get worse if we do not stop them now."

Saul swings around and peers at the women. "If my very own brothers became one of them—do you know what I would do?"

He turns toward the men. "I would not hesitate to do whatever is necessary to stop them. Betrayers and blasphemers are all alike and must be punished alike."

Stephen is relieved when the final benediction is offered, and the back doors are opened.

He slips out, leaving Philip behind, and heads for home. When his family arrives soon after, he is sitting cross-legged in the middle of their courtyard, his head in his hands.

"Stephen, darling," Livia says. "What happened?"

"It's starting all over again. Only this time, instead of be threatened as a Jew, we are being threatened as Christians. We should not have come here."

"Sweetheart, he is not after us. He doesn't even know we are here. We can stop attending the Jewish synagogues; then, we won't run into him again."

Stephen looks up at his wife only briefly. Little Abraham lets go of his mother's hand and sits cross-legged next to his father.

Livia looks up at her mother-in-law. Tullia sits on a bench nearby where she does not have to struggle to get up and down.

"Son, their father was a tentmaker. Andronicus and Junias are certainly tent makers too. Let us look for them. You were young enough they wouldn't recognize you. Let us find them and see if they have become Christians. If so, we can warn them. We can even hide them if we need to."

Stephen looks up at his mother. He presses his lips together and nods. "You're right, Mother."

The following day, Stephen finds where the tentmakers are and walks over to the far edge of the market. He thinks he spots Andronicus and Junias.

"So, what do you hear about all those Christians?" Stephen asks, looking over the kind of seams a sample two-person tent has in it.

"We hear good things from them. They take care of their own and stay out of trouble."

"Seems to me the Sanhedrin has found someone to get them under control," Stephen responds.

"Could be."

Stephen walks around to look at a tent that is much larger. "Where are you from?"

"Tarsus up in Anatolia."

"Junius, who are you talking to?" Andronicus looks over at

Stephen and squints.

"Do I know you?"

"Uh, I do not think so."

"Yes, I do. You lived in Tarsus a long time ago. Fifteen or twenty years ago. You used to play with my little brother, did not you?"

"What do you mean?"

"You look just like him. Ezekiel was his name. He was a scribe and a good one."

"Well, yes, that was my father."

"You just moved here. Come back here the day after the Sabbath. Bring your family. Do you have a family? We may have something to offer you whenever you travel. But come early."

Stephen looks at the two brothers, unsure whether his Christianity has been discovered. He leaves without saying anything more.

The rest of the week goes by in slow motion.

"Livia, tomorrow morning at dawn, we are going to see Saul's brothers. I do not know what they have in mind. They did say to bring my family. I will drop you and the children off around the corner from their business, and motion to you if it is safe."

"How exciting," Livia says. "Okay."

The following morning at dawn, Stephen takes the family to the far edge of the market where it backs up to the city wall. He leaves them around the corner from the tentmakers and walks on alone.

"Hello, Stephen," Junias says. "You did not bring your family?"

"Well, what did you have in mind?"

"Come in here," Andronicus says, standing by the flap of a large tent.

Oh, God. I do not know what to do. Should I go in? Are they going to kill me?

"I do not think I can do that," Stephen objects, turning to leave.

"Hello there, Stephen. Glad you could make it."

Stephen turns at the voice. "Trophimus?"

"They are Christians," Trophimus says. "Saul's brothers are secret Christians. I told them all about you, and they have invited you to their secret worship."

Stephen presses his lips together, grins, tips his head, then shakes it. "Wait here."

He walks back toward where he had hidden his family and motions for them to join him.

When Stephen enters the tent with his family, he estimates there are thirty or forty people inside.

Another man walks up to Stephen and offers him his hand. "Remember me? We played together when Saul would let us and wouldn't beat up on us."

"Elegius? Is that you?" Stephen says, grinning.

"Yes, and the only reason Saul got by with beating up on us is that you and I were both sons of slaves. I have since been freed. How about you?"

"Yes, my father was freed, so I was too."

"Here is someone else you may remember."

"Your father used to buy leather from my uncle's butcher shop to dry and make parchment out of it. I am Silas. I played with you too, but I never beat up on you."

The three men who had grown up together in Tarsus laugh, then remember where they are. They stop, look around, listen for movement outside the tent, then resume. Only this time, they whisper their laughter as they recall earlier times.

"I was twelve years old when I left Tarsus," Stephen says. "Little did we know then that we would see each other in Jerusalem fifteen years later and with families of our own."

Junias joins them. "It looks like this is the Tarsus congregation of Jerusalem," he says.

"What about us?" Trophimus says with a smile.

"Well, and a little bit of Antioch."

"I think everyone has arrived," Andronicus says. "Everyone be seated. Let us meditate a while on our Lord Jesus and what he did for us."

"Remember, everyone," their chanticleer warns when he finally stands to lead them in their psalms. "Whisper your songs."

At the end, people leave by ones, twos or threes. It takes them two hours to empty the tent. When it comes Stephen's time, he smiles at Trophimus. "We're home."

The following year is a happy one. Tullia walks to the *insulae* every day and gathers the widows around to learn more about the prophecies of Jesus or learn a psalm of David, but always to pray for each other and the church.

The men take turns preaching but are not forced to participate. Stephen volunteers.

Do not be fearful of evil men.

Do not envy them either.
They will wither like grass.
Their blossom will fade away forever.

"Brothers, those who are after us will not last. Some day we will be free of those who come after us for our faith. It may be a lifetime or two lifetimes away, but someday we will no longer fear, for our enemies will have withered away."

The secret congregation continues to grow a little at a time. It is a good year. Hiding and surviving is better than declaring and dying. Stephen is happy again.

On Abraham's third birthday, Andronicus and Junias disappear, and the tent is burned to the ground.

45 ~ EXPOSURE

"**N**o, we do not know how we were discovered," Secundus tells him.

Stephen is at the scribe school. "I knew if anyone knew what happened, it would be you men."

"Our guess is that someone was tortured. And since Andronicus and Junias are gone..."

"You mean, they weren't killed?" Stephen asks.

"Andronicus and Junias saw the men torching their tent, so came here to decide what to do," Achaius says.

"They think it was their brother, Saul, who burned it down, so decided they would be safer up in Tarsus where their friends would protect them," Justus says. "Silas went with them."

"We gave them what money we had," Trophimus says.

"So, what do we do now?" Stephen asks.

"We do not know which of us were named," Secundus says. "Nicodemus has been telling us we were fools to hide our faith."

"But the events of last night just prove we cannot grow unless we hide and do it in secret."

"Who said?"

They turn and see Nicodemus standing at the doorway of the empty classroom. He walks toward them.

"I hid it, and what did it benefit? I did not vote to acquit Jesus, so he was killed. I did not tell any of the Jews, I did not tell any of the Romans. It was as if my faith was a shadow, a mist."

"So, you are saying we need to resume meeting with the apostles on the very temple grounds where the greatest enemies of Jesus are."

"That is right. There are thousands of us. If they try to stop us, they could be ousted from office as high priests, priests, Sanhedrin members. The Christians are becoming stronger all the time."

Stephen takes a deep breath. "I have tried it both ways. Both ways work a while, then do not work. But, since I respect you, sir, I will go public again."

"Good for you, Son," he says, pounding Stephen on the back. "My daughter has been pestering me to talk you into returning to the temple. Now she'll have to find something else to pester me about."

The first day of the following week finds Stephen, Livia Abraham, and Naomah heading into Solomon's Portico to worship openly with the other Christians. Although Tullia lives with them, she prefers to sit with the widows of Cyrene.

"Ha, ha," Livia says while grabbing Naomah, so she doesn't toddle away, "can you just imagine ole High Priest Caiaphas over there on the second floor of their *officium*, peering out the window, or up on the roof spying on us? I will bet every first day of the week he stomps around in a bad mood."

"I hope that is all he does," Stephen says.

They hear a booming voice coming from in front of the assembled masses of Christians. Abraham sits up as tall and proud as he can next to his father.

For the next two hours, they pray, they sing, they listen to the prophecies of the Messiah being read.

The Lord's Supper takes up half of that time. For Stephen and the others, it is a solemn time. A sacred time. A time of tears and painful memories of the agony. A time of awe and remembering him actually alive again. A time when thoughts of the Savior run deep—deep into their hearts, their souls, their very being.

It should have been me on the cross that day, Jesus, Stephen prays. *It should have been me.*

Parents in the audience do the best they can to pacify restless children. By now, both Abraham and Naomah are asleep on their parents' laps.

Near the end of the service, people stand in place and tell of someone in need of money, personal care, teaching, encouraging. The basket is passed around for those needing funds—for the apostles so they can support their families while teaching every day, for orphans, widows, Christians traveling through.

A final announcement is made by John, the apostle who everyone says was Jesus' life-long closest friend.

"The apostles are starting a new class on the prophecies Jesus fulfilled," John explains. "The previous class has learned all we know to tell them and is ready to go out and teach for themselves. We will be meeting on the third floor of our hostel the second evening of each week. We urge you to become teachers of the lost. That is why Jesus came—to save us from hell. We must spread the word as fast as we can."

On their way home, Tullia hears her name called. She turns and sees two old friends.

"Well, well," Tullia says. "Nicholas and Lucius. I heard you were here in Jerusalem but did not know how to find you. Stephen, do you remember Nicholas and Lucius?"

"Barely. I was only seventeen at the time. That was eleven years ago."

Nicholas looks over at Stephen with his mite-sized eyes. "You have certainly filled out and matured since your Antioch days," he says, holding out his big hand to Stephen.

"When did you become a Christian, Lucius?" Tullia asks.

"The bigger question is when did I leave paganism and become a Jew. I became a Jew in Antioch after you left, and I became a Christian when I came here to Jerusalem."

"I should have visited you while you were in Cyrene," Red-haired Lucius says, pulling on his long nose. "Born and raised there, but all my relatives are gone now."

"Will you join us for our noon respite?" Tullia asks.

"We did want to spend some time talking to you," Nicholas says, looking over at Stephen.

"If you do not mind two children crawling over you uninvited, you are welcome to spend the afternoon with us."

"Or all night, if you have a lot to say," Livia snickers.

Nicholas and Lucius follow Stephen's family home. After eating a few figs and a wedge of cheese, Livia takes a nap with the children, and Tullia excuses herself to go see her widow friends.

"We think the three of us would make a good team," Nicholas begins. "We could choose a different street to walk down each day, just to see if the children playing outside seem fed and well, and to see if there are any women at the neighborhood well with cracked pots or are struggling with the weight of the water."

"Nicholas would be able to guide us around the city because he has lived here longer than any of us," Lucius says. "One of us could keep track on a clay tablet, and return the next day or two with whatever they need. I inherited a salt pit in the SaHara, and it is doing very well. So I can finance us."

"Where do I come in?" Stephen asks.

"You make locks, do not you? You could provide locks for people, most of whom only rely on a board across the inside of their gate, which makes it hard to secure on the outside."

"Okay, so I give people locks that you pay for," he says, grinning at Lucius, "—well, only the materials. My labor would be free. What then?"

"Then we teach them," Nicholas says.

"Then we save their souls from hell," Lucius says.

"Well, since we would be doing a service, perhaps we would be safe."

"What do you mean, safe?" Nichols asks.

"I had a lot of problems in Cyrene teaching the people, but then there was a lot of prejudice against Jews there."

"Oh, yes, I remember that," Lucius says. "So, should we start tomorrow?"

"No, I want to go hear the apostles explain all the prophecies Jesus fulfilled. People cannot see him perform miracles anymore, so the prophecies is the only proof we have left."

"The apostles perform miracles as proof they are telling the truth."

"But they won't live forever. Knowledge of these prophecies is something we can pass on to our children."

"So, how about the third morning of each week?"

They come to an agreement. The next evening, instead of going home after hammering out the last slab of iron he needs for the next locks, Stephen heads south, then east through the city, and stops at the apostles' hostel.

The third-floor room is full. He finds a seat and introduces himself to the men on each side of him.

"I am Nicanor from Corinth." He has red hair and a face full of freckles. His mouth is small and taunt when he speaks.

"I am Timon from Thessalonica." When he shakes hands, Stephen notices his muscular but short arms and big hands. *They do not seem to fit his small head,* he snickers to himself.

"What are you doing here so far from home?" Stephen asks them both.

"Probably the same reason you are so far from Cyrene."

They hear a voice at the front of the room and come to attention.

On his way out two hours later, Stephen sees another

familiar face. "Hello, Philip. I have not seen you lately."

"You are right there. My daughters want to come to your house and spoil your children again."

"Someday, when Livia and my mother and I want to go somewhere without the children, I will send word."

"Excellent. And how did you like the lesson tonight?"

"I felt I was back at the university. Except, instead of poring over the writings of famous philosophers, we were poring over the writings of the living God."

The following morning, Stephen rises before dawn and meets his friend in front of the Antonia Fortress as pre-arranged. Nicholas leads them to their first street.

Two of the women at the well are crying as they lift their heavy loads out of the water. The men approach.

"Here, let us take those for you," Nicholas says.

"Thank you. My lower back hurts all the time. It nearly kills me to lift anything heavy anymore."

"Would it help if I hired a young lady to lift it for you?" Lucius asks.

The other woman, also crying, hears the conversation. "I have a strong daughter. She could go to work for you."

"Madam, that would be perfect. But I think your tears are for something far more than your daughter needing a job," Lucius says.

"My husband. He is very sick and cannot walk anymore, and no one knows why. I try not to cry in his presence."

"May we follow you home, ma'am?" Stephen asks. "I have a little apothecary knowledge."

The other two men look at Stephen. "You do?" they ask in unison, their eyes sparkling.

Nicholas carries the jar home for the first woman. "Let us join the others so you can meet the girl who will be helping you from now on."

They catch up with the others and enter the small apartment where they meet the invalid. Stephen examines the man.

"I am not a *medicus,* so do not know what is wrong with you. But I do believe crushed stinging nettles brewed in a tea would help your pain. I will check to see if an apothecary has any."

"There are some behind our *insulae*," the girl says.

"Perfect," Nicholas says. "Now, is there anything else you need?"

"Yes, the wife says. "Why are you doing this?"

"We do not even know you," their daughter adds.

"Because of Jesus, who they crucified outside the city a few years ago."

"We heard about that, but just moved here."

The three Christians spend the next hour explaining his fulfilling all the prophecies of God coming to earth to save mankind from the power of Satan.

"So, you see," Stephen concludes, "he wasn't just a criminal they hung that day. God was in that body, and God's words were heard from that body. The body God used was Jesus. He became a human so he could die in our place."

"How can someone die in our place?" the woman asks.

"As far as Satan was concerned, the debt of death incurred by all sinners, the fine, the punishment was paid," Nicholas explains. "We are now free of Satan, but only if we believe Jesus was who he said he was and did what he claimed he did."

"Everything you said makes sense," the man says. "I want to be his follower and saved. I am sorry for all the sins I've committed. I really am sorry."

"In that case, we can take you to the Pool of Bethesda right now," Lucius says. "I am tall enough, I could carry you. "As a believer, you can be baptized into the death, burial, and resurrection of Jesus. You can imitate what he did for you and me."

By the time Stephen, Nicholas and Lucius are through with the two families, the sun is high in the sky. They part to go to their regular jobs.

As Stephen slams his heavy hammer down to flatten his white-hot bar of iron into something workable, he smiles to himself.

"Take that, Satan!"

"And that!"

"And that!"

When evening comes, he takes off his heavy leather apron, arm protectors and leg protectors, and heads for home.

Today was a good day. Jesus, I was wrong to hide you. Oh, how wrong I was. I promise to never hide you again.

When he arrives home and opens the gate, he sees his mother sitting on a bench in a corner, hugging his two-year-old daughter and weeping.

"Mother," he says, stepping over to her and kneeling. "What is it? What happened? Did you have to rescue Naomah from something? Is Naomah all right?"

Tullia loosens her grip on her granddaughter and takes her other hand down from her eyes.

"They have run out of money."

"Who has?"

"The widows. My widows. The widows from the plague. We cannot move them all in with us. This is a small house. They and all their children wouldn't fit."

Stephen lifts his daughter off Tullia's lap, kisses her on the forehead, and motions for her to go play with her brother.

He sits on the bench next to his mother and embraces her. Her frame seems smaller than it used to be. He realizes how frail she is now.

"Mother, I will go see the apostles tomorrow. They have a fund for widows. I promise they will not lose their homes."

"You have turned out to be such a fine man, Stephen," she says, holding both sides of his head in her hands. She reaches up and kisses him on the forehead, and he remembers how she had always done that to comfort him as a child.

The following day after work, Stephen goes to see the apostles for enough money the widows of Cyrene can keep their little apartments for another year. He is sent to a room full of donated dried food.

The man in the room looks up from pouring a sack of corn into a larger vat.

"Keeps the rats out better. May I help you? My name is Simon, by the way."

Stephen holds out his hand.

"My name is Stephen, and I have a good friend from Cyrene named Simon. I guess I will have to call you apostle Simon."

"Whatever keeps you from getting mixed up."

Stephen explains the situation. Apostle Simon takes him to a smaller room full of baskets piled up in each corner. He pulls out a scroll and looks through it.

"Hmmm. Seems like some widows over in the old City of David section are in need of the same thing. How many of your widows did you say?"

He looks back at his ledger. "Uhhh, well, uhhh we need to pay the apothecary for the medicines of five men who were injured when a wall they were building fell on them. Uhhh, how many did you say there were?"

Stephen tells him. "Twelve widows and thirty-five children between them all."

"Uhhh, I think we can help them. But you will have to wait until our next worship and contribution. Can you come back? And I will try to be more organized then."

"Did you say you were from Cyrene in Libya? Isn't that where that outlaw TacFarinas was?" Simon chuckles. "I used to be an outlaw myself." But those days are gone. See you next week."

Meeting this Simon reminds Stephen of his old friend. He makes a point to stop at his Berber friend's apartment on the way home.

"So good to see you," they tell each other.

"Are you any better?" Stephen asks. "You know—about dealing with, well, you know, carrying his cross?"

Simon stares at the blank wall and back at his friend. "I struggle with it every day. But what is strange is that everyone wants me to tell about it. I do not want to."

"You are the last one of his followers to touch him. They need you to help them keep Jesus alive in their hearts," Stephen replies.

"I suppose. But there's a man who has been stalking me," Simon says. "I am worried. Alexander is eleven now and Rufus ten. They need their father. I do not know what that stalker intends."

"Who?"

"Saul. Saul of Tarsus."

46 ~ THE STRUGGLE

"**T**hat concludes the events surrounding Jesus' birth. Does anyone have any question?" Thomas asks the crowded room on the top floor of the apostles' headquarters.

Stephen raises his hand.

"These apostles are pretty busy," Permenas says, sitting next to him.

"We need to let them rest now," Prochorus on the other side of Stephen says.

"This question is actually for Peter," Stephen calls out. "Peter, when you preached that first sermon, is this how you were saying Joel's prophecy had come true?

"Anna, Simeon, and Elizabeth were the sons and daughters who prophesied. Joseph was the young man who saw a vision. Zechariah and the Magi were the old men who dreamed dreams.

"The sign in the sky above was the star over Bethlehem, the sign on the earth below was the dove at Jesus' baptism.

"Blood and the sun turning to darkness occurred at the cross. When all this was fulfilled, God poured his Holy Spirit on all mankind who would believe."

Peter stands in front, shaking his head back and forth and grinning. "Friend, you are very astute. You and I shall have to get together and talk. Oh, and bring those two children of yours. They can play with mine."

When the class is dismissed, Stephen works his way through the crowd to the front.

"Simon. I am looking for Simon. I saw him a moment ago."

"I think he has taken a couple of widow ladies—Sarah and Esther, I believe—to his storeroom to fill their sacks with corn," Thomas says. "I am sure he can see you tomorrow.

"He is doing the best he can, I guess," Stephen tells his

partners the next morning as they walk to their chosen neighborhood. "But Simon—the apostle, not my Berber friend—is really disorganized. He promised me money for our Cyrenian widows three weeks ago. I cannot convince the owner of the *insulae* to be patient much longer."

"I will loan you the money," Lucius says. "Take your time paying me back. Oh, I think we have a soul to reach over there. Look at that man with the missing leg." He leads the others to the beggar.

"Sir," Lucius says, pulling out several coins. "We can help you monetarily. But what else can we do for you?

The man looks up at Lucius. "Well, to start with, you can quit acting superior to me, and get down here on my level."

"Good point," Nicholas says.

"What you can do for me is give my leg back so I can return to work, support my family, and be a man again. That is what you can do for me. Anything less than that, I do not want. Now, get out of here. All three of you."

The men rise. Lucius calls back, "Well, may Jesus Christ bless you anyway."

"Do not know him. Do not want him. Just get my leg back."

"Rejection is going to happen," Stephen says. "I have been through it so many times. You try to save someone from going to hell, and all they can think about is how miserable they are here."

They continue on down the street. Stephen stops and turns in a circle in place.

"What?"

"I did not realize this is where we were. I never come this way. This is where the widows live. That is their *insulae*."

The three men go inside and knock on the door of a first-floor apartment.

"Mother?"

"Stephen? What are you doing here?"

"Looking for people to help."

"That is wonderful. The apostles got the money to you? Oh, come in. This is Chloe's apartment. Remember, Carpus, who joined your secret synagogue for a while? He was her husband."

"Do I have company?" Chloe asks as the men file in. "Oh, Stephen. I haven't seen you in a long time. How are your wife and children?"

"They are fine. Uh, we have uh…"

"We have come to tell you we are going to pay your landlord

later today," Lucius intercedes. "You will be able to stay here another year."

"All eleven of us?"

"Yes, all eleven."

"I have an idea," Stephen says. "If your oldest will round up the other children, we will meet them behind the *insulae* and have a race."

"I am sure the mothers will be happy for the break," Tullia says. "Well, I am on my way home now. You can catch up with me. Your legs are stronger than mine."

Months pass. Stephen, Nicholas, and Lucius continue rescuing neighborhoods and introducing them to the real Jesus. Then telling them all about heaven. But the old problem of finding funds and food continues.

It is the first day of the week once more. The Church of Jesus Christ has just been dismissed.

"You go on home," Stephen tells Livia. "I need to have a talk with Philip and Andrew."

Stephen works his way through the crowd, which is going in the opposite direction. At last, he reaches the front. He looks among the smaller, but significant group gathered around the apostles.

"Philip! Andrew! Philip! Andrew!"

"You called?"

"Oh, Andrew, there you are."

"What about me? You called me too?"

"Perfect, Philip. Walk over here with me. We've got to talk before we have a crisis."

"Huh?"

"I am not complaining about Simon. He's doing the best he can. But he is overwhelmed. Oh, here come Nicholas and Lucius."

"Did Stephen tell you the problem?" Lucius asks Andrew.

"Part of it. What is your view?"

"We work on the north end of Jerusalem, the newer part by the Fortress of Antonia where mostly Greek-Speaking Jews and Pagans live," Lucius says. "We are helping and converting people, but we sometimes run low on our own funds."

"When we come here to ask for help," Nicholas continues, "we are usually told the funds are low because of helping the Jewish-born Christians in this part and the old part of Jerusalem. Our widows and their children are suffering."

"I do not think we really knew things were that bad," Philip says. "We knew Simon had been asking for help because he has hardly any time to teach the gospel any more, and that is what Jesus commanded of us, his apostles."

"Find us next week after worship. We will have an answer for you."

"Not before?" Stephen asks. There is no answer.

The week passes slowly for Stephen, his mother, and everyone else involved in helping the widows at the north side of Jerusalem.

With anxious hearts, they walk over to the temple and find a place to sit in the expansive portico. As they do, Stephen looks toward the front and sees Andrew. Andrew smiles and nods his head.

Worship begins. Worship of Jesus. Nothing like temple worship which goes on across from the portico with trumpets blasting and choirs bellowing, incense and candles burning, priests with fancy clothes, and the smell of meat cooking.

They worship with the simple psalms of David, prayers spoken and unspoken, reading of the prophecies,
silent meditation, and the Lord's Supper. "Do this to remember what I did for you," he had said.

How Stephen agonizes over what he had seen with his own eyes, heard with his own ears. Torture and love. Death and life. Evil and good. Hell and heaven. Sin and forgiveness.

Worship together with the other saints comes to an end. Now they rise to serve.

"May I have your attention," Andrew calls out. "Sit back down if you please. It has come to our attention that not all our widows and their children are being helped. The Greek-Speaking widows are being neglected." He waits.

"Things are becoming too complicated as we grow. Jesus told us apostles to teach what we have seen and heard. But we are being distracted by good works that should not be neglected. People in our congregation need help." He pauses.

"Therefore, we want you to choose seven men to oversee this work. They must be wise and full of the Holy Spirit. We apostles will now leave while you make your decision."

Achaius stands.

"Each man who served the Lord's Supper to you earlier is ready to take your votes. They have clay tablets to pass down each row. Each of you write one name and one name only. We will tally them, and the seven men who receive the most votes will be our deacons."

The process is slow. Six thousand votes must be counted in a corner away from the congregation. Achaius, Trophimus, Secundus, and Justus, along with their scribe students, divide up the tablets—three hundred for each. They make tallies on blank clay tablets. Many of the congregation, especially with restless children and no husband to help, leave before learning the results.

Two hours later the apostles are brought back and given the list of the top seven votes:

Stephen of Cyrene & Antioch
Nicholas of Antioch
Philip of Caesarea
Nicanor of Corinth
Timon of Thessalonica
Permenas of Pergamum
Prochorus of Paphos on Cyprus

The seven chosen ones walk forward and face the apostles. The apostles work their way down the row to place their hands either on their shoulders or head. The new deacons face the congregation, the apostles now standing behind them. The congregation is pleased but tired. They pray for their new deacons, rise, and head for home.

"Please stay," Apostle Simon tells the seven. "We want you to go home to our hostel with us. Bring your families. I know they are tired and hungry. We will take care of that. And, by the way, thank you for relieving me of that heavy duty. Even with help from the other eleven, it was too much."

The group leaves the temple complex and goes down the ramp and around to the apostles' headquarters. They eat and are refreshed.

Late in the afternoon, they assemble in the third-floor room. The families stay at the back. They fall to their knees and pray. The apostles pray. Stephen and the other six new deacons pray.

"Help us use your money wisely so we can save them from hell," Stephen prays.

The seven stand, facing the twelve. James makes the announcement.

"We have decided to give you the power."

Stephen and the others look at each other as though checking to see if everyone else heard what they had heard.

"Jesus gave us the power himself. He also gave us the

ability to pass the power on to others. We have not used it yet. But have decided now is the time."

Stephen's lips tremble. *Miracles? Like Jesus performed? The supernatural? Not me. Why?*

"As you divide up your work of helping the widows and their children, you will learn of special occasions that need your attention. Go to them. Heal them. Teach them. Save their souls."

Seven of the apostles—the seven who had seen Jesus by the Lake of Galilee after his resurrection—approach Stephen and the other deacons. They place their hands on each man's shoulders. The other four apostles kneel and pray for the church's new deacons.

"Your lives will be in more danger now," James says. "The temple hierarchy will hate you as they hated Jesus and now us. May Jesus give you courage to face it as he did and as we apostles have."

It is over. As Stephen walks home with his family, he is silent.

"What's wrong with *Abba*?" Naomah asks.

"Shhh. Your *Abba* has been given an awesome responsibility."

"What's awesome?"

"Beyond comprehension."

"What's compr'n?"

"Beyond human understanding," Tullia says.

That night Stephen tells Livia, "I know who I am going to help first. And I am going to do it first thing tomorrow morning."

Livia smiles. "The man with no leg."

"Yes. He was bitter, but he couldn't help it."

At dawn the next morning, Stephen leaves his home to find the neighborhood where the beggar lived.

"Maybe I came too soon." He squats on the side of the street and watches as the neighborhood comes back to life.

"No, do not put me over there," the gruff voice declares. "That is where I was yesterday."

Stephen looks in the direction of the voice and sees two older children with their hands locked together, carrying the man in a seated position.

"Stop!" Stephen says, rushing over to them. "Stop!"

"What do you mean stop? Get out of my way!"

Stephen motions to the children to set the man down.

"Do not you dare," he counters.

"What is your name, sir?" Stephen asks.

"None of your business."

"Jesus wants to do something special for you because he loves you."

"He doesn't even know me. Who is Jesus anyway? Set me down over there before you drop me."

The children scoot their feet a little at a time. The man throws down his mat. They set him on it.

"You still here?" he says, spotting Stephen.

"Sir, Jesus wants to do something special for you because he loves you."

"You already said that. Go away."

Stephen kneels and puts both hands on the man's stump.

"What are you doing? Get away from me."

Looking up at the man, he smiles. "I have to confess I have never done this before. But Jesus is with me." Then looking up at the sky, he calls out, "Jesus, heal this good man."

"Who's good? Get out...huh?"

Stephen slides his hands down from the stump. As he does, there is more leg under his hands. He slides them down and down, a knee, a calf, an ankle appears. A heal, toes.

"Huh? Huh? What happened? Huh?"

The man looks at Stephen, still kneeling in front of him. "My leg. My leg is back. What did you do?"

Stephen smiles. "I told you. He loves you. Jesus, your creator, caused your leg to come back."

He stands and offers his hand to the man. The man reaches up, takes Stephen's hand, and leaps to his feet. He stares down at his new leg, then back up at Stephen. "What did you do? Who is Jesus?"

The one true God came down to earth for a while in the form of Jesus. He lived among us as the perfect one. Then he took the punishment for all your sins, and mine, and everyone's."

"He did? Are you sure?"

"It was his power that brought your leg back. This was done to prove what I have just told you is true. You believe he brought your leg back. Now believe he wants you to live with him in heaven. Just obey his commands and worship him and try not to be so grouchy."

"I believe. I believe. I want to be in heaven with him."

"I would like to pray for you every day, but I still do not know your name."

"Oh, I am sorry about that. My name is Kyros. And yours?"

"I am Stephen, a servant of Jesus, the Christ."

"Mister!" a young man says. "My little girl is blind. Do you think Jesus would love her too?"

Stephen looks around and realizes a crowd has gathered.

"Certainly. Where is your little girl?"

The man reaches behind him and guides a shy child to step out. "Her name is Alala."

Stephen squats and smiles. "Would you mind if I touch your eyes?"

"I guess you can."

Stephen reaches over, puts his hands on Alala's eyes, and looks up at the sky. "Lord Jesus, heal this little girl. Make her see again." He gradually slides his fingers across her eyes until they are no longer covered.

"Open them up now."

"*Abba.* What's that?"

He kneels. "Turn this way."

"That is different. What is it?"

"My sweet Alala. You are using your eyes. They tell you what people and things are without having to touch them. What you see right now is me, your *Abba.* Would you like to see what your mother looks like?"

"Uh-huh."

The father stands. "If Jesus caused this to happen, then he really is Lord. I believe that now. I want to be his follower so I can be with him in heaven."

Just then, Stephen hears a scream. Two horses pulling a wagon have broken loose and are galloping up the street. Stephen rushes out to the street. He holds out his hands. Instantly the horses stand still, the wagon behind him intact, as though they had been in that spot to begin with.

"The horses aren't even breathing hard," someone says.

"It's as though they were never running."

"Jesus wants to keep you protected," Stephen responds. "Come to Solomon's Portico the first of next week. Come worship with us. Everyone come."

In the weeks and months that follow, more Jews—no matter what their nationality—become Christians, including many of the priests. So many are now coming to worship together, they flow beyond Solomon's Portico.

Sometimes they see priests and Levites, teachers of the Law of Moses, and even the High Priest himself walk out of the holy part of the temple complex to the outer courtyard and stare at the Christians.

Every time they do, the apostles stand and lead the congregation in a very loud psalm of David to make sure the spies hear them.

"I've got a plan, Livia," Stephen tells her often in private. "I think I'd like to return to Cyrene. Now do not interrupt me. I have powers now. I can heal them, and then they'll believe me. Then, I want to go back to Crete and Antioch and Tarsus. Maybe even to Rome. There are souls out there going to hell," Stephen says, his eyes tearing. "I must get to them."

One evening at home, there is a knock on Stephen's gate. He opens it and sees his Simon, his Berber Simon.

"Come in, dear friend," he says, putting his arm over Simon's shoulder and escorting him in. I am ashamed I have not been to see you in the last few weeks. I have been so busy. I swore when we moved to Jerusalem, we would spend more time together. Instead, it has been..."

"Stephen, I have to tell you something."

For the first time, Stephen sees the expression on his friend's face.

"We've been through a lot together since that day a dozen years ago when you fished my parents and me out of the undercurrent and saved our lives."

"I am here to save your life again, Stephen," Simon says.

Stephen wrinkles his brow and forces a nervous smile. "What do you mean? Things are going so well. The church is growing. We are saving souls."

"That is why. Remember I told you a year ago I was being stalked?"

"By Saul of Tarsus? Yes, I remember. Bad news, that man. He doesn't want you talking about helping Jesus with his cross."

"His spies have reported to him that you were made a deacon. And since you are the most visible of the seven deacons, he is going to come after you."

"Come after me how?"

"I do not know. But he is mean. He is evil. And someone like that who believes God is on his side is the most dangerous man on earth. Watch out. Watch for dark corners, shadows, men pretending to be sick beggars. Please, Stephen. As your best friend, I am begging you."

Stephen forces his smile again. "Why would he want me? There are thousands of Christians in the city. Why me?"

"Stephen, your son is five years old now. Naomah is three. They need their father. Be careful. I must go now. God bless you, Stephen. Be strong."

Simon stands, and Stephen walks him to his gate. Stephen opens it. The two men face each other. They embrace. They pound each other on the back.

"We have always been there for each other, haven't we?" Stephen says.

A week later, a messenger arrives at Stephen's gate while he is at work. Livia answers it and takes the message. She does not read it.

When Stephen arrives home, she hands it to him, and both she and Tullia sit with him, awaiting the news.

It is written on a small scroll with a fine, bold hand. He breaks the seal and reads it aloud.

You are hereby summoned
to the Greek-Speaking Freedmen Synagogue
for a debate on Sabbath Day next.
The subject and your opponent will be
announced after your arrival.
If you do not appear,
you will be branded a blasphemer.

"Is it signed?" Livia asks.

"No. But I know who wrote it." Stephen says.

"I know too," Tullia says. "He has turned out as mean and vicious as his father."

"Who?"

"Your husband has been challenged to a debate in a hostile synagogue with Saul of Tarsus, sent to Jerusalem to be educated at the feet of now-high-priest Caiaphas, and Gamaliel," Tullia says.

"He has the reputation of being the smartest and shrewdest student the temple school has taught in a hundred years. And now he is the youngest member of the Sanhedrin. They brought him in for one reason—destroy Christians."

Stephen stands and faces the women. "Well, he has never faced the grandson of the smartest and shrewdest student of the temple school just before the arrival of Pompey," he says for the sake of Livia.

Stephen pulls out the notes he had taken at the apostles'

class on prophecies Jesus had fulfilled in his birth, life, and death.

The Sabbath arrives. He and his family walk north toward the Sheep Gate to the familiar Greek-Speaking Freedmen Synagogue.

Stephen stops in the middle of the street and looks into his wife's eyes. "Livia, I love you and always will."

"Oh, I know that," she responds. "And I love you."

Silence.

"Well, I had to tell you again."

He takes her hand, and they resume walking toward the synagogue.

He takes a deep breath, holds his head high like his father had always told him to do when he was afraid, and walks inside. The building is full to overflowing.

He stares at the podium. Already seated are Solomus, Rabbi of the Greek-Speaking Freedmen Synagogue in Cyrene. Down in the front row, Stephen spots Usirus, Xenon, Balios, and Helios of his former synagogue in Cyrene.

Next to them are Joshua, Ebron, Eben, and Midyan, former merchant friends of Stephen's father and members of the new Merchant Synagogue in Cyrene, who had turned on Stephen and helped run him out of the city.

"He did not!" Tullia sneers in a whisper, still looking at the men on the podium. "Saul brought his father down here, old Lucius."

"There is Tobit, Rabbi of this synagogue," Stephen whispers back, "and of course Saul himself."

"Hey!" Stephen hears in a loud whisper from near the back row.

He looks over and sees Achaius, Trophimus, Secundus, and Justus.

In front of them are the other six deacons plus Lucius of Antioch. Berber Simon is there too, of course.

Stephen says a prayer, lifts his chin, and walks forward, just as his father had always told him to do. There is one chair left empty on the podium. He takes it. Solomus and Tobit are to his right. Lucius and his son Saul are to his left.

Saul stands, and the congregation comes to an anticipating hush. He lifts his hands heavenward to pronounce the benediction.

"Ohhh, Lord..."

A noise in the back. Saul stops and looks toward the door. In walks Nicodemus. Behind him are the twelve apostles

47 ~ SURRENDER

*T*obit, Rabbi of Jerusalem's Greek-Speaking Freedmen Synagogue stands. "These are the rules:"

One: The first man will affirm; the second man will deny.
Two: Each man may speak as long as he deems best.
Three: No interrupting

Saul stands. He raises his hand high. "The prophecy of Micah states that the Messiah will be born in Bethlehem. Jesus of Nazareth was born in Nazareth."

"Stephen stands. He raises his hand high. "Birth records in Bethlehem state Jesus was born there thirty-seven years ago during the great census."

Those sitting on the back benches grin. Those sitting in the front frown.

Saul raises his hand high. "The prophecies all say the Messiah will be the descendant of Abraham, Isaac, Jacob, Judah, and David. Jesus was not."

Stephen raises his hand high. "Oh, but he was. In the birth records of Bethlehem, the registration of Jesus' birth lists his ancestry back all the way to Adam. I believe you will find he met all the criteria."

Those sitting in the back nod in approval. Those sitting in the front squirm.

Saul raises his hand high. "The prophecies state that the Messiah will rule from Jerusalem. Jesus of Nazareth never did."

Xenon, sitting in the front, stands and shakes his fist in approval.

Stephen raises his hand high. "He did. The scriptures also state that he would enter Jerusalem riding on the colt of a donkey.

At that time, the people declared him their king. And he ruled the leaders so much, they had to kill him so they could keep their jobs."

"That is the truth," Nicodemus growls, standing in the back. "We all knew it."

Saul frowns. He raises his hand high. "The prophets all state there will be no end to his government. Jesus did not even organize a government."

Usirus in the front stands and barks, "Yeah!"

"Stephen smiles. He raises his hand high. "First, you missed the same prophecy in Isaiah that said he would preach mostly in the province of Galilee. Second, he did organize his government. He set up twelve ambassadors who, I believe, are with us today."

Everyone in the synagogue turns and sees the twelve lined up along the back wall. The apostles wave at them.

Saul raises his hand high. "The Law of Moses was given to the Jews forever. The Law of Moses can never be repealed. Jesus tried and failed."

Stephen raises his hand high. "Jesus declared that the law of God is now in our heart. All Christians are now priests, not just the Levites. Christians need no sacred candles because we are the light of the world. Christians no longer recognize Caiaphas as the high priest because Jesus is now our high priest. Christians no longer tithe because we give from our heart and give even more."

Eben, the butcher back in Cyrene, stands and faces the crowd behind him. "That is rubbish. Who can read a heart? I see hearts all the time, and there is no writing on them."

Laughter.

Saul raises his hand high. "The prophet Hosea stated the Messiah would be in Egypt. Jesus never lived in Egypt and never ruled from Egypt."

Stephen raises his hand high. "Oh, but he did. His parents took him to Egypt the night Herod ordered all male babies in Bethlehem killed, and stayed until Herod's death. And, by the way, you missed the other point Hosea made—that he would be God's Son."

Midyan in the front row stands. "Never! It's impossible. You cannot kill the Son of God."

Others in the audience join him.

"Never!"

"Never!"

"Never!"

Saul raises his hand high. "The prophecies say all nations of the earth will be ruled by God, the king. I did not see Jesus ruling anyone from that cross."

Stephen raises his hand high. "I am surprised you missed it, Saul. On the Day of Pentecost, after his death and coming back to life, three thousand people of all nations agreed to make Jesus king and were baptized. A few weeks later, another five thousand made Jesus king and were baptized. People come here from throughout the earth to hear Jesus' apostles, and leave with Jesus king of their heart."

Rabbi Solomus and Rabbi Karpos on the podium jump up. Saul's father, Lucius, jumps down into the audience, Saul following, their faces scarlet with anger.

Immediately, the women scatter and run out the door.

The men in the front rows all jump up from their seats. The two rabbis, Saul, and his father lunge at the men in the back row who support Stephen.

Men are wrestled to the floor. The Christians try to control themselves. "I do not want to hurt you, my friend," they grunt while being pounded in the face.

The fight moves to the outside. Gradually, people break away and run toward home or wherever they consider the safest place for them. All that remain in front of the synagogue are the men who had been on the podium, minus Stephen. Staring and angry and shouting with fists in the air. "We will get you for this!"

"Come with me!" Simon shouts at Stephen.

"No! I will put you in danger," Stephen shouts back.

Simon stops his friend as they round a corner out of sight of the synagogue.

"Saul and his supporters are after me," Stephen objects. "I cannot go with you."

"Our families are safe at home by now. We're cannot go there. Follow me. Just trust me."

Stephen follows close. The two men with scrapes and bloody faces stumble up another street.

"Is it much farther?"

They stop at a small home near the Jerusalem gate leading down into the valley, then up to the Garden of Gethsemane. Simon calls out as he pounds on the gate. "It's Simon. I've got Stephen with me. Open up!"

The gate soon opens, and the two men rush in. The gate closes, and Stephen looks back at his new savior.

"Draco?"

"Here and ready to help. So, what do you have going on?" he says with a grin.

"When did you get here?"

"A few days ago. I looked up Simon just last night. He told me about the debate this morning, but I had to sign the deed for this house. I figured there would be more debates, knowing you, Stephen. I still remember that debate at the university you had with ole Cato. He never got over it. So, the debate today did not end so good?"

"Not at all, Draco. We won," Stephen says, feeling around his face to discover where all the blood on his tunic is coming from.

"Hey, what's going on here anyway? What is Draco doing in Jerusalem?" Stephen asks, looking over at Simon.

"Ask him."

"Come sit, and I will tell you about it."

They step over to two benches in the still-sparse courtyard.

"After our secret synagogue was discovered," Draco begins, "I went to Antioch. You always said you liked it there, and the mountains were cool, so I gave it a try. I met Manaen there. He had become a Christian on the Day of Pentecost, came back to Antioch, and a few of us believed him and became Christians. He kept encouraging me to go to Jerusalem to learn from the apostles themselves, so I finally did."

"Just you?" Stephen asks.

"Yes. I haven't married," Draco says. "How about you, Stephen?"

"Married to the daughter of a former member of the Sanhedrin, and I have a son who is now five and a daughter who just turned three."

"Well, when things settle, you and Simon will have to come over so the little ones can meet their uncle. But first..."

"Yes, but first," Simon repeats, "we have to hide Stephen."

"And you, my brother," Stephen tells Simon.

"You both can stay here as long as you need to. But I do not understand why Simon has to hide."

"He carried Jesus' cross," Stephen says in almost a whisper."

"Oh..."

"He is the last one of his followers to touch him and talk to him."

"I agonize over it every day," Simon says.

"He shouldn't," Stephen adds. "The other Christians keep wanting to ask him what Jesus said along the way that the mob couldn't hear. And how bad his face was battered when seen up close."

"I do not want to tell people of the Master's suffering," Simon says.

"Because of this, the Sanhedrin is after him," Stephen explains. "They want to kill him. He knows too much."

"Oh. I see," Draco says.

The next morning, Draco gets word to the families of Stephen and Simon. That afternoon, there is a hard pounding on Draco's gate.

"You two stay out of sight," he warns on his way to open the gate.

"We are searching for Stephen of Antioch and Cyrene, and Simon of Cyrene. They are wanted for blasphemy."

"Hurry, while Draco stalls them," Simon whispers to Stephen. "Up on the roof."

They take three steps at a time, look around on the roof, make their decision, and jump, hoping not to break any bones.

"Where to?" Stephen asks, crouching.

"Out the city gate. We will hide in the Garden of Gethsemane."

Stephen follows Simon as he works his way down into the valley around the city, then up the Mount of Olive Trees.

"I think it's right over there," Simon says, slowing down and walking over to a clearing. He looks around. Yes, I think this is where they used to hide out."

"Who?"

"Jesus. Whenever he was in Jerusalem and things got dangerous, instead of spending the night with his friends in Bethany, he came here. Look. Over there. See those logs around that old campfire? I am sure that is where they sat around with him at night."

Stephen stares at the hiding place.

"There is one more spot. More sacred to me than this. Where he begged God not to have to go through the crucifixion and take the blame of all our sins onto himself."

Simon walks into a thicket of trees closest to the campsite. Stephen follows him.

"I cannot find it. I guess we will never know. It's been too long. I've asked some of the apostles to show me where it is, but they all say it is too painful for them."

They return to the logs and sit on them. "Do you have any fire on you, Stephen?"

"Yes, I always carry a piece of curved glass with me to fire up my forge."

Simon gathers up some dried leaves and piles them in the fire pit. Stephen kneels before it, and soon has a fire started.

Silence.

"Stephen, remember when we ran for our lives up in those desert mountains?"

Stephen grins. "Yeah. I never told you, but I did not think we were going to get out of them alive."

"Sometimes those thoughts crept into my mind," Simon says. "If it hadn't been for little Alexander..."

"I guess your toddler is the one who saved both our lives. How old is he now?

"Twelve. And Rufus is ten."

"They're getting to that age when boys really need their father, not just a mother," Stephen says.

"Yes, I guess you're right."

"We've been through a lot together," Stephen whispers. "Simon, you have to live."

"Huh? Well, of course. You too. We're going to get out of this mess somehow."

"Simon, I have been getting into messes like this all my life," Stephen says. "I have run all my life."

"Then run again. And keep running."

"Things are all mixed up again, Simon," Stephen says. "What are we going to do? We cannot ever deny him. Simon, you've got to live."

"You too, Stephen. You've got to live too."

Silence.

Near dusk, they walk around the grove, gathering up dry firewood and piling it near the campfire to keep it going through the night. They check around and find a few sparse olives left on the trees for their dinner.

It is mostly dark by the time Simon returns to the campfire. He falls asleep, waiting for Stephen to return from the thicket.

Stephen does not return.

48 ~ GOING HOME

hadows.

Wondering.

Sorting things out.

"Jesus," Stephen whispers, "is this garden where you struggled? It's so hard. Help me. Help me know what to do."

He kneels.

"I am so mixed up." He pauses. "I guess that is what I used to tell my father. Now I am telling you. I have tried to bring people to you so they can be saved from hell, but they hate me. Well, not all of them, but..."

By a sliver of moonlight, he looks up through the branches high overhead.

"Why, God? Why do they hate me? Why do they hate you?"

He falls forward onto his forearms.

"Your throne. What is it like? Is it gold? Is it like pearls or diamonds? What's it like?"

He stands and looks out toward the campfire and Simon now asleep on the ground, his robe wrapped tight around him.

Stephen gathers up more dry firewood, puts it carefully in the fire, gathers up more for a reserve, and returns to his spot in the thicket. He kneels.

Silence.

"He has to live, Jesus. Simon has to live for his family. So people can talk with the last one on earth to ever do anything for you. Comfort him, Jesus. He's really struggling."

Clouds bump into each other overhead.

"Livia. I always loved that name. Live. Livia. She gave me new life. Over and over she has given me new life."

Silence.

"Well, no. She has given me life, but you, Jesus, are my life.

I love her so. And my little Abraham and Naomah. So innocent. Will they…”

The question goes unasked.

He walks back to look at Simon again. “Protect him, Jesus. He must live. Protect him.”

He sits on one of the logs the apostles had sat on with their Master. And where the Master, still in his body, had sat. He stares once more at Simon.

“There is still so much work for him to do,” he whispers. “They have been stalking him for much longer than they have me. He’s such a good man. Did I ever tell you about the time he saved my parents and me out of the maelstroms offshore from Cyrene?”

He smiles. “I do not guess I need to tell you. You were there helping him.”

He sighs. “That was a lifetime ago. I have started my life all over again so many times. Tarsus to Antioch. Antioch to Cyrene. Cyrene to Jerusalem. And now what? Where do I run to? What do I put my family through? I cannot do it, Jesus. I cannot put them through what I have been through. I cannot. I just cannot.”

Stephen stands and stumbles around the thick hiding place. He stands still and stares at the stars above.

“Letting go. How do I let go? Maybe not. You need me here, Jesus. Didn’t I shut the mouth of the enemy—Saul? He is trying to destroy you. I am smarter than him. If I stay, I can stop him.” He looks into the shadows, then back up.

“And the Sanhedrin at the temple. They will be over there, destroying people a hundred years from now. Someone has to stop them. Nicodemus and I together—we could stop them. With your help, we could.”

He sits on the ground, hugging his raised knees.

“So much to do. Enemies to shut up for you. Brothers and sisters to protect for you. My family. Souls to save for you.

“I must run. I must run away. Take my family and escape.”

Silence.

“But what about Simon?”

Stephen stands and walks around the grove of trees. He looks at the moon overhead. He walks to a tree and hugs the trunk.

“You’re so gnarled. How did you get to be so old, olive tree? After all these years, you’re still standing. You weathered all the storms. The heat. The cold. Drought. Flood. How is it done?”

Stephen steps away, stands in place, and turns around and

around until he falls from dizziness. He sits cross-legged and looks up through the high branches.

"Jesus. Where are you? Do you want me? My wife wants me. My children. The church. Do you want me more?"

He leans over until his head and one shoulder are touching the rocky, sandy ground with slivers of dead branches strewn among them. He weeps.

His shoulders shake. He shakes his head back and forth.

"No, no, no. No, Jesus!"

He curls up and hugs his knees. "Jesus, help me."

Silence.

He stands. He raises his hands heavenward. "Do not make me do it. I cannot. I cannot do it. I am too young. Do not make me!"

He puts his hands on each side of his head as though doing so will change what was and what is. Once more, he stumbles out to watch Simon sleep.

"Sleep on, my friend," he says, stooping, his hair down in his face, his eyes red and swelling. He puts his hands on his knees and stares at his loyal friend.

"You are so good, Simon. I never heard you say an unkind word about anyone. So good. The church needs you. You must live. You have to live. What will we do without you? What will they do without you? Oh, Simon, Simon. My dear, dear friend."

Stephen stumbles over to where Simon is sleeping and kneels next to him. "Breathe on. Live on. Oh, Jesus. Oh, Simon."

He thinks he hears something from the edge of the grove. Maybe down on the road at the bottom of the little mountain. His insides jump. He stands.

"Are they coming after us? I've got to get to them before they find Simon. I have to let them think I am alone. Hurry. Hurry before they find Simon."

He stumbles and works his way to the edge of the clearing where they had first entered the garden that afternoon. He walks through some of the olive trees, then notices the lights.

"They're coming. What do I do? Do I hide? Do I run away? Do I walk forward like he did that night?"

He walks a few steps forward and realizes what the lights are.

"The temple. Lights from the temple on the other side of the valley. Candle lights. Everywhere. Silence, though. No singing at night. Not much of anything at night. They are all in their own night. The night of their making. The dark valley of their own destruction."

Stephen turns around. "Simon. I've got to go back to Simon. I must protect Simon. He must live."

He stumbles back, falling sometimes on something unseen. He struggles to his knees and stands again. He works his way finally back to the campfire.

He watches Simon in his peaceful sleep. "Oh, my friend, my heart."

He straightens and smiles.

"If I stayed here, Jesus, the apostles could dictate to me the things you did and said while you were on earth. I am a good scribe. Matthew and John have already mentioned it to me. You would like that, wouldn't you, Jesus? That is what you would want me to do."

Once again, Stephen moves back into the deeper darkness of the grove.

"Help me know what to do. Help me save Simon."

He looks back in the direction of his friend though he cannot see him.

"I cannot give you up, Jesus. But I cannot allow my family to suffer because of me. Always on the watch for danger. Always on the run. Always...."

"How do I say goodbye?" he rasps as he finds his way in the darkness. "How? How can I say goodbye? Can I even? My wife? My children? My mother? Never to see them again?"

He sucks in breath through a throat that is parched with agony.

"My mother. She will take care of my family. She is strong. And maybe Draco. Maybe he will help them. And of course, Philip.

"And Nicodemus. Maybe his smaller home will be large enough for my family. He and Naomah are strong. And my mother. And Livia. Oh, Livia. How can I live without you, my own heart?"

He chokes on his words. He groans.

Once more on his knees. Tears running down his cheeks. He clasps his hands and puts them on his knees like a child saying his prayers.

Silence. For a very long time now. Silence.

"Jesus," he whispers. "Jesus, are you calling? Are you calling me?"

He looks up into the sky, now pale gray. "What is heaven like, Jesus? Is there peace? And love? And angel songs? Are there misty glows? Rainbows? Shimmering waters of life?"

Silence.

"What is your throne like, Jesus, my God? May I worship at your feet? May I give you my heart? I've never done this before. How do I go about it? Dying? Are you calling me?"

The sky grows a little lighter. Now a slight red glow.

Silence.

"Yes," he whispers. "I know. I've got to protect Simon. Simon has to live."

He sighs. "Jesus, wait for me."

He takes a deep, full breath.

The decision has been made.

Stephen holds his head high like a soldier reporting for duty, and makes his way out to Simon. He takes off his father's eternal ring, sets it in Simon's open hand, then slips into the shadows.

As the sky becomes red, he enters through the gate into Jerusalem, his head bowed to hide his identity.

He slips over to Draco's house and looks around to see if any soldiers are watching. He knocks on the gate and, at the same time, notices the sun has turned from red to gold.

The gate opens.

"Get in here. They're watching my house. I do not know why," Draco says. "I just arrived in the city. And you look terrible. What have you been doing? What is going on?"

"Someone followed Simon and me. It was probably Saul. Well, we do not have much time. This is what you must do. Listen carefully."

"Stephen, do I want to hear this?"

"There are two men in this city you must contact. One is Nicholas. The other is Lucius. They are both from Antioch. They must help Simon escape to Antioch. Do you have a clay tablet I can draw a map on?"

Draco looks among the baskets he has not unpacked yet. He finds one and gives it to Stephen along with a stylus.

"They are both Greek-speaking, so both live in the new north end of the city near where you are. Okay, Nicholas lives over here." Stephen draws his line. "And Lucius over here. This is your house." He hands the tablet to Draco.

Stephen turns his head.

"They're banging on gates up and down the street again."

Stephen hunches his head down close to Draco's. "Simon is asleep up in the Garden of Gethsemane. Tell Nicholas and Lucius it's where Jesus and his apostles used to hide. Tell them to go get him while you get his family. Do not give them time to pack anything. They must leave the city immediately."

The banging is now on Draco's gate.

"Open up! Open up! We know you're in there."

"Take his family to the garden," Stephen says. "Nicholas and Lucius are to take them to Jericho, cross the Jordan River and work their way up to Antioch."

More banging on the gate. "If you do not answer it, we will break it down!"

"Do not go by sea. The Sanhedrin probably has soldiers at all our ports."

The banging grows louder. Spears are being jabbed into the wood around the hinges.

"What about you?" Draco says.

"I will hold the Sanhedrin off until they are safely out of Jerusalem. Then you need to come to the courtroom and signal to me so I will know they are safe."

"No, Stephen! Don't do this. What about your family?"

The hinges give way, and the soldiers charge in.

"Take care of them, Draco! Take care of my wife and children."

They grab Stephen, pull his arms back, and chain his wrists.

"Tell Livia I will always love her. Tell my mother, thank you!" he shouts as they push him back through the gate.

"Tell my children I will always watch over them!"

As the soldiers push Stephen up the street, Stephen calls out one last time, hoping Draco can hear over the wall. "Tell Livia I love her!"

Stephen stumbles forward as the soldiers push him in the direction of the Antonia Fortress. Being Levitical soldiers, they do not enter the Roman stronghold

The soldiers laugh among themselves. "There is going to be a bonus in it for us," one says. "Saul has been after Stephen a long time. Simon will be next."

Stephen looks over at the soldier and manages a brief smile. The soldier slaps him with the back of his hand.

Once around the fortress, they turn south, paralleling the wall of the temple complex on top of Mount Moriah. They go past houses, an *insulae*, then a large three-story hostel. They pass that. When they come to the palace of High Priest Caiaphas, they turn east. They march onto the ramp leading from the street in the middle of Jerusalem up to the top of the temple mountain.

Stephen stumbles ahead of them. He is bent over. His tears have returned. He hears his father. *Do not do that, Son. Hold your head up. Make them believe you are not afraid. Hold your head up.*

As Stephen does, he looks at the sky above. He looks directly at the sun. He feels the sun looking directly back at him. The sun glows for him.

"Jesus," he cries out. "It's for Simon. It's for you. It's for the world."

He grits his teeth. He takes a deep breath. He presses his lips together. He keeps his head high, even as the soldiers push him ahead. "We can do this, Jesus. Together, we can do this!"

"What's he mumbling about?" one of the soldiers asks.

"Something about Jesus. Well, we got rid of him. Stephen is next."

They make their way through the massive outer Courtyard of the Gentiles.

Stephen looks over to his right and sees the Portico of Solomon, where he had worshipped Jesus with thousands of Christian brothers and sisters. Where he had heard the teachings of the very apostles themselves. Where he had sat next to his Livia, Abraham sitting up proud next to him, and Naomah on her mother's lap.

"Live on, church. Live on!" he calls out, just as they arrive at the Song Gate up to the Treasury and Women's Courtyard. Stephen manages all eight steps.

Crossing the courtyard, one of the soldiers moves up beside Stephen, puts his foot out, and Stephen trips. He struggles back to his feet, his wrists still bound behind his back.

Hold your head up, Son, continues to ring through his mind.

"Jesus. We're going to do this. Together," he calls out. "Just keep Simon safe. He has to live. He has to live."

They are now at the Nicanor Gate leading up to the Courtyard of the priests and sacrifices. He bows as he manages all seven steps, then straightens up once more.

In front of him is the grand temple itself, the gold-lined building only priests are allowed into. He smiles. "This is nothing compared to where I will be soon," he says aloud.

They turn left, walk around the altar of sacrifice, then work their way beside the temple to the attached building used by the Sanhedrin.

As he walks closer, Stephen presses his lips together. He

takes a deep breath. "Jesus, let me see your throne. Jesus, open the door. I am ready. Open the door now."

The door opens to the Sanhedrin's building, and Stephen is forced up the steps to the courtroom at the top. Another door is opened. They shove Stephen ahead of them.

When Stephen enters the courtroom, there is a gasp.

Stephen stands just inside the large ornate room, his head high. *Is that your door, Jesus? Thank you.* He smiles.

The Sanhedrin and court observers stare at Stephen and then each other.

"His face. It's glowing."

High Priest Caiaphas steps toward Stephen. "Stop that glowing right now. Do you hear me? Only Moses was allowed to glow." He turns to the jury, the seventy members of the High Council. "Let the proceedings begin," he announces.

Witnesses step forward as they called.

"Is it true, Rabbi Solomus of Cyrene, that you heard him say the Law of Moses is to be done away with?"

"Yes, I heard him say it many times."

The next witness is called forward.

"Is it true, Ebron of Cyrene, that you heard him say the temple is worthless now and should be destroyed?"

"That is what I heard him say, your holiness."

"Is it true, Lucius of Tarsus, that you heard him say all followers of Jesus of Nazareth are now priests?"

"Oh, yes. Heard him say it often, your worshipfulness."

High Priest Caiaphas turns toward the assembled seventy of the Sanhedrin. "What need we further? We have had three witnesses."

Priest Selig stands. He smiles. "I think we need to hear some of his dribble. He will be fine entertainment before we...you know."

High Priest Caiaphas turns toward Stephen. "Fine. You may have your say. Make it good, because it will be your last."

Stephen is alone now in front of the powerful Sanhedrin. They leave his wrists chained behind his back.

Jesus, speak through me. Give me the words. Jesus, I know you are here. I can see your door. I can still see it. Thank you. I know you are...

"Get on with it!" someone shouts from the assembly. Stephen recognizes the voice. It is the voice of Saul.

Unwanted tears return to Stephen's eyes briefly. "Stand

tall, Son. Stand tall. Smile."

Stephen lifts his chin a little higher. He smiles. He wants to raise his hand as he had always done in debates. *Jesus will raise his hand for me.* He takes a deep breath.

"Brothers! Fathers! The God of glory appeared to our father, Abraham, when he lived long ago near the remains of the Garden of Eden." His voice grows stronger.

God promised Abraham this land for his descendants. Our father obeyed."

Stephen looks from man to man as he speaks. He reads their eyes. He sees hatred. He looks up and sees the door, now glowing.

"Our God repeated the promise to Abraham's son and grandson, Isaac, and Jacob. He predicted Abraham's great-grandson would sojourn to Egypt, where Joseph had become second only to Pharaoh. God said the rest of Abraham's descendants would sojourn there and become slaves for four hundred years, and it came about just as God said."

"So, what?" a member of the Sanhedrin shouts out from the back of the courtroom. "We know all that."

Stephen looks up. The gold door. It is brighter now.

"At last, Moses was born, and God sent him to bring our ancestors out of Egypt. They were stubborn and refused to believe Moses. They turned on him, and hated him and remained slaves another forty years. But Moses returned and freed our ancestors, even though they hated him."

"Well, you're no Moses!" one of the witnesses shouts.

The golden door grows larger and closer.

"God took care of our ancestors as they wandered as nomads for forty long years. During all that time, they rebelled over and over against Moses and God. Despite that, God brought them into this land he had promised Abraham centuries earlier. And God promised he would raise up a great prophet like Moses someday. You know that. You have always known that."

Stephen looks over at the door leading into the courtroom. It has not opened. He must continue.

"Our ancestors had judges and kings to rule over them," he bellows. "When David became king, God promised David his throne would last forever through one of his descendants. God's other prophets said the same thing. You know that. You've always known that."

Stephen looks at the door of the courtroom. It opens. Draco stands by it and smiles. "They're safe," he whispers. Stephen smiles back. A faint smile.

It is time.

He looks up again. The golden door. The door is opening.

With one final blast, Stephen attacks.

"You! You, and you and you!" he says, looking all around the courtroom at his judges. "You killed that prophet just like your ancestors killed all the prophets who described the Messiah," He bellows. "You killed the prophesied Messiah! You are nothing but heartless murderers!"

"How dare you!"

"Blasphemer!"

"Murderer of the Law of Moses!

"You have condemned yourself!"

Stephen looks up. "The door is open! I see him! I see Jesus, who you murdered! He is standing at the right hand of the throne. Standing. Is he saluting me?"

"Stop that!"

"You see nothing!"

"You're a lunatic!"

"A blasphemer!

"Silence him!"

The younger men in the back of the assembly climb over and between the older men sitting in front.

"Kill him!"

"Stop him!"

"Kill him!"

Saul rushes to the outer door, opens it, and thrusts his fist into the air. "Kill him, I say. Kill him!"

They grab Stephen. They rush him down the steps. The rest of the Sanhedrin follows. They rush him out into the holy Courtyard of the Priests, past the altar of sacrifice, down the steps into the next courtyard.

Saul works his way around and is now in the lead, his fist still punching the air.

"Kill."

"Kill."

Hold your head up, Son, Stephen hears. He looks ahead, and still, he sees the brightness. "I am coming, Jesus. I am coming."

Pushing.

Shoving.

"Kill him!"

"Kill the blasphemer."

Down more steps from the Courtyard of the Treasury through the Song Gate to the last and most expansive courtyard.

They push him to his knees. Stephen looks up at the glowing sun. "Jesus. I am coming."

They grab him by the chains at his wrists and pull him up, always shoving him forward.

He sees ahead Solomon's Portico. "Keep worshipping him!" he shouts at ten thousand Christians in a mist.

Out the austere Golden Gate. Across the dizzying bridge spanning the precipice below. The great bridge to the Mount of Olive Trees.

Saul stands tall and proud. The mob of holy men stops. It is time. Stephen knows.

"Jesus, I am coming," he whispers.

He stays still. As a lamb waiting for the slaughter, he waits.

Hold your head up, Son. Hold your head up.

The first stone is thrown at him. "Ughhh." Stephen reels. He puts his head down to protect his face.

Do not do that. Lift you head up, Son.

Another blow on the other side. "Ughhh."

He loses his balance, then straightens again.

Another blow. This one to his head. "Ughhh." Blood. Blood flows down into his eyes.

"Jesus...show your throne to...Livia, my childr...," he groans, "Make Livia...ughhh...strong."

Now at his legs, his arms, his chest. "Ughhh." His head again. "Aghhh."

Blood on his arms, his legs. Bones. "Ughhh." Bones hurting. Bones screaming.

Another to his back. "Ughhh." Another and another. Ducking, bending, leaning. "Aghhh." Blood and burning and fire.

Stand tall, Son. Hold your head up. Do not let them see you afraid.

More stones. Blood. A stone hits him in his eye. "Ughhh." Another to his nose. His cheek. The side of his head. "Aghhh." He loses his balance and falls to his knees.

"Jesus!" Stephen calls out. "I am...almost there. Meet me...Jesus. Meet me."

Stand back up, Son. Hold your head up. Stand tall.

Stephen struggles to his feet. He does not know how he does. More stones. "Ughhh."

Stones all around now. Stones stained with blood.

Stephen's blood. "Ughhh. Ughhh."

Stones at his back, his arms, his chest, his head. "Aghhh." Bending, ducking, shifting. Bones crushing. "Aghhh." Skin breaking. Blood smearing everywhere.

"Jesus, meet…aghhh…me at the…door!"

He reels again. He falls to his knees once more. He raises his head toward the sky and the door and the throne and Jesus.

"Jesus!" he calls out.

The clouds shift and churn overhead.

"Do not…charge…Forgive them…Ughhh…Keep loving …."

Another stone. To his throat. One more. To his heart.

A haze.

Mist.

Swaying.

Reeling.

Falling.

Collapsing.

Sinking.

Cold. So cold.

Now standing.

Climbing.

Rising.

Soaring.

Emerging.

Silence.

Calm.

The mist now gone.

Fog now gone.

Golden sun.

Rays of warmth.

Drawing.

Lifting.

Carrying.

Wings.

Angel songs.

Love.

A smile.

A touch.

"Welcome home, Stephen."

It is Jesus.

Godly men buried STEPHEN and mourned deeply for him.
On that day,
a great persecution broke out against the church at Jerusalem,
and all except the apostles were
scattered throughout Judea and Samaria.

Those who had been scattered
preached the word wherever they went.

Acts 8:1b, 2, 4

Now those who had been scattered
by the persecution in connection with STEPHEN
traveled as far as Phoenicia, Cyprus and ANTIOCH,
telling the message only to Jews.

Some of them, however, men from Cyprus and CYRENE,
went to ANTIOCH and began to speak to GREEKS also,
telling them the good news about the Lord Jesus.
The Lord's hand was with them,
and a great number of people believed
and turned to the Lord.

Acts 11:19-21

49 ~ I WILL NEVER FORGET YOU

"I remember when Stephen came to my crucifixion, and I was so scared, and I hurt so much. He cried for me. *Thank you, Stephen. I will never forget you.*" –Abraham of Antioch

"I remember how Stephen used to call me a jaguar behind my back because I could run fast. He called me a sea bird because of my long, skinny legs. He called me a tiger because of my big teeth. He called me an alligator because of my big nose. We knew why he did it—to remember our names. We had so much fun being around him as a teenager. *Thank you, Stephen. We will never forget you.*" –Justus, Secundus, Trophimus, Achaius of Antioch, Cyrene, and Jerusalem.

"I remember when I first met Stephen in that jail on Crete waiting to be sold as a slave. Then, after I helped him escape, he challenged Cato, the university bully. Then he started a secret synagogue so we could convince pagans to believe in God. And then...Oh, Stephen. I do not think I will ever understand. He gave his life for the sake of Christianity. He was only twenty-nine. He was always so strong. *Thank you, Stephen. I will never forget you.*" –Draco of Cyrene, Antioch, and Jerusalem

"I remember when Stephen and that mother of his stood up to me by bragging on his famous grandfather who tutored Augustus himself—Athenodorus—so I would let a Jew into the university. What bravado. *Thank you, Stephen. I will never forget you.*" –Censor Rabannas of Cyrene

"I remember when Stephen and his father made sure we had a full set of the Torah and Prophets for our Slave Synagogue. *Thank you, Stephen. I will never forget you.*" —Rabbi Obadiah of Cyrene

"I remember when Stephen tripped over himself making enthusiastic suggestions to the Greek-Speaking Freedmen Synagogue scroll committee. Were they mad. But I liked his naïve enthusiasm. *Thank you, Stephen. I will never forget you.*" –Brother Benjamin of Cyrene

"I remember when Stephen wandered into the wasteland of the mountains where TacFarinas was hiding with his outlaw gang. There he was with an arrow sticking out of his leg, still determined to save his friend and that baby of his. What young nerve he had. *Thank you, Stephen. I will never forget you.*" –Centurion Theophilus of Berea

"I remember how hard Stephen trained to win the javelin-throwing Olympics. He had strong arms but did not know how to control them until I got hold of him. He won too. I was sorry they lied and took his crown from him. He held his head high, though. *Thank you, Stephen. I will never forget you.*" –Achilles of Cyrene

"We remember when Stephen formed a guild for the smiths so people wouldn't take advantage of our skills. He paid for it later with that beating. He was brave. *Thank you, Stephen. We will never forget you*". –Ianos, Nikon, and Sethos of Cyrene

"I remember when Stephen stood up to Governor Blasius, who wanted to cheat him out of his locks for the fortresses. Stephen made him give in. *Thank you, Stephen. I will never forget you.* –Centurion Cronos of Cyrene

"We remember when Stephen and Simon showed up on the edge of our oasis nearly dead. Alexander wasn't even Stephen's son, and Simon wasn't his brother. But he loved those strange Berbers like they were his kin. *Thank you, Stephen. We will never forget you.*" –Gwafa and Tazerwat of the Nasamonian Tribe

"I was falsely accused and put in jail just because I was a Jew. Even though Stephen had just been beaten by pagan priests and had broken ribs, he came to the jail and helped me escape. *Thank you, Stephen. I will never forget you.*" –Cheber of Cyrene.

"We remember how Stephen and his mother came to us after our husbands died in the plague and helped us. He defended us to the Jewish-Born Freedmen when they wouldn't accept us. Then he took us to Jerusalem and watched over us and our children there. *Thank you, Stephen. We will never forget you.*" –Aello and Chloe on behalf of all twelve widows.

"I remember the first time I saw Stephen, surrounded by all those widows with all those children. He was one brave man to take them hundreds of miles from home so he could take care of them better. Everyone in Jerusalem was talking about it. *Thank you, Stephen. I will never forget you.*" –Deacon Philip of Caesarea and Jerusalem

"Little did we know when Stephen fled Antioch as a mere boy we would meet up with him again years later in Jerusalem with a wife and children. He had such a big heart as we walked with him through all those neighborhoods seeking people to help and save. *Thank you, Stephen. We will never forget you.*" –Nicholas and Lucius of Antioch and Jerusalem.

"I was so mean to Stephen when I met him. I admit I was bitter. I had lost my leg in an accident and could no longer support my family. I hated myself and everyone else. Stephen came into my life and brought my leg back. More than that, he brought my dignity back, and my soul back from hell. *Thank you, Stephen. I will never forget you.*" –Kyros of Jerusalem

"He saved my daughter from being trampled by runaway horses. Somehow, they got spooked and broke loose. My little girl was crossing the street just then. Stephen ran out and stood facing the charging horses, his hands up. Suddenly they stopped, just like that. *Thank you, Stephen. I will never forget you.*" –Miriam of Jerusalem.

"Did I ever misjudge Stephen when I first met him. Never was he ever going to marry my daughter. But, when I saw his love and patience, and how much he loved the Lord who I had been ashamed of, I took courage. *Thank you, Stephen. I will never forget you.*" –Nicodemus of Jerusalem

"When the entire congregation of over six thousand Christians made Stephen their top choice as a deacon, we knew we had a unique young man before us. But we did not know just how unique. He had more courage than a hundred other Christians. We will tell about him where ever we go. *Thank you, Stephen. We will never forget you.*" –Peter on behalf of all twelve apostles of Galilee and Jerusalem

"You were the best son a mother could ever hope for. You were brave when we did not understand why. When you fell, you got back up. Your father and I were so proud of you. You had a heart of gold. Then you offered it up for someone else. *Oh, thank you for your example, my son. I will never forget you.*" –Tullia of Rome, Tarsus, Antioch, Cyrene, and Jerusalem

"Stephen, my heart. You were the best husband a woman could ever have. How can I tell you how much I loved you? My heart is breaking. How can I go on without you? You were my everything. My darling, you gave your life for the cause of Jesus Christ. Will I ever understand such love? *Thank you for your undying love. I will never forget you.*" –Livia of Jerusalem, Cyrene, and back to Jerusalem

"*Abba*, we did not want you to go away. *Abta* says you went to heaven, but when we are all grown up, we can see you again. She also said you can see us right now, even when we cannot see you. Will you be here for all our birthdays? *Thank you for being our Abba. We will never forget you.*" –Abraham and Naomah of Cyrene and Jerusalem

"Stephen, you were the best friend a man could ever hope for. The day I saved you out of the sea when you were just eighteen, I thought I was the strong one. How wrong I was. I never knew such strength and determination in anyone such as what you had. Then the ultimate sacrifice. How could you have done it? You were twenty-nine. I was thirty-nine. I am in Antioch now, safe with my family. I will make you proud. My dear, dear friend and brother, I owe you my very life. *How can I ever say thank you? I will never forget you.*" –Simon of Cyrene, Jerusalem, and Antioch

THANK YOU

Thanks for reading my book! I'm so honored that you chose to spend your precious time with my characters. You are appreciated. I'm an independent author who relies on my readers to help spread the word about stories you enjoy.

Would you take a few minutes to let your friends know on Facebook, Pinterest...wherever you hang out online? Also, each honest review at online retailers means a lot to me and helps other readers know if this is a book they might enjoy.

I welcome contact from readers. At my website (below), you can do so. You can also sign up for my monthly newsletter (below) for half-price paper and 99c ebooks for the whole family - novels, non-fiction, storybooks and first peek at my newest release.

GET ALL 8 BOOKS IN THE HISTORICAL SERIES
INTREPID MEN OF GOD

Novel 1 ~ Lazarus: The Samaritan
Novel 2 ~ Paul: The Unstoppable
Novel 3 ~ Luke: Slave & Physician
Novel 4 ~ Mefiboset: Crippled Prince
Novel 5 ~ Joseph: The Other Father
Novel 6 ~ Michel: The Fourth Wise Man
Novel 7 ~ Stephen: Unlikely Martyr
Novel 8 ~ Titus: The Aristocrat

TO READ MORE ABOUT
ABELIA, ALEXANDER, & RUFUS TEN YEARS LATER
AND SAUL'S BROTHERS:

PAUL: THE UNSTOPPABLE
http://bit.ly/PaulUnstoppable
Book 2 in *Intrepid Men of God* series
International Buying Codes

TO READ ABOUT THEOPHILUS
DURING THE REST OF HIS CAREER:

LUKE: SLAVE & PHYSICIAN
http://bit.ly/LukeSlave
Book 3 in *Intrepid Men of God* series
International Buy Codes

TO READ MORE ABOUT
JESUS' LIFE AND DEATH:

THEY MET JESUS
http://bit.ly/TheyMetJesus
In 8 Novels
International Buy Codes

SOME HISTORICAL BACKGROUND

POMPEY (GNAEUS POMPEIUS MAGNUS) besieged Jerusalem in
63 BC, set up his headquarters in the temple complex, and
killed 12,000 Jews. Stephen belonged to the Freedmen
Synagogue in Jerusalem; therefore, he was probably born
in slavery. He also was in charge of Greek widows, so I
surmised he was a Jew but raised in a Greek area.

CLEOPATRA, QUEEN OF EGYPT, went to visit her lover, Marc
Antony, in Tarsus in 41 BC. The "Cleopatra Gate" through
which she entered the city still stands.

ATHENODORIS, THE STOIC PHILOSOPHER, died AD 7 in Tarsus
at age 67. He was born near Tarsus, and became the tutor
of Octavia, later Augustus Caesar. When Octavia's uncle,
Julius Caesar, was assassinated in 44 AD, he followed the
young man to Rome where he continued to tutor him.
Later, he returned to Tarsus, rewrote the constitution,
expelled what we would call the mayor of Tarsus, then
became the mayor himself.

POSIDONIUS was probably the most famous philosopher of his
time. He was a teacher of Athenodoris and died c. BC 50.
He wrote on physics (including meteorology and physical
geography), astronomy, astrology and divination,
seismology, geology and mineralogy, hydrology, botany,
ethics, logic, mathematics, history, natural history,
anthropology, and tactics.

TYCHE was the patron goddess of Antioch, Syria. She was the
goddess of fortune and prosperity as well as misfortune.

ANICETUS was a pirate born in the Roman Province of Pontus
(northern Anatolia/Turkey) which adjoined the Province of
Cappadocia. In Cappadocia were the Clitae mountain
people who rebelled against Rome. Anicetus died AD 69.

CRETE was notorious for its popularity with pirates. Balo Lagoon in the northwest of the island, had a successful slave market there, though the selling of slaves occurred in all seaports. Phaistos with its famous dark castle was a seaport a few miles southwest of the capital city of Gortyn. Phaistos Palace was built in the Late Minoan Period. It was mostly in ruins and deserted by the first century. It was located at the top of a cliff overlooking the ancient Amyklaion Harbor.

QUINTUS JUNIUS BLAESUS was proconsul of Africanus (all of northern Africa except Egypt) AD 21-23. He was also governor of Creta Cyrenica which was formed into a single Roman province headquartered in Gortyn, Crete. His army captured the brother of Tacfarinas and he was rewarded with his own arch in Rome.

CYRENE was a city within the Roman Province of Creta Cyrenica which covered a large part of Libya except the Sahara Desert.

BERBERS were the original inhabitants of the northern half of Africa. Ancient paintings and statues show them with long black hair, many of whom had a strip of hair draping down in front their ears. Many of today's Berbers have red hair. In the paintings and statues, they look sometimes Egyptian and sometimes Ethiopian and sometimes with characteristics we see in today's Libyan Berbers. They all wore multi-colored tunics with capes, and flat skull caps.

INSULAE were apartment buildings as high as five stories. They were build throughout the Roman Empire. More people lived in insulaes than houses.

WEST AFRICAN BARB HORSES are small and hardy with much stamina. They have a fiery temperament and gallop like a sprinter.

TACFARINAS was a Berber of Libya who was an auxiliary soldier in the Roman army. In AD 20, he deserted and joined a rebellion of Berbers against Roman invading and taking over the little bit of green coastland Libya had. In AD 22, he declared war on Augustus Caesar. Rome had little success in subduing him until it sent Junius Blasius to be governor and general of Africa (Libya). Tacfarinas was killed in AD 24.

PERSECUTION OF JEWS in Cyrene began in 74 BC when Rome took over. Tensions grew until 73 AD with an insurrection of the Jews under Vespasian. It was called the First Roman-Jewish War.

THE JEWS were extremely class conscious as was most of the world in the first century. They divided themselves by (1) born-Jew or born-Non-Jew/Gentile. They were further divided by (2) language, (3) slaves, (3) freedmen, and (4) Roman citizens (5) "barbarian" such as Berber. They did not associate with the other classes unless absolutely necessary. The good Jew never even entered the home of a non-Jew and hesitated to if they had been converted to Judaism from paganism. Therefore, I have broken down these divisions to be represented by the following synagogues both in Cyrene and Jerusalem:

Jewish-born Synagogue
Jewish-born Freedmen Synagogue
Jewish-born Slave Synagogue
Greek-Speaking Roman Citizens Synagogue
Greek-Speaking Freedmen Synagogue
Greek-Speaking Slave Synagogue
Berber Synagogue

The synagogue that accused Stephen in Jerusalem was the Freedmen Synagogue made up of people from Cyrene, Alexandria, Asia (the province Ephesus was in), and Cilicia (the province Tarsus was in). This would have been a Greek-Speaking Freedmen Synagogue.

FAMOUS philosophers, mathematicians, astronomers, etc. from Cyrene included by the first century AD:

ARISTIPPUS - Founder of the university at Cyrene
CALLIMACHUS – Descendant of 1st Greek king of Cyrene, Battus, and famous poet.
THEODORUS - Famous mathematician and called The Atheist because he believed in only one god and creator.

ERATISTGEBES - calculated the circumference of the earth, distance of the earth to the sun, and the <u>365-day year</u>

LIMES were small Roman forts, sometimes only a watchtower, set up at intervals to mark the borders of the Roman Empire and to keep out the "barbarians" on the other side. Some were later substituted with a wall such as Hadrian's Wall in England.

THE "ESTHER QUEST" that Stephen tried in the book, read the book of Esther in the Bible, only about nine pages long. She married the emperor of the Persian Empire, but never told that she was a Jew. But, years later when the emperor ordered all Jews killed, she told it and was able to save the Jews from annihilation.

THE "DANIEL QUEST" that Stephen later tried was taken from the Bible where Daniel declared in Babylon/Persia that he was a Jew and was thrown into a den of lions to be eaten by them. But God kept the lions' mouths closed. This story is in the Bible book of Daniel, chapter. 6.

MEDICAL CURES and treatments referred to in this book all came from plants used for those purposes by the Berbers.

NERVOUS SICKNESS referred to is what we today call Mad Cow Disease. In the fifth century BC, Hippocrates described a similar illness in cattle and sheep, which he believed also occurred in man.

THE TEMPLE COMPLEX sat on Mount Moriah, adjacent to Mount Zion where the original Jerusalem (City of David) was located. The temple complex had four levels according to Josephus. The first level was the expansive Court of the Gentiles which was half a mile long and quarter of a mile wide. In order to go up to the Courtyard of the Treasury (also called the Courtyard of the Women), one had to ascend eight feet of steps. In order to go on up to the Courtyard of the Israelites (Men), one had to go through the Nicanor gate and climb ten more feet of steps. In order for the priests to enter their courtyard with the altars, they had to climb three more feet of steps. To finally be on the ground floor of the temple building itself, the priests had to climb another eight feet. So, the temple building was 29 feet above the level of the Courtyard of the Gentiles.

SOLOMON'S PORCH/PORTICO was the only part of the original temple complex to never be destroyed. The temple complex was approximately one-half mile long; the portico was eight feet deep (according to Josephus). It had columns all along where it jutted out into the Courtyard of the Gentiles and had a roof covered with cedar, so was perfect for worshippers to get out of the rain. If a person was allowed three square feet to sit in, you could fit approximately 6900 people within Solomon's Portico. Therefore, when the Bible says the early Christians met here, apparently they stayed together and had one "church building" with the apostles doing the leading. There were such porticos all the way around the temple complex; only the one on the east side of the temple complex was Solomon's Portico.

JEWISH HOLY DAYS are explained in the Bible in chapter. 23 of Leviticus, third book of the Bible. Passover (Feast of Unleavened Bread) begins in verse 5, Pentecost (Feast of Weeks) begins in verse 15, Day of Atonement begins in verse 26.

WHO WAS SIMEON ALSO CALLED NIGER?

One of the teachers and prophets in early Antioch of Syria was Lucius of Cyrene in Libya. He is listed right after Simeon AKA Niger. Niger could have referred to his skin color or the region where he lived before Antioch.

To the Ancient Greeks, Libya was one of the three known continents along with Asia and Europe. In this sense, Libya was the whole known African continent to the west of the Nile Valley and extended south of Egypt. Herodotus described the inhabitants of Libya as two peoples: The Libyans in northern Africa and the Ethiopians in the south. According to Herodotus, Libya began where ancient Egypt ended.

Niger as we know it today is in the southern half of the Sahara Desert. Since its few inhabitants were nomads, there is little history of Niger before the 19th century. 80% of today's Niger is in the Sahara Desert. About 75% of Libya is in the Sahara Desert. Archaeological research is scarce in the Sahara. There are some pre-historic cliff etchings in an area where Libya, Tripoli, and Niger meet today.

Therefore, for this novel, I allowed Simon of Cyrene, Libya, to be Simeon of Antioch. Of course, we do not know this because all we are told is his name. But I have always thought this.

Did Stephen lecture the Sanhedrin in order to buy time for Simon to escape? The Bible does not say this.

Blacksmithing. I made Stephen a blacksmith because I think he was very strong. When they were stoning him, he did not fall to his knees until almost the end.

Did Stephen leave behind a wife and children? I Timothy and Titus state that a deacon was to have one wife and children.

BUY YOUR NEXT BOOK NOW

HISTORICAL NOVELS FOR ADULTS

THEY MET JESUS Series of 8
http://bit.ly/TheyMetJesus

INTREPID MEN OF GOD Series of 8
http://bit.ly/IntrepidMen

HISTORICAL STORYBOOKS FOR CHILDREN

A CHILD'S LIFE OF CHRIST Series of 8
(Parallels Adult *They Met Jesus*)
http://bit.ly/ChildsLifeOfChristSet

A CHILD'S BIBLE HEROES Series of 10
http://bit.ly/Bible-Heroes

A CHILD'S BIBLE KIDS Series of 8
http://bit.ly/bible-kids

A CHILD'S BIBLE LADIES Series of 10
http://bit.ly/BibleLadies

DISCUSSION QUESTIONS

CHAP. 1:
*When you were a teenager or even a child, did you have a strong desire to defend or promote some good cause? Do you still have that strong desire? Is it stronger or weaker? Why do you think that is?

CHAP. 2:
*We do not know if Stephen's parents did or did not agree with his desire to prove statues were not gods. What we do know is that they went to as many extremes as was needed to protect him from the backlash. Are you close to anyone involved in a cause who is suffering backlash? What can you do to help the person (not the cause, but the person)?

CHAP. 3:
*Have you ever been "between a rock and a hard place" where it seemed no choice was the right choice? Romans says God will make all things work together for good if we love him. Notice it does not say "for the best", but for the good. When you made your choice, what good can you see that came out of it?

CHAP. 4:
*Have you ever spoken to someone about your beliefs in God only to be persecuted by them for saying it? If you have never been persecuted or even yelled at, do you know someone who did go through it? What does persecution reveal about a person?

CHAP. 5:
*Did you ever decide to do something that ended up changing the course of your life? If you made a life-changing decision right now, what do you think it would be?

CHAP. 6:
*Sometimes we find ourselves in a hole, try to get out, and end up with a deeper hole. What kinds of bad situations can a person with a problem make that just makes it even worse?

CHAP. 7:
*Do you think trying anything you can think of (grasping at straws) to get out of the bad situation is worth it? What about asking for God's help in a helpless situation, but still trying yourself?

CHAP. 8:
*How does others teaming up to work through a mutual problem help the individual? Are you or a friend trying to get out of a problem alone, even though there are others who share that problem? How is it working for you or them?

CHAP. 9:
*In this CHAP., Stephen and his family randomly met a man and his family who they ended up being close friends with the rest of their life through thick and thin. Have you experienced this?

CHAP. 10:
*Are you the kind of friend who will walk away from someone as soon as you find out something bad about them? Or have you lost a friend because you "told too much" to? Do you have any friendships that have lasted through good and bad?

CHAP. 11:
*Have you experienced prejudice because of your beliefs, nationality, occupation, etc. or just because people in a group wanted to maintain control? How can such prejudice change to acceptance?

CHAP. 12:
*How much difference does it make when someone stands up for a person being persecuted? Do you have the nerve to do it? Do you have a friend who is enduring prejudice? How will you stand with that person? Or are you enduring prejudice right now? What do you need? Be specific.

CHAP. 13:
*I remember as a child in the 1940s there were "white" churches, "black" churches, "Spanish" churches and "Chinese" churches in the same city. I also remember Polish immigrants settling in one neighborhood, Italian immigrants settling in another neighborhood, German immigrants settling in yet another. What benefits are there for the individual to associate with people with

their particular cultural background? What are the drawbacks?

CHAP. 14:
*Sometimes people fight the status quo of prejudice (or even a family feud) by doing something good for the "opposite side". Why do both sides end up taking their anger out on you?

CHAP. 15:
*Queen Esther was a secret Jew. There are people in the Middle East, Community China and much of Russia who are secret Christians. Under what circumstance might you be a secret Christian? Or are you already a secret Christian, such as at work or in a club? Why?

CHAP. 16:
*If you lived in a country as a Christian where it was illegal and dangerous, what kinds of things could you do to spread the gospel anyway?

CHAP. 17:
*In what ways is it dangerous to expose your enemy to the rest of your group, congregation or even the world for what s/he really is? Is it worth doing this? In what ways can you prepare for his promised revenge?

CHAP. 18:
*Have you ever headed out for a "quest" and the outcome ended up so bad, you wanted to fall through the floor and disappear? How did you pull out of it?

CHAP. 19:
*Does someone need you right now and you do not know how to help them? Are they in uncharted territory to you? Do you need to wade in after them and hope the undercurrent doesn't get you? What kind of person would do this? If it were your child, would you go?

CHAP. 20:
*Did you ever known a famous person before they were famous? What about them do you remember that might have helped them become famous?

CHAP. 21:
*What is it like to search and search for something, know it could be within your grasp, but still unable to find that thing? Do you think it would be better to search alone or other another person or with a group?

CHAP. 22:
*What is it like to lose something and not find it for a very long time until you are looking for something else? What lesson is there for you in such a situation? Are you looking for something right now? What else could you look for in the meantime?

CHAP. 23:
*What is it like to survive something that seems hopeless? How do people treat someone who is now called a survivor or a hero? What about someone who has survived a health issue that lasts for years? How can you make that person feel like a hero?

CHAP. 24:
*What kind of person survives an impossible situation, then jumps right in to another one? Do you know any children like that? What kind of adult do you think they will turn out like? Were you like that as a child? Are you still like that?

CHAP. 25:
*Here goes our friend, Stephen, on another quest, trying to make society better. Remember, he has a "fixer" personality. Do you know anyone with a fixer personality? Always trying to fix people or things or society? Do you like being around such a person? Do you consider them fun or a trouble maker?

CHAP. 26:
*Did you ever ask someone for help who needed the help worse than you did but you did not realize it? Did they help you anyway? If someone asked you for help at a time when "I have my own problems", what will you tell them?

CHAP. 27:
*What is it like to always want to go to a special place and finally be able to go? How can you relate this to your life's journey on your way to heaven?

CHAP. 28:

*Did you ever go to hear someone preach and never saw them again after that, but what they said influences you even today? Who was it? If you have never experienced, who do you think you would like to go hear speak? What do you think you will get out of it?

CHAP. 29:
*Who, other than family, do you think influenced you the most as a child? Have you run into that person as an adult? Who was it? How do you feel about that person now?

CHAP. 30:
*Did you ever spot greatness in a young person? What about them made you think that, or would if you ever met such a young person? Jesus spoke out and said thing to the leaders no one else had the nerve to do. Is that one thing that makes a person great?

CHAP. 31:
*Why do you think Stephen and Livia made a good match? Do you think it is better to be married to someone just like you or the opposite of you? If you compromise, which traits should be the same and which the opposite? Or is it ever good to be married to an opposite?

CHAP. 32:
*Knowledge is power. Do you know someone who just does not like you? How do you think it would help to get to know them better? Sometimes it helps and sometimes it doesn't. Have you had the experience of getting to know an enemy better and they end up your friend?

CHAP. 33:
*Have you ever exposed someone to be the enemy of other people and the enemy nearly destroyed you? What did they do to you? Or have you seen this happen to someone else who was nearly destroyed? Is it true that, as we go through life, we keep repeating the same types of actions over and over?

CHAP. 34:
*Remember a time when you were at your lowest with no hope of recovery. Then someone—perhaps a relative, a friend, or just an acquaintance—knew just the right thing to pull you out of it? How

did they do it? Do you know someone right now at the "end of their rope"? What can you try to help them stand again?

CHAP. 35:
*Have you ever had someone demand you do something outrageous in order to obtain what they can give you? Did you do it? Was it worth it? What is it like to have a dream come true so suddenly, you do not believe it is really happening?

CHAP. 36:
*Have you ever run into someone you used to be very close to, but went separate ways for ten, twenty or more years? Did you feel like complete strangers now around each other? Or did you "pick up right where we left off" those many years ago? Why do you think that was?

CHAP. 37:
*Did you ever go somewhere expecting it to be nice, but it turned out to be something earth-shaking? Or were you ever drawn into a cause (club, congregation, etc.) thinking it would be nice, but it was nothing like what you had expected?

CHAP. 38:
*What is it like to deal with guilt? Or do you think people today more and more do not feel guilt? In what ways can allowing yourself come right out and admit the guilt help or hinder you?

CHAP. 39:
*Have you ever been baptized? Look up Acts 2:38, Acts 22:16, Romans 6:3-4, and I Peter 3:28. What do they say baptism is for when done after believing?

CHAP. 40:
*It seems sometimes deaths within a family or among friends come close together. How can someone handle such personal devastation? Do you think it is easier to have a chance to say goodbye while the person lingers, or not say goodbye when death is sudden?

CHAP. 41:
*Jesus said we are not to cast our pearls before swine. Under what circumstance is it best to just walk away from a situation and try somewhere else or with someone else? How might thinking you at

least planted a seed help you?

CHAP. 42:
*Have you ever known someone to tackle a project that was way too big for them? If they succeeded anyway, why do you think they did?

CHAP. 43:
*Did you ever or do you now see an enemy in your midst and no one believes you? What can you do to keep standing for what is right, knowing the enemy wants to destroy you (in a club, neighborhood, nation, congregation, etc.)?

CHAP. 44:
*Once again, Stephen tries the "Esther Quest" of worshipping in secret and hiding one's beliefs in public. Is anything ever really a secret? If you are hiding your faith to a club, neighborhood, or etc.? How far do you think you are willing to go to make your faith known? Will you do it?

CHAP. 45:
*Stephen and two of his friends went public by doing good works among the "enemies" of their beliefs. Make a plan now to do something good to those you have been hiding your faith from, then confessing your faith. Share it with your friends.

CHAP. 46:
*Do you know someone right now who is standing alone against the enemy of their beliefs? How can you be supportive of that person in public and in private?

CHAP. 47:
*Sometimes in life we must choose between ourselves and someone who accomplishes more than we do. How hard is it to admit someone passionate about the same things you are is more effective? What would you be willing to do for that person?

CHAP. 48:
*Think hard before answering: Would you be willing to give up your life for Jesus? There are Christians in hiding right now around the world who are faced with this. If they went public and knew they would be killed for their faith, what can you tell them

to give them courage to do it? That means giving up their plans to grow the Kingdom of God in secret. How can one person's death accomplish more than anything they could have done in their lifetime? What things can they think about when making this decision? What would you think about?

ABOUT THE AUTHOR

Katheryn Maddox Haddad spends an average of 300 hours researching before writing a historical novel—ancient historians such as Josephus, archaeological digs so she can know the layout of cities, their language, culture, and politics.

She grew up in the northern United States and now lives in Arizona where she doesn't have to shovel sunshine. She basks in 100-degree weather, palm trees, cacti, and a computer with most of the letters worn off.

She is author of 77 books, both non-fiction and fiction. Her newspaper column appeared for several years in newspapers in Texas and North Carolina ~ *Little Known Facts About the Bible* ~ and she has written for numerous Christian publications. For over twenty years, she has been sending out every morning a daily scripture and short inspirational thought to some 30,000 people around the world.

She spends half her day writing, and the other half teaching English over the internet worldwide using the Bible as textbook. She has taught some 7000 Muslims through World English Institute. Students she has converted to Christianity are in hiding in Afghanistan, Iran, Iraq, Yemen, Uzbekistan, Somalia, Jordan, Tajikistan, Sierra Leone, Pakistan, Indonesia, and Palestine. "They are my heroes," she declares.

With a bachelor's degree in English, Bible and social science from Harding University and part of a master's degree in Bible, including Greek, from the Harding Graduate School of Theology, she also has a master's degree in management and human relations from Abilene University. She is a member of American Christian Fiction Writers, Historical Novel Society, International Screen Writers Association, and is also an energetic public speaker who can touch the hearts of audiences.

CONNECT WITH KATHERYN MADDOX HADDAD

Website: **https://inspirationsbykatheryn.com**

Facebook: **bit.ly/FacebooksKatherynMaddoxHaddad**

Linkedin: **http://bit.ly/KatherynLinkedin**

Twitter: **https://twitter.com/KatherynHaddad**

Pinterest: **https://www.pinterest.com/haddad1940/**

Goodreads:
https://www.goodreads.com/katherynmaddoxhaddad

GET A FREE BOOK

Sign up for Katheryn's monthly newsletter with half-price books for the whole family and insider tips on what's coming next.
http://bit.ly/katheryn

JOIN MY DRE
AM TEAM

Members get the first peek at my newest book and have fun offering me advice sometimes. I have a point system of rewards for helping me get the word out. Check it out here:
http://bit.ly/KatherynsDreamTeam